A BROVELLI BROTHERS' MYSTERY

THE CASE OF THE 1950 VOLKSWAGEN HIPPIE BUS

TOM MESCHERY

CAVEL PRESS

KENMORE, WA

CAMEL
PRESS

A Camel Press book published by Epicenter Press

Epicenter Press
6524 NE 181st St.
Suite 2
Kenmore, WA 98028

For more information go to: www.epicenterpress.com

Author's website: Warrior 14.com and TomMeschery.com

Cover design by Rudy Ramos
Interior design by Rudy Ramos

The Case of the 1950 Volkswagen Hippie Bus
Copyright ©2025 by Tom Meschery

ISBN: 9781684922680 (trade paper)
ISBN: 9781684922697 (ebook)
LOC: 9781684922680

Produced in the United States of America

To my grandchildren Grace, Ruth, Carson, Leo, Moses, & Van
I am grateful for all of you

Acknowledgments

Bob Aldrich, a true Deadhead historian, thank you for so much useful information about The Grateful and for taking the time to read The Grateful Dead chapters to make sure I had the scenes right.

To Ned Averbuck who lived in the East 14th neighborhood, for background.

As always, Don and Ron Dirito, the anecdotes you shared with me enrich these novels.

To Matthew, my son, musician and song writer, your take on the Grateful Dead gave me some important insights into the Grateful Dead's music.

A big thank you to Jennifer McCord, my editor at Camel Books for your faith in the Brovelli Brothers.

And, finally, but never least, to my wife Melanie, my line editor and Muse, none of mysteries would have been written without you.

*The spirit of a deceased person who bestows benefits
upon the one responsible for his burial.*
Grateful Dead

He who seeks revenge digs two graves, one for himself.
Attributed to Confucius

CHAPTER 1

A MISSING PERSON

"The childless have one trouble, but those who have children have a thousand."
Armenian proverb

East 14th Street begins in downtown Oakland, California and extends as far south as Hayward where it becomes Mission Boulevard. If you continue driving south on Mission Boulevard, you'll wind up in the sleepy city of San Jose. Our section of East 14th, called the Fruitridge District, is home to stores selling all kinds of goods: hardware, furniture, auto parts, carpets, jewelry, paint, groceries and liquor. There are restaurants, taverns and a few nightclubs. There are other used car dealerships like ours and some new car dealers, although most of the new car dealers are found on Broadway in downtown Oakland.

The Brovelli Brothers' Used Cars is located near the High Street Bridge which takes a driver from the Fruitridge neighborhood of Oakland to the Island City of Alameda. My twin, Vincent, and I were born and raised in Alameda. I'm Victor Brovelli, Vincent's other half and technically speaking, the younger, as he entered the world three or so minutes before me. Our used car lot is two blocks north of the clubhouse of one of the most notorious motorcycle gangs in California, the Satans, whose now-deceased honcho almost killed my twin and me two years ago. I still occasionally revisit this nightmare in my sleep.

Our business is within ten miles of the Oakland Municipal Airport and the Alameda Naval Air Station which, for the last four years of the Vietnam War, has filled the air with the sound of military planes taking off and landing. East 14th reverberates with city noise: cars honking, trucks slamming brakes, rumbling motorcycles, the sirens of ambulances and police cars, and voices raised to be heard above the din. This racket is my kind of rock and roll. I'm a city boy down to my Italian toenails.

1

It was almost June 1970, Thursday, May 28th to be exact. I was counting because my fiancé, Dila Agbo, was scheduled to return home in a week for summer break from NYU where she was enrolled, working on her master's in theater arts. We had less than two months to get our unresolved marital status resolved before she had to return. Thinking of Dila made me happy; thinking of our marriage plans made me nervous, particularly since there'd been a lot of indecision recently on Dila's part. I was not sure where this was coming from. I was all-in and excited about the prospect of being a husband to Dila. I didn't believe Dila had any questions about being my wife. We had long ago given up worrying that ours would be an inter-racial marriage. Recently, however, I'd sensed that there was something new bothering her. That "something new" was contributing to an unhappy silence between us. The British poet Archibald McLeish was once asked how he knew a poem was good. His answer was when the hairs on the back of his neck stood up. I could have answered in the same way if someone had asked me how I knew there were impending problems between Dila and me. I hoped it had nothing to do with her membership in the Black Panthers. Her membership was a source of great pride for her, even if she wasn't working for them at the time. In the last six months law enforcement, including the FBI, had increased its pressure on the BPP, and it was rumored that a major confrontation was imminent.

I finished placing the last of our discount sales signs on the windshields of the cars we wanted to get rid of quickly and returned to the office. I was determined not to think about Dila. When she was ready to tell me what was going on, she would. Until then, it was futile to try to pry anything out of one of the most stubborn minds I'd ever encountered. I had paperwork that needed my attention. As it turned out, the paperwork continued to need my attention, and I wound up sitting at my desk staring out the window, my mind wandering between Dila, the traffic on East 14th, my twin out on the lot talking to a customer and back to Dila. *Always, back to Dila.*

I was berating myself to stop worrying and get busy with the invoices, when I saw Nick Parsegian, the owner of Discount Furniture across the street, begin jaywalking in our direction.

Jaywalking is not a smart move since East 14th is one hell of a busy street. Why risk his life when there was a crosswalk a half block away? To find out why our local furniture salesman never takes the crosswalk, you'd have to ask a psychologist who deals with death wishes. One year at Flynn's, the boys had set up a pool and picked specific days of the year Parsegian would become bumper food. Everybody put in twenty bucks.

Nobody won, so Body Flynn, the owner of Flynn's, threw a gigantic party with the cash. We all decided that Parsegian was being protected by the God of Jaywalkers and gave up betting.

A horn blasted as a garbage truck nearly hit him. The furniture salesman was holding up his hand like a cop stopping traffic while dodging bumpers at the same time. *Roba de matti*, crazy, I thought. I held my breath as a yellow cab almost nailed him. He made it to our side of the street. I hoped he was going to Flynn's tavern, which was next door, but he began walking up our driveway. *Merda.*

Parsegian was not one of my favorite people. Not that I totally disliked him, but he was one of those kinds of unctuous salesmen that didn't register very high on the trust meter. He was always dressed in expensive-looking pin-striped suits that upon closer inspection were probably a knock-off he had bought from the back of a van and never quite fit. That annoys the hell out of Vincent and me. We consider dressing sharp an important part of being salesmen; in our case that means blue blazers, button down oxfords, well-creased gray trousers and blue and red stripped ties, the colors of our alma mater, Saint Mary's College.

As for Parsegian's sales technique, it was a combination of pleading and arm twisting. In his favor, his furniture was reasonably priced and of modestly good quality, but in all the years he'd been in business in the neighborhood, I didn't remember him ever buying a round of drinks for the boys at Flynn's tavern, while never turning down a freebee.

Parsegian stopped to speak to my twin. Vincent pointed to the office and shrugged his shoulders in my direction as if to say sorry before turning back to his customer. I watched Parsegian approach. He poked his head in, nodded at Theresa, and said, "Victor, could I have a word?"

"You promise one word," I said. He looked puzzled at my remark. Not swift on the uptake, our furniture salesman.

"In private," he said.

From her desk, our office manager, Theresa Bacigalupi, said, "I got to go to the bank." She stood up, grabbed her purse and left.

Parsegian let her pass, then stepped inside.

"Okay," I said, "what's so private?"

"It's my daughter, Merriam. I don't know what happened to her."

The next thing I knew Parsegian was slumped in my chair, sobbing. He was about my height, 6 feet. He had a tiny mustache above a tiny mouth. He wore his graying black hair plastered back over his pate with pomade. He looked pathetic bent over my desk, slobbering on my office calendar. Maybe I should have put my arms around him to console him, but like I said, he was not one of my favorite guys. I waited for him to get control of himself.

Finally, he took a deep breath. He looked up at me. His words came out in gulps. "They found Merriam's bus. It had blood in it. She wasn't in it." He took another deep breath and between gulps continued. "It's her blood type. It's been a week. My wife is frantic. Oh, God, she's, my baby. Victor, the cops aren't doing anything. I don't think they care. They called her a Deadhead. They called her a groupie. I thought they were calling her a dead fish. My wife fainted. I had to ask what that meant. She's not one of those kids who follows bands around. You know Merriam. She's a good girl."

I knew nothing of the sort. Half the teens in California were *Grateful Dead* groupies. I wasn't crazy about the band, but some of their songs were definitely energetic.

"Why are you coming to me with this?" I asked. I probably should have sounded a little more sympathetic.

"Victor, you've solved two crimes. You have the know-how. I want you to find Merriam for me."

Parsegian had purchased his daughter's first car, a neat little red and white Nash Metropolitan, from us in the spring of 1969, as a high school graduation gift. I remembered the next day, her driving to our lot and thanking us for her car as if we were responsible and not her father. She had brought a dozen homemade Armenian cookies called Simits as a thank you present. They were covered with toasted sesame seeds and had the flavor of vanilla and were perfect for coffee dunking. She was a gawky teen, all legs and nervous smiles, black hair cut short, wide dark eyes with long eyelashes, and sort of teenage pouty lips, not especially pretty, but the potential was there. As a car guy, I appreciated how much she enjoyed her Nash.

I also remembered the following year when Merriam drove to our lot, looking to trade in her Nash. I'm not sure what I had expected to see that day stepping out of the driver's side door, but it certainly wasn't the Merriam Parsegian I remembered from a year before, not that incarnation at least.

One long shapely leg followed the other, her body now fully developed—and I mean fully. Parsegian's daughter must have had a growth spurt. She'd changed the color of her hair, or I should say she had added a number of different colors to her previously black curls that now swept down to her shoulder and were being held in place by a green headband. She was wearing a tie-dyed blouse and a long flowing tangerine skirt and sandals. How that gawky teen had changed so radically in a year seemed almost unnatural. She'd known exactly the car she wanted. She pointed her long fingernails to our 1950 Volkswagen Type 2 Transporter Bus.

The VW Transporter had been launched in November of 1950 to compete with the popular VW Beetle. By 1970, over two and half million had been sold. The one Merriam had been looking at that day was the first model and had already become a vintage classic. Vincent had found it on a lot in in the town of Merced, body in perfect shape, but the engine needed a serious overhaul. He bought it cheap, and Jitters, our savant mechanic, rebuilt the rear-mounted horizontal air-cooled engine. When we got it, the Transporter had been painted a classic dove-blue. I loved the look of the Transporter from the front, the silver band from the sides joining together above the front fender to make a V with the VW insignia in the middle below the windshield like the S on Superman's chest. We were asking big bucks for it. The price was not negotiable.

She'd looked at her father, spoke a *pretty please, Poppy* with her pouty mouth and he nodded. She smelled like incense. I imagined some Buddhist temple. She had not hugged her poppy. I remember feeling embarrassed for him. Her poppy grumbled but wrote a check minus the trade-in. Fair Merriam drove away, toodle-ooing her long fingernails out the driver's side window. Parsegian had jaywalked back to his store across the four lanes of East 14th Street, probably hoping that a truck would hit him. That might have been what he'd been thinking today.

Recalling the high school Merriam and the transformed Merriam, I'd forgotten the weeping father who was looking up at me with red eyes, waiting for me to say something. I had to think for a moment.

"I'm not doing detecting any more, Nick," I said, even though I knew it was not exactly the truth. "But I know a couple of names of private investigators that I can put you in touch with. Have you talked to Jay?"

Parsegian shook his head.

Jay Ness was a Detective Sergeant in the Oakland Police Department's homicide division and my friend. Given that Jay was known around the neighborhood and frequently took his lunch at Flynn's Tavern, I would have thought he would have been the first person Parsegian would have gone to.

"Why don't you talk to him?"

"I don't think Officer Ness likes me."

That hadn't occurred to me, but knowing Jay, it was a fair guess.

"I went downtown to the homicide office," Parsegian said. "They told me the blood could have been anybody's, someone who'd cut himself shaving. I didn't appreciate the joke. They said Merriam's disappearance belongs to the Missing Persons Department."

"Have you checked with Holy Names College? Her roommate? Friends?"

Parsegian looked into his lap and didn't say anything.

"Well," I said.

"Merriam quit school after her first semester."

I didn't know what to say. Parsegian had bragged that his daughter earned a full academic scholarship to Holy Names, a Catholic college, which was sort of sister college to the all-male Saint Mary's College that was Vincent's and my alma mater.

I remembered Parsegian a year ago bragging about his daughter's academic prowess, her talent playing the cello and violin. A proud father, now not so proud.

"Okay, how about at her job?"

Parsegian looked even more glum. "She'd moved out of our home and in with friends. She wouldn't tell us where she lived or with whom. I don't know if she had a job, and I don't know the names of her friends."

This sounded like a huge family mess, what we call a *casino* in Italian. I definitely didn't want to be involved. "Like I said, Nick, go talk to Jay. He's just kidding about not liking you. I bet he'll be at Flynn's this afternoon.

"It's Thursday, you know how much Jay loves chili," I said. Parsegian knew the lunch schedule: Tuesdays and Thursdays at Flynn's were I-Dare-You- Chili, that came with grated cheddar cheese, crackers and a fire hose. Mondays and Wednesdays, Body prepared Irish stew, in his words so rich and thick a mouse could run across it without drowning, and being a good Catholic, the Irishman served clam chowder on Fridays. On most days of the week, half the working population of our business district found their way to Flynn's for a brewski and good chow. "You might want to buy him a drink. Jay's got juice. He can help more than I can."

"If he won't help, will you?" Parsegian asked.

"I can't, Nick. Let me put it another way: I won't. What happened in January was too much violence for me. I want to get back to selling cars."

"Victor, please."

I hate to see a grown man grovel. I thought of Merriam — of Armenian cookies and incense, Buddhist temples, long fingernails and sweet smiles. I thought of my mother and father grieving over Mario's death and said something stupid.

"Maybe, but go see Jay Ness first."

CHAPTER 2
GEMELLI

"Le Flamme gemelle bruciano piu luminose.
Twin flames burn brighter."
Italian proverb

I love being a twin, and I particularly love my twin, Vincent. However, there is a problem with twinness. Twins can't put anything over on each other. Vincent walked into the office, looked at me and said, "Okay?"

"Okay, what?"

"What did you do, Victor?"

I have no idea what my tells are. I swear to God I had my poker face on. "What are you talking about?" I answered a question with a question.

"*Vittorio…*" Vincent said.

When he calls me by my Italian name, there is no use in lying. I explained, beginning with the Nash Metropolitan sale, which he remembered; the sale of the Van, which he regretted; and ended with Nick Parsegian slumped in my chair weeping over his missing daughter.

"What does 'maybe' mean?" Vincent asked.

"Maybe means if Jay can't help, maybe I will."

"*Odio,*" Vincent said, looking up to a heaven he didn't believe in. "I feel for Parsegian, but she probably just ran away. With a father like him, by high school, I'd have had the motor running."

"The bus was found abandoned," I explained. "There was blood in it. "

"Tell me the bus was okay, no damage. That was my baby."

"You're thinking of a machine; Parsegian is thinking of his daughter."

"Stuff it, Victor. You know what I mean."

"What if something happened to your daughter?" I asked.

"Cristina is two years old, for craps sake, Victor. Let the cops figure it out."

"Vincent, don't you remember Merriam's cookies and her cute smile?"

After Merriam had her new little Nash, she'd drive to the lot in the mornings with a fresh batch. When she finally stopped, I remembered us feeling like cookie addicts going cold turkey.

"All I remember is after Christmas how you being a frigging detective almost got you and your girlfriend killed. I didn't like it, but I understood. It was about Mario, family, *onore*. I had your back, didn't I?"

I nodded, remembering Vincent holding his trusty softball bat down on the San Francisco docks during an episode that became known as Victor's folly, and the year before, him holding a pistol to the head of a Mexican gangster and swearing he'd put a bullet into the *chooch's* ear if he touched me.

"But this is not family," Vincent continued. "You don't even like Parsegian."

"I don't dislike him, and it's his only child." This was only partially true. I actually found Parsegian very unlikable.

"I need you on the lot. It's summer. People are buying cars."

"I only promised him I'd do some research, like find out some names of Merriam's friends, places she hangs out, put together some leads. After that Parsegian can hire a real P.I."

I could tell I was not convincing Vincent. I raised my right hand.

"Don't swear, Victor. *Per favore*. If that gun battle in Monterey didn't cure you of being a Private Eye, I don't know what will. You need to make up your mind about what you want to be. Like Pop, I know I'm a car salesman. You need to start thinking about yourself."

Another thing about being twins is knowing when one is telling the absolute unvarnished truth. There was no denying that in the past I had often enjoyed being a detective. It was also true that I had researched what the requirements were to get a Private Investigator's license in California. It was true as well that I was also feeling enormously guilty about Dila's injuries, the cause of which had been my stubborn refusal to give up trying to prove Mario had not committed suicide but had been murdered even when all the facts were against me.

"I know, I know," I said. "Look, I'll do the minimum. I feel like I have to do something for the poor guy. He's part of our neighborhood. That's sort of like family."

"Total bull, Victor."

"Now, don't get started." I said.

"Who's starting? Neighborhood family, give me a break. You've told me a number of times how guilty you feel about Dila. *Oh, woe is me, poor Victor.* And now you want to go get yourself mixed up in another possible crime. You're lying to yourself. That may be okay for you, but lying to me is not."

Another thing about twins is that they manage to provoke each other faster than normal siblings. My hands turned into fists. So did his. One does it, so must the other. It's a rule written in *The Book of Twins.* Fists clenched, we stared at each other. But I blinked.

"Okay, okay, Vincent. You're right. I like solving crimes. It gives me a rush that car sales don't. At least not for a while. But I'll do as you say. I'll tell Nick Parsegian I'm out. And I'll concentrate on selling cars. You can count on me."

We embraced. *Americans hug, Italians full body embrace. We learn from our parents, don't we?* Our pop, Big Sal Brovelli, embraces everybody, sometimes much to their astonishment, occasionally lifting them off the ground. He doesn't lift women off the ground except our mama though.

Theresa walked into the office.

"You guys dancing? I don't hear any music?"

"Go vacuum," I said.

"Up yours, Victor," she said and sat down at her desk.

"I'll tell you what I'll do," Vincent said.

"Do what?" I asked.

"If all you were going to do was get some names, do a little research. . ."

I interrupted. "So, you're saying I can go ahead?"

"No, no, no. You got to work the lot. I'll do it. I could use a break. Do something a little different. I'll find out stuff tomorrow morning and play with my kids in the afternoon. It will be a working vacation. With the lot all to yourself, you can begin figuring out if selling cars is what you want to do in the future? *Capite?*

I thought for a moment, then nodded. *Si, Capito.*

As it turned out, I really didn't understand.

CHAPTER 3
VINCENT STRIVES TO HELP

"I know many songs, but I can't sing."
Armenian proverb

Vincent had told his wife Gloria that he wouldn't be on the lot this morning and that they could take the kids to the zoo in the afternoon. He had explained what he was doing, and his wife had warned him that it was a bad idea, getting involved with the machinations of his twin. Gloria loved using big words that she acquired from her addiction to Sunday morning crossword puzzles. She'd said, "You know the kind of trouble Victor gets into. You're not single like him. You have two children to consider."

Vincent had loved Gloria from the first day he'd seen her as he had strolled all cocky-like into the mixer at Holy Names High School for Young Ladies. Gloria had been standing by the punch bowl. Their eyes had met and that was the end of the story. It hadn't hurt that she was Italian, and her parents had emigrated from Napoli, like our parents. They had two gorgeous children, the baby Mario, named after our deceased older brother, and two-year-old Christina.

Vincent had promised not to follow in his twin's footsteps, only to hear Gloria reply skeptically, "Yeah like that crazy time down at Pier 5?" He couldn't argue with his wife. That incident had almost turned into a huge *casino*, or as Sweets, the neighborhood's resident burglar and quasi-friend, had put it, *a mess of magnificent magnitude.*

Sitting in his car, waiting for green light, Vincent wondered what his twin would do first.

He probably should have asked Victor for advice. *Nah*, he thought, *how hard can this detecting stuff be?* The light changed. Vincent stepped on the gas. He was driving his recently purchased 1969 Dodge Charger 4 door sedan, having left the Chrysler Town & Country station wagon with Gloria. He'd had a Motorola telephone installed—in case of a children crisis, he'd explained to Victor. Not to be outdone, Victor had had one installed in his Mustang. Even though car phones had been around for a while, they were still a niche item, so for his twin it was all about car phones being the ultimate symbol of masculine cool. Vincent smiled. Victor had calmed down some since Dila had come into his life, but his twin couldn't fool him. Victor's favorite TV show detective was Mannix who had a Motorola telephone in his car and drove a Dodge Dart GTS 340.

Vincent decided Victor would start with Merriam's college friends. Even if Merriam had dropped out after the first semester, she'd have had a roommate and must have shared ideas and plans. He took the Nimitz freeway figuring he'd make better time to Holy Names College. A minute later he regretted his decision as the traffic on the freeway came to a halt. He veered into the verge and saw bumper-to-bumper as far as he could see. To make matters worse, an ambulance came roaring and whooping down upon him. He barely got back into his lane. The ambulance was followed by a sheriff's patrol car, its siren blaring. Some weirdo ahead of him began blowing his horn. On the other side of the freeway, a truck slammed on its brakes, rubber on asphalt, call-and-response to the driver behind him who did not apply his brakes in time.

Now both lanes of the freeway were backed up.

Vincent closed his eyes and wondered why his twin loved living in the city. He couldn't wait for the time when the Brovelli Brothers' Used Cars would make its fortune and move their dealership to a quiet suburb. Maybe they would get a new car dealership. Marin County or the West Bay around Palo Alto looked good to him. They could check out Lafayette or Walnut Creek, which were on the other side of the Caldicott Tunnel, closer to Oakland, but those areas didn't have enough population. But maybe someday… If the Brovelli Boys were already there, they would have a jump on the competition.

That is unless Victor stopped playing detective. Then the dealership might belong to only one Brovelli brother. He'd discussed the possibility with his wife. She had wisely not tried to convince him to buy out his twin, but he could tell she was not against it if this was the path he chose to take. He knew Victor was a hell of salesman when he put his mind to it, but he was also a complicated man. Imagine a car salesman who read classical literature! Vincent was sure that his twin didn't think he knew about him reading novels and poetry. Didn't Victor understand by now that twins know everything about each other?

And then there was his twin's strange relationship with, as their mother put it, *la donna nera,* the black woman. Dila wasn't just black, she had at one time worked for the Black Panthers. The Black Panthers were high on J. Edgar Hoover's list of organizations that needed extermination. Vincent was sure his twin had never mentioned this factoid to their parents. As it stood, Big Sal and Lucia, their mom, were worried about the engagement, not because they didn't like Dila or were prejudiced against the Negro race but because they believed that interracial couples faced terrible obstacles in their married lives, and interracial children, *bambini,* would be discriminated against in schools. Even if it was the Seventies and times were changing, as Victor had pointed out, their parents didn't believe society had changed that much. Vincent agreed with his parents.

He wondered if he and Victor were drifting apart. It worried him. When they were young, they were inseparable. They thought alike and spoke alike. They both had black curly hair, hazel eyes, dimples and a swarthy but smooth southern Italian complexion. If they wore the same clothes, which they often did, they were mirror images of each other.

Vincent smiled, remembering how many times they'd tricked teachers. Sometimes they could even confuse their parents. Those days of tricking people ended in college when Victor's complexation had been marred by a line drive that tagged him as he tried to steal second base, leaving him with a cradle-like scar that extended from the middle of his left eye to his ear.

Ironically, that scar, rather than ruin his good looks, wound up providing his twin with the sort of bad-boy image that for some reason attracted women. Vincent had found that curious and had asked Gloria, not yet his wife, and she'd been vague, shrugging her shoulders and saying something like, *well you know. . .* He recalled that Gloria had blushed. He'd interpreted the *"well you know. . ."* to mean you know women. He didn't think he knew women very well, but that was okay because the only woman he needed to know was Gloria.

While he was pondering his relationship with his twin, the traffic finally began to move, first slowly, then faster. He kept his foot on the gas, moving into the fast lane, passing as many cars as he could before moving back into the correct lane to take the exit that would lead to the Oakland

Hills and Holy Names College.

From the freeway, he turned onto Mountain Boulevard and drove toward the campus. The sentinel of trees lined the road into the hills. He lowered the window and breathed in the scent of eucalyptus. Cloud cover with flashes of sunlight made him blink and pulled down his sun-visor. A jackrabbit sprinted across the road. The scent changed from eucalyptus to laurel and sagebrush.

There was nothing like California spring to juice the senses. The last time he'd been here was to attend Gloria's graduation. That brought back another memory when he and Victor were double dating. Gloria had fixed Victor up with one of her friends. They drove down from Holy Names to a party in Berkeley at which there were a lot of University of California football players. As he recalled, the night had turned into a catastrophe when Victor got into a fight with the star of the Cal Bears football team, a quarterback known for his street-fighting prowess.

What started it, Vincent couldn't remember, but he recalled the escalation had occurred when one of the football player's buddies pinned his twin's arms behind him to make it easier for the Cal Bear guy to land a punch. That's when Vincent had picked up a chair and smashed the attacker on the head. Another rule in the *Book of Twins* is it's back-to-back against all comers. From there, it was a free-for-all. The police arrived and the bunch of them were all hauled off to the Berkeley Police Station. Gloria and her friend were left to drive home alone.

There were still occasions even many years later, Gloria reminded him, as more examples of why her husband should be very careful about involving himself with his twin. "You just can't seem to help yourself when he's in trouble."

And he'd remind her, "You know, in sickness and in health, in blah, blah, blah, until death do you part. It does not apply only to a couple getting married." Gloria had looked at him as if he was nuts, but Vincent knew this to be truth about him and Victor, and perhaps of all twins.

Vincent parked his car and walked to the chapel. From there, his wife had given him directions to the freshman residency hall, while reminding him that no males were allowed entry except on special open house occasions. This presented a problem. He decided if Holy Names was constructed in the same way as Saint Mary's College, which it looked like to him, there would be a common area between buildings where students could buy snacks, coffee and essentials. A store would be open to faculty and there were males on the college faculty. When he reached the residency hall, he realized that his guess had been correct. There was a sign pointing to a mezzanine that connected two dorms. It read "Student Store." He walked in and was relieved to find a male in a janitor's uniform sitting at a table drinking coffee and reading the *Sporting Green*. He ordered a coffee at the counter and looked around the room. There was only one other table occupied by three students. This store serviced both sophomores and freshmen. The girls looked young to him, so maybe freshmen. They were drinking coffee and eating muffins. He approached them.

"I was wondering if you might help me," he asked, smiling. He knew smiling would produce his dimples, and he knew that his twin used his dimples when talking to women the same way women use cologne to attract men. He also knew if he said that to his wife, she would have called him a sexist pig.

The girls looked up and smiled. "If we can," an Asian girl said.

"Are you by any chance freshmen?"

"We are," the speaker said. "Proud class of 1969."

"I'm looking for friends of Merriam Parsegian."

"Merriam dropped out of school half way through last semester."

"I know," Vincent said.

"Are you related?" the Asian girl asked, her tone turning suspicious.

"I'm a friend of her father. The family hasn't heard from Merriam and are very worried."

The girl sitting next to the Asian girl said, "And for a good reason, Merriam went kind of beserko. A friend of mine was her roommate. According to her, it was totally weird. I'd let her tell you but she has the flu.

"I remember Merriam started listening to Grateful Dead tunes though. Next thing you know, she's wearing hippie clothing and not coming to class. She began learning to play the guitar. She was a really terrific violinist, but she was determined to play the guitar, not just an ordinary guitar, but a twelve string. My roommate said it was driving her batty listening to Merriam practicing all the time. She had to go to the library for any quiet to study. The next thing we all knew, Merriam was, *poof*, gone. Just packed up her bags and drove away in that Volkswagen bus of hers."

"Yeah," another girl said. "Gone real flower child."

Vincent asked if it would be okay if Merriam's father talked to them, and all three agreed. Was there anyone else at the college who knew Merriam he could talk to, he asked. The Asian girl, who'd introduced herself as Linda Fong, said the music professor would be his best source of information. His name was Brother Gaspare.

The third girl, who had not yet spoken added, "Brother Gaspare chose Merriam to be first violinist for the school orchestra over the previous first violinist, a senior. It caused a huge uproar."

Where could he find Brother Gaspare? he asked. They directed him to Ambrose Hall next to the Student Union. Miss Fong drew him a map on a napkin. Vincent thanked the students. As he walked away, he heard: *Did you check out his dimples?* Vincent smiled.

At the door he dropped his stale undrinkable coffee into the garbage bin. He was reminded of all the stale undrinkable coffee he'd put up with when he was in college. And the inedible food in the cafeteria. As he walked in the direction of Ambrose Hall, he thought of guys from his class in college who said that those four years were the best of their lives. He thought they were crazy. He remembered those torturous years of academic bullshit when all he wanted to do was get out into the world and sell automobiles like Big Sal. Victor had liked college, and Vincent thought that was sort of breaking the twins' code of togetherness.

As he passed the chapel, the bells rang. It reminded him of the school anthem, *The Bells of Saint Mary's. "I hear they are calling, the young loves, the true loves. . ."* he sang the school anthem softly to himself. Maybe college wasn't so boring.

Soon, Vincent found the music department. Through the office window, he saw a man dressed in black sitting at his desk, bending over a book, deep in concentration. Vincent assumed it must be Brother Gaspare. He knocked.

No response.

He knocked louder. The man looked up. Vincent recognized the collar that identified the man to be of the teaching order of his alma mater, the Christian Brothers. He had expected an older man. Brother Gaspare looked not much older than him. He was wearing a Giants' baseball cap, and his dark hair hung beneath it framing a thin face from which two brilliant green eyes shone above slender nose. He remembered a word his twin had used once to describe one of their cousins, an artist, that would apply to this man, *aesthetic.* The Brother beckoned him to enter.

Vincent opened the door and stepped inside. "I'm sorry to bother you, Brother. My name is Vincent Brovelli. I'm a friend of Merriam Parsegian's father. I was wondering if I could speak to you about Merriam. I was told she played first violin in the Holy Names College orchestra that you conduct."

"I'm also professor and chairman of the one-person music department," Gaspare said, pointing to a chair. "How can I help you?"

Guy has a sense of humor, Vincent thought. He sat down. "I went to Saint Mary's College," he said. "We didn't have a music department."

"Ah, a Galloping Gael," Brother Gaspare said. "But, yes. Merriam played first violin in our orchestra, but she left school suddenly without a word. Enormously talented that one. I elevated her to first violinist and alienated half the upperclass women of the orchestra. One day she was here, the next day she was gone."

On closer inspection, Vincent could tell that Brother Gaspare was not as young as he first believed. He put the Christian Brother's age closer to a young forty. The brother spoke with a slight accent that he thought might be Italian. Brother Gaspare was also in some kind of pain. There was a bottle of aspirin on the desk, and his brow was sweaty. He might ask about it later after he explained about Merriam. "Merriam's parents don't know where she is, Brother, and are very worried. I'm trying to help find her."

"The college made numerous attempts to find her," Brother Gaspare said. "I investigated as much as I was capable of doing. Finally, the college and I gave up."

Vincent was reminded of something that Victor told him about interviewing witnesses. Often, they remembered something helpful after the fact, which was a good reason to conduct two or even three interviews with witnesses. "Is there anything you can tell me that has crossed your mind since? Something new that comes to mind."

"No, not that I can think of. Merriam became enamored of the Grateful Dead Band. God knows why, such a marvelous classical talent as her. She completely changed her lifestyle."

"Yes, we've heard that," Vincent said.

"I wish I could help you more," Brother Gaspare said and wiped his brow with a handkerchief he pulled out of his pocket.

"Are you okay, Brother?" Vincent asked. "Can I get you a glass of water?"

"I'm fine, thank you. A couple of days ago I tripped and fell down a flight of stairs. Luckily, it was a short flight, but I broke a couple of ribs."

"I know how you feel, Brother. Broke a couple of ribs myself playing rugby."

Vincent probed a little longer but discovered nothing more that he could pass on to Victor. For a while they chatted about Saint Mary's College. He learned that Brother Gaspare was originally from the Basque area of France, which accounted for his accent, but had gone to seminary in the United States. He had taught for a year at Saint Mary's before taking the position at Holy Names. He spoke lovingly of the Saint Mary's campus. He had Brother friends teaching there and often spent his free days among his pals.

Vincent asked Brother Gaspare if there was any small detail that might help him discover where Merriam had disappeared. Brother Gaspare felt that he should look anywhere there was a Grateful Dead concert, the same advice the three freshman students had given him earlier. Brother Gaspare also added that he might try investigating the Haight-Ashbury district in San Francisco, which was becoming a hippie haven. He thanked Brother Gaspare and left. It was time to head back and report to Victor.

As Vincent was walking to his car, a thought occurred to him. If it was true what Brother Gaspare said, that he and the college had tried their utmost to locate Merriam, how come her father hadn't known she was missing from college when they showed up at the lot to buy the van? He remembered back to that day, watching Victor talking to the transformed and sexy new Deadhead and her father. If that were true, Parsegian must have known at the time that his daughter had dropped out of college. Why would her father spring for a new car if that were the case? Victor needed to talk to Parsegian.

Anyway, with the ball in Victor's court, he'd completed his mission. He'd report his findings to his twin and head home. Vincent was looking forward to an afternoon at the zoo with his wife and kids. Perhaps a swim in Fleishhacker's pool next door to the zoo. The day had turned sunny and warm. He'd take the family to Fisherman's Wharf for an early Friday supper. He could have cared less about the Catholic tradition of meatless Fridays, but Gloria insisted. So did his twin, who was a Catholic traditionalist, something he had always found curious, given his twin's less than saintly lifestyle. Vincent thought he'd order fish and chips at the zoo.

CHAPTER 4
TRUTH BE TOLD

"Ogni verita non e buona per essere detta.
Every truth is not good to be told."
Italian proverb

Saturday at the Brovelli Brothers' Used Cars was known around the business district of East 14th Street as Barbeque Saturday. By noon, the grill was hot and the chicken, along with Italian sausages, were sizzling fragrantly. Theresa had raised the red and blue Saint Mary's College banners above the office door, the signal that the barbeque was ready to be served to all comers. Theresa had brought two large plastic containers of cannellini bean salad she'd prepared at home for which she'd be reimbursed. It was her family recipe. We provided water; otherwise, it was BYOB. On our speakers, Creedence Clearwater Revival was looking out their backdoor. Theresa and Vincent were manning the serving table. I was in the lot ready to talk to customers.

The barbeque, which was my brainchild, posited that the tantalizing aroma of barbeque would attract buyers to our lot. Father Dunnican, our parish priest from Saint Joseph's, had told our father that this sounded a lot like the Bible story of Esau and Jacob. Esau, unable to resist the aroma of onions simmering in the potage Jacob was cooking, gave up his birthright for the meal. As I recollect, our pop, Big Sal Brovelli, had no idea what the good father was talking about. My theory has yet to be proven to Vincent's satisfaction. Vincent might be right because so far no one has given us their birth right, and no cars have been sold between noon and three o'clock when the barbeque officially ends. But, we reasoned that our barbeque Saturdays were good publicity and had become such a neighborhood tradition that we never gave it up.

The neighborhood freeloaders began to appear. Jitters, owner of the gas station next door and mechanic extraordinaire, who we kept on a retainer, was followed by other guys from Flynn's tavern. Some were already waiting in line. Jitters waved me over.

"I wonder if I could borrow Theresa later this afternoon," he asked.

I didn't need to ask him why. After we had hired Theresa Bacigalupi, our distant Genovese cousin, to be our accountant and office manager, we found out, much to our surprise, that she was a trained automobile mechanic. When she was in high school, without telling her parents, she had signed up for auto shop and outperformed the rest of the class, made up entirely of boys. According to her, she'd been doing a few engine rebuilds to make a little extra cash. Jitters called her an engine-whisperer. I told Jitters no problem. I had my eye out for Nick Parsegian. After hearing what my brother told me yesterday, that Parsegian had not told me the whole truth, we needed to have a little chat.

I spotted Parsegian approaching. He'd fooled me and used the crosswalk this time instead of defying death jaywalking.

From our sound speakers the Grateful Dead were singing something about taking their time drinking their wine. My private investigator's manual that was cleverly entitled *How to be a Private Investigator* advised me not to believe in coincidences, but this had to be one. Theresa was responsible for our Saturday music. We'd also have to have a talk.

I waved Parsegian over and lit into him. I didn't want to give him a chance to think of another lie or half-truth.

"I'm sorry, Victor, truly," he said finally. "The whole thing was so embarrassing."

"If you want me to help you in any way, and I'm not saying I will for sure yet, you got to level with me. Right now, the way I see it, when you bought Merriam the VW bus, you already knew she'd dropped out of Holy Names and was on her way to being a Grateful Dead groupie."

"I didn't know what that meant, Victor."

"For Christ's sake, stop, Nick, you're not an immigrant just off the boat. You know the scene around here. This has been flower power country for the last four years or so. It's tie-dye everything. The country is going through a complete remodel. Tim Leary, LSD, half the soldiers returning from Nam are addicted to drugs and hanging out in the Haight. You were witnessing your Merriam go hippie and now you're scared shitless that something bad has happened to her."

When I started to light into Parsegian, I didn't begin with the idea of being too rough on him, but the more I talked the angrier I got. I thought of what Vincent would have done in Parsegian's place had his first born, his little Christina, as a teen, suddenly showed up dressed as Mother Earth. When Dila and I got married and had a daughter, how would we react?

Then, I thought *if*. The image appeared of me standing at the altar without a bride. My side of the church filled with family and friends, looking bewildered, her side, all the pews empty. I blinked a couple of times to shake the image away.

I stuck my finger into Parsegian's chest. "And where the hell was your wife when all this was going on?" He stumbled backward. Some of the folks around the grill looked over at us. The Grateful Dead were singing about working around the clock and wanting a little whiskey.

"My wife is a good Armenian woman," Parsegian said. "She leaves the big decisions to me."

Menchia. This was one of the many reasons I never liked Nick Parsegian. He thought women were not his equals. Vincent and I learned from childhood that our mom was every bit as important in our family as our dad, and Big Sal Brovelli never made one decision in his life without consulting our mom, Lucia. Okay, so our mother made the decisions always attributed to our pop. Vincent told me that was just a game they played with each other, Italian families being pretty traditional. I remembered telling Dila this and her response, *cute but never in my lifetime.* I heard Parsegian saying something.

"I didn't hear you, Nick. What did you just say?"

"Jay said he was going fishing for three days. He told me that I'd be better off dealing with missing persons because he was in the homicide division."

I'd forgotten Jay's fishing trip. If any cop needed a break away from the chaos that was the Bay Area these days, it was my friend Jay, one of the hardest working cops there was. "You should follow Jay's advice," I said.

"Victor, there was blood in the bus."

"We talked about that already."

Parsegian threw his arms around me. It caught me by surprise, and I almost fell over.

"Help me, Victor. I don't know who to turn to."

"My list of private investigators is in the office. Let me get their phone numbers for you." I tried to free myself from the furniture salesman, but he clinging to me.

"I already talked to four. They want a lot of money before they do any work. How can I trust them not to just keep taking my money?"

Well, there it was, I thought. Parsegian was worried about his daughter, but he was equally worried about his bank account.

"You can let me go, Nick. People will start getting the wrong idea." He released me and stepped back. "Please," he moaned.

Saying please was probably not an easy thing for Parsegian, whose ego was as big as a Cadillac El Dorado. Over his shoulder I could see Vincent shaking his head vigorously.

Jerry Garcia was singing about a sleepy alligator in the noonday sun. The sun had broken through today's cloud cover just to prove there is a strange synchrony between music and nature.

I shrugged in the direction of my twin. I saw him close his eyes. I suspect he was praying that I was not about to do what he thought I was about to do.

"I'll make one run for you, Nick, to the Haight-Ashbury in San Francisco," I said. "I'll check around there. Lots of runaways wind up in the Haight. But that will be all I'll do."

"You're a good friend, Victor," Parsegian said.

I was no such thing.

"Go get some chow," I said to Parsegian. "After I get back from the Haight, I'll check in with you." He opened his mouth to say something, but I walked away before he became maudlin again.

I wanted to avoid my twin, so I took a stroll counter-clockwise away from where he was standing. If I was going to spend any time in that weirdo place, I thought, Sweets Monroe might be someone to take along with me. Sweets was our neighborhood burglar and one of the most complicated men I'd ever met. Around the neighborhood, Sweets Monroe was known as a quasi-Robin Hood. There was never any doubt that burglar was his job title, but at the conclusion of Sweet's burglaries, single moms always found a basket of food and an envelope of cash at their doorstep. The cynics in Flynn's, our local tavern, were quick to remind us that the moms were always good lookers, but it never ceased to surprise me how much arcane knowledge Sweets possessed. Like he could name all the North

American species of butterflies, and, despite Sweets's skinny biceps, it was the rare man who could beat him in arm-wrestling. This accomplishment he explained was attributed to some kind of ju-ju passed down to him by his Cajun – or was it Creole? – ancestors. Sweets' genealogy was always a matter of speculation. One of his girlfriends claimed he'd told her of a great aunt who was a Seminole Indian.

The neighborhood burglar was standing by the grill chatting up a woman who worked at Sears in men's clothing. She was staring at Sweet's Goodwill wardrobe with a horrified look on her face. Sweets was holding a plate of chicken and sausage that could have provided dinner for the poor of Bangladesh. I took Sweet's arm and guided him away.

"Very impolite, Victor," Sweets said.

"I need to talk to you. After the barbeque, hang around. We'll go to Flynn's and I'll buy you an after-barbeque-drink."

CHAPTER 5
FLYNN'S TAVERN

"For whomever is lonely, there is a tavern."
Georg Trakl

The familiar Irish voice of my friend and tavern owner Body Flynn greeted me and Sweets as we entered into the dim light of the tavern.

"Victor, me boy-o, how does an Italian get into an honest business?"

I knew that one. I grabbed Sweets by the arm and pulled him next to me so Body could see him clearly. "Through the skylight with the help of the greatest burglar in the Bay Area."

"Ah, shist, Victor, you didn't bring *fooking* Sweets Monroe into my establishment, did you?"

"Greatest burglar in the state of California, I'll have ya'll know," Sweets intoned in his Cajan accent. "And ah deeply take offense to the word fucking, which you can't pronounce you *fooking* mick."

"You stay right there, Sweets," Body said. "I'm going to get my baseball bat."

"Ah'll be right here with my switchblade, daddy-o."

"Stop with the bullshit, you two" I said. "You know you love each other."

"You're out of your dago mind, Victor," Body said.

On weekends, the usual neighborhood denizens were not in attendance to appreciate the ruckus. The bar seemed empty without them. A couple of guys playing pool in the back stopped and moved closer to what might be something interesting. They were not regulars, so they didn't know it was all play-acting that had been going on for years between Body and Sweets.

Well, maybe not entirely acting on Body's side. Sweets Monroe, who claimed to be a descendant of Jean Lafitte, the pirate, was not bragging when he said he was a great burglar—considering he'd never been caught by our city's finest, which drove my friend Jay Ness, homicide detective

24

for the Oakland Police Department, up the wall and over the edge. Two years ago, Vincent and I had saved Sweets from being prosecuted for the murder of his ex-girlfriend. He owed us, but it was a two-way street since Sweets, a few years before Pop turned the keys to the business over to us, had saved our pop's life from a violent gang called *The Amigos*. How he had managed that has remained his secret. All the guys that frequented Flynn's tavern knew of the connection between Sweets and the Brovelli family. City neighborhoods are not unlike small towns in that everyone knows everyone else's stories.

Both Sweets and I were full of barbeque, so I ordered two Irish Shandies, which is a mixture of a pilsner beer and sparkling lemonade that Body swears is far more refreshing than the bloody British variety of beer and ginger-beer. I knew Sweets liked Shandies. We took our drinks to a booth.

"You never invite me to Flynn's, Victor, so I'm guessing you need my burglar skills once again."

"You're wrong this time. I just need your presence. I'm going to the Haight tomorrow, and I'll be asking the transient weirdos questions. I think they'll be more likely to be forthcoming with you by my side."

"Are you implying that I'm some kind of hippie. Victor, those freaks wear tie-dye, believe in free love and drop acid."

"You believe in free love and your wardrobe is straight out of Salvation Army."

"Ah most certainly don't believe that love is free. Ah always pay for my chicks' meals."

Sweets took a couple of pieces of hard candy out of his pocket and offered me one. I shook my head. Sweets got his nickname because of the amount of candy he ingested daily.

"That's not exactly what free love means, you *chooch*. Anyway, it will only take a morning out of your life, and it might help me find Nick Parsegian's daughter."

"Parsegian is a *saleau*."

"What the hell does that mean?"

"Cajun for dirty old man."

"Sweets, this isn't about Parsegian. It's about his daughter. I'm only doing him this one favor. He's part of our East 14th happy family, right?"

"Okay, Victor, I be your guide into psychedelic land. I'll need to sleep at your place Sunday night if we getting up early on Monday."

"You don't have an alarm clock?"

"My present squeeze dances 'til closing time, and she needs her beauty sleep."

I didn't ask Sweets who the *squeeze* was. With his cockatiel-style blond hair, wildly spaced blue eyes and a body that was skinny from top to bottom, Sweets Monroe was not the kind of man that I'd think women would find attractive, but he had to have some kind of mojo with the ladies because he was never long without a live-in girlfriend.

The two guys that had been playing pool walked by. The tallest looked familiar, but I couldn't place him. He nodded at me as he passed.

"You know who that tall guy was?" I asked Sweets.

"No, but that was one cool Aloha shirt he was wearing. With that tan, he be living in Hawaii or someplace down south like Tee-whan-a."

"Yeah," I said. "Can't get a tan like that up here."

Sweets stuck another piece of candy in his mouth. "So, do I get to bunk on my favorite couch?"

"You driving your hog or the Plymouth we sold you that you're two months behind in payments?"

"Don't start, Victor. Now that I have to pay like all the rest of your customers, it takes a little getting used to."

What Sweets was referring to was the deal that our pop made with him for saving his life: Sweet could purchase any car on our lot, pay tax and license and drive away. It was an unspoken agreement that he wouldn't have to make payments, but after a certain amount of time, we'd repossess the car, clean it up and put it back on the lot. After an appropriate amount of time Sweets would return to the lot, pick out another car and the dance would begin all over again. After Pop turned the business over to us, he made us promise on our honor to continue his handshake agreement with Sweets. *Onore* is a big thing with Italians. It's huge with our pop. However, two years ago, after we saved Sweets' butt, Vincent and I told Sweets our family honor was satisfied, and we were even. In the future, if he bought a car from us, it would be on the same terms as all of our customers. There had been a lot of whining, but Sweets finally saw we would not change our minds.

"One more month, and Vincent and I show up with the jumper cables," I said.

"Two months or I won't go to hippie land with you."

"Two months, but you have to come up with half a payment. Something Theresa can show on our books."

He grumbled something about having to sell some of his stocks or I'd misheard and he'd said something about money in his socks. I stood up. Sweets followed. We said our goodbyes to Body and the two salesmen from Sears whose names I never remembered, both too busy arguing about the Belmont Stakes winner to notice us leaving.

Walking back to the lot, Sweets said, "A friend told me to bet on High Echelon, but I didn't do it."

I wasn't a big horse racing fan but I paid attention to the Triple Crown. "I wish you had too," I said. "You would have taken care of your back car payments."

"We could have used your help cleaning up," Theresa said as we walked onto the lot.

"Didn't Vincent tell you Sweets and I had something to discuss?"

"He was too busy selling the turquoise '60 Chevy pickup you said we'd never sell."

I didn't respond to the zinger. Sometimes, Theresa can be a pain in the ass. Instead, I asked, "Is Vincent in the office?"

She nodded. I told Sweets to keep Theresa company while I talked to my twin. In the office I explained to Vincent what I needed to do Monday morning. Morning only, I promised. It was a promise I wasn't able to keep.

CHAPTER 6
HAIGHT-ASHBURY

"Someone told me there's a girl out there
with love in her eyes and flowers in her hair"

The Love-In-Her-Eyes message was written in chalk in huge rainbow-colored letters covering most of the wall of a store on the corner of Masonic and Haight Street. On the other corner was a Catholic Church. The bells were ringing, announcing to the neighborhood that it was ten o'clock in morning. The bells reminded me yesterday I'd slept in and forgotten to attend Sunday Mass, not something I normally do. I may not believe in all the tenets of my religion, but basically, I'm a believer and take confession and communion seriously, unlike my twin, who sort of shrugs his shoulder at the mention of anything religious. The sign about love made me think of Dila, who was still in New York City at NYU and had not been very communicative recently, so uncharacteristically uncommunicative that yesterday after we closed the lot, I let Sweets off at my apartment and went to visit my ex-girlfriend.

No, don't take it the wrong way. My ex-girlfriend, Rene Sorenson and Dila were friends from the time they both were counselors at a music camp. Their nicknames at the camp, they'd told me was Vanilla and Chocolate, Renee being blonde with super white skin and my Dila being African-American with a latte complexion. I went to Renee for advice. Did Rene know what was going on with Dila? As it turned out, Renee had not heard from Dila either. We tried a couple of times to call her, but with no luck. We gave up and went downtown to see M*A*S*H. It was funny as hell but didn't cheer me up. *Dila on my mind.*

• • •

We'd driven to the Haight in Sweets's Plymouth Belvedere, an upgrade from his previous automobile, a piece of junk 1961 El Dorado Caddy convertible. The Plymouth was far less conspicuous than my new 1970 royal-maroon Mustang Mach One Fastback. Between Sweets crunching on his hard candy and the Zydeco tunes coming from the cassette in the pocket of the driver's door that Sweets refused to turn off, I was relieved to arrive in the Haight. Sweets parked. I got out and walked to Sweets's side and opened the door for him. Smiling, he stepped out. Smiling, I reached inside and pulled out the cassette and smashed it on the cement.

"Dude," Sweets said.

"I'll gladly buy you a new one, so long as I don't have to listen to any more Louisiana cracker songs "

"A C note," Sweets said.

"It's used. Seven bucks," I said. "Let's get to work."

I looked around at the scene in front of us. It was not the *Summer of Love*; more like the summer of insanity. For about two years beginning with the summer of 1967 to 1968, the Haight and surrounding neighborhoods had been filled with flower children who had nothing but peace, music, and free love on their minds—and freedom from parents, someone had quipped. As the decade changed so did the residents of the Haight. Today's 1970s flower children were more likely to be eating what was distilled from the bulbs of orange flowers from Afghanistan, or were tripping on LSD or following the advice in Carlos Castaneda's *Don Juan: the Yaqui Way of Knowledge*. I looked over at Sweets. He was smiling broadly and sort of slip-sliding his body to the rhythm of a flute that was coming from an alley across the street.

"Far out, Victor. Let's see if we can score a little Mary Jane?"

I smacked Sweets on the shoulder. "No dope, *babbo*." The word in Sicilian slang means dope. I knew Sweets knew because I'd called him a dope on many occasions.

"You are a funny man, you," Sweets said. "Let's get this over with. My main squeeze will be waking up wondering where her lover boy is."

We started walking down Haight Street. A couple of large cardboard boxes on the sidewalk moved, revealing feet or heads. This seemed like the extreme definition of sleeping rough. I wasn't sure what I was looking for, or even where to begin. I spotted a sporting goods store across the street with a large going-out-of-business sign 50% to 70% off in the window.

"Let's start over there," I said to Sweets and pointed to the store.

"All you'll get from them is how the country is going to the doggies."

"I'm betting they've been in business a long time on this street and know the lay of the land." I tugged on his sleeve, and we jay-walked across. I opened the door and chimes rang. A portly man stood up from a chair in the corner.

"It's all got to go," he said.

"I'm looking for information," I said.

"I'm not in the business of information, but I got a lot of jock straps."

A comedian, I thought. I started again, holding out my hand. "My name is Victor Brovelli. I really am not in the market for sporting goods. But I could sure use some help."

"I know a Sal Brovelli. You any kin?"

"If you're talking about Salvatore Brovelli from Oakland, I'm his son."

"Big Sal's son. By God, I was sure sorry to hear about your brother. Big Sal used to come down to our Italian club meetings at Salesians every once and a while, and we reciprocated by going to his club in Alameda. My name is Lou Moretti."

I looked at Sweets and gave him a told-you-so-wink.

"Mr. Moretti, pleased to meet you."

We shook hands. "Thanks for your kind words about my brother," I said. "It's been hard on my parents, on all of us." I wanted to move on quickly from the subject of my brother's death. "Let me tell you what brought us here." I pointed to Sweets. "I'd like to introduce you to a friend, Sweets Monroe."

Sweets stepped forward and stuck out his hand. Moretti hesitated, looked Sweets up and down, probably wondering if he might catch some dread disease, decided it was safe, and shook his hand.

"My man is looking for a young woman," Sweets said.

"There are plenty to choose from," Moretti winked.

"That's not what my friend meant, Mr. Moretti." I took my time explaining, trying to get in as many details as I could. According to my P.I.'s instruction manual, the more precisely you explained things, the better chance you had of jogging a person's memory. I was particularly careful to describe Merriam; as beautiful as she was, she'd be hard not to notice.

"Well, yeah, come to think of it, I have seen a young woman that looks like that around, but not in the last month."

"Was she with some people? Would there be anyone I could talk to who might know if she's still living hanging out here?"

"Those kids come and go," Morelli said. "I didn't mind the early days in 1967, but now. . ." He paused and pointed to the For Sale sign in the window. "I've had my shop on Haight Street for 30 years. Time to move on."

"About my missing girl," I said to forestall more talk about how bad things had gotten.

"Yes, you should talk to Father Boniface at Saint Agnes's. It's on the church on corner of Masonic. The good padré has a clinic and safe house. He helps runaways. He's seen it all. You may not like what he tells you. Don't expect good news."

We left Lou Morelli's store with some expectations. "Moving on," I said to Sweets.

CHAPTER 7
SANCTUARY

"Hey Mr. Tambourine Man"
Bob Dylan

Above the open doors to the nave of the church, there was a sign that read:

YOU WANT TO CLEAN UP,
SMELL GREAT AND FLY STRAIGHT
FOLLOW THE ARROWS.

The arrow, painted the colors of the rainbow, pointed to our right in the direction of a staircase where similarly gaudy arrow pointed us down the stairs. All the arrows had wings. *Clever,* I thought. We descended into a large room that at one time must have been an auditorium. At the far end was a stage. On either side of the stage on the floor were doors marked EXIT. The wall furthest from us contained a row of windows. Ten single beds were placed perpendicularly against the opposite wall, spaced about five feet apart. Each bed had its own curtain like the kind you see in hospitals that can be drawn completely around the bed to provide patients with some modicum of privacy. All the curtains were drawn back against the walls and all the beds were empty. A nightstand with a lamp stood next to each of the beds. The stage had been turned into a combo rec room/living room with sofas, easy chairs, a coffee table, two bookcases, a large TV set, a ping pong table and a pinball machine. There was music coming from a stereo system. I recognized the song, Simon and Garfunkel's "The Sound of Silence." One of the sofas was occupied by two young women. As we got closer, I could see they both had sandaled feet propped on the coffee table. One was reading a book, the other a magazine.

Sweets tapped me on the shoulder.

"Dude, that one chick with all that red hair is like knockdown gorgeous."

"We're not here to scope out the chicks."

"You're missing a treat, man."

I was about to say something nasty to Sweets when a voice behind us interrupted my thoughts.

"May I help you?"

I turned to see a tall man in black Levis and black polo shirt. He could have been any guy off the street, but his clerical collar gave him away as a priest. His dark hair reaching to his shoulders was held back by a headband advertising the Grateful Dead. My first thought was I'd come to the right place.

He walked toward us. He had dark penetrating eyes under bushy eyebrows. He had high cheek bones and a square jaw. His complexion was swarthy. He was not smiling. I gave him my best smile. Car salesmen can pull a smile at a funeral. "Hi, Father. Sorry to barge in. Mr. Moretti at the sporting goods store suggested we come talk to you. He said you might be able to help us."

"Lou Marelli is a reactionary who is not fond of our mission."

Ok, a reactionary, I thought, he'd established his creds as the hip priest for the benefit of the two teens on stage who had put down what they had been reading and were listening.

"My name is Victor Brovelli and this is Sweets Monroe." I pointed at Sweets. Sweets turned back from the two girls he was watching. He was sucking on a hard candy. When he smiled, his teeth were orange.

"Padré," Sweets said.

"Love your hair," one of the girls yelled from the stage. Sweets turned back to the stage and gave the girl the peace sign.

Odio, I thought.

"I'm Father Boniface," the priest said. "I ask you again, what can I do for you?"

He had a slight accent, maybe from the South. *How about being polite*, I thought and almost said. I didn't like the suspicious way this priest was treating us. But I didn't understand the neighborhood either. This was like a foreign country. It reminded me of the first time Vincent and I drove into West Oakland to repo a car. Our pop, Big Sal Brovelli, told us to be careful. That's all he said. Two white Italian college boys in a neighborhood predominately black, we should have guessed. We got halfway into the street we were looking for and knew we were in deep shit if anyone saw us repossessing a car.

That's when an elderly woman stuck her head out of a window as we were hot-wiring the car and yelled that would teach Perry, whoever Perry was, that he had to stop messing around and get himself a job. She asked us if we wanted a soda. She introduced us to her neighbors. They all agreed Perry needed to get a job. Two large bottles of Cokes and a brief chat later, we drove off with Perry's repo'd car. We have sent Miss Rhoda Christmas cards ever since. Foreign neighborhoods never frightened us again.

The priest was looking at us, waiting for an answer. At that moment, Sweet must have decided he needed to do something to make up for my present lack of communication skills. He began with a little flourish of his hand.

"*Mon pere*, your priesthood, we be looking for a young lady who disappeared. Ya'll have heard such tearful stories before, being that you help these sweet runaways, and let me say this over in Oakland where my *bon frere* here lives, we be hearing of the fab job you do at Saint Agnes's, but we be grateful for any help y'all can find it in you *bon coeur* to help us."

I wasn't sure what I was hearing coming out of Sweets's mouth, a synthesis of Creole, Louisiana Cajun, street jive and just plain bullshit. By the surprised look on Father Boniface face, he didn't either. "You understand, you?" Sweets finished with another flourish, pointing a long skinny finger at the "*bon frere*."

The priest's expression turned into a grin. "I've heard a lot of BS in my business before, but the Cajun accent sounds authentic enough. Where you from in Louisiana, *mon ami?*"

"Born and raised in Abbeville, Vermilion Parish before moving to the Big Easy."

"*Moi*, I was born and raised in Lafayette."

"Happiest town in America," Sweets said.

"*C'est vrai*," Father Boniface laughed. "That *is* the truth. I went to LSU, then left Louisiana for the seminary."

The detectives in the mystery novels I read are wrong when they say coincidences don't exist. I was witnessing one. For a while priest and sinner chatted, each trying to outdo the other in Cajan. I looked up at the girls on the stage, and they were grinning and snapping fingers. I thought the way things were breaking lucky, I should jump into my Mustang, drive to

Tahoe and do a little gambling. I hated to interrupt them, but I needed to move the conversation to Merriam.

"Gentlemen, "I said. "I was wondering, could we talk about the missing young woman? Her parents are extremely worried." Father Boniface turned around and stared as if he'd forgotten I was there.

"Yes, yes, of course. I forgot. Could you give me a name and a description."

I did, once again paying attention to details.

"Yes, I know the girl, but she went by the name of Samantha. I'll ask my two assistants. I call them assistants but they are more like meeters and greeters, help to relax our part-time tenants, make them feel at home. He took a couple of steps toward the stage and spoke, "Kayla, do you remember Samantha, you got any idea where she might be?"

"None, father. She was only here one night."

"How about you, Ginger?"

"She came here scared," the redhead said. "I can tell you that."

"You find out why?"

"She didn't want to talk about it, and you know, we don't pry. Her business. By the time she went to sleep, she was doing okay and feeling better. I was surprised she took off."

Kayla and Ginger went back to reading, and Father Boniface turned to us.

"Sorry, men. House rules. We don't pry and never interfere unless we're asked. She had a violin case in her backpack. That one night she stayed here, she played. It was *Mendelsohn's Violin Concerto in E minor, opus 64*. She also played the piano, a jazz piece our clients liked a lot better. We have a piano and an organ in the church."

"That's our missing young lady all right," I said. "Did she make any friends while she was here that we could talk to?"

"Not that I recall. You wouldn't get anywhere anyway even if you did find a friend." He paused, "Well, maybe, if your bribe was enough. Bribes work in the Haight, but the best you'd get would be half-truths or out-and-out lies. Most kids around here are looking for cash to support their habits. It's my experience that the body has to heal before the mind does. I know that sounds upside down, but it's the reality I've come to witness." He lowered his voice. "The two girls seated on the stage were skin and bones when they wandered in here. They slept for two days straight. We fed them in return for giving up their stash of LSD and weed. They've been here now for a week. They're going to eat me out of home and church, but we have a chance with them. You see all the empty beds. They'll stay empty until the sun goes down. By midnight, this basement is full."

As the priest talked, I began to feel less lucky. Father Boniface described the Haight as a maze you'd have to be Daedalus to get out of. He called what the runaway inhabitants of the Haight suffered from was the Minotaur of the soul. The good padré had the face of a rock and the soul of a poet. I gave him my card and asked him to call if he saw Merriam. He agreed, but only because I had a good Cajun to vouch for me. He was joking, but maybe not.

Sweets and I walked up and down Haight Street. I let Sweets do the talking. A couple of times, Sweets dug into his pocket and pulled out a ten-dollar bill or a twenty. In return, he received an ounce of Jamaican. I scolded him, but he explained he paid double the price for the weed for information about Merriam.

It was going on noon before we got back to Sweets's car, and we were back in my apartment by one, but I wasn't dissatisfied. What Brother Gaspare had told Vincent didn't mean that the blood in her Volkswagen bus was not hers, but what we learned from Father Boniface was that Merriam was alive. I would clean up and drive to Parsegian's Furniture store and tell him in person. He'd be relieved.

CHAPTER 8
GOOD COP, BAD COP

"Oggi di persona, domaini della tomba.
Today, in person, Tomorrow in the grave."
Italian proverb

The sound of the doorbell buzzing woke me. I rolled out of bed and looked at my bedside clock: 5:10 a.m. *Minchia.* Who the hell would that be this early? I remembered my mother explaining to Vincent that now that he had children, every phone call he and his wife Gloria would receive at an odd hour would strike fear into their hearts. I was unmarried and had no children, but since the murder of my brother Mario, and Dila's near death, I was more sensitive to the frailty of life. The buzzer sounded again, this time with more insistency.

"I'm coming," I yelled as I padded barefoot down the hall. I unlatched the chain and opened the door. Two men in business suits were standing there, Detective Sergeant Mark fucking Halpern and one of his buddies of the Oakland Police Department. Halpern and I had a history that dated back to 1968 when I was responsible for stopping his Oakland Police Department's Flying Squad from illegally raiding the regional headquarters of the BPP, the Black Panthers Party, and later that same year landing a very satisfying right-cross to Halpern's nose.

"This is Alameda, what are you doing here?"

Halpern said, "We'd like to ask you a few questions, *sir.*"

The "sir" came with a wicked smile.

I wasn't going to satisfy him with some snarky retort. "All right ask your question." I didn't move from the door.

"Can we come in?" Halpern's buddy cop asked. I'd never seen him before, but his question had been delivered politely. I nodded and walked down the hall to the living room.

In the living room, I turned around. "Okay, ask away."

"Nice place you have here." Halpern said with a smirk. "Nice little love nest for you and your Black Panther girlfriend."

"*Va fangul*, you bent sunavabitch."

The punch came before I could shut my big mouth, and I doubled over, unable to breathe. The next thing I knew I was on the floor being handcuffed. As my breathing returned, I heard Halpern reading me my rights. "You have the right to remain silent, you have the right to counsel-"

I interrupted, "I have the right to kick your ass."

". . . you have the right to . . ."

Halpern was enjoying himself. His partner was standing to the side with a bored look on his face. Not the polite cop I'd thought, but another jerk.

"You're a dago moron, Brovelli," Halpern said once he finished with my rights. "We were only here to question you. Now we're going to haul your ass downtown and charge you for threatening and assaulting a police officer."

"I never threatened you or assaulted you; it was the other way around. Halpern, I thought bent was your middle name."

Halpern kicked me in my side. A couple of my ribs were not happy. I lay, dizzy on the floor thinking I must be getting stupid in my old age, letting Halpern get under my skin.

"Add resisting arrest to threatening and assaulting an officer of the law. Isn't that so, Officer Lazlo?"

"No doubt about it, Officer Halpern." His partner said.

I didn't remember this cop from Halpern's flying squad that had terrorized black neighborhoods in Oakland two years ago. With some fancy camera work during a riot at a candle light vigil for Black Panther Little Bobby Hutton, I'd managed to capture Halpern's Flying Squad at their violent worst, the result of which forced the Oakland police chief to disband the squad. From then on, according to my friend Officer Jay Ness, I'd become a pariah to the Halpern faction of the police department, the guys I associated with men who used the law to satisfy their need for power. Bullies, all of them. I knew there were a lot of good police officers, like my friend, Jay Ness, on the force and the guys with whom he'd graduated from the academy that called themselves "The Knights of the Roundtable." I'd met many of them, a good bunch of dedicated lawmen, unlike these two goons.

"Okay, Halpern," I said. "You take me down to the station and arrest me, and I'll call my lawyer. I'll make a big deal about our history and your almost being kicked of the force for excessive violence. Let's see who wins that battle. Your badge is so dirty you're lucky there's a shortage of cops or you'd be working as a security dick at Sears Roebuck." I watched as Halpern raised his leg to kick me again. This time his buddy, Lazlo, stopped him.

"Hold up, Sergeant," he said. "We don't need a lot of publicity right now. Remember?" He moved between Halpern and my prone body. He leaned down. "Mr. Brovelli, I'll take the handcuffs off, if you promise not to cause a scene. We can go into your living room, sit down, and we can question you. Does that sound like a reasonable thing to you?"

I realized that I'd assumed Halpern was the lead officer, but from what I was hearing the top cop was his partner. He introduced himself as Officer Jack Lazlo. Despite how my ribs were feeling, the thought of Halpern being busted to sergeant gladdened my heart. I needed my handcuffs off to tell him *Vai a quel paese* which without an accompanying gesture means, simply get lost, but with an obscene gesture has more the meaning of stick it where the sun doesn't shine. Meanwhile, I was on the floor, hands cuffed behind my back with my ribs hurting and remembering that my mother didn't raise a foolish child.

"That sounds okay by me," I said.

"That okay by you, Officer Halpern?" Lazlo asked.

"You make one false move and the cuffs go back on," Halpern said.

Lieutenant Lazlo uncuffed me and helped me up. He steered me straight ahead and sat me on the couch. "Now then," he said. "We're all copasetic, right? No fuss."

"Yeah, you bet. No fuss. Now tell me what all this *merda* is all about."

"Hardly shit, Brovelli," Halpern said. "There's been a crime committed, and you're a suspect."

"Not a suspect," Top Cop corrected. "But you might be able to help us."

"What crime?"

"In a moment," Mr. Brovelli," Lazlo said. "Would you mind telling us where you were yesterday, say, from around four in the late afternoon until this morning?"

"Why?"

"Answer the question first," Halpern said. "Then we'll tell you why."

If I wanted to know what was going on, I thought, I'd better cooperate. The answers were pretty easy. Not a problem. "I closed our dealership. Being Sunday, we close up at five. I'd missed morning mass, so I caught the 6:00 pm mass at Saint Joseph's. After that I went straight home and stayed there until I went to sleep around midnight."

"What did you do at home?" Top cop Lazlo asked. "Did you watch TV, for example?"

Aha, I thought. I'd seen enough Mannix shows to know what was up. "I made *linguine con vongole*. Poured myself a tall glass of *vino* and had my meal in front of the television watching *Hogan's Heroes*. I like Sergeant Schultz. Hogan got him into trouble with his commandant, then got him out of it, so Sergeant Schultz owed him a favor. You want me to tell you how the episode ended?"

"Not need," Lazlo said.

"After that I read until about ten o'clock. Then went to bed."

"What did you read?" Halpern asked.

"What the hell difference does that make, Sergeant?" I said, drawing out the word so even dumb ass Halpern would get the sarcasm. He glared.

I continued, this time trying to sound like a private eye, "I could tell you anything and there is no way it would prove or disprove where I was." I saw Halpern ball his hands into fists.

"So, other than the TV show, you have no other way to substantiate you were home alone all evening? You didn't go out for to the store and buy something for which you'd have a receipt, for example?"

"No, and now you need to tell me what's going on," I said.

"Do you know a woman by the name of Renee Sorenson?" Lazlo asked.

Odio, I thought. I felt my stomach clench. "Yes, I know Renee. What's happened to her?" The minute I asked the question, I knew what their answer would be. Death was written all over their faces and fouled the air in the room. I groaned. "She's dead, isn't she?"

CHAPTER 9
JAIL TIME

"Dei morti, parla bene.
Of the dead, speak well."
Italian proverb

My wrists were bruised from the handcuffs and my ribs hurt from being kicked, but my soul ached for Renee Sorenson. Renee was no longer my girlfriend, but she had remained my friend. I made the mistake of agreeing to return with Halpern and Lazlo to the police station to be officially interviewed. I thought of calling our family lawyer, but I was not being arrested, just interviewed. In Lazlo's words with the hope I could assist them solve the murder. Not a smart move on my part as it turned out. What started out amiably enough in a claustrophobic room sitting at a desk answering questions into a tape recorder. As close as the police doctor could tell, Renee had been murdered somewhere between the early morning to late morning. Forensics could provide a closer time once her body was examined properly. Of course, that left me with no alibi other than my own word. I found myself becoming increasingly nervous as the question became more personal.

"We found a framed photograph of you in Miss. Sorenson's bedroom," Lieutenant Lazlo said. "How do you account for that since you said you have been broken up for two years?"

"I have no idea," I said.

"You weren't cheating on your Black Panther chick, were you, Brovell?"

"I'm outta here, " I said. "No more interview. I know where this is heading. I'm not a suspect so you can't hold me unless you charge me."

"That's not entirely true," Lazlo said. "We found a bunch of fingerprints in Miss. Sorenson's apartment. My understanding is you applied for a California State Private Investigator's license. You see where I'm headed."

"Sure, I've been in Renee's apartment. We're friends. Proves nothing. You don't have near enough to arrest me," I said. "So I'm going home."

"Ah, come on, Brovelli," Halpern said, "you got a rep with women. You were into a little hanky panky while your black chick was gone. You know like after tasting dark meat, you went back to white. Right, Brovelli?"

He was smiling and making little sexual movements with his fingers. That's when I did something foolish but extremely satisfying.

"Sonavabitch!" he yelled as he stumbled backward off his chair, landing on the floor, grabbing his nose that was bleeding all over his dirty badge.

Five minutes later, I'd been read my Miranda rights again and was sitting on a bunk inside a jail cell, waiting for Vincent and our family lawyer, Carter Innis, to show up. Once again, Halpern had provoked me, and I was calling myself *uno stupido gumbah*.

Well, if I was stupid, I'd just have to get smarter fast. I was anxious for Carter to bail me out so I could get busy finding who murdered Renee Sorenson. A moth fluttered into the cell and began attacking the single ceiling light. The moth had a death wish. Was Renee like that moth, looking for danger?

I was thinking of the murderer as a man because I didn't believe a woman could overpower Renee to strangle her, not six-foot, muscular Renee. Renee had been an Ingrid Bergman-like Swedish beauty—a musician, a musicologist, a woman with a great sense of humor. *What kind of monster are you to kill such a vibrant creature?* There was so much to admire about Renee that the great sex we'd shared seemed almost an afterthought. But, yes, Renee was passionate about everything she did and I had been fortunate that she had shared her passion with me. I lay back on the bunk and closed my eyes. I wasn't trying to go to sleep. In the screen inside my brain, I was playing various special moments of our times together. There were so many, they began to spin like one of those early experiments in making movies that looked like a merry-go-round.

The cell door rattled. I looked up and saw my twin and Carter looking at me from the other side of the bars. Carter Innis, son of our family lawyer, Harvey Innis of Innis & Innis, Attorneys at Law. Like Vincent and me, Carter was a Saint Mary's College grad. In college, we'd always thought of him as a little dim—that it had taken him three tries before passing his bar exams added to our negative impression of him. But in May of 1968, during the time Vincent and I were working to keep Sweets Monroe out of the gas chamber, Carter had demonstrated some legal acumen. I was happy to see him. Happier to see Vincent. Behind the two was a police officer holding a set of keys. We talked through the bars.

"Victor, I'm so sorry to hear about Renee," Vincent said. "It's awful. I don't understand how they can suspect you, of all people."

"He's not a suspect," Carter corrected Vincent. "He's here for being stupid and slugging a cop."

"Got to be Mark Halpern," Vincent said.

I shrugged. "They found fingerprints in Renee's apartment. When they check them out, mine will be among them.' I said. "I'd visited her the day before yesterday."

"Victor, keep quiet," Carter said, pointing his thumb over his shoulder to cop behind him, standing by the open cell door. "When we leave this place, we can talk privately. Then I need to know everything."

"Right," I said. 'There's nothing to know. I know nothing. There was a framed photograph of me in Renee's bedroom. That's how they got on my tail. Why Renee would still have a photo of me, I haven't a clue."

"Would you let my client out, please?" Carter requested." He showed the guard the document in his hand.

The officer inserted a key and opened the cell and I stepped out into Vincent's equivalent of a Big Sal Brovelli Italian bear hug that nearly took the breath from me and sent an electric shock through my rib cage.

Vincent leaped away from me. "What's wrong, what's wrong, Victor?"

"Fucking Halpern kicked me in the ribs," I said. "A couple are broken, I think."

"Officer," Carter said, "You are a witness to my client's pain and his accusation. I'll need your badge number."

The officer with the keys did not look happy as Innis wrote down his badge number. I was happy the cop was not happy. I was looking forward to Carter filing assault charges against the Oakland Police Department and fucking Sergeant Mark Halpern. Was I going to break my promise to Officer Lazlo not to make any trouble? *You're damn straight.* Bad cops don't deserve to be cops.

Let's get the hell outta of here. My prints are on file with the State of California. Once they I.D. them, who knows what those two bent assholes will do. I don't plan to go back into a jail cell." I hurried to the exit, Vincent and Carter following behind.

Once we got into Vincent's car and began driving, I explained everything I knew to Carter. We dropped him off at his office. Vincent pulled away into traffic. I told him I wanted to go to my apartment. I was curious to see if Renee's murder had made the morning papers. Probably not, considering she'd been murdered that early in the morning. I'd have to wait for the afternoon edition.

I had been clenching and unclenching my jaw for hours and it was aching. For a while Vincent and I did not speak. He knew I was mourning and angry. He was also grieving. Vincent had always liked Renee and had hoped that maybe she would have been the woman that settled me down. I was reasonably sure he liked her better than he did Dila. It was not that Vincent was racist, it had more to do with Dila's association with the Black Panthers. That, like lots of whites, terrified him. The Panthers terrified me too, but not for the same reasons. I'd seen firsthand how much good they had done in African American neighborhoods. As Dila recently told me proudly that the Panthers were serving free breakfasts to poor black children in twenty-three cities across the United States. For that they deserved a lot of credit.

I also knew first hand through my fragile friendship with Terrance Bowles, the Black Panthers' Minister of Education for California, how unfairly the Panthers were targeted by the FBI and law enforcement across the nation. At the start of the year many people believed a shooting war was imminent. I was terrified for Dila. I knew in my heart that my love for her would never stop her from grabbing her M1 carbine and joining her brothers and sisters of color on the front lines. It would not be a war I could be a part of. As a white, I would be unwelcome by the Panthers. At the same time, I could not in good conscience side with the law.

Thinking of Dila, I dreaded having to get on the phone and tell her what happened to Renee. A few years ago, they'd renewed their friendship from their days working together at a music camp. Two days ago, when I visited Renee, she'd told me she and Dila were planning on going on a road trip up the coast to Canada when Dila returned to the Bay Area. It had annoyed me because while Dila was in communication with Renee, Dila's silence to me was palpable.

We pulled onto the Nimitz freeway.

"You think it's a good idea to be alone?" Vincent asked. "Why don't you come home with me, Gloria will cook a nice meal. We'll talk. You shouldn't be alone, Victor."

"I can handle it," I said.

"You're angry. You sit around stewing; it won't be good for you. I don't want you running off half nuts trying to solve this murder without calming down and figuring things out carefully."

I was relieved to hear Vincent acknowledge that I would have to become a detective again. There was certainly no doubt in my mind. "I need to call Dila," I said. "She and Renee were close. I don't want her parents to tell her before I do."

"You can call her from our house."

"You need to be on the lot," I said.

"Theresa can handle it for half a day."

"Really, Vincent, I'm fine. I may be angry, but I'm also tired and hurting." I touched my ribs to make my point. "I'll talk to Dila and then try to get some sleep." Vincent remained concerned but agreed if I promised to rest.

I promised.

• • •

The noon church bells at Saint Joseph's were ringing by the time we got to my apartment building in Alameda. My building has an elevator, and normally I never use it, but today as tired and aching as I was I passed on my usual routine to stay in shape. I reached my door on the third floor. I unlocked it and walked down the hall to the living room. On the coffee table was a huge bouquet of flowers with a note. I opened the note card. It was from Sweets.

> Mon frere, Renee, one fine chick.
> You need help finding who off her
> you count on Sweets Monroe.
> We kill the muthafuckas. We do.

The flowers were in a large vase that was too expensive to come from a florist. It might even have been an antique. I smiled. It probably belonged in the home of some rich person in Pacific Heights in San Francisco or on our side of the bay in Oakland's upscale neighborhood of Kensington, probably worth a few bucks. "Sweets," I said aloud, "You sweet damn burglar, I'm sure as hell going to need you."

I went to the telephone and dialed Dila. There was no answer. I went to the kitchen and pulled out a beer and returned to the telephone. I dialed again.

This time a man's voice answered.

I asked to speak to Dila.

She wasn't home. Did I want to leave a message?

I did. "Tell Dila it's urgent that she call me. It's about Renee Sorenson. Doesn't matter what time."

"Can I tell her what the problem is?" he asked.

"No," I said. "Just tell her." I hung up. I had no idea who the man was and didn't want to know. My emotions were too ragged, like parts of me were loose and the slightest breeze could blow them away. I finished my beer. There was a phone extension on the nightstand next of my bed. I took off my clothes and threw them into a corner. I'd give them to Saint Vincent de Paul charity. They could clean the stink of a jail cell.

I took a quick shower with the shower door open in the event Dila called. I toweled off, shaved, slipped on a Gael Rugby team T-shirt. Then, I propped the pillows up on my bed and lay back to think.

I'd met Renee at a Mills College mixer in my senior year of college in 1966, but didn't start going out on a regular basis until a year later. Orphaned at the age of nine after the death of her parents in an automobile accident, Renee had been shuttled from one temporary home to another. Because of the instability of her own childhood, she enjoyed the Brovelli family gatherings. She would come to dinner and after dinner, play the piano, play with my sisters' kids, and talk recipes with my mom. Yes, there was an edginess to Renee, her fascination with danger, but she was one sharp and caring lady.

As I thought of Renee's murder, it occurred to me that her murder was more than just a death, it was the destruction of an original. Sorenson was not an uncommon Norwegian name, so there had to be Sorensons somewhere, but as far as Renee was concerned, she had no blood kin. With her murder, it was possible the killer had wiped out one entire blood line of Sorensons. The thought of it made my gut tighten, and I felt sick.

All thoughts of Merriam disappeared, replaced by how to start tracking down a vicious unknown killer. Jay would be home tomorrow from his fishing trip. I'd have to talk to him. I needed facts from the crime scene. I could see out of my bedroom window that the gray day had turned sunny.

I thought I might be able to get some help by reading my manual: *How to be a Private Investigator*, but I had left it on the back seat of my Mustang. I put my head back against the pillow and closed my eyes.

The dream was psychedelic nonsense accompanied by the voices of the Grateful Dead, something about death leaving me crying. Renee appeared in a tie-dye Mother Earth dress, flowers in her hair. I said, "Renee, don't tell me you're a Deadhead."

She didn't answer.

I didn't expect her to.

The phone ringing woke me up.

It was Dila. Her first words were, "Victor, what happened to Renee?"

I couldn't think of anything else to say except the truth. "Someone broke into her apartment early this morning and murdered her."

Dila began to cry. I waited. The crying went on. Finally, I heard her breath deeply. "Oh Lord," she moaned, "Who'd want to kill Renee?"

"I'm going to find out," I said.

"The two of us will find out," Dila said. "I'll be on a plane tomorrow. I'll call you at the lot to let you know when I'll be arriving." She began crying again. In the background, I could hear a male voice asking her what was wrong. Dila hung up.

I could have answered the man's question. Everything was wrong.

CHAPTER 10
LA FAMIGLIA

"Devi defendere il tuo onore. E la tuo famiglia."
You have to defend your honor. And your family."
Italian proverb

Once Vincent had dropped Victor off at his apartment, he stopped at a gas station and called Theresa. He explained what was going on, and he asked if she could handle the lot for the rest of the day because he had to help his brother. Theresa agreed, saying how hard this must be for Victor. Theresa had not been working for them during the time Victor was dating Renee, but she was a cousin in a close-knit Italian family that, according to an old Italian proverb, lived inside everybody else's pockets, so she couldn't have helped knowing how much Victor cared for Renee.

Vincent thanked her. He called his wife at home and explained to Gloria that he would not be at the lot for the rest of the afternoon. He'd be at his parents' and then he had to do some work for Victor. Vincent had already told Gloria earlier what had happened, so he didn't expect her to argue with him as she usually did whenever she believed he was going to get involved with his twin's on-going *casinos*.

This was not a simple screw up, but a full-on tragedy. *"Vai ora, aiuta tuo fratello,"* she had said. He'd replied that he'd do what he could to help his brother. His wife kissed him through the telephone. Vincent touched his lips to the receiver.

Back in his car, Vincent was reminded how much he loved Gloria who was a nag about little things, but when it came to important matters, especially if they had something to do with family, she could be counted on. *Mia famiglia,* he whispered.

He started the engine and pulled away from the curb. Alameda was a small island community. It would take him less than ten minutes to get to his parents' home.

• • •

His father poured three glasses of red wine and placed them on the kitchen table. Vincent knew the ritual. Whenever his pop sensed a serious topic was about to be discussed, out came the wine and up went his suspenders. His mom was already seated. Big Sal sat down next to her. Vincent pulled out a chair and joined them.

For a moment they didn't speak. Vincent traced his finger over the few burls in the walnut grain of the tabletop. Where his mom was sitting, Victor had used his newly purchased boy scout pen knife to carve what looked like a little beetle. Their pop had taken his belt to both of them because he wanted to make sure he spanked the real culprit. There were other marks and scratches on the wooden surface of the table, each one evidence of he and his twin's artistic history.

His mother spoke first, "*Vincenzo*, you look like a man with a story to tell."

Vincent saw a troubled look on both his parents' faces. Having suffered through the death of their son, his older brother Mario only four months ago, Vincent hurried to explain. He told them about Renee's murder and Victor being under suspicion and that he needed to support his twin. "Pop, I need a favor."

"Whatcho want?" Big Sal asked.

I need you to run the business for a week or so while I help Victor. Theresa will be there. She knows the finances."

"You think I forget so easy? Theresa good Italian girl. We do okay together. You take time. *Onore, Vincenzo,* we cannot have peoples think bad of *Vittorio.*"

Vincent thought he should have expected his father to bring up his favorite word, honor. It was the foundation upon which Big Sal based his life

"Right, *La famiglia,*" Vincent said, hoping he didn't sound sarcastic.

He watched his father's face turn proud, as he rose from his chair, hooking his fingers into his suspenders and puffing out his enormous chest. Big Sal Brovelli knew how to strike a pose.

Vincent stood and embraced his pop. He kissed his mom on the on her on the top of her head and nodded when she said, "*Stai attento.*"

He would definitely follow his mother's advice to be careful. He had a bad feeling about this murder, nothing he could point to specifically. Victor had once explained his version of gut feeling to him as an annoying little noise some cars made that no mechanic could figure out. When he had told his wife, Gloria, about it, she'd called it intuition. He felt intuition was more a female thing. What he felt was not so dramatic, simply a bad feeling, why complicate matters? Vincent considered himself an uncomplicated man, unlike his twin who could complicate a children's nursery rhyme.

His next stop was back to Victor's apartment. He looked at his watch. It was 3:34 p.m. Time enough for his brother to have rested. They needed to decide what to do. To start with, the fate of Merriam Parsegian would have to be put on hold.

• • •

There was no answer when Vincent rang the doorbell. He rang it again. Then knocked loud enough that Victor would have heard even if he was asleep. So, where would Victor have gone? He left and drove to the car lot, hoping to find Victor there. No, Theresa told him, she hadn't seen Victor. Vincent walked next door to Flynn's tavern. He entered and heard Body's voice.

"Ah, it's about fooking time, Victor, you told us what's going on."

Vincent was relieved Body hadn't started with one of his sick Italian jokes. He could never figure out why his twin put up with them. He stepped out of the shadows. "Wrong Victor," Vincent replied. "You need glasses."

"I need better lighting, Come to think of it, maybe you should get a scar somewhere on your face. Man-you-up some."

"I'll pass," Vincent said.

"You want a beer?" Body asked.

"No thanks. Has Victor been here?"

Body shook his head. "Jay was in," he said. "Just got back from his fishing trip. He told us about Victor's ex-girlfriend, Renee, being murdered." Body tapped an open afternoon Tribune on the bar. "Second page," he said. "Not a lot there. According to the Oakland police it was a brutal murder. Police investigating. Nothing concrete. Is Victor in trouble?"

Vincent could see a number of the tavern usual customers, Larry Hughes, one-time Oakland Raider and owner of the DoNut Hole, sitting farther down the bar with Jitters and a few guys from Sears a couple of bar stools down from them. They all turned in his direction. At the end of the bar sat Jack Swann, owner of the auto detail shop. Everyone called him Swanee for the Suwanee River in Tennessee, the state of his birth. Swanee waved, then moved up a few seats to hear better. A couple of pool players in the back stopped their game and stepped closer to listen. One of the guys worked at Sears. Vincent couldn't place the other tall, skinny fellow-- not from the neighborhood. Except for those two, Vincent knew all of the men of the tavern by their first names. He explained what had happened. A cheer went up when he described Victor punching Halprin's nose.

"Those two sure d-do hate each other something f-fierce," Jitter stuttered.

"Remember when Victor head-butted Halpern on his sneezer last year?" Body asked. A cheer went up again.

"Nose got to be getting a bit tender," Larry Hughes said.

Vincent went on to explain that Victor was out of jail after posting bond. Was Victor in trouble? Just for assaulting a police officer.

Swanee explained that the newspaper described that Renee's murder had been particularly brutal, that she'd been beaten badly and strangled.

"Victor loved that woman," Body said. "He told me the breaking up was without any, you know, angry stoof."

Around the bar, heads nodded in agreement.

"That's the story, for now, Body," Vincent said. "If Victor shows up, tell him I need to talk to him. I'm not going to be at the lot, but he can leave a message for me with Theresa."

"I'll do better than that," Body said, "If Victor comes in, I'll hold him here. You check in with me."

"I will. Thanks, Body." With a wave to the guys at the bar, Vincent left and walked back to the lot. In his car, he thought about what he should do next. If only he could find his twin, then they could make plans. Jay Ness was back from vacation. Perhaps Victor was with him. The police department would be his next stop. As a detective sergeant in the homicide division of Oakland police, Jay would be able to provide him with crime scene details. In the automobile business, the more you knew about your product, the better chance you had to make a sale. That had to be true of solving crimes. He started the engine and drove away.

At the police station, the desk sergeant, who often came to their Saturday barbeques, told him that Victor had not been there, and that Detective Ness was at the crime scene.

Mills College was off McArthur Boulevard. Vincent took Broadway Street north. He took Broadway through downtown and through what used to be called Auto Row, home to numerous new and used car dealerships. The freeway had cut into the city of Oakland. Many dealerships had already moved into the suburbs.

Vincent dreamed of a dealership in the suburbs. If he'd believed in religion, he'd have lit candles. His twin was the true believer, which had always seemed odd to him, since between the two of them, Victor was by far the greater sinner. Maybe that was the point. His twin needed the confessional.

Vincent turned left onto McArthur and a mile or so later turned through the campus gates to visitors' parking. It didn't take long to find two police cars in front of a three-story building with a sign in front that said Unmarried Faculty Residency. The door to the building was open. He stepped toward the door just as Jay walked out.

"For Christ's sake, Vincent, what are you doing here?"

"I've got a twin brother, if you haven't forgotten."

"This must be hard on Victor. You still shouldn't be here. This is a crime scene."

"And my brother is a suspect."

"You don't think I understand? Why else would I be here and not at home in a hot bath on my last day of vacation?" Jay was dressed in jeans and tan fishing vest over a white T-shirt. "Look, Vincent, I can tell you this much," Jay said. "So far, Victor is not a suspect. They found a photograph of him in her bedroom. But, considering they had a relationship, it's understandable. There's no word yet on fingerprints, Vincent."

"When will the fingerprints be identified?"

"Crap, Vincent, you're not going to start playing private investigator too, are you? Please don't tell me that. One Brovelli playing detective is all I can handle."

"You know me better than that, Jay. I don't approve of Victor playing P.I. One of these days, he's going to get himself killed. But Victor is my twin. I want to know everything I can. Let's say, if his fingerprints show up in the apartment, will that be enough to get him arrested? If he's arrested for the murder, we already have a lawyer. I need information."

"If I talk about this, it could cost me my job."

"If you don't, it could cost you our friendship." He hadn't meant to sound as if he was threatening Jay, but it had come out like that.

"Jesus, Vincent," Jay said.

"I'm sorry, okay. I'm sorry. Our parents are really worried. Mario's death just happened. They don't need any more trauma in their lives. Is there any possible chance Victor would be charged with the murder?"

Jay sighed. "Ask your questions. I'll answer if I can."

"Other than the fingerprints and photograph, what hard evidence is there that would affect Victor?

"Time and opportunity. Some kind of witness testifying they heard them arguing, like that. Yeah, the fingerprints. If they find his prints in her bedroom, that would hurt. It's a lot of times how the investigating officers deal with the evidence. Halpern is not a fan of your twin. I'd say if Victor's fingerprints are found on Renee's body, it's a sure bet they'll arrest him. Whoever murdered her took her underpants. That's between you and me. You hear."

"Absolutely. Anything more you can tell me?"

"That's all I can say, Vincent."

"That's all you will say, you mean."

"Yeah, Vincent, that's exactly what I mean."

"What floor is the apartment? I want to go and look around."

"On the 3rd floor, but only the police can go in. Go home, Vincent. Leave this investigation to the professionals."

"Well, how about-"

"Go home, Vincent," Jay cut him off. "Go home to your wife and kids. I'll help Victor, but I won't stand for any interference. Understand?"

The look on Jay's face told Vincent that it would be best to leave before Jay got mad.

He walked slowly back to his car down paths bordered by eucalyptus trees and lawns and past halls of higher learning. They brought back memories. He had entered college already having sold cars, gotten paychecks, opened a bank account, and set up an investment plan. What else had he needed to learn? Not about Greek plays that were so depressing he and his business major pals felt compelled after class lectures to buy a couple of six-packs of Bud and try to think of chicks or sports. It had been a revelation to him many years later to find that Victor actually liked those dreary lectures, and an even greater revelation later that Victor had a bookcase in his bedroom filled with novels and poetry. It had made him question the theory that twins thought alike. Not wanting to embarrass his twin, he had kept what he'd discovered to himself.

Vincent reached his car. On the drive home, he wondered if Jay had told him all of the facts. At least, so far, Victor was not a suspect. But things could change rapidly. . . and what kind of sicko killer would take his victims' panties?

CHAPTER 11

CONUNDRUM

"When you have eliminated all which is impossible, then, whatever remains, however improbable, must be the truth."
Sir Arthur Conan Doyle

There was a loud noise. Someone was banging on my door. This was getting to be a habit. *Fuck 'em*, I thought through the pillow I had over my head; they weren't going to take me back to jail. *I'll barricade myself in my bedroom. There'll be a siege. I'll negotiate. I'll call for takeout. In the end, they'll break the door down, but I'll have slipped out the window and leapt on to the billboard with its Marilyn Monroe likeness, paid my respects and jumped to the sidewalk and made my escape. Public Enemy #1, Victor Brovelli.*

I woke up.

I wondered if I'd been dreaming. I removed the pillow to see if I was in the middle of a dream. No, it was my bedroom. It was still daylight. I was home safe, and Renee was dead. I pulled the pillow back over my head.

The next thing I knew it was dark. I looked at my bedside clock. 10:46 p.m. I tried to go back to sleep but it was no use. I staggered out of bed. I watched a late-night movie on TV. It was *Picnic*, a 1956 flick I'd seen a number of times, the last time with Dila. After the sexy dance scene between William Holden and Kim Novak, I turned it off. Listening to music didn't lessen my growing depression. At midnight, I went to bed with a copy of *Finnigan's Wake*. I figured if anything could put me to sleep, Joyce's stream of consciousness would. Ten minutes later Joyce's words were closing my eyes.

I woke up angry and sad. I was out of jail on bond, I'd beat the assault charge. Carter would see to that, but I was feeling vulnerable. Lazlo and Halpern were the officers in charge of the case, I could anticipate being hauled back to jail on some trumped-up charge. I knew some dirty cops planted evidence. This had that feel about it. The Oakland Police Department, overworked, under-manned and anticipating a shooting war with the Black Panthers, would want to solve ordinary murder cases quickly. *Talk about an edgy national and local atmosphere.* Renee's murder would not be a huge priority.

It was getting light outside. I walked down stairs for the morning *Tribune*. Back in the apartment, I drank coffee while I skimmed the paper, looking for something about the murder. I found it on page three. It was less than an inch column about a homicide at the all-women's Mills College with few details and no name given. I wanted to talk to Vincent. I needed to talk to Jay Ness as well. I wasn't planning on working so I dressed casually in khakis and a polo shirt. I grabbed my bomber jacket just in case the weather turned colder.

The drive from my apartment in Alameda to East 14th took less than fifteen minutes. I parked my Mustang in my space in back of the office. I turned the corner to the building and saw Theresa standing outside, having a smoke.

"Oh, Victor, I'm so sorry about Renee," she said as I stepped toward her.

"I can't get my head wrapped around it. It's too awful."

"Vincent was looking for you all day yesterday," Theresa said,

"I was sleeping."

"He said he tried your apartment."

"I was in a coma."

"He'll be in soon. You also got a message from Dila. She's flying in at 4:50 this afternoon on United. I wrote the flight number and put it on your desk."

"Thanks, cuz," I said, and went to the office. Theresa followed me in.

At my desk, I stuck the note with the United flight number in my pocket. I stared out the window at the cars that filled our lot, the source of our income and additional retirement income for our parents. When I'm anxious, checking out our inventory of cars always soothes my nerves. They are solid hand-picked vehicles, declared mechanically sound by Jitters, our genius mechanic who made our cars run like new. In the center of the lot, on a podium, stood a dusty blue 1937 Ford Deluxe station wagon, a classic Woodie. I loved those horizontal door panels of golden pine. It was not for sale. We called it our shill, like a beautiful woman that casinos pay to play at gaming tables to attract customers. This was one of many spectacular promotional ideas that I took credit for. The real credit went to my twin for finding it and having it towed to Jitters for repair, after which it took its exalted place on the platform. *It was a beauty.*

My attention was drawn across the street to Discount Furniture, and I was reminded of Merriam. As I was looking, Nick Parsegian opened the doors to his business and stepped out on to the sidewalk and looked at our lot. It made me feel bad. I saw Vincent's bronze and cream Chrysler Town-and-Country station wagon turn into our driveway and disappear behind our office. A few minutes later, Vincent appeared in the window. He entered the office.

"Where the hell have you been, Victor? I was all over yesterday hunting for you."

"I was asleep."

"I rang your doorbell, I banged on your door."

"I was in a coma."

"Some frigging coma. Okay, it doesn't matter. We need to talk. Pop will be here any moment."

"Pop? Our father?"

"Yeah. I recruited him to take over for a couple of days. You and I have to get busy solving this murder. I can't have my twin brother in San Quentin."

"Calm down, Vincent. They put you in San Quintin for assaulting a cop?"

"You can't sell cars behind bars," Vincent said.

"You're a poet," I said.

"Like Cassius Clay," Victor said.

"Like Mohamed Ali," I reminded him.

"Whatever," Vincent said. "Boxers don't sell cars either."

Our pop coming to help out surprised me, but in a good way. It sounded like Vincent was ready to kick butt, and when Vincent decides to take something on, he's like a dog with a bone. Together, the Brovelli Boys would find out who murdered Renee Sorenson and bring him or her to justice. Then, I remembered Merriam.

"We can't forget Merriam," I said.

"I was afraid you'd say that, Victor. She's not on the top of our priority list, you are."

"I understand, but listen. Doesn't it seem strange to you that Merriam disappears, possibly murdered, then shortly after, Renee *is* murdered."

"There were two weeks in between, Victor."

"I know. But Merriam's disappearance and Renee's murder could be linked."

"How?"

"Music. Renee is a grad student in music at Mills. Merriam is a gifted violinist and starting her first year in college at Holy Names. Renee was in the Oakland Youth orchestra. Merriam is now. According to her father, Merriam wants to major in music. Renee and Dila were music camp instructors. I wouldn't be surprised if Merriam as a kid went to the camp. It's in Travis City, Michigan and pretty famous."

"All that makes some sense, Victor, but Merriam's disappearance has to do with her father and family stuff. Renee connects back to you. I just don't buy the link."

"You're just being argumentative. I've been thinking about this since I woke up, and I'm hearing my annoying-car-noise."

Victor Brovelli intuition," Vincent said.

"Be as sarcastic as you want, asshole. I know what I'm feeling."

"Who are you calling an A-hole?"

"You, you *cretino*," I said standing up from my chair.

"*Calme, bambini*," Theresa called from her desk. "*Calme!*"

I looked at Victor. He was staring at me clenched jaw and fire in his eyes. I looked at Theresa, and burst out laughing. Here I was a murder suspect and my twin and I were going to duke it out. Vincent laughed. Then, Theresa started laughing.

"Is good to see my sons having laugh when they should be on the lot selling cars."

Vincent and I turned toward the door at the same time. Big Sal Brovelli, our pop, was standing in the doorway, preventing the light from entering. He was wearing a navy pinstriped suit, white dress shirt and red tie that was his salesman's uniform for as long as we had known him. The color of the tie was optional. The suit smelled a little like mothballs.

CHAPTER 12
PUTTING OUR HEADS TOGETHER

"Don't always look ahead.
Sometimes the answer is behind you."
Chick Nguyen, "The Greatest Lady Burglar"

Vincent and I stepped through the door of Flynn's Tavern. Body saw us, and I braced myself for the bad Italian joke that usually accompanied my entrance. But there was only silence. Not to hear Body say, *Victor, me boy-o, have you heard about the Italian yada, yada* was a new experience for me, and considering what was going on, a welcome one.

We took the two empty seats closest to the door.

"Victor, we're all with you. It's terrible what the garda did, arresting you. You had every right to punch him."

Voices down the bar echoed, "Here, here." I knew that Halpern was not a beloved member of the East 14th neighborhood, but I didn't realize how much he was despised.

"Sonava bitch tried to squeeze me for free bottles of wine," Ozzie Averbuck the owner of A & B Liqueurs said.

It gave me a warm feeling to witness the support my fellow East 14th Street neighbors gave me. These were middle class law and order Americans all the way, but they knew what a bent cop looked like.

"That damn Jay," Body groused. "He should set his Halpern straight."

"Cut Jay some slack," I said. "He just got back from vacation."

"Jay was at the crime scene, Victor. I forgot to tell you. I talked to him there."

I turned to Vincent. "So, what did Jay say?"

"He told me if I started playing detective like you, he'd kill himself."

"Not funny. We need Jay to help."

"He's willing. But you know. He gets nervous when you start sticking your nose in."

"This assaulting a cop thing is too bogus for me to worry about. Did Jay say anything that might put me into the picture?"

"Well, he mentioned your framed photograph in Renee's bedroom. He also said if your fingerprints are found in Renee's bedroom, Lazlo and Halpern might think they have enough circumstantial evidence to arrest you. Jay doesn't think they could get a warrant unless they had additional hard evidence."

"Well, that's a relief," I said.

Body placed a mug of Anchor Steam in front of me and a bottle of Bud in front of Vincent. "You guys want chili?"

I hadn't eaten breakfast. "With lots of cheese and chopped onions," I said. Vincent shook his head.

"Let's grab a booth," Vincent said.

We took our drinks and moved into one of the empty booths that lined the opposite wall.

"All right, Victor, how do we start? Where do we start?"

"I'd like you to work on the Merriam side of things." I saw the question mark in Vincent's eyes. "I'm serious," I said. "I have that feeling. Somehow Merriam's disappearance and Renee's murder are connected."

"I don't think so, but I'll go with your instincts. I'll work it for a couple of days and see how it shakes out."

I was relieved because Dila was coming home, and the two of us would take on solving Renee's murder. I gave Vincent all the information Sweets and I had managed to acquire in the Haight. He wrote it down in the little pocket-sized notebook he always keeps in the inside pocket of his sports coat.

Body brought me my chili, a spoon, napkin and bottle of hot sauce, as if his chili wasn't hot enough already. While I ate, Vincent and I talked. I couldn't figure out who the hell would want to kill Renee. She was smart and talented. She was highly educated and both a skilled musician and a PhD candidate in music. She had no character flaws that I could think of except, well, I wouldn't call it a flaw. . .

Renee was turned on by danger. Nights at Grizzly Peak turnout came to mind. Renee and me in my Mustang, me telling her a story about how my brother Vincent stuck the barrel of a pistol in a gangbanger's ear in order to save my life. The more dramatically I painted the scene, the more aroused Renee became. There were many such nights of different exciting tales during our relationship. She even turned down the idea of going to a motel, explaining the close quarters of a car produced stronger pheromones. *You gotta love a woman like that.* If Vincent knew that I used his exploits to increase Renee's libido, he would have been shocked.

Maybe not entirely shocked but certainly disapproving. I was not about to tell him now. It would remain Renee's and my secret. Mine, now that she was dead. The thought depressed me, then made me angry. I suggested to Vincent that he keep exploring the Haight district and investigating the Grateful Dead aspect of Merriam's life. I also told him he should find out more about Brother Gaspare. I told him I'd call him from time to time to discuss our progress.

"What if they re-arrest you?" Vincent asked.

I thought we'd already dealt with this subject, so the question surprised me. "You think they will?"

"Let's say that Jay didn't seem really confident they wouldn't."

"*Merda,*" I said. "If that happens, call Carter Innis. But for a while I'm not taking any chances. I'm going to check into a motel for three or four days. I can't investigate if I'm behind bars."

"Geez, Victor. You don't want to be a fugitive."

I love that Vincent hardly ever swears. *Who the hell says, geez?* As for me, I don't know how to talk without swearing. I said "I'm not a fucking fugitive yet. I'm just going to keep a low profile." That seemed to relieve my twin. I told him I'd let him know which motel once I made up my mind. He left to see how Pop was doing on the lot. I remained to finish my chili and have another beer.

And, to do some more thinking. I would check my *How to Be a Private Detective* manual to find out if there was anything in it about avoiding being arrested. I didn't recall anything like that in the book. I continued eating and thinking.

Swanee stopped by on his way out to say how sorry he was about Renee. I nodded and thanked him. He warned me not to play pool with the guy in the back, pointing in that direction of the tall, skinny guy wearing a cowboy hat.

"He's a pro," he said.

"Did he hustle you?"

"No, I'll give him credit, he warned me when I wanted to play for money." Swanee left then turned back and said, "He has his own pool cue."

"I'll keep it in mind," I said. Swanee didn't have to worry. I was no pool player and never played for money.

Ten minutes after Swanee left, I used the door myself. When I stepped on the lot, Pop and a customer were standing next to an adobe beige and Sierra gold 1957 Chevy Belair mid-range Two Ten. Pop's hands were busy talking. I walked away quickly so he wouldn't see me and poked my head into the office.

"*Tuo padré e um uoma felice,*" Theresa said.

"He looks happy to me too. Vincent gone?"

"He took off about fifteen minutes ago."

"Did he tell you that both of us will be off the lot for a few days?"

"Yes." Theresa said. "He filled your father and me in. *Buono fortuna.*"

"Thanks, cuz. We'll need all the luck we can get."

With that, I stepped out of the door and headed around to the parking area behind our office and my Mustang. As I pulled onto East 14th, Parsegian was standing in front of his store. He waved to me to stop. I felt bad but kept driving. I looked at my watch: 2:40 p.m. I needed to go to my apartment and pack enough for at least three days in the wind.

In my apartment I pulled out a small suitcase from under my bed. I put in three changes of casual clothes, three days' worth of underwear, socks, my dope-kit and *Finnegan's Wake* in case I needed help going to sleep. On top, I folded a hoodie and some workout clothes if I found time for a run. In the top compartment, I placed a pair of dress shoes. Some of the jazz clubs I intended to visit were classier than others. I took a sports coat, slacks and dress shirt out on a hanger and placed it in a garment bag. I hung my bomber jacket over the garment bag. I checked the back door then phoned Sweets.

"You need a house sitter?"

"What did I just say? I don't want anyone inside my place."

"Bad ass cops, you mean?"

"How'd you guess?"

"I gots powers, *mon ami.* Beeg powers."

"I'll put the keys in the. . ."

"No need," he interrupted, "ah put a shazam on your lock."

I was about to hang up when Sweets said, "You know, Victor, sometimes people make fun of Sweets Monroe, *tu sais?*"

Yeah, I knew, but I didn't know how to respond.

"It's okay. Sweets understands. But that tall drink of water, Renee, she always treat Sweets like I was no joke."

"Renee was real," I said.

"You find the killer, you."

After assuring Sweets that I would find the killer, I hung up and checked my watch. Even with rush hour traffic starting, I had more than enough time to get to the San Francisco Airport and meet Dila.

CHAPTER 13
THE GREEN-EYED MONSTER

"Oh, am I fortune's fool."
William Shakespeare

Watching my fiancé, Adila Agbo, walking toward me, I got a lump in my throat and a pain in my heart. It had been four months since she'd returned to New York City to resume her studies at NYU. So many calls to her apartment, so few return calls. And recently when I called to hear a man's voice answering the phone and a man's voice in the background while I told Dila about Renee's murder: *Dila, honey, what's wrong?* Did he actually say the word *honey* or was that my imagination?

Dila waved to me, and I waved back. I was smiling; she was not, but she did fall into my arms and we stood there embracing. Over her shoulder I saw some people staring at us. Even in the liberal Bay Area, it was still unusual to see a white guy with a black woman in an embrace. I winked and the starers stared elsewhere. Some people can't find the way out of their own racist hearts, Dila liked to say whenever she noticed people staring at us, and if she caught anyone glaring, *Odio*. Dila with her battle-face on was a sight to behold.

"Oh, Victor," Dila moaned, "I've been crying all the way across the country. One of the stewardesses stopped and asked me if I wanted one of her ludes. A woman behind me told me that her sweetheart had also been killed in Vietnam. She gave me a telephone number for a grief support group that meets at Saint Mark's Episcopal."

"You should have taken the lude."

"Maybe I should have," Dila said.

"Your luggage will be coming in over there," I pointed to an United Airline sign.

"This is all I have, Victor." She was holding onto the handle of a small carry-on suitcase. "I have enough clothes at home. We're going to find out who murdered Renee then I have to fly back to New York."

The lump in my throat and pain in my heart that had disappeared with our embrace returned. "I thought we were going to have the whole summer,"

"I thought so too, but there are a lot of crazy things going on. The FBI and the cops around the country are gathering their forces. We all have to be ready. Terrance wants me to assess what's happening on the East Coast. I told him about Renee. He's cool about my taking time to help you, but he wants me back on the job as soon as we're finished."

The Terrance Dila was referring to was Terrance Bowles with whom I had a tentative friendship. "I thought your job was your PhD."

"When was the last time you talked to Terrance?" Dila asked, avoiding answering me.

I thought. "A month, maybe a little longer."

"He would have told you that we're in a crisis."

Five months ago, Terrance Bowles and I and Giant James, Bowles's bodyguard, were sitting in my Mustang across the street from the Monterey docks, waiting for trouble. I could hear Bowles's voice. "*Victor, when push comes to shove, Dila will choose her people over you.*" I wondered if this was going to be that time. I couldn't bear the thought of it, so I didn't say anything. Instead, I took Dila's suitcase and began walking out of the terminal to the parking area. Dila caught up and walked next to me. We didn't speak until we reached my Mustang.

"You have anything to eat at your place?" Dila asked.

"I do, but Sweets is housesitting. Jay told Vincent that there's a chance that I might be re-arrested. I decided to check into a hotel for a few days, just in case."

"Oh, Victor, this is all so insane."

"Don't worry. It might just be rumors, but better to err on the side of caution. There's a real nice hotel, the Forest Hill Inn in Lafayette, not far from our college. It's where the school puts up visiting dignitaries. It's got a good restaurant, sort of continental cuisine. They don't make a bad lasagna, but their steaks are some of the best meats ever. They have what they call their Hungry Cowboy Special for two. Good old American chow."

"You talked me into it." Dila said. "But first we should make sure their beds are comfortable."

"Traffic on the Bay Bridge will be awful this time of day but considering the possibilities, I think I can make it in about ten minutes."

"Lead on, McDuff," Dila said and smiled broadly at my exaggeration. It was my Dila talking, not the Black Panther warrior. A distinction between the two was something that I thought I had come to grips with, but perhaps not completely. There was the Dila Agbo whose face turned to stone when listening to reports of Southern bigotry, who'd one time shown me how fast she could break down and reassemble her M1 Carbine. On the other hand, there was Dila, the musician who worked at children's music camps, the same Dila who was an actress and a playwright who laughed at silly jokes and swooned over banana splits, and wept as the TV announcers counted the week's Vietnam body bags. I breathed a sigh of relief that the Dila I liked best, my future wife, was the one sitting in the passenger seat, her head resting against the window, her green eyes half-closed, looking peaceful.

I started the engine and drove out of the airport area faster than the speed limit.

• • •

First, we treated ourselves to some long overdue love making, and then in the hotel restaurant we launched into the sirloins. It was served with a baked potato the size of a Nerf football and green beans in a mushroom gravy.

We avoided talking about Renee. We talked about Dila's PhD dissertation, some about the Brovelli car business, our parents. Her father was planning another trip to West Africa, this time with a group of African American business men for the purpose of investing in a number of the post-colonial countries, one of which was Benin. Mr. Agbo's ancestors were descended from Benin's Betamaribe tribe.

"My daddy has been studying French like crazy preparing to go back to Benin."

Her dad was a nut in my mind. He was the one who'd insisted Dila go through the Betamaribe tribal ritual of scarification even though it was hardly practiced anymore even in the rural villages. In his daughter's case, luckily, not on her beautiful face, but below her belly button. Dila had explained to me proudly that it signified her coming of age. That such craziness had not bothered her had at first been surprising, but as I got to know Dila, I realized how deeply she was invested in the cultural roots of her race. Unlike her father whom I believed was a phony, there was nothing contrived about Dila. The scars were tiny dots of raised flesh like braille that were artfully created to look like the spread wings of a bird. As I'd gotten used to them, they reminded me of body art, kind of like a tattoo.

Dila's father was large, smart, arrogant and wealthy. He did not approve of the Black Panthers or any of the other combative Black organizations from the separatist Nation of Islam to Martin Luther King Jr's non-violent Southern Christian Leadership Conference. He did not approve of Dila and me getting married. Dila's mother was somewhat better about us. She might have even come to like me a little, although I'm sure I was not her choice for her daughter's husband.

The day we told *my* parents we were engaged, Pop said, "*La mamma dei cretini e sempre incente.*" The literal translation is: The mother of idiots is always pregnant. In Italy one says this when seeing a person or people acting foolishly. When Dila asked what he'd said, I told her he'd called us idiots. These days when the subject of our marriage comes up, Pop just shrugs. My mother sighs.

I did not ask about the man on the phone in her apartment, and Dila did not bring up the impending war between law enforcement and the Black Panthers. We ordered dessert. In keeping with the All-American Cowboy themes, it was apple pie with vanilla ice cream along with coffee.

Back in the room, I uncorked a bottle of champagne I'd ordered before we went to dinner that had been chilling in a bucket of ice. We clinked glasses.

"So, how do we proceed, Detective Saturday?" Dila asked.

It was the name she'd given me after I'd told her she was my Girl Friday. I explained about my jazz club theory that Renee loved jazz and could have met her killer in a club.

"That makes sense," Dila said. "Renee was really getting into jazz the last couple of years. She had some ideas about creating jazz concertos and jazz symphonies. There was some musician or perhaps he was a music teacher she spoke about who was a composer. . ."

I interrupted, "What was his name?"

"Let me finish, you macho Italian. I know she told me, but I can't remember. He didn't teach at Mills."

"Try to remember. It would be the first actual name we can connect to Renee. Did she say she was romantically involved?"

"No, that I would have remembered."

"But maybe he thought they were."

"Give me some time and I'll come up with his name. In the meantime, let's do the jazz clubs. We might be able to get more names."

"Was she dating anyone?"

"No. She said once you ditched her for me, her romantic life was over."

I had not told Dila about the photograph of me, Renee had by her bedside. I'd have to at some point, but not now. *Coward*. I looked around for the voice.

"Come on, get serious, Dila. This murder was so violent it looks like hate."

"Sorry. Look, you need to drop me off at home so I can check in with my folks. Why don't you pick me up at eleven? Things don't start really hopping at jazz clubs until around midnight. Also, if folks are drinking, they tend to be a little looser about talking to strangers."

"Where will we start?"

"San Francisco. They have the best clubs with the best jazz artists. Renee would want to hear the top musicians."

We had tested the firmness of the mattress one more time before leaving. I pulled out of the hotel parking lot and headed west to Oakland. I asked Dila if she wanted to hear some music. She nodded. I told her to look in the glove box and pick out what she wanted to hear. She looked at me oddly. I said, "Check out the dashboard."

"You have a cassette player," she said. "That's not standard on this Mustang, is it?"

"I had the factory install it. It's worth every penny. There's a Billy Holiday compilation."

She found it and inserted it in the player. Billie Holiday is good driving music. The moon was not blue and Victor Brovelli was not alone.

Before getting out of the car, Dila kissed me hard. She waved to me from the porch. I drove away feeling much better about us. I'd heard from other people what jealousy can do to a relationship. I did not want the monster with green eyes in my life.

CHAPTER 14
NORTH BEACH

"By and large Jazz has always been like the kind of man,
you wouldn't want your daughter to associate with."
Duke Ellington

In the middle of the week, at ten o'clock at night, traffic across the Bay Bridge was light. Behind us, the lights of the cities of Berkeley and Oakland were shimmering like costume jewelry, while ahead of us the Pacific fog had snuck in under the Golden Gate Bridge like a white ghost ship and had slipped into the hills beneath Coit Tower and reached the pinnacle of the TransAmerica building. Soon the fog would swoop down and blanket North Beach. But so far, lights still shone in the windows of some buildings and the street lamps along the Embarcadero directed us to Fisherman's Wharf and our destination, the clubs along Broadway.

Dila and I were in my Mustang, listening to a cassette of Art Tatum whom Dila told me was one of Renee's favorite jazz pianists. I was happy to show off my new toy and had placed a bunch of cassettes in my glove box that I knew Dila would like. Tatum was playing "Willow Weep for Me", as I took the Embarcadero exit that dropped down to Broadway and the North Beach night club district. There were four jazz clubs on Broadway, so we could park and walk from club to club.

"Remember when we went to the Monterey Jazz Festival?" Dila asked.

I was concentrating on a jerk in a Chrysler in front of me weaving, either drunk or having a heart attack and wasn't listening. "What?"

"The jazz festival in Monterey, remember last fall."

"Yes, what about it?"

"Remember that clarinet player with the funny name, Peanuts Hucko?"

It took me a moment to focus. "Oh, yeah. Part of the opening act. There was a vibraphonist Renee kept saying was the best she'd ever heard. A Red something."

"Red Norvo," Dila said.

"Were you making a point?"

"Sort of roundabout," Dila said. "There was bass guitarist with them that Renee had her eye on all night. He was in the audience when MJQ came on, and she was flirting with him. He had tattoos all over him. He looked like a con. I told Renee. You know what she said?"

I shook my head.

"It was classic Renee, 'Doesn't he look deliciously dangerous?'"

"Was he a local musician by any chance?" I asked.

"I wouldn't know, but it's worth asking around once we get in the clubs."

On the corner of Broadway and Columbus was *The* Condor Club where the voluptuous Carol Doda performed. I thought of the steering wheel knob with her half naked torso picture on it. Vincent and I had attached the knob to the steering wheel of the 1966 Mustang we'd given our older brother Mario as a gift when he had returned from Vietnam, which he'd removed after he met his girlfriend, Grace.

And then, both of them dead. I didn't want to think about it. So much death recently in my life that I wondered if I was cursed. Would Renee's ghost appear to me like the ghosts of the past had: Sweets's girlfriend, the beautiful Winona Davis of two years ago; Mario and Grace's ghosts four months ago? Every once and a while out of the corner of my eye, I see Mario, not as a specter, but as he was when we were growing up, helping Vincent and me: homework, showing us his collection of Boy Scout badges. Vincent says he sees Mario like that too, but he does not call them "ghost memories" as I do. Ghosts are not part of Vincent's world like they are in mine. I have come to believe that my great Aunt Maddalena's prediction that seeing *fantasmi* would become a permanent part of my life had come true.

I found a parking space on Columbus Street just down from Bimbos 365 Club. It used to be a successful supper club that my mom and pop went to occasionally because the owner was an Italian.

"He was called Mr. Bimbo," I said when Dila asked if my parents knew every Italian in California. "His real name was Agostino Giuntoli."

"You're a wealth of Italian lore," Dila said.

We were walking the two blocks back to Broadway. I said, "North Beach is like Little Italy in New York."

"I've been to a couple of Italian restaurants in Little Italy," Dila said.

While we walked, we held hands. Out of the corner of my eye I watched Dila, beautiful, tall, at 5'10", almost my height, her Angela Davis afro like a dark halo. Thinking back over girlfriends, it occurred to me that I must have had a thing for tall women. Renee had been tall, and the girlfriend before her, Gina or Sophia, was taller than me. I didn't need a photograph of Dila. Whenever I wanted to see her all I had to do was close my eyes and there she was looking at me through those green irises, the right one with a speck of amber in it.

"Renee was attracted to dark-looking men," Dila said.

"Black men as well as white guys?"

"No, I'm not talking about skin color. Guys that had that bad boy thing. You know like a dark side. She always mentioned your name. Guys like you."

"*Madonna.* Like I'm a bad boy?"

"Well, you and your brother get in a lot of predicaments, don't you?"

"Not of our own making," I replied.

"Maybe it was that sexy scar under your eye or all those wild stories you told her."

I felt myself blush. "That was before I met the love of my life."

Dila squeezed my hand. "Cool it, Brovelli. I'm not accusing you. I bet you don't know that Renee keeps a framed photograph of you on her bedstand."

At least I didn't have to tell Dila about the photograph that led Lazlo and Halpern to my door the morning of the murder. "I didn't know that. And I don't understand."

"Easy, Renee still loved you. She confided in me right after she broke up. It was one of the reasons she left the country and went traveling around. Leave us to ourselves. Renee was a real fine woman."

I needed to change the subject. "Which club shall we start with?" I asked.

We'd reached the corner of Columbus and Broadway. To the left were most of the nightclubs, to our right up the avenue in the direction of the Broadway Tunnel were mostly restaurants, my parents liked one where the waiters sang arias. The fog had reached the crest of the hill above the tunnel and was drifting down. Straight ahead of us across Broadway was City Lights Books, famous for publishing and distributing the poetry of the Beat Generation.

"We could go down Columbus and do a little nostalgic trip to Vesuvios."

When Dila and I were first dating, rather than meet in Oakland where there might have been a chance of someone we knew seeing us, we'd meet in San Francisco. The first tavern we met in was Vesuvios. "That would be fun, but we better stay on the job."

"Right, Detective Saturday."

"Right, Girl Friday."

We turned left and crossed the street and passed the Condor Club. We continued up the street past Finochios that featured female impersonators. We arrived at Basin Street West, walked in, paid the cover charge and found an empty table.

Dila said, "That's Oscar Peterson on the piano."

Most of what I knew about jazz I'd learned from Renee and Dila. I liked some of it. Some of it got too strange and made me uncomfortable. My pop would have said, "give me Franco Corelli singing an aria any day."

My eyes adjusted to the gloom. The waitress came to take our order. We asked for beers. I showed the waitress a copy of a photograph of Renee and asked if she remembered her. She shook her head. I explained that Renee was my sister, and she was missing. I could have said murdered, but it might have freaked her out. Instead, I turned on my dimples. She sighed, said she was really jammed tonight, but she'd show the photograph around to the bartenders and other waitresses. I thanked her. She left and returned with our beers. I gave her the picture.

Oscar Peterson's music was interesting. The crowd was attentive and appreciative. I asked Dila if she knew the tune. She shook her head.

"So?" I said. "See any dangerous men?"

"Those dimples of yours are dangerous, Brovelli," Dila said.

I was about to say something smart-alecky about my dimples when our waitress touched my shoulder.

"I'm sorry, I asked around. No one remembers a girl that looks like this."

She handed me the photograph. "Keep it," I said. "Ask your bartender to show it to other shifts, okay." I handed her a few more photographs, some of my Brovelli Brothers' business cards and twenty bucks. "Could you ask him to call if she shows up."

The waitress smiled and said she would. We left our beers half drunk and Oscar Peterson's set half completed and left. It was past midnight.

Our next stop was the El Matador. The Modern Jazz Quartet was playing there and the place was so full we could barely squeeze in. No waitresses or bartenders remembered anyone who looked like Renee being in but with the caveat that shifts of waitresses and bartenders changed. We left more photographs of Renee and my business cards to pass around. On the way out, one of the bartenders waved the photograph at us and yelled above the sound of the music. "Foxy lady."

At the Jazz Workshop we got lucky.

"Carl, the bartender at the far end over there," the waitress said, pointing, "He remembers your sister. She came in about a week ago,"

"Alone?" Dila asked.

"No, he said she was with a man."

"Could he describe him?" I asked.

"All he said was that he was tall, well-built, you know, kind of rough looking, but he remembers she called him daddy, like it was a joke. The guy was not laughing. Carl's got this crazy memory. He said they didn't look like they liked each other very much."

"Was that the only time they were in?" Dila asked.

"As far as Carl is concerned. He works a ton of shifts. Got an ex, three kids and a new wife. I asked the other girls. They don't remember her."

It was now one o'clock and bars closed at 2:00 a.m. We had only an hour to hit the other clubs. Sugar Hill was next. No help there. Neither Dila nor I recognized the singer, Jay McShane, but I really liked the tune, "I'll Catch the Sun". We stayed to listen to it. On the way out I told Dila I'd give the sun to her if I could catch it. When we first met, her *hrumumphs* always signaled her disbelief or annoyance with me. Now the sound felt a little more loving.

We crossed to the other side of the street.

"Let's skip the Hungry I," Dila said. "I just can't see Renee in there. Besides it's mostly folk music and comedy. We kept walking. At the corner, we looked down Columbus. We were tempted to go to Vesuvio's for one drink, but decided to go to The Cellar Club instead.

"Some kind of poetry and jazz combination performances going on there," Dila said.

"Groovy," I said.

"You sound like Sweets," Dila said.

"Sarcasm noted," I said.

We walked to The Cellar and down the stairs. It was shadowy and full of cigarette smoke. I don't smoke, so I found a corner table away from the crowd seats around the bandstand. No one came to serve us, so I went to the bar. I asked for a Bud for me and a Coke for Dila.

"Twenty-minutes to closing," the bartender said.

"Is there another set?"

"Yep, about to start."

He left to get our drinks. I pulled out the photo of Renee and placed it on the bar. When the bartender returned with our glasses. I asked him to take a look, telling him the story about Renee being my missing sister.

"Nope, and I got a good eye for good-looking chicks. Not so much of that runaway stuff goes on around the North Beach. You might be better off hitting the Haight for your missing sister."

I explained about Renee being a musician and loving jazz.

"Yeah, that sounds right. I'll ask my waitresses."

We drank our drinks and listened to a bass and a flute back up a poetry recitation of Allen Ginsberg's "Howl".

Dila said, "Could be the revolution is coming."

I thought "Howl" was a bunch of bullshit but didn't say anything to Dila. We listened and waited until the bartender got back to us with the information that none of his waitress remembered seeing Renee, then we left.

As we were walking up the stairs, one of the waitresses stopped us. She said she'd seen Renee or someone who looked a lot like her at an afterhours jam session in the Haight that a folk singer named Faith Petric, held every Friday at her apartment. I asked for an address. She didn't know the numbers, but it was on Clayton Street. She wished me good luck finding my sister.

"Well, we know more than when we started," I said, as we stepped onto the sidewalk and began our way back to my car.

"Yes, we know Renee was seen with a dark-haired guy she called daddy."

"Maybe like a sugar daddy," I said.

"Could be," Dila said. "I don't think sugar daddies like to be reminded that they're sugar daddies."

"So that was why he wasn't looking happy, according to the bartender," I said.

"It's a start. On Friday, we'll go to this folk music jam session."

"Vincent is handling the Haight district looking for Merriam. I'll ask him to check it out. We stay with Renee's murder. Vincent will deal with the Grateful Dead crowd. And I want him to take a look at Merriam's VW bus. By the way, you wouldn't remember when you guys were music camp instructors whether Merriam Parsegian had been enrolled?"

"I see where you're going, trying to connect the two, but I saw Merriam Parsegian perform for the Oakland Youth Symphony last year. Renee and I were also camp counselors then. We got to know the kid musicians well."

We were walking through wisps of fog. Dila shivered. I put my arm around her.

"Alright," Dila said. "I'm jet lagged. Let's go to your hotel and get some sleep."

On the drive to the Forest Inn, Dila rested her head on my shoulder and a hand on my thigh. In my mind, I rewrote Shakespeare: *To sleep or not to sleep, that's an easy question.*

CHAPTER 15
RENEE

"La gratitudine e la memoria del cuore.
Gratitude is the memory of the heart."
Italian proverb

In the morning after a lazy room service breakfast, I drove Dila to Berkeley and home. I saw the door to her house open and watched her mother, whom I'd nicknamed Queen Agbo, embrace her daughter. I pulled away from the curb and went looking for a telephone booth. I called Vincent. My twin didn't sound happy.

He explained that Theresa had raised her right hand and sworn she'd kill herself if one of us didn't come down to straighten our pop out about how things were run. I felt bad for my twin. According to him, he'd spent the morning bringing Big Sal Brovelli up to speed. Our speed, not Pop's speed, which was the way Vincent described it me, *deja vu* all over again, a Big Sal Brovelli & Sons' way of doing business. In those days before it became our business, there was never a question who was the boss.

"Victor, it's driving me crazy."

I told Vincent to go home at noon and relax with his children and Gloria. I'd take the afternoon. No cops had come looking for me and no warrant had been issued, so I figured I could take a gamble I'd survive the day without being arrested in order to help Vincent. Vincent apologized that he'd missed a day of detecting. I gave him absolution and hung up.

The rest of my morning, I spent tracking down and talking to Renee's friends from her graduate school. All of them had been shocked and frightened by Renee's murder. Many of them had already been interviewed by the police. A couple of them remembered me as Renee's boyfriend of a

76

couple of years ago and were not friendly. None of them had any idea of Renee's present male friends, although all were sure she must have had one or two. One woman told me that Renee was too attractive to be without suiters, a word that was too old fashioned to be associated with Renee, who was certainly a modern enlightened female. None of Renee's friends provided me with anything useful.

I looked at my watch. It was a little after eleven. I was hungry, and I wasn't far from the lot. I'd have an hour for a quick meal at Flynn's. It was Thursday, Body's famous I-Dare-You-Chili.

Ten minutes later, I pushed in the doors to Flynn's Tavern and sat down at the first open seat at the bar next to Larry Hughes who was so large across the bottom that he flowed over on either side of his stool. His mouth filled with chili, he grunted a hello. I was hungry, but knew I'd have to suffer one of Flynn's awful Italian jokes before he would serve me. He approached with an evil smile on his round Irish face.

"Victor, me boy-o, what does an Italian have when he has one arm shorter that the other?"

Given a little time, I probably could figure it out, but the chili Hughes was eating smelled delicious. I said, "Tell me and make it quick."

"A speech impediment."

Body laughed all the way back down the bar and into the kitchen. He was back with a bowl and a mug of Anchor Steam in each hand.

He placed both down in front of me, then took a spoon and fork out of his apron pocket. "You'll need a lot of water today," he said.

"Bring the fire hose and some crackers," I said.

"Make it two fire hoses," Hughes said, mopping his massive brow.

I dug in. Body returned with a basket of crackers and small bowl of shredded cheddar cheese. Hughes nodded at the empty cheese bowl in front of him.

"I'm going to start making you pay, Hughes," Body said. "That was your second. Three strikes and you're out."

"I was a football player. Baseball metaphors don't count. I need the cheese to control the flames."

"Metaphors is it? You'll be having me thinking you're educated next."

"I got through the fourth grade, one grade higher than you."

"Got you there, Brother Body," a guy a couple of seats down from Hughes said. I looked up to see it was the new guy to the tavern, the one who carried his own pool cue. I nodded at him. He smiled and raised his hand.

"Been meaning to say hello. I'm Dustin Kramer. Just moved to these parts."

"Victor Brovelli," I said. "Nice to meet you."

"Sorry to hear about your trouble."

I didn't want to get into a conversation about my troubles or his troubles or trouble in general. To my relief, he didn't pursue it with a follow up comment or question.

"Sure do enjoy Brother Body's vittles," he said. His accent was from the South, but not the Deep South. The word hillbilly came to mind, but that was sort of like saying my pop had a dago accent.

"Can't beat it," I said.

"Join me in a game of pool after you're finished?"

"I'm not much of a pool player," I said.

This exchange brought Larry Hughes's head up out of the trough.

"Better you don't, Victor. Man torched me. Lucky we weren't playing for money, he'd have owned the DoNut Hole. Got his own cue, which indicates professionalism to me."

The guy named Dustin Kramer reached down and lifted a black leather cylinder and held it up so I could see it.

"Brother Hughes is right, got three more of these babies. This one is my favorite. It's partly how I make my living, playing pool and snooker. But I never hustle amateurs."

"That hurts," Hughes said.

Kramer smiled again. It was a friendly smile. I was about to ask him where he'd come from when Body interrupted.

"Here's your cheese, Hughes, me boy-o. I'm running out. I have to keep some for the rest of my customers, so this one is it."

"Why don't you come over for a few of the donut holes you like so much tomorrow morning? I'd like the opportunity to act like an asshole too."

Listening to my two friends' back and forth and the spicy chili and cold beer helped me to forget Renee's murder and that I was under suspicion.

Kramer, the pool pro stood up, gave me a quick salute and walked to the back in the direction of the pool table.

The big hand on my watch told me it was almost noon. I finished my chili and said my goodbyes. On my way out I heard Larry calling for more chili and Body yelling some Irish expletive as the door closed behind me.

I had parked behind Flynn's Tavern. I was about to get in my car when a police cruiser turned into the driveway and parked beside me. Jay Ness stepped out.

"How hot is the chili today?" Jay asked.

"Lots of fire hoses," I said.

"You want to join me?"

"I was just inside. I got to relieve Vincent."

"Thank God, no private detecting," Jay said.

"Jay, we're talking about Renee, not to mention two very unfriendly cops are looking to pin this murder on me. Tell me if I'm wrong." I looked in Jay's eyes. Jay will usually be straight with me, but if he is silent or equivocates, that means Victor Brovelli is in deep *merda*. "Am I in deep shit, Jay?"

"I can't talk about it, Victor. Look, you're not going to be arrested today, okay?"

"How about tomorrow?" I listened to Jay's silence. Maybe that was the silence people in the Midwest hear as the sky turns green before a tornado lifts their houses off their foundations.

"I'm hungry, Victor. And I just got back from vacation and my good friend's fingerprints are all over a murdered woman's apartment. And there's another anti-fucking-Vietnam march scheduled for tomorrow. So, do you get the picture?"

I stared at him squinting my eyes. "Maybe," I said.

"Fuck you too, Victor. No, you will not be arrested tomorrow, can't make any promises after that. The captain is in consultation with Detectives Lazlo and Halpern. They're the lead on the case, not me. You know how Halpern feels about you. Whatever you do, Victor, stay away from the crime scene and don't go sticking your dago nose into the investigation. Now, I'm going inside and eat. I'm due back in an hour and I'd truly like to relax."

I felt bad for my friend. I should have had a little more empathy. I knew how overworked all the cops in the Bay Area were.

"They still have you working without a partner?" I asked.

"Yeah, and a few other detectives as well. We're stretched thin. Captain doesn't like me much, so when things ease up, if they ever do, the asshole will probably hook me up with a rookie."

"That's tough," I said. I gave him a little we're-still-friends fist-tap on his shoulder. He returned the favor. Jay lumbered around the corner of the tavern. He looked like he'd gained weight on his vacation. If he sat next to

Larry Huges, it would look like an elephant and a hippo at the watering hole. I got in my car, fired up the engine and drove down the driveway, turning onto East 14th and next door on to our lot. I had paid for three nights at the Forest Hill Hotel, but Jay said I wouldn't be arrested tomorrow. I'd risk sleeping in my own bed. I'd keep the two nights in the hotel in reserve, just in case. I'd call Sweets and to tell him to vacate for the night.

• • •

My twin was smiling as he drove away. Vincent smiling made me smile. It wasn't often I could do him a favor. He could play with his kids. Maybe try for a third baby while his kids napped. I sometimes find myself jealous of Vincent's single-minded belief in the benefits of marriage. I had a feeling that my marriage to Dila, if it ever came to pass, would not be as comfortably settled in as Vincent and Gloria's marriage. I waved to him as he turned on to East 14th. I headed for the office.

My first order of business was talk to our pop. Our pop's first order of business was to tell me he'd paid Sweets Monroe to help me clear my name. When I asked him whose idea it was, of course, it had been Sweets. I was actually thinking that the next step in my investigation would require a burglary, but I did not like it that Sweets took advantage of Pop and Mom's generosity. I'd have to straighten the distant relative of Jean Lafitte's ass out.

"Is not a problem and not your biz-e-ness what I pay Sweets to help you, Vittorio. Go home. You and Sweets find killer. You keep your *onore*."

I could see from the set of my pop's jaw that I shouldn't say another word. Our mom and pop's relationship with Sweets was inscrutable and frustrating. Vincent told me once that it had to be more than Sweets saving Pop's life. He reminded me that Sweets was one of the first people Mom and Pop met when they set up the car business on East 14th, to which I'd said so what, and Vincent had replied it was like our parents were birdwatchers and had just discovered a Cebu Flowerpecker, one of the rarest birds in the world, a piece of arcane information that my twin comes up with because he watches strange shows on late night TV when he can't sleep. Given that Sweets looks like a cockatiel, I remember I had a hard time stopping laughing. My twin never had much of a sense of humor, so when he occasionally comes up with something funny, I've always tried to encourage him.

I knew if I left, Theresa would put her hands around my throat, so I told Pop I was staying but we could close early if it wasn't busy.

By 5:30, I was putting the key into the door of my apartment. The first thing I did was yell at Sweets to take his shoes off if he was going to lie on the couch. I made coffee and we drank it. I explained what I needed, and he assured me it would not be that difficult. I left him sitting on the couch, munching hard candy and reading Playboy. I went to my room and stretched out the bed. Since Sweets and I were going to start a little clandestine work at midnight, I intended to take a nap, but sleep didn't come. What was Dila doing at home with her parents?

I turned to my P.I. manual. I'd review the important chapters. Some time ago, I'd decided that most of the crucial information in the book could be found in John D. MacDonald's Travis McGee novels. I was halfway through *A Purple Place for Dying*. I suspect I read the manual out of habit to keep in P.I. shape, like athletes keeping themselves from getting rusty. One of the primo instructions in both the P.I. manual and MacDonald novels, was follow the money, phrased differently in both cases, Agatha's being more literary. I worried about that instruction for a while. Money did seem like a possible motive for Merriam's disappearance since her daddy was as rich as Midas and doted on her, but the Parsegians had not received a call or letter demanding payment.

As for Renee, there was nothing I could think of that connected her to money. The motive for murdering Renee that seemed most plausible to me had more to do with passion—maybe jealousy. Since renewing my friendship with Renee, I'd queried her on several occasions about her love-life, and her answer had always been the same: *I don't have the time for men these days*. After being rebuffed a couple of times, I stopped asking. I didn't want to pry. As I thought about it now, Renee's protestations, given her passionate nature, didn't seem credible.

I spoke to the ceiling, "Not a chance, not the Renee I knew from the back seat of my Mustang."

I put down my P.I. manual. Why the hell couldn't I be a P.I. and be a good car salesman at the same time? All that either-or *merda*. The Bay Area was full of *Love-it-or-Leave-it* bumper stickers. Vincent had a right to worry about my commitment to selling cars, but he'd have to wait a while for me to decide. I would have to be a detective for a while.

I closed my eyes and pictured Renee: Tall, slender, high-waisted and long-legged, she could have been a high jumper or a runway model. She possessed the kind of Norwegian beauty that comes to mind when thinking of a young Ingrid Bergman. Most of last year, Renee had been traveling, but when she'd returned, we renewed our relationship, this time as friends.

While Dila was studying in New York City, it was comforting to talk to Renee who was a friend of Dila's from their years being counselors at a music camp. There was no jealousy on Renee's part and no regrets on my part. I was going to marry Dila. Renee was supportive.

Sometimes, I'd bring coffee and donuts to her place. Occasionally, we had dinner. We attended concerts. I began to enjoy classical music. She played in a string quartet and I'd come attend. Since we parted without any hostility, our past intimacy was a memory we both believed took our friendship to a higher level. I had shared this idea with Dila, and she had agreed. Dila's words came back to me: "*Brovelli, you might be finally beginning to understand women.*" A great wave of gratitude flowed over me for Renee, for allowing me into her life as her lover, but mostly as her friend. I had my sense of *onore* and I owed her plenty. I would repay my debt.

• • •

Sweets woke me up at midnight. I had fallen asleep in my working clothes. I got out of my sport coat and slacks and put them in the cleaner's pile. I told Sweets there were leftovers in the fridge and went to the bathroom to take a quick cold shower to wake myself up. What I had in mind that needed Sweets' expertise was getting into Renee's apartment without the cops knowing it. The front door would have a yellow scene-of-crime tape across it, so it would have to be a window. Since Renee's apartment was on the third floor of a five-story building, it would make it difficult no matter what Sweets believed. Over the last couple of years when I'd been faced with solving murders, Sweets had helped me break into apartments to search for evidence. You could say we were developing a symbiotic relationship. I was pretty sure the State of California private investigators' licensing board would not approve of our relationship.

I returned to the living room wearing my burglar's outfit: black jeans, black hoodie, zipped to the neck, and black Converse Chuck Taylor All Stars. Sweets was similarly dressed in a skin-tight outfit that looked sort of like a diver's wet suit. His shoes were low-cut somethings. The burglar was standing at the kitchen counter eating cold lasagna and drinking coffee.

He pointed at my Mr. Coffee that was emitting a fragrant aroma. I poured a cup and tasted. "What's in this?" I asked.

"Chicory, *mon frere*, I brought some with me."

"Tasty," I said.

Sweets finished the lasagna. Our coffee drunk, it was time to go.

"Before we leave," I said, "give me the money my pop gave you."

"Say what?" Sweets said. "I didn't hear you, Victor."

"You heard me. I'll pay you if the job gets done to my satisfaction. It may not be the same pay scale you talked my pop into. You understand. Give it up."

"You think I carry that kind of bread around on my person, you crazy, you."

I backed Sweets skinny ass up against the counter. I reached inside his pocket and withdrew all the bills. Five hundred bucks in all. I stuffed a C note back in his pocket. "I'm returning the rest to my pop. Consider the hundred as a retainer."

"I'm insulted," Sweets said. "I should go home; leave you to climb the wall. See how you like falling a couple of stories."

"But you won't because you know another hundred is waiting for you. And that's fair, right?"

"Two bills for a five-story job, you're low-balling *moi*."

"Sweets," I said, lowering my voice down to a warning level.

"Okay, you win, *mon ami*. Sweets give up. I do this for Renee, not you. Let's boogie. Get this over."

It was close to 1:00 a.m. when we drove into Mills College campus. All was quiet. Mid-week, students were asleep or studying, not out and about. The moon, however, was out and shining brightly, so two men on a women's college campus might be more easily seen and raise some suspicion. We needed to be careful. The unmarried student residency hall was at the back of the campus and away from the undergrad dorms. We chose a parking space in the back of the building. Sweets had brought a backpack. We walked quickly to the side of the building Renee's apartment was on. It was past midnight. There was only one window with a light on. From it came the faint sound of a saxophone playing some mellow jazz.

"I scoped this out for you earlier," Sweets whispered. "I got to go in from the roof. I hope you're not afraid of heights, Victor."

"Heights?"

"You stay here out of sight. I'm going to do my thing. You'll see what you have to do when I do it."

"Can you be a little more specific? I thought we were going in through the door."

"No can do," Sweets said. "Fuzz put a big old chain on the door. There is a sign on it. It's from your friend the cop. I kept it for you." Sweets pulled a square of cardboard out of his pocket. On it I read:

Victor
Just so you don't do something dumb.

Sweets was grinning. "No worries, *mon frere*. Sweets get us in. I be the best burglar from here to the Big Easy, *non*?"

I had graduated from *mon ami*, my friend, to *mon frere*, my brother. I controlled myself.

"Okay, bro," I replied. "Guess the best burglar should get started."

Sweets ignored the sarcasm and nodded, strolling casually away and around the corner of the building. The bright moon cast a light over him and he and the backpack combined to cast a weird shadow on the ground of a deformed creature. He turned the corner and disappeared from sight. I hunched down between two parked cars and kept my eyes on the roof. I had no idea what to expect. Fifteen minutes went by before I spotted Sweets leaning over the top of the roof. He turned around so his back was to me.

Che cozzo, what the fuck, I thought as Sweets stepped backwards into the air. I leaped from my cover, hoping to reach him in time to catch him, or at least break his fall when I saw the crazy Cajan was tied to a rope and was repelling down the wall. He was no longer a cockatiel but a spider. At Renee's third floor window, he stopped. With one hand he reached into his backpack. I could see him doing something to the window. He reached down, the window rose, and he swung inside. A minute later a rope ladder dropped down, the last rung about a foot off the ground. *Minchia*. Was I supposed to climb up? I answered my own question. Yes, I was.

I looked around. It was still all quiet on the western front. Did I mention that I'm not really happy with heights? But I was all in. I sprinted to the ladder and began climbing, hand over hand over hand, vowing not to look down. I reached the window and swung my leg over the sill. My body was delighted to follow my legs inside. Sweets hauled the ladder in behind me and whispered, "You be one fine burglar if you decide to give up selling cars."

"Piece of cake," I whispered back, feeling pretty damn good about how fast I'd made it up, even though I was trembling. Sweets began duct taping black cloth over the window. Once the window was sealed against light shining through, he turned on his flashlight.

"Stay here, *mon frere*. I gotta black out the other windows before we can turn on the lights and do some searching." He was gone. Ten minutes or so passed before he returned.

"As soon as I stuff the crack under the front door, we good to go. He knelt in front of the door and sealed a strip of black duct tape to the bottom of the door and the floor.

"You can turn on one floor lamp," he stated. *Pro burglar in command of amateur sleuth.*

I obeyed, switching on the standing lamp next to the couch. I looked around Renee's living room: the framed posters of famous musicians and composers. The furniture was straight out of Ikea. The real Afghan rug that Renee was so proud of, in the center of the room, supported a couple of huge pillows facing the couch. I remembered the last time I was in the room, sitting on one of those pillows. Renee had made a Bundt cake. We were drinking coffee, talking about Dila. Renee was giving me advice, not to crowd Dila. We'd talked some about music and a little about politics. We had gone to a movie.

"Okay," I said. "I'll take this side of the room. You take the bookcases."

I began with Renee's desk. I sat down on the straight back chair in front of the desk and opened the drawer. My P.I. manual listed important things to look for: diaries, telephone address books, bank statements, letters, bills from the telephone company and bills from stores. It was important to go through wastepaper baskets for discarded notes, as well as look for possible hidden areas in the desk, the author of the manual advised. People make an effort to hide personal items of importance. There was hardly anything in the drawer except writing materials. I sat back in the chair.

In my last two cases. . . I stopped myself and thought. *I am not on a case. I am an automobile salesman who is investigating the murder of a friend. I have no private investigator's license. Therefore, I have no cases.*

"Shh, Victor."

I looked across the room at Sweets. "What? I didn't say anything."

Sweets put his fingers to his lips and pointed to the front door of the apartment.

That's when I heard someone was in the hall outside very slowly turning the doorknob. I pointed to the standing lamp. Sweets shook his head. We sat and waited. Soon whoever it was stopped trying the knob. We continued searching. After searching the rest of the apartment, we returned to the living room. It looked to me that whatever had been in the apartment that might have been a clue, the police had taken. I was not unhappy.

In her bedroom closet I'd found a couple of skirts and blouses that were definitely made to be worn by earth-mothers. Earth-mother was not Renee's style.

I also found in the wastepaper basket in the bedroom a bunch of sheets of music with musical notes written on them in pencil. At the top of one page was the title "Concerto for the Grateful Dead." It had been crossed out and written above it, also crossed out: "Gratitude: Concerto for the Grateful Dead." Obviously, Renee had been trying to compose a concerto for the band or based on the Grateful Dead's music. I remembered Dila telling me that Renee was trying to do something classical with rock and roll. I'd listened to Grateful Dead songs and didn't like their kind of psychedelic sound. I didn't think Renee would have either. Here was evidence to the contrary. Coincidently, it also established a link between her and Merriam. In detective fiction that I'd started to read a couple of years ago, the detectives never believed in coincidences, but I was Italian and I did. I couldn't imagine what the connection could be, but I was satisfied we would not find anything else that might be a clue.

I told Sweets we were done, and he instructed me to turn off the lights. He removed the duct tape from the bottom of the door and the black outs from the windows and stuffed them into his backpack.

"I'll let down the ladder and you scoot on down, Victor. I got to go to the roof and remove the anchor for my rope. Can't have the cops thinking stuff. I'll meet you at the car."

Climbing down was harder than going up. By the time I got to the car, Sweets was already climbing over the lip of the roof. Ten minutes later, I saw him walking toward me, and five minutes later, we were driving down McArthur Boulevard. When we got back to my apartment, Sweets asked if he could sleep over since he was having a slight problem with his main squeeze. Sweets's living arrangements were always dictated by problems of one kind or other. I agreed. I was in a good mood.

In my apartment, I brought out a couple of bottles of Anchor Steam. I handed a bottle and four one-hundred-dollar bills. Damned if he hadn't earned it.

"You are fair man, *mon ami.*"

I ducked his embrace. I was happy to be back being his friend and not his brother.

"How did you learn all that mountain climbing stuff?" I asked.

"I'm a professional, Victor. Took lessons in Switzerland. Climbed the fucking Eiger."

"What's that when it's home?"

"Dude, it is the tallest and most dangerous peak in the Alps."

One more tall tale to join numerous tall tales from the lips of the pirate Jean Lafitte's relative. I would not question it or bother to research it. When it came to the truth, Sweets was a skillful fiction writer, and I was okay with that. I bid him sweet dreams and left him on the couch, drinking beer and sucking on hard candies, then climbed into bed and dreamed about tall mountains.

CHAPTER 16
IN DISGUISE

"Quardo il diavola ti accarezza, vuole l'anima.
When the devil caresses you, he wants your soul."
Italian proverb

At seven o'clock, Vincent was up and making breakfast for his first born, Christina. Gloria was still in bed, for some much-needed rest after walking their colicky son, Mario, for half the night until the sun had risen and both mother and infant had fallen asleep. He and Christina ate bowls of Honey Kix together and drank orange juice. Then, Vincent placed his daughter in front of the TV to watch *Dasterdly and Muttley* along with a bowl of dry Kix, while he went to take his shower and get dressed for work.

But this morning Vincent was not going to work. He was going to drive across the Oakland Bay Bridge to the Fillmore West where the Grateful Dead were preparing for a concert that would play for three nights beginning tomorrow and ending on Sunday. He had read the information Victor had given him. After the Fillmore appearance, the Grateful Dead would be off to tour the East.

Vincent was a little nervous. Individual hippies, in general, made him nervous. But hippies in a bunch, well you never knew. He'd been told by one of the guys at Flynn's that a hippie on LSD could be dangerous. Up in the attic, in some box, was a pair of brass knuckles—might not be a bad idea to take them. The thought of rummaging through the attic nixed the idea though. He and his twin had boxed in the CYO League Juniors. A coach had told him he had quick hands. He imagined a dangerous hippie bearing down on him and he, Vincent Brovelli, with quick hands, ready to punch the guy's lights out. The image made him smile. He'd be fine on his own.

But first, before heading across the bay to San Francisco, he would do what Victor had suggested and visit Discount Furniture and inspect Merriam's Volkswagen Transporter bus for clues. Victor had not defined clues, so he was not sure what he would be looking for.

Vincent decided not to shave or comb his hair. Unbrushed, his natural tight curls would look like a bird's nest. He dressed in jeans, a Grateful Dead tie-dyed T-shirt Victor had bought at a used clothing shop in the Haight because he'd need to "blend in". He laced up black Converse Keds and checked himself in the mirror. His jeans looked a little too clean. He went to the closet and took out his shoe polish kit. He rubbed some black polish in spots around the knees and ankles, then rubbed them with a cloth until they were dry and looked like oil stains. He turned to the bed when he heard his wife's voice.

"If you smoke any dope, I'll divorce you."

"Okay, I'll just do a little peyote," he said.

"Don't joke," Gloria said. "Where's Christina?"

"Fed and sitting in front of the TV."

"I'll be up in a second. Don't leave until I check on the baby and Christina."

Fifteen minutes later, Vincent was in his Dodge Charger driving to East 14th. He pulled to the curb in front of Discount Furniture and walked in the front door. Nick Parsegian saw him and rushed toward him, his hand outstretched.

"Do you have news?"

"Sorry," Vincent said, "It's too early. Nothing to report. Victor told me to come here and inspect your daughter's bus for clues."

"Yes, of course. The bus, right. I'll get the keys." Parsegian turned toward his office. He returned with a set of keys.

"These are extras. The police never found Merriam's set of keys. The bus is in the back parking lot." Vincent followed Parsegian through the showroom and into the parking lot. The parking area was enclosed by a ten-foot-high link fence. The Transporter Bus was standing in the far corner, covered by canvas.

"That bus is going to be a classic in the future," Vincent said. "Any car thief with half a brain finds out about it, that gate won't keep them out."

"Don't worry, Ajax has the run of the building and the parking lot at night."

"Who is Ajax?" Vincent asked but then remembered the monster dog that had almost eaten Victor a year ago when his twin and Sweets had attempted to break into Parsegian's store looking for evidence in the murder of Sweets's girlfriend, Winona Davis.

When they arrived at the bus, Parsegian removed the canvas covering. Victor gasped. He hung his head and took a couple of deep breaths. He hoped when he lifted his head, the bus would once again be painted its original dove-blue. He looked up. *Odio*, he thought. The bus was canary yellow and covered with decals and paintings. There were peace signs and rainbows and. . . was that a palm tree? And below the tree, sitting cross-legged was a picture of some kind of frigging swami. In the absence of Merriam, Vincent felt like kicking her father in the butt, just on general principles for allowing his daughter to destroy such a one-of -a-kind paint job. No telling what she'd done to the motor.

Then, he felt ashamed. Merriam might be dead.

Vincent opened the side doors and stepped up inside the van. *Mama mia*, it was filthy. He could see where the police had dusted for fingerprints. The little stove was greasy. He moved to the drivers' seat. He liked the way the angle of the wheel was flatter than most vans, so the driver almost looked down on it. With the engine in the rear, the driver was able to see through the windshield straight down to the road, which took a little getting used to. The Van would never be a speed demon, but you could sleep and eat and shower in it. A little home on wheels, the guy he bought it from had called it. Now, Vincent thought, it looked more like a slum on wheels.

"My daughter was always a clean person. She would never have allowed her car to be filthy like this."

Vincent swung around at Nick Parsegian's voice. Nick was staring inside; his mouth was now closed tight and his jaw muscles were twitching.

Vincent couldn't feel sorry for Parsegian. "Your daughter might have changed, Nick. She changed her hair and her clothes. Maybe her habits as well. Hippies don't bathe, you know." The last comment was unnecessary and maybe a little cruel, but Vincent had come to believe that the furniture salesman was a bad father. When little Christina grew up, she wouldn't run off and be a hippie. He and Gloria would have raised her better. Over the years, he and Victor had watched Parsegian spoil Merriam. Spoil a child, bad things happen. He remembered his father saying: *Una rapa viziata ravina la zuppa; un bambino viziata ravina la familia.* A spoiled turnip spoils the soup; a spoiled child, spoils the family. Big Sal was the repository of hundreds of Italian proverbs, some of which Vincent suspected his pop had made up. In this case, Merriam was too beautiful to be compared to a turnip, but the truth of the message was appropriate.

"Why don't you go back to the store, Nick?" he said. "I'm going to poke around a bit. Look for clues, you know. It's detective business. We detectives don't like people looking over our shoulders."

"I understand, Vincent, I'll be in the office. Lock up and drop the keys off when you're finished."

Parsegian walked away, his head down, his shoulders drooping. Vincent almost felt sorry for him. He turned back into the bus and began inspecting drawers and cabinets. Under the driver's seat, he found books. One by one, he took them out and read their titles: *The Teachings of Don Juan: The Yaqui Way of Knowledge, Siddhartha, The Science of Being and Art of Living* by Maharishi Mahesh Yogi. Vincent put the books down and said aloud, "Didn't know Yogi Bear wrote a book." *I made a joke,* Vincent thought and began laughing.

"Knock yourself out, daddy-o."

Startled, Vincent spun around. Sweets Monroe was standing in the doorway, a goofy smile on his thin bird-like face, not a face Vincent was happy to see. Unlike his twin, he had a difficult time even tolerating the burglar, who he blamed for starting the entire *casino* of Victor wanting to be a private investigator. That began the morning they had found Sweets' girlfriend in the trunk of Sweets's '61 Chevy Impala.

"That might be y'all's first joke I've ever heard, Vincent. You growing a funny bone?"

"You don't sneak up on a guy, Sweets's. What are you doing here anyway? Shouldn't you be climbing in windows and robbing people?"

Ignoring him, Sweets stepped up into the bus and shouldered his way past him. As usual, Sweets smelled of candy... *strawberry,* Vincent guessed.

"Ooowee, look at all these spiritual books, Vincent. You teenk Merriam was on a walk-about seeking enlightenment?

"Is that what these books are?" Vincent asked. "I can't pronounce most of the titles."

"Oh, yeah, *mon,* spirituality up the wazoo. Gurus and sheeet like that. You know like sitting under a banana tree, meditating, like that."

Banana tree didn't sound right to Vincent, but what did he know about spirituality? Catholics weren't into all this weird crap. It's go to confession, go to mass, take communion and start your week all over again. That was good enough for him, even if he was not very good at it, and didn't actually, unlike his twin, believe in his religion or religions in general. They were always looking for you to donate your hard-earned money. "Well, whatever these books are about," Vincent said, "I guess they are clues. I'll have to tell Victor about them."

"You be a real detective. You know if the fuzz thought they were clues, they wouldn't still be here. They'd be in an evidence room in the po-leece station."

"Never said I was a detective. Victor told me to tell him anything that I found that was unusual. This looks unusual enough for me."

"Okay, so you no detective, you just lied to old Parsegian. I get it. So, what's your plan?"

"No plan. I'm driving to San Francisco. The Grateful Dead are having a concert at the Fillmore West tomorrow. I want to talk to the people that set up the stage and sound. I was told Deadheads just hang around. I'm guessing if anyone has seen Merriam or knows something about her, it would be the workers and hangers-on."

"You want me to come with you, *mon ami?*"

Vincent was tempted to say yes, but then shook his head. "No, Sweets. I can handle it. I'd kind of like to get a feel for what my brother finds exciting about being a private investigator."

"You want a P.I. license?"

"What are you talking about? What license?"

"It's not a real one," Sweets said.

Vincent watched as Sweets withdrew a leather holder from his jacket pocket. He opened it and held it out.

"I stole one a long time ago and forgot I had it. Made a bunch of copies. Never know when they could come in handy, the bidness I'm in. *Comprend?*"

"Yeah, I understand. You're a thief."

"You so harsh, Vincent. I gave one to Victor last year. He used it a couple of times, you know, when he was investigating your brother's murder. Said it came in handy."

"That's illegal."

"No sheet, you one smart *Eye-talian*, Vincent. Take it. Use it, don't use it."

"I'm not touching it. I don't figure these people like private investigators any better than they like the police. I'm just going to mingle and act like a Deadhead."

"Vincent, *mon ami*, let me tell you. You 'bout the least looking Deadhead any Deadhead has ever seen, you so Italian car salesman, Rotary Club dude. You teenk that Tie Dye shirt you wearing and that whatever you smeared on your pants gonna fool anybody?"

"First of all, Sweets, you are not my friend. Second of all I belong to Lions Club, not Rotary, and this Tie Dye shirt was worn once by a real Deadhead, and I don't see how it matters whether I'm an Italian cars salesman or a Swedish car salesman. And, finally, that fake Cajun accent of yours is really annoying."

"Don't get your shorts in a twist, all Sweets be saying is you need help, I'm ready to provide it. I helped Victor. I help you. We're all one family, *non?*"

The thought of Sweets being part of *la famiglia*, made Vincent nauseous. His mom and pop doted on Sweets. Mom would have Sweets over for dinner and send him home with the left-over lasagna or whatever the meal she'd cooked. If Sweets was invited to dinner at his parents, he and Gloria always managed to find an excuse to send regrets. He sighed. "No thanks, again. I appreciate your asking. Guess I better get going. The traffic across the bridge is still going to be pretty busy."

He watched Sweets shrug and walk away, his cockatiel hairdo swaying from side to side like a rickety fence. *What a piece of work,* Vincent thought. He found a garbage bag that didn't contain garbage and placed the books in it. In Parsegian's office, he replaced the keys. He'd found nothing except some books, he replied to Parsegian's question, ignoring the follow up question, and hurried out of the building.

• • •

By the time Vincent got across the Bay Bridge and took the 9th Street exit ramp, it was 10:34 a. m. He pulled into a gas station parking area and took out the San Francisco Street map plus some general background information that Victor had given him. The street location of Fillmore West on the map was encircled in red ink at the corner of Van Ness Avenue and Market Street. *Odd,* Vincent thought. Why was it called Fillmore? Vincent knew where Fillmore Street was. He'd crossed it a number of times driving to Golden Gate Park when he attended a 49er game at Kezar Stadium. His team was the Raiders, but the 49ers were second best. Got to stay loyal to the Bay Area, he'd explained to the guys at Flynn's who were Raiders' fans or nothing and wouldn't be caught dead in Kezar stadium unless the Raiders were playing the 49ers.

The Fillmore District was pretty much an all-black neighborhood beginning on Sutter Street south to Hayes Street. He took out the information sheet that accompanied the street map. It was typed. Victor didn't know how to type, so this had to be Theresa's work, and it was as if Theresa had anticipated his confusion about the name of the Grateful Dead's venue. She had provided the answer: In 1966, the promoter, Bill Graham, began staging his concerts at the Fillmore auditorium on Geary Boulevard and Fillmore Street. In 1968, the neighborhood was getting raunchy, and Graham bought the present building on Van Ness and renamed it Fillmore West.

The guy who owned the music hall had been murdered, Vincent read. He didn't understand why Theresa had added that information unless he was trying to frighten him. There was also a list of names of musicians and singers who played in the original Fillmore, like Jefferson Airplane and Santana. Vincent had heard of the Jefferson Airplane, but not Santana, which sounded foreign to him. That information too seemed irrelevant. There was an address of the nearest police station and a phone number. Now Vincent was certain Theresa was trying to frighten him. They'd have to have a little talk when he got back to the lot.

San Francisco was no fun to drive in. It took Vincent about fifteen minutes to find a parking spot that was not on a meter. A penny saved, he'd often told Gloria, and she'd made a face at him. So, what if he was a little frugal? He had almost put aside enough in their Bank of America savings account for a down payment on a home in the small town of Orinda on the other side of the Caldicott tunnel and close to his alma mater, Saint Mary's. With the new baby, they needed more space, and two children were not enough to convince his parents that he was worthy to be called a good Italian father.

Vincent knew in the marrow of his businessman's bones that the area east of the tunnel would one day turn into an Oakland suburb and make people who had the forethought to buy land there wealthy. It had been one of his pop's lessons, *buy land, boys, buy land.* Capice? Thinking of wealth,

Vincent decided he liked the sound of the word. It was his immigrant Pop's word, the American dream talking. It was sound advice. Victor never seemed to care about wealth unless it had to do with what he needed to buy: good-looking wheels and the latest fashions. His twin lived for the moment. Well, Victor would learn once he got married. Though the idea of Victor marrying made Vincent think of Dila and that made him nervous.

He forced his mind back to the present. He took a look in the rearview mirror, roughed up his hair, but it didn't do much good. His curly black locks refused to change, falling back into place. He locked the car and began walking. He congratulated himself for anticipating the San Francisco chill by remembering to wear his all-weather jacket with the wool lining. According to some newspaper called *Bagdad by the Bay*, the East Bay was always at least ten degrees warmer than San Francisco. This seemed ridiculous to Vincent since Bagdad was in the Middle East somewhere and never got this cold. The thought left Vincent wondering why San Francisco always seemed to him filled with weird people, and they were snobs about Oakland.

By the time he'd worked up some righteous anger about San Francisco snobs, Vincent had reached the corner of Market and Van Ness Ave and was standing in front of the building that housed Fillmore West.

Market Street was part of one of some of his best childhood memories. The street began at the Twin Peaks tunnel and stretched to the waterfront, obliquely dividing San Francisco into two separate parts, south and north. When they were kids, his parents always drove into San Francisco to see the Fourth of July Parade. After the parade, they would eat on Fisherman's Wharf. The owner was friends with their pop. Vincent remembered each time they left Scoma's, his father saying: *Accanto a tuo madre, I migliori chef d'americ.* Aside from your mother, the best chef in America.

When they first got their driver's licenses, he and Victor had driven to San Francisco and taken the trolley through the tunnel. They had taken rides on the cable cars. They'd driven out to Playland at the beach and tried to pick up girls. They had driven up and down the Great Highway and before leaving for home had eaten at *Fior d'Italia,* another restaurant whose chef, according to their pop, was the best chef in America next to their mom.

A truck blowing its horn brought Vincent back to the present. He looked up at the marquee at the front of the building. It read:

FILLMORE WEST
Market & Van Ness

BILL GRAHAM PRESENTS

GRATEFUL DEAD
NEW RIDERS OF THE PURPLE SAGE
SOUTHERN COMFORT

Lights by Dr. Zerkey

Maybe, Vincent thought, he should have taken Sweets up on his offer to come with him. Who the hell were the "New Riders of the Purple Sage?" This was supposed to be a rock concert, not Country & Western. All he knew about "Southern Comfort" was that it was a fruity tasting kind of whiskey.

Mama mia, he whispered to himself. Vincent suddenly felt a little like he might be walking into a trap set by hippies to attract ordinary American citizens, like flies for the spider who'd turn them into LSD zombies. How would he even begin talking to people like this? *I need to be cool, stand around and listen. Then when somebody notices say I'm a journalist and start asking questions. No, that won't work. These guys travel with the Grateful Dead all over the country. Journalists are probably trying to talk to them all the time to get inside information.*

Vincent began pacing. This was a busy corner. He stayed close to the side of the building to avoid pedestrians. *What if I say, I'm looking for my girlfriend*, he thought. *Said to meet her here, something like that. Said she was here to apply for a job. She's . . .* In his mind, Vincent rehearsed his lines. He had halfway talked himself into going with the girlfriend idea when he saw a girl walking toward him with a big smile on her face like she knew him. She had red hair, pale skin, and her lips were colored purple. She wore a small silver ring in the left side of her nose. As she reached him, he saw her blue eyes, *Odio*, what eyes.

"You sure get around, dude," she said.

Now that she was standing directly in front of him, Vincent saw that her hair was not just red, but flaming red, like the color he remembered from campfires when he was a kid camping, turning different shades of red. And her blue eyes were sometimes dark blue then light blue. He always heard about crooked smiles but never seen one up close like this. She'd moved in close to him so that he could smell a perfume that he imagined was incense. She was wearing a long floral dress belted at her waist, revealing slender hips and long legs. She was as tall as he was and was looking him straight in the eyes.

"Do we know each other?" Vincent asked.

"Sorry, dude. Guess we don't. I mistook you for someone else." She hesitated, then her smile returned. "But you'll do in a pinch."

This girl was the most stunning young woman he'd ever seen, short of some movie actress named Elizabeth Taylor or his wife, Gloria, but so different from both. Irish looking, a cross between a young Rita Hayworth and Maureen O'Hara, two of Vincent's favorite late night movie actresses.

"You lost the power of speech?" She asked.

Vincent recouped. Shook his head. "Sorry, you took me by surprise. I was thinking."

"I know what you were thinking. How to get into the auditorium and get autographs. I was like that a year ago at The Family Dog. Got there way early and tried to con my way in so I could get autographs. It was just my first Dead concert, if you can believe it. You know you're a day early; it's only the roadies in there setting up. 'Course, the roadies are the coolest. They don't mind if you hang out as long as you don't disturb them. It's the best vibe ever watching them do the lights, yelling cool stuff about amps and audio to each other. I told them I was going to be an electrician. They let me run errands for them." She lifted a bag. "Stanley's Hardware down Market Street. They needed batteries. Come on. You can come in with me. I'll introduce you. You get to know them, you'll have better luck tomorrow night, maybe getting in the back to hang out with Jerry and Pigpen and the rest of the band."

This was pure luck, Vincent thought. Then it occurred to him that maybe it wasn't luck at all but a glorious temptation the devil had cast in front of him to test the strength of his four-year marriage.

"Come on, baby, I got to get this stuff to the boys."

The girl with the flaming red hair began walking.

Vincent followed her.

CHAPTER 17
THE ROADIES

"Follow the sweet scent of Mary Jane,
and she'll find you."
Written on the wall of the Fillmore West

There was no one guarding the entrance to Fillmore West, which surprised Vincent. As they made their way up the stairs, the perfume Lydia was wearing was beginning to make him sweat. She kept grabbing his hand, and he kept pulling it away, and she continued taking his hand until he finally gave up. Better for whomever was in the auditorium to believe he and Lydia were an item. Sweets may have been right that true hippies wouldn't believe that he, Vincent Brovelli, was part of them, but with a flower-child holding his hand, they might.

He imagined himself explaining to his wife, who heard from some housewives' source that keeps track of husbands, that his hand was being held by a gorgeous redhead. *It was a disguise, Honey; she was holding my hand, not the other way around. You gotta believe me.* Vincent was working himself up into a panic, and was thinking of turning around and leaving, when Lydia dropped his hands, pushed open two large doors and ushered him into the auditorium to the sound of guitars and drums and voices singing. Vincent saw the source of the music, a large boom box set on a table in the center of the stage. The girl said. "I just love listening to 'Golden Road', don't you?

"Yeah," Vincent said. "Very cool." Golden Road meant nothing to him.

"Hirsh's strange cord at the end blows me away," she said. "I've only heard it in practice. I know some guys who heard it for real in a concert in '67."

He'd never been to a Grateful Dead concert in 1967. It was best not to respond.

"I'm a neon light diamond, you know. The Dead could have written that song 'bout me."

"You sparkle like a diamond," Vincent said and immediately regretted it. *What was he thinking?*

She gave him another one of her crooked smiles. "If you had a scar on your face, you'd look just like the guy I know. You got kin you don't know of?"

"Not that I know. I'm an only child."

"Cool, so am I. Here we are. Looks like the boys are taking a break," Lydia said. "You can smell their morning snack."

All Vincent smelled was marijuana, then, catching on, and not wanting to sound uncool, said. "A little pot in the morning with your coffee. Sounds good." Lydia looked over at him and smiled. She reached for his hand again and began caressing his fingers, one finger at a time. For a moment, he allowed her to continue before he blurted out, "I'm married."

"What does that have to do with anything?"

"Well, for all. . ." he stammered. She didn't give him a chance to continue, pulling him.

"Come on, silly, let's go and get a little bit of what they're smoking."

This was not what he'd bargained for, Vincent thought, when he told Victor he'd do some of the detecting. What he was being led toward by this soft female hand?

A chorus of voices greeted them, "Lydia!"

"Boys," Lydia replied. She placed the bag of materials on the stage.

"Come join us, bring your friend," the chorus said. "Just taking a little break."

The girl gripped the top of the stage and swung up. "Come on, you," she said.

One of the four men in the group looked at Vincent and asked. "Who's your friend?"

"Who are you?" she asked.

All the guys began laughing.

"He's the silent type."

This got the men laughing again. Vincent didn't think it was that funny, but the marijuana might be helping the comedy along. There was enough smoke in the air that Vincent was feeling a little fuzzy.

"Name's David," Vincent said.

"I'm Goliath," one of the guys said and began giggling.

They're all high, Vincent thought. If he stayed here much longer, he'd be high too.

"Here, David," Lydia said and handed him a thick joint she had just rolled.

"Have some chow," Another of the roadies said. "You look hungry."

"He looks pretty well-fed to me," said a smallish guy with a goatee.

"Let me introduce you," Lydia said. "The dude that just said you look well-fed is Road Dog. He handles transportation and equipment. Next to him with the pony tail is Marvin Radish. He's not Goliath, but he knows everything there is about guitars and sound equipment. Next to him with the bald head is Bobby Brillo. He's our new stage manager, directs the construction crew."

Unlike the skinny Radish, Brillo looked like he could be a weightlifter. He said, "Not like the cleaning pad, Lydia, Breee-oh. It's Mexican."

"Right," Lydia said. "Breee oooh's seating partner is Carl Leftwish. He's our crew boss."

"Not your boss, darling, just these ugly guys," he said pointing to the rest of the crew. "You're getting a little possessive, girl. Bobby is ours, not yours." He winked, and continued, "Lydia won't tell us what her last name is, will you honey?"

"I'm Lydia gone-with-the-wind," she said. "David here wants to be an electrician like me."

"You hang out with Lydia," Radish said, "and she'll tell you all you never wanted to know."

"What I want to know," Lydia stated, "is what the set-list is for tomorrow night?"

"You know I couldn't tell you that," Radish said. "Besides, I don't think Jerry knows what tunes they're going to play himself. Times he changes his choice at the last minute. I'd bet he'll surprise everybody tonight with some unexpected tune."

"At least tell me if they're going to do most of the songs from the new album?"

"Album's coming out June 14th," Road Dog said, "should be some songs from it."

"Come on, pretty please," Lydia begged.

Vincent was unsure what the big deal was about knowing the songs that the band would play tomorrow night was all about, but he tried to affect an interested look on his face. He looked down at the joint in his hand.

"Don't push it, Lydia," Radish said. He flipped the cartridge in the boom box that was no longer playing music and pressed the button. The sound of an electric guitar began. He stood up. "We'd better get back to work." He grabbed a donut and the boom box and walked away down the stage and behind a curtain, the music trailing him. The rest of the guys followed.

"You going to smoke that joint or let it burn down?" Lydia asked.

Vincent felt embarrassed that he must be looking like a total Mr. Clean. He placed the joint between his lips and took a deep drag, holding the smoke in, then letting it out slowly the way they had done in college. It hadn't been that long ago since he'd smoked dope but his head began to spin. For a second, he thought he'd have to hold onto the table.

"You don't really do much drugs, do you, David?" Lydia asked. "No sweat. You don't have to put on an act for me. Now what are you really here for? It ain't for autographs. You're not even into the Grateful Dead. You didn't know the name of the song, "St. Stephen", one of the Dead's songs from *Live Dead.*" Lydia paused. "'St. Stephen' was never released as a single in the U.S. and only as a 3" inch side in Japan in 1969, but you wouldn't know that either."

Mama mia, Vincent though, he would never have survived as an undercover agent. Vincent felt that he was blushing. Lydia continued to look at him with those uncommonly blue eyes and with that crooked smile. She wouldn't believe another lie. There were no other options for him but to tell the truth. "Well, it's like this. . ." When he had finished with his story, Lydia took his hand.

"That is so sweet of you, so caring, David. If I'd run away, I would have wanted you to find me. Can't help you. I've never run across the girl Merriam you described. I'm sure I would have remembered. But I've only been on the scene for a year and I don't hang out in the Haight."

"Do you think you could go in and ask the roadies? I'm kind of embarrassed going in and explaining that I was an alias."

"An alien, you mean? Sorry, just messing with you. Yeah, I'll go in and asks the boys. You wait out in the lobby."

Vincent watched her walk toward the stage curtain. He jumped off the stage. In the lobby, he sat in a chair and waited. He was tired. The hit of dope was still with him. He thought that the marijuana they were smoking must have an unusually high percentage of TCP for it to affect him the way it did. What did Victor see in this that was so exciting? Selling a couple of high- profit cars in one day seemed far more exciting to him. He was drowsy and feeling slightly guilty about the way he'd been attracted to Lydia. He wondered if he dared tell Gloria about his morning. She'd ask him, and she'd know if he was keeping anything back. He was rehearsing what he might tell his wife when Lydia returned.

"Sorry, whatever your real name is. The boys don't remember a chick like that." She spun around and slammed through the doors back into the auditorium. Vincent sighed. What was that all about? He stood up. He thought he should go after her and thank her. But she had sounded angry. He left the building and took a last look at the venue marquee with the giant letters FILLMORE WEST. GRATEFUL DEAD.

That song Lydia had raved about that he didn't recognize, what the heck was so great about it? The guy, Weir's voice who wasn't too bad, but how could the drum solo possibly compare to Bobby Darin or Sam Cook? Cook's "You Send Me" was one of Gloria's favorite songs, dating back to their days in high school, when they would dance together at one of the college mixers, her feet on top of his, shuffling softly to the music. One of his favorite songs was Darin's "If I Was a Carpenter".

Vincent was glad to be out of there, happy not to think about Lydia. Already he was feeling less guilty. He felt Victor would be happy with the information about the roadies. It didn't seem to him that being a detective was all that difficult. He thought of the coming afternoon with Gloria and the kids. It was not until he was in his car and driving across the Bay Bridge that Vincent began to wonder what it was that had angered Lydia so much.

CHAPTER 18
DETECTIVE SATURDAY &
HIS GIRL FRIDAY

"Amor senza baruffa, fa la muffa.
Love without a quarrel makes mold."
Italian proverb

Dila and I began our Friday with breakfast at Olie's Waffle House down the street from my apartment. We were greeted by my favorite waitress, Mame, named by her mother after Auntie Mame, of movie fame. She was as redheaded as the actress Rosalind Russell, who played the role, and in some ways just as flamboyant. I'd been eating breakfast at Olie's for as long as I have been out of college and gainfully employed. Mame was old enough to be my mother, but I think I had a crush on her, and she on me. Not enough to do anything about it—the age difference being too big an obstacle. In all the years I had always come to Olie's Waffle House in the morning alone. It took a while for Mame to get used to Dila—to any woman, really. Now they were friends and hugged as we entered.

We found a booth. Mame knew what I wanted, my usual stack of pancakes topped with two eggs over easy and a side of sausage. Dila ordered waffles plain with maple syrup, with three eggs scrambled on the side and bacon. I'm no longer surprised by Dila's appetite. We ordered two cups of strong black coffee for both of us. The two women spoke briefly before Mame left to put in our order. Dila and I sipped our coffee silently. She was the first to speak.

"You made a connection between Renee and Merriam, right?"

I nodded.

"And we found out a few things at the clubs."

"Correct."

"Can we put them together in any meaningful way?" Dila asked.

"Renee and the Grateful Dead had more to do with her career as a musician than anything to do with Merriam. What that tells me is they might not necessarily connect. On the other hand, Renee having hippie-type clothes, particularly the blouse which had a Grateful Dead insignia on it, means she might have been trying to pass herself off as a Deadhead. Perhaps to ingratiate herself with the band."

Dila completed my thought. "Because the band would be more likely to listen to her if they thought she was a fan."

"It still doesn't link the two women." I said.

"They were both into music. By the way, I checked back to the music camp, and Merriam was never enrolled in the one we worked at in Michigan."

"Less of a link. Plus, there was a pretty big age difference," I said.

"You told me Merriam was eighteen. Ten years is not that much."

"No problem with us. We're the same age. In two years, we'll be thirty. Time to get married and start having *bambini*." I knew it was a mistake the second I said it.

Dila scowled. "Time for you to get over being an Italian male."

Outwardly, I laughed, trying to defuse my ill-timed comment; inwardly, I was serious, but I recognized Dila was not ready for another discussion about marriage and children. I had no doubt that Dila would be a good mother. I'd seen her working patiently with the little musicians at an after-school program the Black Panthers had started a year ago to help out single moms. Dila, who could routinely hit bullseyes on the rifle range, would cuddle and whisper encouragement to the kids who needed it: *you're so special, you were made to play the flute; oh, I wish I could have played the piano like that when I was your age.* And the faces of the children lighting up. But this was obviously not the time remind Dila of her maternal side.

I changed the subject back to our investigation. "I need my Girl Friday to work her magic," I said.

Dila was about to reply when Mame brought our breakfast. We tucked in, too busy with food to talk. During our first culinary break, I said, "We need to find the guy Renee kept calling daddy."

"I was thinking the same thing," Dila said. "So, do we go back to the North Beach?"

"It's far too early."

"Okay, where else?"

"Let's visit Holy Names College and the Haight. We need to establish a connection between the two women or we might be spinning our wheels. Do you have the photograph of Renee, I gave you?"

Dila pointed to her purse.

"Good, I have one too, in case we decide to separate for some reason."

We got back to our breakfast.

• • •

Dila gave Mame an extra-big tip. Her reason was that Mame was the hardest working waitress she'd ever known and was raising teenagers. It had come as a surprise that Mame was a mom. Beyond telling me how she'd been named, Mame never spoke of having a family. I didn't need to ask how Dila found out. One look with those green eyes and people opened up the book of their lives to Dila.

I drove to Holy Names College. Eight o'clock classes had already started. There were students standing in front of the student union. We walked to the music department. The thought occurred to me that Vincent had described the music prof, Brother Gaspare as being short, on the slim side with long dark hair. I sent the thought back to where it originated to my over-eager imagination. *Not a Christian Brother hanging out in the North Beach clubs.*

Brother Gaspare was not in his office, but we were told he was in the auditorium preparing for his nine o'clock choir class. The music hall was at the other end of the building. We found it and opened the door. The Christian Brother was standing in front of a lectern. He looked up as we entered.

Dila spoke first, introducing us and explain what we were doing.

"When you entered," Brother Gaspare said. "I thought you were the same man who talked to me a few days ago."

"We're twins," I explained.

"Yes, I can see," he said.

When Dila showed him the photograph of Renee, he nodded. "I do know Renee, or I should say I know of her. We were on a symposium last year together. She was very impressive."

"When was that?" I asked.

"I'd have to look in my calendar for the exact date, but it was, let me think." He paused, rubbing his chin. "It was just before Christmas break."

"You wouldn't happen to have seen Renee with Merriam Parsegian, would you?" Dila asked.

"Merriam is still missing, I presume," Gaspare said.

"Correct," I said. "But we have found some people who have seen her, so despite the blood found in her van, she may be physically okay."

"That is good news," Brother Gaspare said. "No, I'm not sure if Renee Sorenson has ever been on this campus. I wish I could be of more help. If you'll excuse me," he said, looking at his watch. "My nine o'clock class begins in ten minutes."

We thanked the good brother and left. Walking out of the building, Dila asked what I thought.

"I think he's lying. Renee couldn't have been with him at the symposium."

"Right, right. I didn't pick up on that," Dila said. "You told me Renee only got back from Europe in March."

"So why lie?" I asked.

My girl Friday answered. "Because he has some kind of relationship with her. Maybe, he's the man we're looking for that she called daddy."

"He certainly doesn't fit the description we got. Not tall enough and not rugged enough."

"It wouldn't hurt to show his picture around in the North Beach. Maybe there were two guys with Renee," Dila said, adding, "we could get a photograph of him."

"I can do that," I said. "Follow me."

• • •

We were driving to the Haight. The Holy Names College yearbook open to faculty was on Dila's lap.

"How did you get this yearbook out of the building without getting caught?" Dila asked.

"You can't know a guy like Sweets Monroe for as long as I've known him without learning some things."

"You're not going to tell me," Dila said.

"Sweets once told me, pretend you own the store and just walk out with everything you want."

"Hrummph," Dila said.

Dila's growl of displeasure is her way of saying she's not buying something a person says to her. Dila hrummphs me a lot.

On McArthur Boulevard, we found a copy center, made a photograph of Brother Gaspare and had it blown up. I placed the yearbook in my trunk with the intention of mailing it back to the school. Unlike Sweets, I am not a thief.

Forty-five minutes later, we arrived at the corner of Haight and Masonic. It took us five runs through the neighborhood before we found a place to park. Our first stop was Moretti's Sporting Goods.

Moretti looked up from a book he was reading. "You still trying to find your hippie gal?"

We shook hands. I introduced him to Dila and said, "We're looking for a different woman." I withdrew the photograph of Renee from the inside of my jacket pocket and showed him. He shook his head.

"Does not ring a bell."

I withdrew the photograph of Brother Gaspare and gave it to him. The enlargement had turned it slightly grainy. He held it up to the light.

"Well, now, I might have seen this man wandering around, looking kind of lost. He was definitely not a hippie. I pegged him for a father looking for his kid."

We thanked Moretti and left.

"Time for you to check out Father Boniface at Saint Agnes's," I said. "See what you think."

Father Boniface was in the basement with his two semi-permanent helpers changing sheets and pillow cases. He looked up from his work and smiled.

"Carry on, ladies. I just got saved from hard labor."

"I'm still looking for Merriam," I said after we had shaken hands and I'd introduced Dila. "But now I have another missing person for you." I didn't mention Renee was missing her life. Her murder had been covered in the Oakland Tribune on the fourth page devoted to violence in the East Bay, so I figured Father Boniface wouldn't know about it. I showed him the photograph of Renee.

He shook his head. He turned to the two girls making beds and showed them the photograph.

"Ginger, Kayla, have you ever seen this woman around?"

Kayla said, "No, Father."

Ginger shook her head.

They both turned back to their work.

"Well, it was a good try," I said.

Dila stepped forward with the photograph of Brother Gaspare in her hand. "How about this man, Padré," she asked.

"I'm afraid not. He looks like clergy to me. Am I wrong?"

Birds of a feather, I thought. "Not a priest," I said. "He's a Christian Brother. He teaches music at Holy Names College."

"The same college that your runaway, Merriam, attended, correct?"

"Correct," Dila said.

Once again, he showed the photograph to the two hippie girls. They were no help.

We left feeling our trip had been a failure.

"How do you think my afro would look like the color red of that hippie chick's hair," Dila asked.

"You'd look like a stop sign," I said and got a slap on my chest for my honesty.

It was well past noon. We checked out a couple of restaurants serving vegetarian and decided the restaurants might need to be inspected by the health department, so we drove to the Wharf. Both of us had pasta *con mare*. Dila chose a Pinot Blanc. She suggested that it was no sense going back to my apartment before returning to the city at night to talk to some of the people at the clubs at North Beach. We paid for a room at The Wharf Inn around the corner from the main drag and took a nap.

I woke up to an empty side of the bed. Dila was sitting at the desk, talking on the telephone in a hushed voice. From time to time, I heard her swearing. From her profile, I could see her jaw clenching and unclenching. I sat up and leaned back against a pillow and waited. When Dila hung up, she bowed her head down against the desk, her shoulders were shaking. I jumped out from the bed and rushed to her side.

I placed my hand on her shoulder. "Dila, what's wrong?"

She looked up at me. Her eyes were dry. She'd not been crying.

"Oh, Brovelli," She moaned. "That was Terrance. I needed to tell him when I was coming in tomorrow to help with some writing. The news is really bad for the BPP across the country. The po-lice are doing a number on the Detroit BPP. That's one of our smaller city organizations. Don't know why they're being singled out. Total harassment. Arrested a member selling our newspaper and told him they'd killed Hampton and Clark and he'd be next. Arrested a guy driving one of our free breakfast food trucks, took him to jail. Destroyed the food. Food for children."

Dila's eyes began tearing up. I took her hand. She yanked her hand away.

"I'm not the enemy," I said.

The tears spilled over. "Arrested one of the Panthers for stealing his own automobile."

"You got to be kidding."

"God's truth. His own car."

For some reason that made me think of Sweets, the kind of *merda* he'd get involved in and I started to laugh.

"It's not funny," Brovelli.

"His own car," I said. "That's so stupid it has to be funny. Come on, Dila."

"Yeah, maybe." A quick smile surfaced, then faded. "I got to call New York. Terrance said the word is out that the FBI is going to break up a rally in support of the Panthers that are still in prison. There were eleven out of the twenty-one. It's on for tomorrow night in Washington Square. I was part of the organizing committee. I'm pretty close friends with two of the eleven, Joan Robin and Kuwasi Joseph."

"Go ahead," I said. "Charge it to the room."

"I'll need a little privacy, Victor. There's some BPP stuff you shouldn't hear."

"You're serious," I said. Dila said nothing, but her eyes said *serious*. "Okay, I'll go take a long shower."

I was in the bathroom when I heard her give the operator the telephone number in New York. She was calling her own apartment. I undressed, taking my time. I heard her voice say, "Julius, it's me." The next thing Dila said, "I'm okay, but maybe you won't be. I just heard. . ."

I was tempted to listen to her talk to Julius, whoever he was, he was staying in her apartment. Julius could be the voice I'd heard before in the background when I talked to her on the telephone. I didn't want to be jealous. I knew if I kept listening, I would be. It was the tone of her voice, a carrying tone. I turned on the shower to hot and stepped in. I soaped up, washed and rinsed off. It was not the long shower that I promised Dila. I got out of the shower, dried myself. I left the shower running and moved to the door. I opened it a crack. She was explaining some of the things Minister of Education Terrance Bowles must have told her. There was a long pause.

"You know where the weapons are."

Dila paused to listen to his reply.

"I wish I was with you."

Pause

"Don't do anything crazy. It's exactly what the FBI wants you to do."

Pause.

"All right. I understand. You go do what you have to do."

Pause.

"I love you too."

I heard Dila put the receiver down. I hurried back to the shower and stepped back in. I felt terrible faking it. I ran the water to a high heat until I could barely stand it. Then I turned it too cold. I felt a little dizzy. I turned off the shower. I wanted to stay in the bathroom. I knew if I went into the bedroom, I'd say something I'd regret. I took my time drying myself and put my clothes back on.

Dila opened the door and put her head in. "I'm finished," she said. "You weren't kidding when you said you'd take a long shower."

"I'll be right out," I said. And I was, and I did say something that I regretted the moment I said it. "Who's Julius?"

Dila's eyes widened. "You were listening."

I was already committed to the truth. "I was listening. It sounded like you and Julius-"

Dila interrupted me. "Don't say it, Brovelli. I can love anybody I chose to love."

"We're engaged to be married," I said.

"I'm not engaged to my boss or my lord and mastah."

"Not fair," I said. "You have a guy living in your apartment. When I called you, I heard him in the background. He called you honey."

"It's a term of endearment."

"Exactly," I said.

"Don't yell at me, Brovelli. There are some awful things going on. The people I believe in are in danger and you're being jealous about someone you don't know."

"I heard you say you loved him."

"What if I do? What if I told you, you dumbass dago, that people can love more than one person at the same time. You loved Renee Sorenson, didn't you? She still loved you, you know or maybe you didn't know."

"So, now I'm a dumb dago?"

"Oh, for Christ's sake, Victor. Go to hell."

I watched Dila spin around, grab her coat and rush out of the room. I stood staring at the door. It took me a second to think it over and I chased after her. She was looking over the railing at the parking lot below. She was crying. I came up behind her and wrapped my arms around her. "I'm sorry," I said. She didn't say anything. I said, "*Amor senza baruffa, fa la muffa.*"

I heard Dila whisper, "What does that mean."

"Love without a quarrel makes mold."

For a second, I thought Dila had started crying again, until I realized she was laughing. She turned around into my arms, looking up at me.

"Italians are crazy," she said.

"Especially from the south where I'm from," I said. I leaned my forehead down until our heads touched and whispered, "This crazy Italian is really sorry. I'm not your boss. I don't want to be."

"I'm sorry too, Victor. It all just came at me too fast. I do love Julius, as a friend, a dear friend. But you don't have to worry. Julius is gay. He's also deep in the closet. Being gay is not something very popular among African American males, and definitely not the Black Panthers. Which is so nuts because Julius is the most dedicated Panther in New York City."

"I feel stupid," I said.

"There are times it's okay to be foolish, Victor. Let's go back in the room and be foolish for a while."

CHAPTER 19
INCRIMINATING EVIDENCE

"Aiutati Dio ti aiuta.
Help yourself, so God helps you."
Italian proverb

After our long night combing the clubs in the North Beach for evidence of Renee and her mysterious daddy with no luck, we'd decided rather than use up the remaining night we had at the Wharf, we owed ourselves something more elegant, a suite at the *Mark Hopkins* where we agreed we would continue to make up for our argument.

Our suite was on the 10th floor and provided a wide view of all of the San Francisco skyline, the pyramid of the TransAmerica building spiking the star-lit sky. The tops of the Bay Bridge were in the distance, and closer, across the street, the lights of the Fairmont Hotel. I imagined cable cars rattling up and down Powell Street. We stood together holding hands and gazing out the window until it was time to head to the Top of the Mark for dinner. The *osso buco* we both ordered was astonishing, the Cabernet Sauvignon silky smooth and later as promised, so was Dila. I went to sleep *un ragazzo felice*, one happy guy. I woke up feeling all was good between us. No early morning fog in San Francisco. The sun shining over the white city confirmed it would be a good day. My future bride was still asleep.

I shuffled into the living room in my complimentary bathrobe and slippers and turned on the news. Some scientist had synthesized the human genome. The island country of Tonga was about to declare its independence from the United Kingdom. *Small country kicks out big country. Good for them.*

President Nixon was going to make a major announcement about Cambodia at 9:00 p.m. I wasn't interested. Any mention of the Vietnam

War made me think of my brother Mario who had served as a captain in Vietnam and was awarded a Purple Heart and a Silver Star and had returned to America and thrown his medals into a bonfire.

I switched channels. In sports, Bowie Kuhn, the Commish of Major League Baseball was going ballistic over an expose type of book called *Ball Four*, written by ex-Yankee pitcher Jim Boutin. Vincent liked baseball and would know who Boutin was. I liked playing the game but watching it to me is all about the guy selling beer and peanuts. It was already a little before 10:00 a.m. when I ordered room service. I picked up the phone and asked for an outside extension. Theresa picked up. She started with her usual Saturday greeting, "Brovelli Brothers. The barbeque is on us, find the car just for you."

"It's me, Victor."

"Victor, *Odio. Come stai? Dove sei?* Are you okay?"

I didn't like the sound of this greeting: *how was I, where was I?* "Why are you so concerned, cuz?" I didn't need to ask; I knew before she answered. Theresa confirmed my fear.

"Victor, the police are looking to arrest you. Jay says they found more evidence."

"What kind of evidence?"

"I don't know. Jay wouldn't tell us. Here, let me get Vincent."

Theresa put me on hold. A minute later, Vincent came on the line, breathing hard, like he'd been running.

"I've called Curtis. He says go to his office. Go in the back. He'll have the charges by then, and you guys can talk it over. You can turn yourself in with him there to protect your rights."

Screw turning myself in. "Does he have any idea what they found?"

"No, but whatever it was, it was in your apartment. The police had a warrant and searched your place early this morning. I guess you let Sweets sleep over. The cops might have roughed him up a little. He was freaking out."

"*Minchia!*" I swore.

"You can say that again," Vincent said.

In the background, I could hear our loudspeakers playing some rock song, which meant it was Barbeque Saturday. I felt Dila's hand on my shoulder. I looked up.

She mouthed the words, "What's wrong?"

I shook my head.

Vincent was talking in my other ear. "You weren't home last night. Are you in a hotel?"

I told him. "Hurry up and go to Curtis. Remember, the back door. The cops will probably have someone watching the front."

"How's Pop taking it?" I asked.

"You know him. We uphold our family honor. He's saying the police are acting like Mussolini's *Carmicie Nera*, Black Shirts. He might be right. It was that asshole cop, Halpern."

"I'm hanging up, Vincent. Tell Pop and Mom not to worry. I'll get in touch with Curtis."

I hung up the phone and turned to Dila, "I need to find a more permanent place to hide for a while." I explained what was going on. When I finished, I added, "On top of that, it's that fucking Halpern again. I wouldn't put it past him to plant some incriminating evidence in my apartment."

Dila said, "Welcome to our world."

"Incriminating evidence suddenly turns up in my apartment is not the same as my fingerprints in Renee's place. That was totally understandable. This isn't circumstantial any more. My fingerprints plus whatever this evidence is puts me behind bars, and I won't be able to bond out. I know Vincent would try to find out who put the evidence in my apartment, but finally, it's up to me to save myself. That means I'm in the wind and need to find a secure place to hide."

Dila suggested Sweets might know of a rabbit hole. She understood when I explained that I didn't want any of my family or friends to know where I was; that way they wouldn't have to lie to the police.

"Terrance," she said.

She was talking about the Black Panthers' Minister of Education Terrance Bowles with whom I had a semi-friendly and mutually beneficial relationship. Searching back through my memory to Monterey of January and a certain suitcase of hundred-dollar bills that was now in the hands of the Panthers because of me, I figured Bowles owed me.

Dila said not to worry about lying to the police with Terrance, that Bowles enjoyed lying to the pigs. I wagged my finger at Dila for her use of pigs. "Jay would have his feelings hurt if he heard you."

"I know your friend is a good cop," she said. "I know there are a few around. But they're like rare birds you got to use binoculars to find."

That was a pretty funny, but I withheld my laughter. There were few African Americans that weren't terribly suspicious of the various branches of law enforcement. I had faith in Jay and some of his cop buddies that sometimes sat in at the poker games at Flynn's to be honest and hard-working police officers.

West Oakland would be a perfect hideout. The cops would not think to look for a white Italian car salesman in the predominately African-American neighborhood. I couldn't risk going to the hotel by the college or to my apartment. I'd have to buy some duds and other essentials for possibly a longer period of time. I didn't know how long I'd need to be a fugitive.

"I'll call Bowles," I said. "You shouldn't try to find out from him where I am. I don't want you to lie to the cops."

"Terrance and I think the same way about po-lice officers," she said, stretching out the word to appease me without appeasing me.

"Still," I said.

"Fine, go underground on me, see if I care."

"I'll make contact with you," I said.

"How cloak-and-dagger of you."

"Don't joke," I said. "This is serious." Dila leaned over and patted my cheek.

A knock on the door startled me. Dila stood up and went to the door. She asked who it was. Room service with our breakfast. Too late, I was no longer hungry. We drove back to Oakland and I dropped Dila at her house. Then, I drove to West Oakland.

CHAPTER 20
THE RABBIT HOLE

"The time is always right to do right."
Martin Luther King Jr.

The weekend was always a busy time at the Black Panthers headquarters, Saturdays and Sundays being the days they made their food deliveries to the poorest of West Oakland. Over the telephone, I could hear the activity. I explained my problem to Terrance Bowles. Given what I was involved in, I also knew the FBI watched the Panthers' office as a matter of course. I wanted to be sure I wouldn't be walking into a pair of handcuffs. He told me it was all clear, that he'd checked an hour ago. Too early for them. Got to get their beauty sleep.

Minister Bowles met me at the door. It had not been that long since we'd been together, so I didn't expect to see any change in his dignified face, but I was wrong. Bowles looked years older. The gray of his afro had moved further up from the temples. His usually clear, severe eyes, looking at me above his granny glasses, were swollen and red. He waved me in. He still walked ramrod straight but appeared thinner to me.

"I got coffee," he said.

"Black," I said.

"You're learning," Bowles said.

We reached his office. He'd done a little rearranging since my last visit. A new desk and a more comfortable chair for visitors. He'd replaced a couple of his posters. Along with his poster of Minister of Defense Huey Newton, sitting regent-like in a high-back wicker chair holding a spear and a rifle, was his poster of Dedan Kimathi, the leader of the Mau Mau rebellion. Then, there was a new poster of Cassius Clay, now Mohammed Ali, in the ring with his arms over his head after winning the World Heavy

Weight Championship by defeating Sonny Liston. Surprisingly, there was also a poster of a dignified white-haired Fredrick Douglass.

I pointed to the Douglas poster. "You getting a little conservative, aren't you?"

"Can't ignore history. Huey preached the importance of it. Dila probably told you how Huey learned to read."

"She did. At the same time, she was showing me her carbine."

Terrance laughed.

"I like the new Angela Davis poster," I said.

He turned his head to the wall I was looking at. "Sister is a little young for me, but I've always been a little bit in love with her."

I was surprised by Minister Bowles' admission. He was a taciturn man, not known for talking about his personal life.

"Dila keeps her hair like that,"

"Half the sisters in America do," he said.

Terrance handed me my coffee and motioned for me to sit down. He moved behind his desk and sat. For a while we chatted about sports. Bowles was still thrilled by Lew Alcindor and the Milwaukee Bucks winning the NBA Championship. He'd heard rumors that Alcindor was going to become a Muslim and change his name. "Not the Black Muslims," he added, "but the real Islamic faith." He mentioned he had an Aretha Franklin autograph.

Bowles was sounding nostalgic, so I filled him in on some car news that bored him, which got him back to our relationship. Terrance brought up the Monterey incident and thanked me again for my help.

He surprised me by admitting that since then, he'd been feeling really sorry that Little Eddie had been killed on the Monterey dock that day. He explained that Big Eddie had raised his cousin since he was two-years-old. "Stupid man, but a good dad," Terrance said. Big Eddie had made his escape. I could still see that fishing trawler filled with millions of dollars' worth of illegal weapons turning toward the ocean beyond the bay.

"We need more good black fathers, Vincent," Terrance said, his voice dropping to sadness. "I believed Big Eddie had given up crime when he and Little Eddie joined the Panthers. He sure did love Eddie, but I guess he didn't love himself enough."

Terrance had a faraway look in his eyes. It was not like him to be so emotional. It worried me.

"How're you doing, Terrance?" I asked.

"Compared to what?"

I smiled. Bowles was referencing one of his favorite tunes, a song called "Compared to What", made famous by pianist Les McCann and tenor saxophonist Eddie Harris. How did I know this? I'd been to the headquarters of the Black Panthers often enough to be an expert on the music Bowles provided for his office staff. I even knew that the first recording of the song was by Roberta Flack. And how did I know about Roberta Flack? Easy, she was one of Dila's favorite soul singers.

"Put the record on if you want to, but I'd say compared to someone deeply worried."

"I won't go into the FBI shit that's coming down," he said, rubbing his eyes. "We're handling it the best we can, but I'll tell you, Victor, it's not good. There's going to be a reckoning. I can feel it in my bones."

"I hope you're wrong, Terrance." I changed subjects. "Dila is back."

"I know," Bowles said. "She called from the airport."

Why wasn't I surprised?

I wanted to stay on the subject of Dila, but Bowles said, "Let's talk about how to keep you safe."

"I was thinking the cops wouldn't look for an Italian white guy in a black neighborhood."

"I was thinking the same thing. Big James has a great aunt who'll put you up for a while. Her grandson is in Vietnam. She says she knows you."

I couldn't imagine how.

• • •

A half hour later I was standing in front of Miss Rhoda's apartment ringing her doorbell, and remembering the last time I was here two years ago, this dead-end street in the heart of what was often referred to as Oakland's ghetto. Looking around, the street looked pretty tidy to me. Vincent and I had been here repo'ing a car in front of Miss Rhoda's apartment. How could this sweet old woman who'd leaned out her window and offered us oatmeal raisin-bran cookies be related to James the Behemoth, Terrance Bowles' bodyguard, who hated my guts?

The buzzer to let me in sounded. I walked up the stairs. I reached her apartment and knocked. It opened to Miss Rhoda smiling broadly. All I'd seen of her leaning out of the window as we applied the jumper cables was an elderly woman of an uncertain age. The woman before me was certainly of an uncertain age, between forty and sixty. I figured her height at around 5'2" or 3" with a figure clothiers would call petite. Her skin was the color of caramel. Her oval face featured two amber eyes. She wore her hair in an afro, with just a hint of gray, neatly configured to the shape of her head. Because of her age, you could not call her cute, but that's how I saw her.

She welcomed me in a cheery voice and took me by the arm. She walked on the balls of her feet, like she could have been an athlete as a young person. She led me to her grandson's bedroom. It was as clean and as neat as the rest of Miss Rhoda's apartment. Theresa, our neat-freak accountant, would have had to go some way to equal Miss Rhoda's cleaning skills. Her grandson's photograph in a gold frame stood on a chest of drawers. Written on the bottom of the picture was his name and rank: Lance Corporal, Isaiah Teagarden.

"Handsome child," Miss Rhoda said. "Raised that child ever since my daughter died giving birth to him and his no-account daddy disappeared. I was pleased that Isaiah took his mama's maiden name. The boy come home safe, his room be exactly the way he left it."

"I don't want to mess it up, Miss Rhoda. I can sleep on your couch."

"Don't fret, Mr. Brovelli. I wash the sheets before he comes home."

I saw a little spark in Miss Rhoda's eyes. Not a woman to pass up an opportunity, I thought. "Please, call me Victor," I said.

She nodded.

"Will your grandson be home soon?"

"Next month, he writes. Gonna be a First Sergeant in the Marines."

"Wonderful," I said.

"You make yourself comfy, now. I'll call you in a bit. I got apple pie in the oven."

Miss Rhoda disappeared. It seemed to me that hiding a man from the cops was an everyday occurrence for her.

I put away my things and went to the bathroom to clean up. The bathroom was spotless. I could have eaten off the floor. There was no way this bathroom could be this sparkling unless she cleaned it every day. I finished and hurried to the kitchen. Apple pie was a favorite.

Sitting at the kitchen table with a plate of pie and large dollop of vanilla ice cream in front of him was Giant James, scowling at me. "Just thought

I better check on you, White Bread," he said, "make sure you was treating my auntie nice-like."

I hated being called white bread but resisted a comeback.

"Don't you worry about me, James," Miss Rhoda said. "Me and Mr. Brovelli goes back some."

"Yeah," I said. "I wouldn't dare give Miss Rhoda any trouble. She'd kick my butt uptown and downtown."

"See to it," James the Giant Bear said. He shoveled the last slice of pie into his humungous mouth and stood up. "Just passing by," he said. He kissed Miss Rhoda on the top of her head. There was a tenderness there.

"Don't you worry, Mr. Brovelli," Miss Rhoda said after the door closed. "James only likes one white I know of and he's that little freckle-faced boy, Opie, in *The Andy Griffith Show*."

Weird, I thought. I started laughing. Miss Rhoda joined in. Her laughter was so heartfelt with pleasure that I knew someday the races would manage to do what was right.

CHAPTER 21
THE CONCERT

"LSD is a psychedelic drug which occasionally causes
Psychotic behavior in people who have not taken it."
Timothy Leary

Gloria had just cleared off the dinner dishes. The baby, Mario, and his daughter, Christina, were already asleep, when Vincent sat in his armchair by the fireplace and brooded over the predicament his twin was in. Despite his advice to turn himself in, he knew Victor would not do it. The phone rang. He had no doubt it would be Victor. It was.

"I'll be fast, Vincent. I want you to go to the Grateful Dead concert tonight and follow up with that gal Lydia you told me about. All the crap coming down on my head I completely forgot. Also, it seems to me that Merriam could very well be at the concert. She's a Deadhead, she wouldn't miss a concert at Fillmore West. If you find her, see who she's hanging out with. Any particular guy. Take a camera. At the end of the concert, follow her. If you can."

Vincent had not explained to Victor that he and "that Lydia" had not parted on good terms, but he understood the importance of going to the concert. *Of course, Merriam would be there.* He assured Victor that he'd handle it. He began to tell Victor to go to Curtis' office when he realized the phone had gone dead. Vincent recalled cop shows on TV, talking about tracing calls. The thought made him wonder if their telephone was bugged. He dismissed the idea. He was a good American citizen. He cradled the receiver and went to ask Gloria if she wanted to go with him.

"I can't get a baby sitter so late, *caro*. You'll have to suffer without me. Besides, I don't like the Grateful Dead too much. Have fun. Don't smoke any weed. You're a family man now."

It was with Gloria's words in mind that Vincent set off for San Francisco. If he was being honest with himself, he had to admit that he wasn't unhappy that Gloria was not with him. Lydia may have been mad at him for some reason, but she still remained vividly attractive in his memory as a woman with great sex appeal, and, if her flaming red hair was real all over, *Mama mia!* The thought made him angry with himself.

He was a family man! Not only that, he was an Italian family man, and he'd remain such a man for whom *La Famiglia* was at the heart of the culture he'd grown up with! He was a man of honor; he would not be tempted. "I will *not* be tempted," he said aloud.

He'd look for Merriam. She was a tall woman. He could not count on the color of Merriam's hair because it seemed that hippie girls were changing their hair color to match their clothing or whatever whim compelled them. He had her photograph. He'd studied it. If she was there, he'd recognize her.

It was going on 7:30 when Vincent arrived at the Fillmore West. He lucked out and found a parking spot a block away and sprinted to the venue. He'd been told tickets might be sold out, but he lucked out again. There were a few still available. He walked up the stairs to concert hall in the direction of the music. It sounded to him like it was a drum solo. At the top of the red carpeted stairs to the right were two large gleaming copper buckets filled with red delicious apples.

There were two couples standing by the buckets talking, their voices high and excitable, something about a celestial synapse. Vincent remembered from college that synapse had to do with nerve cells. He walked past them and stopped for a second and bent down pretending to tie his shoelaces, so he could hear what they said, without them thinking he was eavesdropping.

It was difficult to hear. The woman kept repeating the word "Aoxomoxoa", which sounded like a foreign language to him. She was twisting her limbs into odd angles as she spoke as if every word she said required a particular part of her body to illustrate her meaning. There was something she was explaining about a Tibetan monk. Aoxomoxoa was probably a Tibetan word, Vincent thought. The woman's words were followed by lots of "far outs", "whoas" and "dig its".

All four of them were eating apples. Vincent thought their faces were kind of glowing. They were either overly excited or already wasted.

Vincent pulled a small yellow apple out and took a bite. *Nice, different taste*, he thought, but he wasn't hungry. He placed it in his pocket for the ride home.

The drum solo ended and a guitar and harmonica took turns leading into a voice. Vincent couldn't make out the lyrics completely but the singer was pleading to his "baby" to "please come on". The stage was too far away to be sure, but it had to be Jerry Garcia singing. Vincent was surprised that he found Garcia's voice appealing, kind of gruff, but full of emotion.

He moved toward the wall of bodies at the back of the crowded room. To his right was a table with a cot next to it and a sign that read MEDICAL. He wondered what that was all about. He and Gloria had gone to concerts and never seen that before. If he wanted to get closer to the stage, his best bet was to hug the walls. Above him were huge disco globes that spun around and sent multi-colored lights swirling over the auditorium. Behind the stage more lights charged into the air. Vincent was reminded of World War Two movies he'd seen on late night TV of English spotlights on the ground trying to find German bombers.

There was a rhythmic instrumental background barely audible, not part of the band's music, emanating from somewhere, creating a sort of hypnotic effect on the crowd. Vincent found himself swaying a little before forcing himself to control his body. He inched closer to the wall. Trying to look over the tops of the crowd was impossible. Vincent began to feel a little lightheaded. He took his handkerchief out of his pocket and sneezed hard. The apple fell out of his pocket and rolled away on the floor. He watched it bounce from leg to leg like a pinball. He could be inside a pinball machine, Vincent thought. He took a deep breath. His eyes began to water. He staggered back against the wall for support.

"You okay, chief? If you're freaking, our medical station is in the back of the hall."

Vincent didn't realize his eyes were closed. He opened them and saw a bone-thin man with a red bandana covering his head, two pigtails hanging from either side of the bandana. "Tonto," Vincent said and began to giggle.

"No, dude, you're the Lone Ranger. I'm Tonto. If you can joke, it means you're okay."

"Far out," Vincent said and began giggling again. The bone-thin Indian medic turned away and hurried toward a guy who was on his knees and shaking.

I need some air, Vincent thought. He saw a possibility in the form of a small empty platform protruding from the wall ahead of him. He pushed hard past a number of swaying Deadheads. He reached it and clamored on top, beating a young woman with hair down to her waist and little rings in her eyebrows. She looked up at him mournfully. He shrugged. He might have shared, but there was barely room for him.

Now, he could see above the crowd, but the view was almost dizzying to watch, like oil moving on water. Bobby Weir was singing "Mama Tried", but he could barely hear the song: there was a lonesome whistle blowing and a freight train and dreaming, dreaming of something. And then, Mama was trying again. *That's one hard-working mama*, Vincent thought. Standing where he was a little above the crowd, his head cleared and he regained his focus.

Vincent had not expected to hear a song he knew at a Grateful Dead concert, but "Mama Tried" was on the jukebox in Flynn's tavern and was a favorite of Swanee's and a couple of the other country and western music lovers, only the tavern's version was sung by Merle Haggard. He'd have to report to Swanee that his favorite singer had competition from a psychedelic rocker. He could only imagine the look of disbelief on Swanee's face. Flynn's tavern was not home to hippy lovers. Vincent remembered Body saying when a lunchtime discussion had turned to the Summer of Love that their women didn't shave their pits.

About the time mama had tried for the third time with no success, Vincent spotted Lydia's red hair. She was talking to the roadie named Grillo. They were standing in the corner next to the back stage entrance. Vincent jumped down and began shouldering his way through the kaleidoscope of bodies. As much as this was supposed to be a peaceful audience, most of them higher than cloud cover, some of his attempts to pass were met with a number of elbows and one furious kick by a boot attached to a fine-looking female leg.

Vincent was close enough to Lydia to call her name. She looked over prepared to smile, but her smile evaporated.

"Lydia," he called again, "I need to talk to you."

"Fuck off," she said. She grabbed Grillo's arm and moved past the guard and through the back stage entrance.

Victor watched them disappear. He stepped forward and was met by an elephant-sized guard wearing a T-shirt two sizes too small for him that fit him like skin over what was definitely muscles. He'd been in a weight room since childhood. Vincent found himself smiling and shrugging as if what the hell, it was just a love thing.

He backed away, back into the delirious crowd of Deadheads. It was time to go home. He was tired and definitely partially high, a contact high it was called. He edged his way around this side of the auditorium until he was at the door. There were two apples left in the barrel. One of them was a Red Delicious, his favorite apple. This one was perfect, crisp and sweet. He looked back into the auditorium. Two guitars were competing with each other and a harmonic was wailing and a keyboard was joining in and Vincent was suddenly feeling like the drums were not on the stage but in his head.

He shook his head, but the drumming continued followed by a shadowy figure of a Lydia dancing forward. The auditorium was suddenly empty. It was only Lydia floating on a cloud of marijuana smoke. She was swinging a long sword in her hand and crooning, "come on baby, come on. . ."

Vincent wanted to run, but his legs wouldn't move. She was so close he could reach out and touch her, but suddenly she disappeared and a rainbow of lights began to circle around him. He started to turn around. Around and around he went. He thrust out his arms and raised his palms up. From somewhere in the distance, he heard a voice yell, "Blazing!" He felt an arm around him and another, more familiar voice.

"It's Tonto, Lone Ranger."

Vincent felt if he kept spinning, he'd take flight. He shook his head, and the spinning took the form of an image. Oh, man, was that him driving a Mercedes 300 SLR Uhlenhaut Coupe? Yes, it was.

Vincent had never felt happier in his life. He couldn't wait to tell Victor. He'd be so jealous.

CHAPTER 22

THE TRUTH, THE WHOLE TRUTH, AND NOTHING BUT THE TRUTH

"La mela mancia, rovina tutte le altre.
The rotten apple spoils the others."
Italian proverb

Vincent expected to hear from his wife again how stupid he'd been last night. Instead, she brought him the Sunday edition of the Oakland Tribune, placed it in front of his Grape-Nuts cereal and pointed to the column that read:

Sunday, May 7, 1970

Oakland Automobile Dealer, Victor
Brovelli Indicted for Murder.
Last night, new evidence was uncovered that
led to. . .

Vincent didn't want to read any further, but he forced himself to finish. *"Che casino,"* he groaned.

"A mess is a huge understatement," Gloria said. "What are you going to do?"

The anxiety in Gloria's voice belied her normal exasperation with his twin's life style. He knew his wife deep down was actually fond of Victor.

"I have no idea," he said.

"He's probably already read the paper, don't you think? Can you get a message to him?"

"I doubt it." Vincent was thinking maybe if he called the Black Panthers office, Victor's pal, Bowles would know how to get a hold of him. His thoughts were interrupted by the telephone. It was Jay.

Vincent listened to Jay's worried voice and promised to call him the second he heard from Victor. He knew he wouldn't without his twin's approval.

The phone rang again. He figured it would be Curtis, their lawyer, also worried and wanting to talk to Victor. To his surprise it was his twin.

"Victor, are you okay? We're all worried. Mama is crazy worried."

"What?"

"Haven't you read the newspaper?"

"*Minchia*, what now?"

"The cops found new evidence. You are no longer the principal suspect, now you're wanted for Renee's murder. They're going to arrest you. It's on the front page of the paper this morning."

"*Stronzata*. This is really bullshit."

"Cops have been hanging around before this like they're just cruising normally, but they're keeping an eye on our lot. I can't imagine what they'll do now. You know Curtis is upset you didn't come to the office. He says you're a fool to hide. It only makes you seem more guilty."

"Does the paper say what kind of new evidence?"

"Yeah, and it's not good. It says it's Renee's underwear with blood all over it."

"And where was I so stupid to hide it?"

"In your closet."

"Where no one would ever look, right? These cops are setting me up."

"No doubt, brother. But that's not how the majority of the police are going to see it. To them, you're a murderer on the loose. And you know how things have been in the Bay Area recently. The cops are totally antsy. Jay just called. He said you have to turn yourself in. He's talking to Halpern and his buddy who are leading the charge to arrest you. I have the feeling that Halpern would just as well bring you in dead. He really hates you."

"And vice versa," Victor said.

Vincent saw Gloria at the kitchen door. She mouthed the word, "Victor?"

He nodded.

"What do you want me to do, Victor?" he asked.

"I've got a safe place to stay while I figure this out. Look, I'll need a car to drive instead of my Mach One that will not be noticeable. Pick out something gray or any light color. A sedan. Could you bring it by this afternoon?"

"Where? No, don't tell me. I don't believe the cops could be listening in, but you know."

Vincent listened to Victor breathing. Finally, he spoke. "Remember the place we were repo-ing a car and that drunken *chooch* shot out the back window with a shotgun?"

"Yeah, that was hairy."

"Do you remember the street?"

"Sure, burned into my memory."

"My car will be parked on that block with a tarp over it. The keys will be on top right front tire. Put the tarp over the car you drive down in. Leave those keys on the tire. Park my Mustang behind the office and stick a tarp over it.

"Jeez, Victor, isn't that street in. . . "

"Like you said, bro, no need to advertise."

"Sorry, I wasn't thinking. I'll see it gets done." He was picturing a couple on the lot that would work. Before Victor hung up, Vincent reminded him to call their mom.

Gloria came into the dining room and put her arms around him. "What does he want you to do?" She sounded worried. He had to reassure her, but he wasn't so reassured himself.

"He wants me to drop off a car in West Oakland that won't be as noticeable as his Mustang."

"Is he hiding in West Oakland?" Gloria asked.

"Sounds like it."

"He'll stick out like a sore Italian thumb."

"His pal at the Black Panthers is probably helping him out."

"*Odio,*" Gloria said and crossed herself. The teakettle began whistling. She took it off the burner and turned back to him. "I have to get the kids ready for mass."

Gloria didn't ask him if he was going to mass. She knew he'd shake his head. His twin may be a believer but Vincent preferred not to believe for a long time. He preferred to be on the lot among his cars.

By 10:30, Vincent was toweling off cars after last night's shower. He was trying to stay busy to distract himself from worrying about Victor. It was not working. The Sunday Tribune was laying on his desk. He'd read the article through a couple of times. Victor was in deep *merda*.

And what was he, Vincent Brovelli, doing? *Niente!* Nothing! Toweling off cars. Victor has told him he'd be in touch. He'd wait. But he should be doing something! He had things to report to Victor from Saturday's concert. Wasn't he the one who was supposed to be doing the detective work about Merriam? That had been their bargain to begin with, but now that Victor was a wanted man, Merriam's fate seemed to Vincent like an afterthought.

Then, there were other responsibilities, he promised Victor he'd take care of. Somebody had to deal with the Big Sal Brovelli problem. He understood that, but still. . . His twin was in a serious jam. The more he thought, the more his dark mood turned darker. He looked up to the eastern horizon and the sun mocking him. Theresa drove in. Normally, Theresa took Sundays off, but with the stuff going on, she had agreed to work on the Lord's Day, a big deal on her part because, like Victor she too was a believer. A few minutes later, to his surprise, Big Sal drove in, parked behind the office. Vince went to meet him. To Vincent's question, shouldn't he be with his wife at mass, his pop explained it was better to help save his sons than listen to Father Dunnican speak about saving souls.

The rest of the quiet Sunday morning, with no customers in sight, Vincent listened with amazement to Big Sal Brovelli on the phone, making cold calls, happily talking to strangers in his big voice with its Italian accent and sounding as if he was a long lost relative. It was the only reason Vincent could figure why people on the other end of the line weren't hanging up on him.

Theresa had mentioned it too—that his pop had some kind of miracle voice. "You know, Vincent," she'd said to him. "By 10:00 a.m. yesterday your father had seven people promising to be in today—on Sunday, for goodness sake, and I don't think they were putting your dad on. He had names, addresses, phone numbers, places of employment, banks. I mean I was flabbergasted. Honestly."

Vincent looked at his father and shook his head. So far, the promises had gone unfulfilled unless the customers were disguised as empty space.

Vincent left his pop in the office and began a stroll around the lot. At street level, he opened the door to a silver and black 1967 Fleetwood Cadillac Eldorado and climbed in behind the steering wheel. He adjusted the seat so that he was facing East 14th Street. Without its normal busy traffic, so unlike the rest of the week, the atmosphere seemed sort of funeral, or maybe it was the mood he was in. A Mexican woman carrying a string shopping bag walked slowly by. The once mostly white neighborhood was changing. He imagined his dream house in the suburban town of Walnut Creek, east of the Berkeley hills.

Seeing Nick Parsegian pull into the driveway of his store, Vincent turned his thoughts back to Victor. What could he do to help his twin and keep his eye on Pop? The answer came to him as he saw Jay Ness's ugly police car pass the lot on East 14th Street, Ness at the wheel, his elbow on the window panel. He turned into the parking lot of Flynn's Tavern. If Jay was on duty on a weekend, it was not unusual for him to stop at Flynn's for an early morning pick-me-up.

Vincent sat up and swung out of the seat. He'd talk to Ness. Maybe there was some way to find out something, anything that would help his twin. If it was the cops framing Victor, as Victor believed, Jay might have some ideas.

• • •

Flynn's was a different tavern on Sundays. Body took the day off. Stuart Tanberg, the night bartender, was behind the bar. Stuart lived in the apartment above the tavern and was an insomniac. With his gaunt features and slicked back black hair, and his normal black attire, Stuart was their resident vampire. He was also gay, which didn't seem to bother the beer drinking macho denizens of Flynn's, something that Vincent found curious. It was sort of like as long as Stuart didn't hit on them and didn't forget to pour a free round once in a while, who really gave a shit? These were a bunch of good guys. Victor was one of those good guys.

Across from Stuart sat Abbot and Costello, the two cab drivers shaking dice. The rest of the barstools were empty except where Ness had planted himself. A man and woman were in a booth, and two men were playing pool. Gordon Lightfoot was on the jukebox singing "If You Could Read My Mind". If only he could read Victor's mind right now, Vincent thought as he sat down on the stool next to Ness. Stuart came over and Vincent ordered what Jay was having, an Irish coffee.

When Stuart was out of earshot, Vincent said, "I've got a problem."

"There's a riot going on in cell block number nine," Jay said.

Vincent remembered the Coaster's song from high school. "Not funny, Jay."

"Neither is the riot that's scheduled to happen in front of the Alameda Naval Airport that's bringing some of our boys home from Vietnam this afternoon. I can't believe these fucking Anti-Nam assholes."

Vincent interrupted. "Victor is in deep trouble.

"You're telling me."

Jay took a long sip of his Irish coffee. "It's as if those troops were responsible for getting us into the war instead of dying for our country or being wounded for life."

Vincent agreed wholeheartedly with Jay and the majority of Americans that supported the troops. His brother Mario, rest his soul, was a captain in Vietnam and had come home bitter. If he were alive today, he'd have joined the protestors.

"Jay, I understand. I'm on your side, but this is about my twin brother."

"You don't think I know that? Look, Vincent. Victor and I are friends, but he's stubborn. He won't turn himself in, what the hell am I supposed to do? Stop what I'm doing, to help him? There's talk the protestors are going to be carrying weapons. At this moment in my life, your twin is not at the top of my priority list."

Mama mia, weapons, Vincent thought. *What would Mario think about that? So much violence.*

On May 4th, the Ohio National Guard had fired into a crowd of protesting students on the campus of Kent State University. Four students had been killed and nine wounded. There'd been protests and candlelight vigils all over the country. Things had just started settling down, which gave Jay a chance for a brief vacation. Victor told him that Jay hadn't had a vacation in two years. He didn't want to place any more stress on Jay.

"I don't envy you having to deal with those protestors," Vincent said. "But can we talk about Victor? Just talk."

"I can't say anything about your bro. He's in deep mayonnaise."

"Jay. You know as well as I do that Victor didn't rape and kill Renee. There's not one person who knows Victor who believes it. Those two had been going together for two years. Come on. You must be able to help somehow without getting into trouble with your superiors."

Vincent sighed as Jay continued to sip his spiked coffee.

"Come on, Jay," Vincent said again. "Any little bit of information about the two cops who found Renee and discovered her clothing in Victor's apartment. It's too damn obvious, don't you get it?"

"I get it, all right. I also get. . ." Jay stopped talking, then continued, "Ah shit, Vincent, the evidence was there. The blood matches Victor's blood type. I agree, only a fool would keep her clothing in his apartment, and Victor is no fool. But our chief wants a conviction. Mill's College has a lot of wealthy and influential alums. They've been putting on the pressure. The papers have been hammering the police force. With this new evidence, they're going to be on our asses even more. It's as if we're the bad guys."

"Is there a way to prove that those cops put the clothing in the apartment?"

"No, we can't, and I'll tell you why."

"I'm listening," Vincent said, feeling a twinge of hope.

"Because they didn't put them there. I don't like Lazlo and Halpern, and there is no doubt they hate Victor, especially Halpern, but I quizzed them pretty damn hard. You don't think I'd let them get away with such shit with Victor and I being friends? They swore to me that they didn't. If a person's a suspect, you get a search warrant and go search. It was a legal search."

"Well, heck," Vincent said. "How *did* the underwear wind up in Victor's apartment?"

"I have no idea, Vincent. And I'll tell you another thing, Halpern is dumb enough to think up a stupid frame like that, but not Jack Lazlo. He'd have thought up something far more clever. Halpern is an altar boy compared to Sergeant Lazlo, a smooth talker, low-key, but the devil incarnate. They play good cop, bad cop all the time, Halpern the bad cop when it should be two bad cops. I'll tell you, Vincent, these days there are enough guys on the force that are willing to accept the bad cops' idea of doing business, which is bashing skulls if necessary. There's not a cop in America these days who's not frustrated and pissed off. But in Victor's case, you need to start looking in another direction to find who's setting Victor up."

This was not what Vincent wanted to hear.

Jay drained his cup and stood up. "Got to go, Vincent. Good luck. If I hear anything, I'll let you know. I'll leave a message with Terry."

Terry, not Theresa, Vincent thought. Since January, Jay and Theresa had been seeing each other, mostly going to operas, which Jay claimed to hate but was willing to suffer through for Theresa. "Ciao," Vincent said to

Jay's back.

"Back at you," he heard before the door closed. A thought came to Vincent and he rushed to the door. He caught Jay as he turned the corner to the parking lot behind the tavern.

"What now?" Jay said.

"Do you know where Halpern and Lazlo live?"

"Don't start, Vincent. This sounds like a Sweets Monroe question to me."

"Look, if we can find something to compromise these two guys, it would help Victor, wouldn't it? You went to law school before joining the police. I'm right, aren't I?"

"Yes, a good lawyer would be able to do something with that kind of information."

"So, how about the addresses?"

"I'm going to do this against my better judgement, but only Halpern's address. Sergeant Lazlo is married with children. I won't be part of Sweets ransacking his home."

Vincent held out his hand.

"Hell, I don't have his address in my wallet, Vincent. I'll find out and call you later at the lot. If Sweets gets caught, I'll disavow any knowledge, you understand."

"Completely," Vincent said. "You're a good friend Jay."

"I'm a stupid friend," Jay replied.

Vincent watched his stupid good friend walk away. He hadn't tasted his Irish coffee. It was probably cold by now.

• • •

Vincent returned to the lot in time to face Nick Parsegian who was standing by the office door, not exactly the person Vincent was eager to talk to. The next half hour was spent answering Parsegian's questions. Did Victor have any news? Where was Victor? How could Victor help find his baby girl if he was a fugitive from the law? Should he hire another private investigator now that Victor was in Brazil? It was after the last question that Vincent had held up his hand. Victor was not in Brazil, he explained to Parsegian, or in any country that did not have extradition agreements with the United States, and that Parsegian should not spread rumors. He wanted to end by saying, you *chooch*, which in English meant moron or the more colorful dumb-shit.

• • •

Vincent was getting nervous. It was three o'clock. If Victor had read the paper, he should have gotten hold of him by now. This morning Big Sal had sold three cars. His pop was standing by the open office door tugging on his suspenders and sticking out his chest. Good for his pop. The old man still had his salesman's chops. His pop was explaining to Theresa some of the nuances of selling cars on Sundays which, according to him, was a trickier day than other days of the week.

The phone in the office rang and Vincent rushed to answer it, hoping it was Victor. It was Ness. Vincent wrote down Halpern's address: 1467 Poplar Street, Oakland, apartment 2B. Jay hung up before he could thank him. Now Vincent had to find Sweets. The thought made Vincent a little nauseous.

The phone rang again. Theresa beat him to the phone. He listened to her speaking. It was for him. She held out the receiver to him, mouthing the words, but he didn't know a man named Rosellini.

CHAPTER 23
FUGITIVE

"Il fuggitivo trova tutto ci oche lo ostacola.
The fugitive finds everything impedes him"
Italian proverb

I hung up the phone and stepped out of the telephone booth. The sun was shining but my mood was too dark for any light to cheer me up. I looked around Jack London Square where I'd driven from Miss Rhoda's apartment. My first morning under her roof, I'd been treated to a lovely breakfast scrambled eggs, sausages and home fries. The Sunday paper had gone unread as we talked and I'd filled her with all the details of my predicament. She'd assured me everything would turn out for the best. After listening to my twin Vincent, the best was a long way off.

I began walking back to my car. Jack London Square was a popular weekend destination for tourists, full of fancy shops and restaurants, but this time in the morning, there was no one about and the silence was interrupted only by the occasional squawk of seagulls. A panhandler sitting with his back against a storefront held out his hand. I didn't have any bills, but I gave him what loose change I had. He spit on the pavement. A seagull swooped down and examined the spittle and flew away in disgust. I hurried on.

I needed to get back to Miss Rhoda's and do some thinking. If I'd arrived at Miss Rhoda's place as a man looking for a short-term hideout, she was about to find out I was a bona fide fugitive. She might not be as happy to have me as a guest.

Using the key Miss Rhoda had given me, I unlocked her front door. The apartment was quiet. The note on the kitchen table told me that Miss Rhoda had left for church and to make myself comfortable. She'd be back in a couple of hours. The coffee was still hot. Coffee with chicory because that's how Miss Rhoda's grandaddy from Louisiana had always made the family brew.

The Sunday Oakland Tribune was open to the *Dear Abby* column and the crossword section. I decided to read the sports page instead of reading about a certain used car salesman that was wanted for the brutal murder of his ex-girlfriend. I felt my eyes stinging and rubbed them. My jaw hurt from clenching my teeth. I sipped my coffee. When Miss Rhoda returned from church. I owed her a complete, detailed account of my predicament.

In the meantime, I decided to visit the BPP office. I knew they'd be open, still preparing for the later deliveries of food and clothing for the West Oakland poor. Their office was less than ten blocks away. It was daylight, so figured I could walk it without being mugged and get back in time to talk to Miss Rhoda. I had questions for Terrance Bowles.

Outside, a few boys were pitching pennies at the wall. I placed my car keys on the top of the front tire of my Mustang. I tucked down the tarp. The biggest of the boys, perhaps eleven looked away from the others at me.

"First place a dude looks if he be wanting to steal your car, Mister."

I asked him how much it would cost me for them to keep an eye on my wheels. We agreed on a flat rate of two dollars per day but only when they were pitching pennies or hanging out. They did other things, he reminded me. We shook hands. I said goodbye; he nodded, half smiling. *Cool kid*, I thought as I walked away. He hadn't introduced himself, so I christened him Big Boy.

• • •

The door to the Black Panther's Headquarters was locked, but the lights were on and I could hear people inside. I knocked, waited then knocked again harder. Finally, I heard a key turning. The door moved open as far as the chain would allow, and I saw Dila's eyes looking at me. Then the chain slid off the door and it was flung open by Dila, her eyes full of concern.

Dila flung her arms around me. "Victor, Victor, what is going on?"

I'd hoped that the Sunday paper hadn't been delivered yet, so I would be the one to break it to her. "It looks like I'm being set up."

Terrance Bowles stepped forward. "Welcome to our world," he said.

"Oh, Victor," Dila repeated.

I saw Big James scowl down at us from the top of a ladder just below an open ceiling trap door. A brief image of me being beaten to a pulp arose and as quickly disappeared. I was here for help. "Don't worry, Dila," I said. "I'll sort this out. I've got some time. Terrance, I need to talk to you."

"Let's go to my office."

I followed him with Dila clutching my arm. We passed the ladder and at the bottom of the ladder was another Black Panther. I didn't know his name, but I'd seen him around. There were a number of long leather bags on the floor next to the ladder. The young Panther had one in his arms, waiting to hand it up to James. There were empty paper coffee cups and donut boxes scattered on the desks. It looked as if there had been up and at work for a long time.

Terrance closed the door to his office and sat down behind his desk. Dila and I sat on the couch.

"I got a guy inside the police headquarters tells me things," Terrance said. "Called me this morning to tell me your portrait is about to be hanging in the post office gallery. Dead or Alive, he says."

"You're not scaring me, Terrance. They don't do that anymore. It's not the Wild West, you know."

"Could have fooled me," Bowles said.

"I don't suppose you're going to tell me what's in those bags that James is hiding so cleverly in the attic that no agent of the FBI would *ever* think of looking there." My concern had shifted from me to Dila. "Whatever you're. . ."

Bowles raised his hands to stop me, so I stopped talking and looked at him. I knew those were weapons, probably rifles of some kind. Why did I bring it up? Dila was here. I was already concerned about Dila and what was going on in New York City. I didn't need more worry at the moment with plenty of my own to deal with.

"Brovelli, what do you think you know?"

"I know you're hiding guns. I know because Dila told me that the Panthers are preparing for big trouble with law enforcement. She's really worried, and I'm really worried for her."

Dila took my hand and squeezed.

"Victor, I have to deal with my life the best way I can. We'll work together to figure out Renee's murder. Now, Terrance, you better tell Victor what he didn't see," Dila said.

I was confused. "What is that?" I asked.

"First of all, Victor, we do have weapons. Thanks to you getting our money back for us from our crooked brothers and the IRA. It bought us a lot of what we're going to need if push comes to shove. That said, what's in those bags you think are weapons are old golf clubs."

Terrance stopped to give me time to think about what he said.

"Like Arnold Palmer," I said.

"Exactly," Dila said.

"And the cops who are planning to do a surprise raid of our offices later today," Terrance continued, "will be very embarrassed when all they find in our attic are golf clubs. Dila has already helped me edit my press release, which I'll hand out to the newsmen and media guys after our lawyer announces we plan to sue the Oakland Police Department and the boys at the ATF."

"Alcohol, Tobacco and Firearms," Dila explained as if I didn't know.

"Got it," I said a little more tersely than I intended. Revealing this plan to me had not made me feel any easier for Dila. I knew from past experience that in any raid things could get out of hand. "I'd feel better if you weren't here when this comes down, Dila."

"Victor, I have to be here. The more women there are around, the less chance there'll be that the cops get violent. As is, they're going to be mighty pissed. The brothers be like sitting ducks without us."

Any time spent in the BPP office and Dila was talking like she was straight off the streets instead of a graduate of the University of California. I placed my arm around her and felt her flinch. If Terrance believed things were coming to a head between law enforcement and the Black Panthers, that same feeling of a reckoning between me and Dila once again surfaced.

Terrance speaking brought me back to the room and Dila staring at me, a quizzical look on her face.

"I attribute the increased pressure and determination to destroy us," Terrance said, "to the recent announcement by the Algerian government that they accredited the Black Panthers as a Liberation Movement that merited support."

Ah, *merda*, I thought. I turned to Dila. "I need my Girl Friday."

"You know, I'm here for you, Victor, but just not for today. Renee was my friend too, don't forget."

"Don't fret, Victor," Terrance Bowles said. "We'll take care of Dila. A number of our sisters will be showing up at any time with hot chocolate and brownies for the cops. We're going to have a party." For the first time this morning, Terrance smiled.

Who was I to break up this happening? My connection to the Black Panthers was a topic of much speculation around our East 14th neighborhood. There were times when I felt that by defending them when they were being criticized, I was being a traitor to the white race, but then I grew up listening to my older brother talk about level playing fields and my pop talk about being honorable, so those feelings never lasted very long.

"I guess I'll go back to Miss Rhoda's," I said. "I'll plot out what our next step in the investigation should be. Frankly, I have no idea."

"We'll think of something," Dila said. "Wish us luck."

I did. At the door we kissed. Big James growled. I stalked out before the bear attacked. Three Panther women walked past me and entered the office holding large plastic containers. I could smell the chocolate. I could also smell fear. My own, I thought.

CHAPTER 24
THE NEW GUY ON THE BLOCK

"Vivame maggoior parte della nostra vita camuffati da noi stessi.
We live most of our lives disguised from ourselves."
Italian proverb

As I reached the front door of Rhoda's apartment, Big Boy said, "Dude said he was your brother took your Mustang and left this piece of crap."

"Yeah, I thought so. Got to wondering 'cuz he didn't have no scar on his face, so the boys and I got into his face some."

Checking the "boys" ages to be between nine and twelve, I bet Vincent had been one frightened "dude". But I went along with the program. "I appreciate your effort," I said.

"Dude showed me his driver's license. You both Brovelli."

I thanked him again and gave him an extra dollar for his diligence. They took off running down the street where there was a small grocery store. A dollar buys a lot of snacks.

I was laying on the couch with my eyes closed, trying to visualize my thinking about what had transpired this last week that led to me laying on Miss Rhoda's couch trying to visualize, when I heard the door open. I stood up.

Miss Rhoda walked in. She was wearing a dress that looked like a florist shop window display and on her head was one of those boxy hats made popular by Jacqueline Kennedy. I asked her how church was. I had completely forgotten mass, but I figured God would understand.

"There was a lot of testifying going on. And our minister lost his voice halfway through his sermon. Clarrisa, my friend, said it was God's punishment for him smiling at Ralph Digg's wife last week at the annual fundraiser."

I asked her if she wanted coffee. I had something important to tell her.

She sat down at the kitchen table and I brought her a cup. The Sunday Trib was still open to the *Dear Abby*. I reached under the section and withdrew the main news section of the paper and pointed to the column about me.

"I'm in very deep trouble, Miss Rhoda. Read this. You might want to rethink providing me with a place to hide out. I wouldn't blame you if you asked me to leave."

"Well, now, that is a mighty fine speech, Mr. Brovelli. Let me read this and see if it merits the drama."

She finished reading and straightened her shoulders.

"I'm being set up," I said.

"If you're talking about the po-lice, that isn't an unfamiliar topic in West Oakland. What does Terrance Bowles think?"

"He said pretty much what you just said."

"I'm a darn good judge of character, Mr. Brovelli. You're no murderer. You stay here as long as you need to."

I thanked Miss Rhoda.

"If you run on the bad side of the po-lice, they're known to pull a few tricks. My nephew James told me all about you at the Black Panthers Headquarters a year back, how that cop kicked your ear. He says you were one brave slice of white bread." Miss Rhoda looked at me and giggled, placing her hands up to her mouth in such a way that it was easy to imagine what she looked like as a girl. What was the expression? Cute as a bug's ear? Cute as a button? Even at her advanced age, Miss Rhoda was that pretty.

"I don't mean to be disrespectful, Mr. Brovelli, but the way James talks about people tickles me. He's got brown bread for the Mexicans and cornbread for the Asians. I asked him once what kind of bread African American peoples was, expecting him to say black bread, but he said, toast. I nearly peed myself laughing."

I didn't find James's sense of humor funny, but Miss Rhoda had started giggling again. I couldn't produce any laughter, but I smiled and left the conversation about racial bread to James and his auntie. I promised myself to remember the toast for future conversations with Big James if I wanted a come-back line though.

Miss Rhoda excused herself, saying she had to go change and go to the roof to visit an owl's nest. Mother owl, she explained, was sitting on eggs. I repeated I was grateful to her for letting me stay on.

"Terrance Bowles vouch for you. You good in my book." She waved her fingers in the air over her shoulder as she walked out of the kitchen.

Through the open kitchen window, I could hear church bells ringing. I counted twelve bells. What the hell date was it? Time was suddenly very important to me. My watch gave me my answer. Sunday, June 7, 1970. Would I remember this first day as a wanted man for the rest of my life? Would I tell my children one day, two bambini sitting on my lap, *you want to hear what happened to daddy when I was a young man?*

I returned to the couch and reclined. This was not the usual way I did my important thinking. It was time to get into my Porsche.

My 1965 silver gray Porsche Cabriolet hard top coupe was parked in the stand-alone garage I rented a block away from the family home. I'd drive across the bay and drive down the coast highway south to Carmel, shifting the gears, my body on automatic pilot and my brain alert. This particular Porsche had been one of twenty built specifically for the Dutch police and could go fast, up to 175 km per hour. Why I think better driving at high speeds around curves is a mystery to me, but as the old Italian saying goes, *E cosi!* It is what it is. I'd leave when Miss Rhoda got back.

Miss Rhoda returned a half hour later. She was dressed in jeans and a McClymonds hoodie over an Oakland A's T-shirt, a pair of black Converse high tops on her feet.

"How are the mama owl's eggs doing?" I asked.

"Hard to tell. Can't very well ask her to stand up and let me have a peek."

"You like birds?"

"It's not a hobby or anything. I grew up in New York City. My daddy, Mr. Teagarden, we always called him Mr. Teagarden, used to have a pigeon coop on the roof. Big competition between neighborhoods. I take care to keep my eyes open for birds. I'm not a serious bird-watcher. At my age, my life is pretty much about our church choir and some volunteering in the BPP kids' kitchen. Our church choir is one fine one group of singers. Did the *Halleluiah Chorus* last Christmas make the Grace Cathedral with all their fancy acoustic sound like amateurs."

I told Miss Rhoda that Dila had started out in her senior year in college volunteering for some of the Black Panthers' community programs before becoming a member of the Panthers.

"Adila Agbo, the daughter of Kahil Agbo? Don't like that man much. Puts on airs. And all that "Back to Africa" bull pucky. Lots of malaria and other diseases, not to mention it's Mississippi hot all year-round in Africa, and there are bugs and snakes. He couldn't convince me."

"We're engaged to be married," I said, testing the waters to see how Miss Rhoda would react.

"Now that you mentioned her, I do recall Clarissa, one of my friends, telling me that a year ago, she was babysitting in the park nearby the BPP headquarters and a white man and a black woman were kissing each other in broad daylight. Now, that wouldn't have been you and Miss Dila, would it?"

I had this feeling that Miss Rhoda knew the answer. I answered affirmatively.

"No wonder James hates you," she said. "He got a big crush on your wife-to-be."

I'd heard this before, so I didn't have to say anything.

"Me, I'll let you in on a little secret, when I was a young woman and singing in a few jazz clubs in New York City, me and a white drummer had a little ro-mance. Now that was back when both sides of the racial divide would have strung us up. Racial mixing be dangerous, Mr. Brovelli."

I told her we both understood the risks. I explained that it was full steam ahead for us.

"Just be sure there's nothing coming at you two full steams ahead from the other direction."

One has to pay attention to a person who thinks in metaphors.

I told Miss Rhoda about exchanging my Mustang for an Olds Cutlass because it would not be as noticeable.

"Now we got to make Victor Brovelli less noticeable."

"How's that?" I asked.

"I will fix you up so you look more like you belong to the neighborhood."

"Like you're going to make me into a black person?

Miss Rhoda shook her head. "Heavens no. First of all, I don't have the skill. Second of all, people around here aren't stupid. They'd spot you in a second. If you keep looking the way you normally do, people will think you're some kind of cop or process server."

"Process server," I said, wondering what the hell that could look like.

"You know, like somebody official. Any white guy wearing a nice a leather jacket, like the one you hung up in the hall, be suspicious. Tell you the truth, I'm surprised you got back here with that jacket."

"Come on, it's daylight. People don't get robbed in the day."

"Maybe not in your part of town," Miss Rhoda said.

I wasn't going to argue. "What do you suggest?"

"You and my grandson about the same build and height. His closet is full of clothes that won't attract attention. Come on, I'll show you."

We walked down the hall. Miss Rhoda opened the closet and withdrew few coat hangers of clothing and a McClymonds' High School letterman's jacket. She handed me the jacket.

"My grandson played some pretty good football. Might have got himself a scholarship, but he was determined to be a marine. He believed in this country. He thought it was his duty to go to Vietnam. I couldn't talk him out of it. Oh, believe me, I tried, Mr. Brovelli. I done tried."

"Miss Rhoda, you must call me Victor. I'm no mister."

"Too early to be calling each other by our given names. It will come natural after a while. Now try on the jacket."

It fit perfectly. I placed the other hangers of clothes on the bed.

"I'll be in the kitchen," Miss Rhoda said. "Try some on and come out and model for me."

Miss Rhoda did that little giggle that I was getting used to and found very sweet. She closed the door behind her. I wasn't sure, but I was getting the impression that Miss Rhoda was the kind of person who could find humor in just about anything. A jazz singer, what else had she done in her life? I wondered.

I checked myself in the mirror and saw a more casual Victor. It would have to do. As I walked down the hall, I heard a throaty alto singing acapella. Unless someone had arrived while I was in the bedroom, the singer had to be Miss Rhoda. I stopped to listen. Not blues exactly. Under Dila's influence, I'd discovered jazz singers and enjoyed listening to them very much. I eased down the hall and to hear better: "You reap just what you sow. . ." I waited until the singing stopped before I stepped into the kitchen.

Miss Rhoda was placing china cups, saucers and plates on the kitchen table. There was a stack of cloth napkins and silverware that I knew were expensive because my mother had some just like them. I could see through to the dining room where the table was covered with a white lace tablecloth in the center of which was a vase filled with carnations and other kinds of flowers I couldn't identify. "You have a great voice, Miss Rhoda," I said.

"Can't help singing when I work. Sort of like breathing to me."

"Great lyrics," I said.

"Made famous by Alberta Hunter. Best female jazz singer that's not named Billie Holiday."

I knew of Billie Holiday. "Did you make any recordings?" I asked.

"I didn't quite make it to the top of the ladder. Sang in small clubs, hung out. Things got in the way."

I didn't want to pry. "Looks like you're getting ready for a party."

"I got my book club coming this evening. Just getting a head start."

It was too early in our relationship for me to admit I loved literature and would have been happy to sit in on the club meeting.

"What book is your club reading?" I asked. Probably a book by an African American author, I thought. Dila had recommended that I read Maya Angelou's *I Know Why the Caged Bird Sings*. I hadn't read it yet. Miss Rhoda surprised me.

"We just finished *Catch 22*. Funny as all get out. Two of our club members were Tuskegee Airmen in the Second World War. They're helping us along with some background. It's a satire. *Catch 22* or any other Catch is something most black folks know all about."

Another novel I'd been meaning to read and hadn't. I asked her about my clothing. She walked around me, looking me over carefully.

"Pull your pants down a little. We have to do something with your hair. How about we make you bald?"

"No way," I said.

"I guarantee it be the one thing that transforms you."

"You mean passing?"

"Some black, real pale can get away with, but a white guy? Hard to do. Blacks don't fool as easy as whites do. Whites want to believe everybody is white. See what I mean?"

I remembered the first time I met Dila, I'd told her that Italians from the south of Italy, where our family came from, had dark skin. Dila had laughed at my weak attempt to convince her to date me. I told Miss Rhoda the story.

"Well, you got yourself a fine young woman in Adila Agbo, that's for sure." I wasn't so certain I had her anymore.

"We got to do something about the scar below your eye. Cops be looking for that."

"Can't go for bald," I said, more firmly this time. "Think of something else."

"I'll use pomade. Lots of the Hispanic men around here use the stuff."

Miss Rhoda placed her finger to her cheek and stared hard at my hair. I knew that to be the truth because I'd seen some of The Amigos, the Mexican gang members in our neighborhood that hung out at the Oasis nightclub, with their hair slicked back like that.

"You sit in that chair. I'm going to get my barbering tools, and I have some makeup cream that will make that scar less noticeable."

A half hour later I was staring in the mirror looking at a semi transformed Victor Brovelli, but no longer an identifiable person of Mediterranean origin. I could have been Hispanic or from some country in the Middle East.

Or, perhaps a Louisiana Cajun. I thought of Sweets and smiled at how offended he'd be if I told him I was disguising myself as one of his people. Of course, no one in the neighborhood knew who Sweets's real people were. Body Flynn had once suggested Martians.

"You know, Mister Brovelli, you Italians are pretty dark anyway. Stay away from the razor. If anyone asks, I'll say you're one of my grandson's army buddies staying until he ships out. They can think whatever race they want. People believe what they want to believe. The McClymond's letterman's jacket and clothes will make the difference. Keep the top collar of your shirt buttoned."

I took another look in the mirror. *Yeah*, I thought, *yeah, people believe what they want to believe.* "Thanks, Miss Rhoda. I'll be out of your hair. I'm going killer hunting."

"There is a baseball cap hanging in the hall. Make sure you wear it backward. The neighborhood is a bit rough at night, but once you turn onto our street, you'll be okay. Crooks know who James is. They don't be messing with the Black Panthers."

Miss Rhoda gave me the key to the front door which was locked at night and wished me luck as I walked out of the house. The sun that had been so blinding earlier in the morning was now hiding behind a layer of cloud cover. Trying to predict weather in June was a crapshoot.

I pulled the tarp from my Mustang and saw it had become a gray 1960 Oldsmobile Cutlass. *Good for Vincent*, I thought. I was grateful that Vincent had made the exchange promptly. I stuck the tarp in the trunk. The engine fired up nicely. Its standard 350 V8 engine purred, no doubt due to Jitter's mechanical expertise. I wouldn't be able to outrun a cop car if I was being chased, but it would cruise to Mexico if I was forced to leave the country. The thought of driving into exile made me a little ill.

I checked my watch. The big hand was approaching twelve. I pulled away from the curb. I was not really sure what I was doing when I said I was going killer hunting. I needed to think. I always thought better when I was driving. I was at an inflection point in my investigation, *our investigation* if I included Vincent and Dila. But both seemed uncertain to me. Theresa had warned Vincent that if our pop worked more than the allotted four days, she'd quit. In the short time Theresa had been our accountant and secretary, she'd made herself indispensable. My twin would have to get back taking care of our business. As for Dila, I was reminded of something out of a Shakespeare poem that she'd given me after I had proposed to her. It had something to do with the marriage of true minds not admitting impediments. I was beginning to sense a bunch of impediments rising up between us and I didn't like it at all. The principal impediment as I saw it, was her loyalty and her sense of mission for the Black Panthers, despite her commitment to theater arts. The question I was mostly worried about was whether her ties to the Black Panthers and the African American struggle was stronger than her commitment to our future.

Vincent had left my *How to be a Private Investigator* manual in the back seat. I remembered reading about inflection points. The author had explained that the struggle with inflection points was the result of not spending enough time evaluating clues the investigator had gathered. The author suggested some deep thinking and discarding the ones that did not light one's fire, which was the way I interpreted it. In my case, I decided discarding wasn't what I needed to do. I had to take what I had and put them in some kind of cohesive pattern to see if they resulted in a change of direction or thinking. He compared evaluating inflection points of which there could be many, was to think of clues as puzzle pieces. Whatever didn't fit, he wrote, had been placed in the wrong box by a malevolent God to fool investigators. *Foolish investigators like me,* I had thought at the time. Now, it occurred to me he really meant to concentrate on who put the ill-fitting puzzle piece in the box in the first place.

I accelerated onto the Nimitz freeway heading south to the Alameda exit. If I didn't see any cops hanging around our house, that meant I could get my Porsche.

• • •

The coastline of the United States from Canada to Mexico rivals any coast in the world for breathtaking beauty. Of the three states that make up our western shore, it's California's shoreline that provides most diverse landscape as well as beauty. Giant redwoods in the North, skin shedding Eucalyptus around the Bay and palm trees in the South. Close to Monterey and Carmel where I was driving, magnificent windblown Cypresses rose suddenly out of craggy hillsides. Vincent was invited by a Cadillac dealer in Monterey to play golf at the very private Cypress Point Golf Club. He broke 90 and has never stopped talking about it to this day.

My Porsche was humming, the horizon between sky and seas disappearing. There were steep hillside to my left, cliffs dropping to my death on craggy beaches to my right. I was close to Pebble Beach and its Lone Cypress when I exclaimed, "*Odio.*" At the nearest turnoff, I pulled off the highway going too fast and almost made a complete yoyo, gravel spraying in all directions, until I slid to a stop. All the way down Coastal Highway 1, I'd been trying to connect the dots, the dots in this case might have been the eyes of the people, subjects of my investigation. I didn't need paper to visualize Merriam and Renee, Brother Gaspare and Father Boniface. Merriam and Renee were linked to each other by their love of music. Both were interested in the Grateful Dead. Merriam was, by all accounts, a Deadhead. Renee was interested in the Dead because of some kind of musical project she was into. Both were linked to Brother Gaspare. He had lied about seeing Renee before Christmas and only knew *of* her. That lie, in my mind, meant he knew her better than he wanted to admit to me. I could link Father Boniface to Merriam, but not to Renee. I could link Renee to the North Beach but not Merriam, nor could I link Renee to the Haight.

Until now. If I was right.

As soon as I saw a break in the traffic, I stomped the accelerator and was back on the highway, back north to the Bay Area.

I needed to talk to Vincent.

CHAPTER 25
CONNECTING THE DOTS

*"Sometimes the problem with putting two and two together
is you don't wind up with four."*
Dashiell Hammet

Once I reached the outskirts of San Francisco, I pulled into a gas station and called our lot. I was taking a risk calling, so before Theresa could start her usual Brovelli Brothers' welcome, I said, "This is Mr. Rossellini. May I speck to Mr. Vincent Brovelli?"

"Mr. Rossellini, how are you?" she replied.

Smart girl. "Is Vincent Brovelli available?" I asked.

"Not at the moment, sir. Can I leave him a message?"

That meant there were probably cops around. "Would you have him call me at the office at this number?" I gave her the number of the pay phone.

"Certainly, Mr. Rossellini."

I hung up and waited.

And waited. I was about to give up when the phone rang. Vincent was on the line, whispering, "Victor, Victor, *come stai?*"

"If you're in a telephone booth, and I hope you are, you don't have to whisper."

"Oh, yeah. Okay. Victor, it's good you called. More news and it's really bad."

I felt my stomach turn over. "Tell me."

"The Oakland Trib article is nothing compared to this. It's on TV and radio. Somebody leaked all the gruesome details. The writer called it an act of sexual depravity."

"What the hell are you talking about, sexual? What sexual?"

"The autopsy showed she'd been sexually assaulted."

"*Minchia*. Renee, raped? Oh, man, poor Renee. What kind of animal. . ."

Vincent interrupted, "They showed your picture on TV."

"They can't do that. They haven't charged me."

"Yes, they have. You're being called a fugitive from justice. And you may be armed and dangerous. You're not armed are you?"

"Are you nuts? Of course I'm not armed! Who the hell is this TV broadcaster that aired this shit?"

"You know, the *cretino* who thinks he's Walter Cronkite."

"I'm going to run over him with my car," I said.

"If only. Our business was named on television, with photograph and address for God's sake."

I listened to Vincent hyper-ventilating and waited for him to calm down. It didn't happen. He was off again.

"Pop's name, Victor. Even our Saturday barbeques got air time. The commentator mentioned that we're located just down the street from the Satan's clubhouse, as if we're somehow associated with that motorcycle gang. Can you believe that?"

I thought of my mom and pop and the pain they must be going through, and my brother, Carlo, and sister, Constanza. I thought of Renee. The shock of the news and my anxiety over it turned to anger. What kind of evil were we dealing with?

"It might be best to turn yourself in and fight this in court," Vincent said. "We'll hire a private detective."

I felt like saying, I *am* a private investigator, sort of, but now was not a time to get into a row with my twin. First, the cops find Renee's underwear in my apartment and now the autopsy discovered she was raped. I couldn't blame the rape on Detective Halpern and his buddy. They were dirty cops known for planting evidence, but even they wouldn't have staged anything that disgusting. The part of me that hated Halpern whispered, *well, he could have bribed the forensic pathologist.* "Nah," I said.

"What did you say, Victor? I didn't hear you."

"Talking to myself, Vincent. Hold on for a minute." I closed my eyes and took a couple of deep breaths, hoping to relax, but all I saw was Victor Brovelli, dead man walking, two prison guards escorting me to the gas chamber. I said a quick prayer to the Madonna that settled my breathing and returned to the phone. "I'm back. Vincent, I have to ask you some questions. Where can we meet?"

"How about Curtis's office when you turn yourself in."

"That's not happening. I'm in the wind until I prove I'm innocent. Look, I think I've discovered something that is important. Where can we meet that's safe?"

For a moment I thought the line went dead. Then Vincent's voice came back on.

"This is crazy, but how about the chapel at the college? They don't do late masses. The chapel will be empty. I don't believe the cops are going to be following me, but remember the shortcut, I'll take that if I have to."

Perfect, I thought. I looked at my watch. We agreed to meet at 6: 30. I wanted to beat the five o'clock traffic. I didn't make it. Even on Sundays the traffic on the Bay Bridge leaving San Francisco was heavy into Oakland. I drove through the Caldicot Tunnel to the Orinda turnoff that would take me to our college campus.

As I drove, I considered my recent brainstorm. The club manager in the North Beach had told us Renee kept calling the dark-haired man she'd been with daddy. Dila and I had assumed it must have been some kind of nickname. Or something to do with the song "My Heart Belongs to Daddy". But it could have been a taunt. Renee had a sharp tongue at times. Why would a young woman call a young man daddy? A sugar daddy?

Somewhere in my brain, this question must have been bugging me, until for some reason I said the word father aloud. Not her father, but a Father, like a priest. Without the black clothing and the white dog-collar you can't tell a priest from a civilian. You call a priest Father. Like Father Boniface. *Bingo!* I had connected an important dot. This meant that Father Boniface and Brother Gaspare had lied. Both of them knew Merriam and Renee. The question I'd want to run by Vincent is why they would have lied? What were they concealing?

Another question would be: could the priest and the Christian Brother know each other? To even consider such a question implied that the two men were involved together in something. A clerical conspiracy? It didn't have to be nefarious, but it was *something.*

"Something," I whispered to myself. I shook my head. Nefarious didn't sound plausible but not impossible. Most Catholics knew of priests and lay brothers that did not keep the vow of celibacy. When Vincent and I were altar-boys, the older altar-boys warned us about certain priests. A young woman had disappeared and another woman had been brutally murdered. As far as I was concerned, I couldn't afford to rule out anyone from suspicion.

I turned into the campus about a quarter to six and parked next to the baseball field. All the buildings of the college were constructed in what was called the California Spanish architectural style, white adobe buildings with red tile roofs. The white chapel with blue trim and its bell tower stood in the center of the quad, the main teaching halls on either side. The four dormitories were backed up to the hillside that surrounded the campus. I remembered the first time Vincent and I saw the college nestled in this small valley. Our college song begins with the bells of Saint Mary's: *I hear they are calling the young loves, the true loves. . .* Vincent and I were hooked then. At the moment, I wasn't feeling very young.

I enjoyed the walk up past the center fountain and flower beds leading to the chapel. The hills surrounding the campus were still green. In a month, they would be yellow.

Near the top of the furthest hill to the right of the bell tower, spelled out in white rocks were the letters SMC. I had spent four fabulous years at Saint Mary's, mostly because of their dedication to teaching the Classics, something I would never admit to my twin. At the mention of Classics, Vincent would either start talking about classic automobiles or nod off, a habit he'd acquired in college the minute a professor began lecturing about a classic book. He still says, "Got to get my *Iliad* nap." My twin doesn't believe he has a sense of humor, but he does.

The door to the chapel was closed but swung open easily, a welcoming for most Catholics but for some, a bit intimidating. In college, I'd been a frequent visitor to the chapel. Unlike Vincent who usually faked illness, I never missed Friday morning Mass. Often, I found myself in the chapel during the days when I needed a quiet place to think. *Peaceful chapels and fast-moving cars.* The incongruity made me smile. Things about us that do not seem to fit turn out to be what makes us the most interesting of God's creatures.

I didn't see Vincent. I took off my cap, dipped my finger in the holy water and genuflected. I arose and moved into my favorite pew on the left aisle, mid-nave closest to the statue of the Virgin of Guadalupe. Even in college when I hadn't given race a lot of thought, I liked the idea that this statue was brown and not alabaster white the way all the other Madonna statues were, which never made sense to me, considering Jesus's mother, Mary, must have been an Israelite, and Israelites were Semitic, brown people like their Arab cousins.

I pulled my rosary beads out of my pocket. Given what was going on in my life, a prayer or three wouldn't hurt. Keeping my rosary with me at all times is a habit and a good one I think, since a sinner like me is likely to commit sins on the fly. Vincent, who doesn't have much use for religion, makes fun of me. It's okay. Twins may look alike, but they don't have to think alike.

I was on my third Hail Mary when Vincent arrived. He slid in to the pew beside me. I was on my knees. I pocketed my rosary and sat back into the seat next to my twin.

The first thing Vincent said to me was, "What the heck have you done to yourself?

"I'm in disguise," I said. "It was Miss Rhoda's idea. She covered up the scar with some magical makeup and darkened my eyebrows some. Her nephew's clothes do the rest. It's not that extreme. I'm just another young stud on the block." I pointed to the M on my McClymonds High letterman jacket. My shirt was buttoned at the neck. I lifted my left foot to show off my Converse basketball shoes. I was sort of enjoying myself. My twin was unimpressed.

"McClymonds High," Vincent said. "We never could beat those guys."

"I wear my baseball cap backwards," I said as if maybe that's what we should have done back then when we were on the Saint Joseph's baseball team.

"Good luck with that," he said. "Up close, you're still Victor Brovelli."

I changed the subject. "You want to walk or talk here?"

"Here," Vincent said. "There's no one else in the chapel. You told me on the phone that you found out something important. But before you start, Victor, I forgot to report to you about the Grateful Dead concert."

"Right," I said. I'd forgotten as well. "Did you find out anything about that Lydia person? I'm assuming you didn't see Merriam or you wouldn't have forgotten that."

"That's about it. No Merriam. That Lydia is a piece of work. I don't know what to make of her. She's real tight with the Grateful Dead's roadies, especially one guy called Grillo. Grillo fits the description of the guy you told me was seen with Renee in the clubs in the North Beach."

Another twist in a road that already looks like a pretzel," I said. "What about Lydia?"

"She wouldn't talk to me and I don't know why. I got close and she bolted back stage. The guy guarding the stage entrance was the size of an elephant. I wasn't going to mess with him. I stuck around and finally gave up."

"That's okay. You stick with Merriam."

"Yeah. There's something else. I hired Sweets to burglar Halpern's apartment to see if we can find any dirt of him. Jay gave me the address. Sweets said he's going to do it tonight, so I'll have his report tomorrow."

"Good idea, bro. What about Lazlo?"

"Jay says Lazlo is off limits because he's married with a bunch of kids."

"Yeah, well, I wouldn't want to be those kids, having a father like Lazlo. But I see Jay's point. Thanks, Vincent. Is there anything else?" I asked.

"No, not really."

"Not really means really, Vincent. There's something else, isn't there?

"I went on an LSD trip."

"You did what? Like on a fucking Timothy Leary trip?"

Vincent hung his head. I listened to my twin's LSD journey. When he finished, I said, "You ate of the fruit of the tree of knowledge of good and evil." My attempt at humor earned me a middle finger.

"What time did you get home?" I asked.

"It was after four. Gloria was totally upset. I told her the truth, and you know what?"

"What?"

"She began laughing. I swear Victor, my wife never ceases to surprise me. She said everyone knows about Bill Graham and his apples, that they were injected with LSD."

"I didn't know that," I said.

"And I sure as heck didn't either."

Now was not the time to tell Vincent how often in college I'd gone tripping. Best to keep a few things secret, even from one's twin. "Let's get back to the case," I said.

Vincent nodded.

I explained my belief that the person Renee had been talking to in one of the North Beach clubs was Father Boniface.

"So? Do you think, the good padré was hitting on Renee?"

"It depends on how you interpret the way she said daddy. Was it with affection or was she being sarcastic?"

"What do you think?"

"Knowing Renee, I'm betting on sarcasm."

"What's our next move?" Vincent asked.

"*Our* move is for *you* to hang with the lot and make sure we don't go broke. I'll take it from here."

"Victor, no way. This is not just about you. As Pop says our family honor is at stake."

"I don't remember you being such a big fan of *onore* in the past," I said. I looked ahead to the chapel altar in front of which were huge bouquets of white flowers. I was too far away to tell what kind, but there was an unusual number. Sometimes after funerals, the families donated the funeral flowers to the church. Instead of cheering me up, their beauty depressed me.

"*Che cavolata,*" I said.

"Bull pucky is right, Victor. Mom is in tears. Pop says he's going to sue."

"Keep Pop under control. Whatever is done is done. I want to dig into Gaspare and Father Boniface's past. I think a lot will be solved once we figure out why they lied. I really need you to keep the business going and care for Mom and Pop. More so than ever now. I'll call you when I need your help. Does that work for you?" I waited for Vincent's answer. My twin can be pretty stubborn.

"*Bene,*" he finally said, pausing for a moment, then adding, "but only for the time being. You understand if I need to step in, I won't ask for your permission. *Capisci?*"

"*Capito.* Now, I want your ideas about why the priest and the brother lied. We need to create some kind of hypothesis. Some place for me to begin."

"Okay. How about this, they lied because they were hot for these women and being a priest and a religious, they could get in trouble if the word got out."

"So, Father Boniface is trying to get it on with Renee, and Brother Gaspare, what? He's hitting on Merriam, maybe putting too much pressure on her, so she bolts?"

"It's as good as I can come up with," Vincent said.

"That might work for Brother Gaspare. In fact, that sounds like it might be it for him. It doesn't work for Father Boniface, unless you believe he murdered Renee."

"Why does he have to be the murderer, Victor?"

I had to think about that. No, he didn't have to be. In fact, the more I thought about, it was unlikely. The way things were shaking out, whoever murdered Renee was trying his best to pin the murder on me. Until we met, Father Boniface didn't know I existed.

Or did he? That made me stop and rethink. Perhaps Renee had mentioned me to him. What if he'd killed her in a violent sexual rage, and afterwards panicked. Maybe at that point, he remembered my name and decided I'd be a good suspect for the crime.

I explained that theory to Vincent. He said it was a possibility. I asked him if he had any better reason for the two men to lie to us. He didn't. He suggested I go to the dioceses. They'd have background on Father Boniface. The Christian Brothers' winery in Napa Valley also housed the general offices of the order. I could get information about Brother Gaspare from them. I asked him why they would release information to me. He shrugged and told me to be inventive.

"But," he added. "For God's sake change clothes and look like you're not some street punk."

I was going to say something like this *is* the new me to piss him off, but decided a chapel was not a good place for one of our brawls. "Before we leave, tell me again about your visit to Fillmore West. There's something you told me that has stayed with me but I can't remember what it is. It's been bothering me, you know, like. . ."

Vincent finished my sentence, ". . . Like the annoying car noise no one can figure out."

"Dila calls it my male intuition." I asked Vincent to go over his time at the Fillmore with Lydia, and the Grateful Dead roadies. I wished that I'd brought paper with me to write it down. My P.I. Manual had advised to have a cassette recorder always available going into an interview. Phillips had introduced the mini-cassette, a magnetic tape audio cassette, in 1967. I'd been meaning to buy one.

"Do you think any of those roadie guys were lying about not knowing Renee?" I asked.

"Hard to tell. They were a little stoned."

"What about the hippie chick?"

"What about her?"

"Could she have been lying? If she was as dedicated a fan as she said she was that meant she'd have been at all the Dead's concerts. She might have noticed Merriam. Merriam is pretty damn striking."

"I'm not sure," Vincent said. "It might be a good idea for you to talk to Lydia. There's a concert tonight. You won't be able to miss her, even with a crowd. That long red hair, I mean flaming red, probably out of a bottle It's hard to miss. She wears it down and flings it around a lot."

Vincent went on to describe Lydia's features in more detail. I could tell by the way he spoke, he'd been enamored of her and, knowing my twin, was feeling guilty about it. I was reminded of the girl with the red hair sitting on the stage in the basement of Saint Agnes's Church. Sweets and I were there when Father Boniface had called her Ginger. Could they be the same person? If so, that would add an unexpected wrinkle.

Behind us the door to the chapel opened and two students walked in. They moved to the right-hand aisle where the confessionals were. I looked at my watch.

"Looks like it's sinner time," I said.

"It will start filling up for confessions. We better get out of here," Vincent said.

Another student entered the chapel, followed by three more. I put on my cap and stood up. Vincent followed me out the side door. He'd parked behind the chapel in the opposite direction of my car.

We hugged. I watched him hurry away, then looked at my watch: going on eight. Plenty of time to make it to the Grateful Dead concert, but before leaving, I turned back into the chapel and waited for my turn in line to confess my sins.

CHAPTER 26
DANGER AT MY DOOR

"Una volta aperta la porta della tua mente, non si chiudera facilmente.
Once you open the door to your mind, it is not easily closed."
Italian proverb

From the college, I drove toward Highway 24 and west to Alameda so I could exchange the Cabriolet for the Olds. As I drove, I turned on the radio to KSAN. Vincent had written in his notes that the station played a lot of Grateful Dead music. As it turned out, the first voice I heard coming out of the speakers was the radio jockey announcing he was about to play some songs from an upcoming Grateful Dead album, *Workingman's Dead*, not due to be released until later this month. He sounded like the news commentator Walter Cronkite announcing some kind of political scoop.

The disk jockey proudly went on to explain this would be a breakout album for *The Dead* featuring acoustics rather than electric for which the band was more well-known, something I certainly didn't know. I *did* know the difference between acoustic and electric but since I never intentionally listened to the Grateful Dead, I didn't have a clue how it specifically applied to the band's music.

The jocky was going to break with tradition and with a song he particularly liked from the B side of the record. The song was "Casey Jones". Jones was driving a cocaine train. I didn't like the song. Garcia's voice sounded too rough, like he had a sore throat. If this was a sample of the recording, I didn't think I would rush down and buy the album. What kind of musical project could Renee, a classically trained musician, have been thinking of that had to do with this kind of quasi country-rock? I remembered that she enjoyed modern jazz, traditional and contemporary. Rock and country had never been her thing.

By the time I got to the Oakland Bay Bridge I'd listened to "Cumberland Blues," Uncle John's Band", "High Time" and "Dire Wolf" which Mr. Disk Jockey introduced by explaining that there really was such a species of carnivore that roamed North America in the prehistoric Pleistocene epoch. The band sounded to me like they'd just got together for a beer, then decided to have a little sing. I knew some of the guys at the tavern liked the Grateful Dead, and Vincent to my surprise, had told me he'd found some of the electric sound enjoyable. Whoever spoke of rock music as enjoyable? Sometimes my loveable twin can sound like such a stiff.

I turned the radio off so I could concentrate on the case. The way I was looking at the problem was that I had four people who were connected to each other in some way. It was the *in some way* part, I was having difficulty understanding. In the case of Renee and Father Boniface, the surface appeared to be romantic or sexual. In the case of Merriam and Brother Gaspare, there was no indication that it was anything more than a professor-student relationship.

I could be wrong. I remembered from my college days that there was a way I'd be able to find out more about Gaspare. Brother Gaspare was a dorm prefect which meant he had his living quarters at the end of one of the dormitory halls. One long attic connected all the rooms of the dorm. By climbing into the attic in one room, you could crawl along the attic and down through a trap door into any room you wanted to. I'd have to do it on a Sunday while he was at Mass or Monday when he was off campus teaching at Holy Names College. I was thinking about how to pull it off when the sign for Alameda appeared and I swung off. I exchanged cars and set off in the Olds for San Francisco.

I crossed the Bay Bridge. At the Van Ness Avenue off-ramp, I swung down onto the city streets. I crossed Market Street with Fillmore West on my left and began looking for a place to park.

When I was in college and afterwards before selling cars took over my life, I'd attended concerts at the Fillmore Auditorium on Geary and Fillmore Streets like probably half the thirty and under population of the Bay Area. My older brother, Mario, rest his soul, was a big fan of Led

Zepplin, The Who and Santana. He spent lots of weekend nights at The Fillmore after he returned from Vietnam. The light shows, I remembered were crazy and dizzying.

When Dila and I were first dating, we took in an Aretha Franklin show there too. I still didn't know much about Soul at the time and had lied to Dila that I liked her voice, which over the years listening to more rhythm and Blues, I discovered that, yeah, I really liked it a lot.

This Fillmore, dubbed Fillmore West, was supposed to have the same funky vibe as its earlier iteration. I was interested to see what the interior looked like. Would it have the same floor and stage configuration? The old carousel ball rotating above? Sweets had attended the opening of the new Fillmore West in 1968 and had come back bummed out. *"Dude, I heard there was going to be a Tibetan monk playing gongs. Anyway, it was cool. Psychedelics, man, like star-gazing, man."* I'd had no idea what Sweets was talking about, and accused him of still being on LSD. His reply was, *"well, yeah, dude, what else is new?"*

My thoughts turned to the August of 1967. Renee and I had attended a Count Basie concert at the original Fillmore Auditorium. Renee's interest in jazz had just begun. Basie was playing with the Charles Lloyd Quintet. Renee had told me there was a pianist named Keith Jarett, in whom she was particularly interested. She'd managed to talk her way backstage to see him, a conversation she kept to herself—musician-talk, she told me when I'd asked. When it came to anything musical, Renee was obsessed. Thinking of Renee brought me brought back my anger over her murder.

A car horn blared, and I swerved back into my lane. I had to drive around the block three times before I found a place to park near the Memorial Opera house.

It was a windblown five-block walk to Market Street. I was told I was lucky there were a few tickets left. I paid my entrance fee and walked into the hall and up the stairs. At the top of the stairs was a bucket of apples. I smiled, thinking of Vincent. As Deadheads passed, some reached in and took one, I took one and put it in my jacket pocket. It was a should-I-or-shouldn't-I moment. My decision would have to wait until later.

Inside the auditorium, there was hardly any room to move. I edged my way through the bodies, slipping sideways in and out, all the while looking for the girl named Lydia that Vincent had described as having flaming red hair. I could barely see the stage. From it, the gravelly voice of Jerry Garcia was singing about laying on his bed and dying. His voice was growing on me; the theme of the song was appropriate.

The lights swirled; strobes flashed. One guitar talked to another. From some dark cavern came the moan of a harmonics. The bass and drums kept the rhythm honest. . . Who didn't want a little peace to die, the song asked. I could have stopped to listen to all of the lyrics, but I was here on detective business. I had to find a way to get back stage so I could talk to the workers. Vincent called them roadies.

I stood on the fringe of the crowd as if I was on the edge of a lake, wondering whether to jump or wade in. A guy behind me bumped me forward and that settled that question. I bumped the person in front of me and he the person in front of him and suddenly I found myself in the midst of bodies swaying, arms swinging overhead, hands like flags in the wind.

I wasn't a novice to concerts. A Crosby, Stills & Nash concert came to mind. They were one of my favorites. Renee and I had rocked out at a Beatles concert. We had also attended a Santana Blues Band at a small club called the Matrix. Dila and I had a great night at a Stevie Wonder concert.

But this Grateful Dead crowd had an altogether different feel than the crowds I was used to, not exactly more subdued, but more mystical, even religious. I thought of a tent revival, without all the halleluiahs and praise Jesus shouting that I remembered from a time I had attended one with Dila because we were both curious. There'd been people speaking in tongues, that's like a weird babble. And there were miracles waiting to happen, everybody jumping up and down like small children needing to pee. No, this Dead crowd may have reminded me of religion, but a different sort completely. The word, cult came to mind.

I continued my forward jostling. None of the Deadheads seemed to mind the body contact. There was frequent touching, a couple of times on my crotch. But when I swung around, it could have been any of the Deadheads near me. I hoped, at least, that they'd been women touching me. I inched and squirmed through the crowd. I decided there was a kind of infectious madness emanating from the stage where Jerry Garcia and others were now singing about danger being at the door. *My door?* I felt a brief chill and shook my head to clear my mind. I made it to the side of the hall where I had a better view of the area closest to the stage.

That's when I saw the unmistakable red hair that Vincent had wistfully described. Her back to me, she was whispering in another Deadheads' ear, a young blonde with long braids with a begonia tucked behind her ear. The redhead gave the girl something that looked like a postcard and moved on. I couldn't see the redhead's face well enough in the strobes that kept their flashing beams dizzily bouncing around the hall. I moved away for a better view, shouldering my way closer and closer to the stage and a sudden hammering drum riff and guitar solo. *Electric, the crowd eating it up.* I was almost standing next to the redhead when she turned so I could see her face. It was the same face of the girl Sweets and I had been introduced to by Father Boniface.

One of the most overused clichés in murder mysteries popped into my mind: *The Plot Thickens.* Thickens was not even close. It was fast becoming a whole gooey porridge of interrelated ingredients. I turned my face away from her so she wouldn't spot me. I stepped back out of sight while keeping an eye on her. Unlike the rest of the madding crowd, she didn't seem to be paying attention to the music. She moved quickly from one young girl to another, whispering and handing out the postcards. Perhaps, I thought, she was hired by Fillmore West to promote future concerts—a way to make a buck or two and listen to The Dead for free. I needed to get my hands on whatever she was handing out. Luck was with me as I saw one girl drop the card. I waited, then as the redhead moved away to talk to another girl, I retrieved it from the floor where it had already been trampled. It was not a postcard but a small pamphlet:

A Safe Haven
To Rest and Find Your Way
No Pressure
Food & Place to Sleep in Peace

The inside of the pamphlet gave a description of Saint Agnes's Church and its mission to provide a safe place for runaways to stay while they figured out how to proceed. It listed a number of Catholic diocese services that were available, from counseling to family reunion mediation to job training and spiritual guidance.

While I read, I kept my eye on the redhead, Ginger. Or was her real name Lydia? Whatever her name was, she seemed to have a knack for finding the girls most likely to be runaways. The majority of Deadheads, it seemed to me, looked like normal humans in costume who'd be back in their classrooms or at their jobs on Monday, the men back in their GQs, the women in dresses and heels. The odd thing was that there were more men in the audience than women. Perhaps, it was the light show and my eyesight.

For a while I lost sight of Ms. Redhead, but saw her again closer to the stage talking to another young girl. She was definitely here to do a job. I'd watched her now for long enough that I began to get suspicious of her motives. She just didn't look the part of a Good Samaritan, not with the cigarette dangling from her lips and the couple of times I'd observed her take a flask from her handbag and sip—not Pepsi, I'd have bet.

I remembered Vincent telling me how angry she'd become with him. Scary, he'd called her. She kept moving down the stage, stopping to talk to another young woman. I followed her the best I could. There was a strategy to negotiating through concert crowds that an amateur concert goer like me was not privy too. If there were rules, one of them was never stop to apologize as you push through. If you have a target you're aiming for, keep your pace. Regretfully, my target disappeared again and only at the last second, I saw her duck past a guard who didn't seem to mind and behind a black curtain leading back stage. The way the guard acted, it appeared to me that the redhead was known to him. It was my understanding that backstage during a concert was considered the Holy of Holies and only the anointed were granted admittance.

The plot thickens even more, I thought and laughed out loud. Self-consciously, I looked around before realizing I could have yelled at the top of my lungs and no one would have heard me above the sound of the electric guitars and drums. What was next? Follow the redhead if I could talk the guard into letting me by him. Keep the pace, I instructed myself and moved in the direction of the guard who, as I approached, looked to be about the size of Big James and just as deeply black. I was holding a twenty-dollar bill in my fist in the event my smooth tongue failed me.

"Where do you think you going, little brother," he said in a surprisingly cultured voice. One of his long arms came down like a railroad crossing barrier blocking my path.

It took me a moment to understand him calling me little brother, then I realized I was no longer an Italian Caucasian. "Yeah, bro, y'all understand, I be trying to hit on this fine white chick with the red hair that just went back stage." His eyes widened. I instantly knew I'd made a huge mistake trying to imitate how Dila talked when she switched from the Kings English to ghetto vernacular.

"Are you fucking with me with that ghetto par-lance?"

"No, no," I stammered, trying to figure the next thing to parlance. "I really want to–" He cut me off.

"That lady has a stage pass. You don't. It would cost me my job, if I let you by, *little wannabe.*"

I heard sarcasm as he pronounced *"little wannabe"* more slowly for emphasis.

"Ah, man, common give me a break." He shook his big head. I opened my fist and showed him the twenty. He shook his head. I reached into my pocket and pulled out two more twenties. He raised his eyebrows, glared at me, snatched my money and his arm dropped to his side. I was let in backstage.

Behind the black curtain was another curtain and behind it was a lot of human hustling about. What to do next? Redhead was nowhere to be seen. It was a bee colony of workers, and I didn't know if I should interrupt in the event whatever they were doing was stage-management-crucial. If I stood around and looked interested, someone would notice me. What then? I'd ask to speak to one of the roadies. I took the list of roadie names Vincent had given me out of my pocket. The crew boss would be the one to talk to, the guy called Brillo. I moved to the side to let a guy carrying speakers past me. I saw a good spot to observe. Perhaps Redhead would show up.

I started forward, but a short, but powerful looking man appeared from behind a tall wooden exploding volcano.

"Lydia tells me you been harassing her. What you want with the girl?"

"Nothing," I said. "It's a coincidence she came back here at the same time as me. I don't know the chick. I just want to meet the head of the roadies. I be looking for work on a band. It's my dream job."

"You full of shit. You look like some punk. You listen carefully. I won't see you back here again after I throw your ass out. And just to be sure you get it, if Lydia comes to me in the future and complains about you, I'm going slice you up a little, *comprende?* "

This guy looked Mexican and sounded Mexican. I was about to answer in Italian, *capito* but remembered in time what I looked like. "Yeah, yeah,"

I said hoping to sound street tough. It didn't work. A switchblade appeared in his hand.

"Just so you don't think I'm kidding," he said.

What was it with switchblade-aficionados that they could make their weapons appear like magic? I'd encountered a few in the past couple of years as I did my P.I. thing, and it always startled me like I was observing a magician pulling a rabbit out of hat. He stepped toward me. Glared. The blade disappeared and so did he. For a moment I stood my ground then decided I'd seen enough. The coward in me said, *Victor, get the fuck out.*

Outside, the windblown overcast I'd arrived in had disappeared and the San Francisco sky was clear. There were too many city lights for a clear view of the heavens, but I recognized the Big Dipper. With buildings in the way, I couldn't see the horizon and the constellation, Scorpio. It was Vincent's and my constellation by only one day; otherwise, we would have been born Libras. Libra, a balanced thoughtful sign, seemed more appropriate to my twin, while Scorpio, the more unreliable sign would better suit me. I walked slowly towards my car, thinking.

The Mexican guy called her Lydia, the name she'd given Vincent, not Ginger. Whoever she was, she was connected to Father Boniface helping him save runaways. For some reason, I wasn't buying it. Coming to the concert had not been a failure. I didn't need to talk to the boss of the roadies. I'd found the man I needed to talk to but it was not going to be easy, since he wielded a vicious looking switchblade. I pulled the apple out of my jacket pocket. I tossed it into the gutter. Several seagulls dove for it and a bird fight ensued. Very soon, the sky would be filled with seagulls flying stoned.

Driving back across the bay to Miss Rhoda's, I felt as if I was very close to solving Renee's murder and even figuring out Merriam's disappearance. I needed to go to the Bay Area Catholic dioceses offices and get the scoop on Father Boniface. I also needed to get in touch with Vincent. I wouldn't have time to inspect Brother Gaspare's room. Vincent knew the trick of the attic leading to the connecting closets. He could do that for me.

CHAPTER 27
WHEN PUSH COMES TO SHOVE

"If there is no struggle, there is no progress."
Frederick Douglas

I woke up not in my own bed. It took a few moments to re-orient myself, to remember I was in Miss Rhoda's apartment in her nephew's bed. I touched my face to wipe away the tears and my fingers came away sticky. They were covered with some kind of brown stuff. I remembered Miss Rhoda's facial cream that had covered the scar below my eye. The pillow where my head had lain was covered with the stuff. I got up and went to the adjoining bathroom, stripped off the T-shirt I'd slept in and took a shower. Under the water, I washed out the pomade Miss Rhoda had flattened my curls with. I rubbed off the makeup. It had been just enough to change my appearance so that I would not have been recognized as the fugitive in the newspaper photographs. I brushed my teeth and combed my hair the best I could as my Italian curls would not behave, having spent so much time drowned in pomade. I found some clean clothes in the closet that fit. After I stripped the bed, I followed the aroma of coffee into the kitchen.

Miss Rhoda was sitting at the kitchen table, drinking from a huge mug that looked even bigger in her tiny fingers. She was reading the Sunday Tribune and smiling. She looked up as I entered.

"Sometimes the Lord provides an old black woman a little Sunday morning entertainment."

She didn't wait to explain.

"That Terrance Bowles is one sly fox, I'm telling you. Right here," she said, pointing to the article she was reading, "He outfoxed the entire law enforcement of the U-nited States. Had them fit to be tied and embarrassed in front of their own newspaper corps that they'd brought with them."

"And," I said, "don't keep me hanging."

"Let me see. I'll sum it up. The FBI, the Treasury cops, the Alameda Sheriff's department and detectives from the Oakland Po-lice department was all at the Panthers Headquarters because there was supposed to be a bunch of guns and ammunition hidden there."

Bowles had pulled off his deception. *Good for him*, I thought, then felt guilty thinking of Jay if he'd been part of the raid. I hoped not.

"And, to top it off, the article is so well written. It's a pleasure to read just for the words."

I felt a surge of pride because I knew Dila was Terrance's main editor. I remembered a number of articles she'd cleaned up for Minister Bowles, one especially I recalled was Terrance blasting the SDS, Students for Democratic Society, for not endorsing a nationwide policy for community control of police that had been initiated by the Black Panthers. Terrance was a fine writer, but Dila was an editor supreme.

"You know what they found instead of guns?" Rhoda asked.

"Golf clubs," I said.

"Well, now. You're no fun," Miss Rhoda said. "You want coffee? I got hot cross buns and an upside-down pineapple cake in the oven ready to eat. A few friends from the book club and church choir are coming over for a snack."

I noticed a stack of plates and cups on the counter. "One of my favorite parts of church is listening to the choir. We have a real decent one at Saint Joe's."

"I know you told me you're a believer, Mr. Brovelli, but tell you the truth I only go to church to sing. Singing praise makes me feel better. You and I are feeling-type people. I tried once figuring out churches with my mind and got so confused I stopped going for a while. I went back because I missed singing in the choir. Kept going ever since."

Miss Rhoda hummed a bit then began singing, *"Rock of ages, cleft for me, let me hide myself. . ."* Her voice trailed off.

All the normal sounds of a kitchen: refrigerator humming, wall clock ticking, the sounds of traffic outside the window had stopped to listen. Miss Rhoda finished the hymn and smiled. "That hymn was composed, lyrics and music, by Thomas A. Dorsey, a black man. I like the old traditional hymns well enough, but I love dearly singing hymns by black folk."

"That was beautiful, Miss Rhoda," I said. "Thank you."

"You're welcome, Mr. Brovelli. And, I'd tell you something else. There are books our book club reads that are like church to me. And what I like about those kinds of churches they're open to all the races."

I loved the idea and was going to respond, but the phone rang. Miss Rhoda went to the wall and answered. She listened, then held out the receiver. "For you," she said.

I listened to Dila, and she said to come to the Panthers office. I asked her why again, but she'd hung up. I placed the receiver back on its hook.

"Got to go, Miss Rhoda," I said. Miss Rhoda nodded. "You back being Victor with a scar, so be careful. Don't forget to button the collar at the top and the letterman jacket."

I was already at the door, hoping that what I heard was a mistake.

There was parking on the opposite side of the street from the Black Panthers' headquarters. Dila was waiting for me outside the front door. I parked and jaywalked. She took my hand and led me down the street. She didn't speak, and it seemed right that I didn't either.

We walked the few blocks to the small playground where she and I had first kissed. That too given the seriousness look in Dila's eyes, seemed appropriate. Beyond the restrooms was a basketball court where a couple of boys were shooting hoops; otherwise, the playground was empty. Dila sat down on the bench next to the children's sandbox. She patted the seat next to her.

"You can't stand there looming over me," she said.

I sat. I took her hand. "Tell me everything," I said.

"There is no way I can avoid this," Dila said. "I have to join my brothers and sisters in New York."

"Why."

"I already told you."

"Tell me again. This time make me understand."

"It's easy," Dila said. "Our BPP has been very aggressive. The FBI is out to stop us. The word is that they are going to set us up on some phony charges. I got a call yesterday from Julius that the protest march we have planned could turn into an armed confrontation. For the last couple of months, we have been arming ourselves for that possibility, but we hoped it would never happen. Considering what happened in Detroit, I think we did the right thing. I've been one of the leaders of our section. If there is real trouble I need to be on the front lines."

Being set up for a crime you didn't commit rang a familiar bell. Even so. . . "You're making it sound like war."

"It is, Victor, my love. It surely is."

"What about Renee? What if I'm charged with her murder?" I asked,

"If things don't explode, I'll be back."

"I don't want you to go."

"No choice, Brovelli. You know how you are always talking about your parents going-on about honor."

"*Onore*," I repeated in Italian.

"I'm a woman of color. When I joined the Black Panthers, I took an oath. I'm on my honor, you see what I'm saying?"

"I'll talk to Minister Bowles. He can give you dispensation."

"This is not the Catholic Church, and Terrance is not the Pope. I'm bound by blood and the color of my skin to live up to my oath."

"Oh, for God's sake," I said. I didn't want to hear some cliché. *Bound by blood*. I was angry and frightened for her.

Dila smiled and patted my knee.

"Victor, my darling, remember a while back when I told you that what you do matters more than words? It's what attracted me to you in the first place, a white man who took our side when you didn't even know us at all, just recognized the injustice of what was going on, cops beating on us. It's what Terrance Bowles liked about you. And if you can believe it, James was equally impressed that a slice of white bread would take our side."

There I was again, just a slice of white bread. The day was sunny, but to me the morning no longer held any brightness or warmth. I could hear the boys on the basketball court yelling at each other. A middle-aged woman pushed a baby carriage into the park and walked toward us. I saw the surprised look on her face as she saw us holding hands. She shook her head and kept pushing.

"When are you leaving?" I asked.

"I'll would like a ride to the airport. I'm driving home now. Can you pick me up in two hours? I have a flight at 2:45."

"So soon," I said. I could hear my voice crack. *Get a grip, Brovelli*, I thought.

"I wasn't kidding about the seriousness of the situation," Dila said.

I wasn't interested in hearing any more about the situation. "Let's get back to the office," I said. We stood up. We were still holding hands. I pulled Dila toward me. "Remember what we did the first time we were here?"

Dila came into my arms.

The boys shooting hoops never gave us a look, even as the kiss turned into the extended kiss of goodbye.

CHAPTER 28
LOOSE ENDS

"Divora l'amore e non perdera mai il suo sapera.
Devour love and it will never loose it's flavor."
Italian proverb

United Flight 1765 rose into the sky and was soon out of my sight. Dila was on that flight, and I was not a happy *paisan*. Before I had picked up Dila at her parents' home, I had called Minister Bowles. I asked him if there was any way he could convince Dila not to return to New York City. He reminded me of the night on the wharf when we were sitting in my car across from the restaurant Harpoon Annie's, talking while we waited for a suitcase of money. He had warned me then that when push came to shove, Dila Agbo would choose her race over her love of me. He had not said this unkindly, and I thought I detected some sadness in his voice. I had recorded it in my memory and it played back to me now.

On the drive down from Oakland to the San Francisco International Airport, Dila and I had barely spoken. I think we were both too sad. I did not want to think of it, but this departure had the feeling of finality. I couldn't explain why I felt that way. Had we not loved each other enough?

I turned away from the window where so many others were still staring into the sky following airplanes and their loved ones disappearing. That window was *not* a window of no return, I told myself.

I forced myself to think about the murder of Renee. What else could I do? The last words Dila had said to me were *"find out who killed Renee, Detective Saturday"*, and the last words I'd said to my fiancée were, *"right, Girl Friday."* Was that pitiful, or what? I felt like getting a couple of six-packs of Bud and getting drunk.

I resisted the temptation and returned to Miss Rhoda's. The apartment was empty. Miss Rhoda had left a note that she was upstairs and would be back soon. I sat at the kitchen table and thought. It was difficult to keep Dila out of my mind. My fear for her safety was palpable and attacking my stomach.

I went to the refrigerator, withdrew a bottle of milk and poured a glass. I returned to my chair at the table and continued brooding. As I downed the last of the milk, one of my pop's sayings came into my mind: *Pensare troppo a lungo all'infelicita e come stare sull'orlo di un precipizio com un piede oltre il bordo.* To think too long on misery is like standing on the edge of a cliff with one leg over the border.

"You're right, Pop," I said aloud. I stood up, washed out my glass and went to my bedroom for a notepad. I would work through one of Dila's brainstorming strategies, that way I'd feel close to her while trying to solve Renee's murder. A psychologist would have some five-syllable name for this, but it made perfect sense to me.

Miss Rhoda returned, carrying a carton of hot chocolate mix. She asked me how it went.

"The plane left on time," I said.

"That's not what I asked."

"It was sad," I said.

"Supposed to be when lovers part. You're welcome to stay. You'll like my friends. Take your mind off Miss Dila."

I thanked her but declined. I continued working on solving the crime and saving my butt. I told her I'd be back in the bedroom. I had to be alone to do some thinking. Miss Rhoda said she keep a few goodies for me for later.

I had not meant to go to sleep. My notepad was resting on my chest. It was filled with my scribbling, arrows pointing to a person or a place or a something that happened that seemed like a clue. I rubbed my eyes. In the bathroom, I splashed water on my face. I returned to the bed and reviewed what I had written. Of all the conclusions that stood out, only one was helpful and that was because it eliminated one suspect of the investigation from my mind.

Brother Gaspare. Having a history of romantic liaisons myself, I should have read the signs better. The good brother was hiding behind his clerical robes and his position as a music teacher to conceal his love for Merriam. It was a good bet that Merriam's disappearance had something to do with that romance being unfulfilled or fulfilled and fraught with misgivings.

I was familiar with loving someone who was culturally forbidden. That Merriam wound up briefly in the Haight in Saint Agnes's basement safe-house could simply have been a desire to flee the stress of their romantic entanglement. I would have to consider her quick exit from the safe-house later when I pursued Father Boniface.

That left the priest as my murderer. I had to restrain my enthusiasm because I had no solid proof beyond supposition. Instead of murderer, I wrote in my notes: *Farther Boniface = person of interest.* Then I crossed it out and wrote: *Father Boniface = person of greatest interest.*

From the hall I heard voices. I looked at my watch and found my wrist empty. I forgot that Miss Rhoda had warned me that my Rolex was a red flag for every small-time crook in the neighborhood. Looking out the window wasn't any help. It was still light. In 1966, Daylight Savings Time had been enacted into law, and without my watch, I was still getting my times mixed up. I removed my watch from the nightstand drawer. It was 5:32.

I put the watch back in the drawer and stretched. I was stiff from sleeping sitting up. I did a couple of knee-bends. I realized that I was hungry. Miss Rhoda had said she would leave a few goodies for me, but I could hear the laughter and the voices from the living room. I didn't want to intrude on their get-together. Besides I was hungry for a real meal.

On my way out, Miss Rhoda introduced me to her friends. Dotty Mae Tolbert, soprano; Charles Haskins, bass and Clarissa Duchat, alto.

Clarissa shook my hand and said, "I remember you; you're the crazy white boy I saw kissing a crazy black girl in broad daylight."

I acknowledged my craziness.

She turned to Miss Rhoda. "You know, Rhoda, dear, I never told you, it just came to me," she turned back to face me again, "that day, young man, after you left a whole bunch of black guys with baseball bats came looking for you. I told them you had driven off. They asked me about the girl. I said she weren't from our neighborhood, but I knew different. I'd seen her coming in and out of the BPP's headquarters."

"She's living in New York City these days," I said and my heart grew heavy.

"Well, our Rhoda here vouches for you and that's good enough for us, right y'all?"

The bass and the soprano nodded their heads in agreement.

I'm heading out for a quick dinner, Miss Rhoda," I said.

"You want me to do away with the scar?" Miss Rhoda asked.

I touched my face. "No, I'm going to drive to San Francisco. Where I'm planning to eat, I think I'll be okay being an Italian." I laughed. "As long as I wear my baseball cap on backward."

Forty-five minutes later, I was sitting at a table in *Nate, the Great's* Soul Food Restaurant in the Fillmore district, a plate of baby back ribs, grits and collard greens in front of me, eating and listening to The Penguins singing about an earth angel and wondering if my angel would ever be mine again.

CHAPTER 29
THE GUYS

"Individually, we are a drop; together, we are an ocean."
Ryunosuke Satoro

On Monday morning, Vincent thought he'd be the first on the lot, but Theresa and his pop were already there. His pop greeted him with a hug but took a quick disapproving look at his watch. His pop didn't bother asking him about Victor. He knew if he had any news about his twin, he'd have shared it with him.

Vincent had hoped he'd have had some time alone on the lot. He told Big Sal he would wash cars this morning. His father grunted his approval. Ten minutes later, he had hung up his sports coat, pulled on waterproof overalls and was hosing down cars on the farthest end of the lot away from the office. Monday mornings were always hectic. He hosed, sponged and wiped. Most of these cars he'd handpicked. Jitters' careful attention to their mechanical condition gave him the confidence to tell prospective buyers that these were the best preowned automobiles in the country.

Vincent was looking forward to hearing from Sweets Monroe about what the birdman had found in Officer Halpern's apartment. How his twin put up with the Creole burglar, he could never figure out. Or was he a Cajun? Who the hell cared? He waved at Jitters who was no doubt heading to the DoNut Hole for some of Larry Hughes' fabulous pastries. He turned his thoughts back to his twin's dilemma.

By lunchtime, there was still no word from Sweets. He tried calling his phone number with no success.

• • •

It was late afternoon without hearing from Sweets. Theresa had already

175

left for home. Vincent stepped out of the office, leaving the door open so he could be close to the telephone if it rang. It was a typical June day in the East Bay, a mild upper sixty degrees with only a few cereus clouds. From down the street he saw this spring's new addition to the neighborhood, the Yoshido Family ice cream truck approaching. It made its way down East 14th Street, playing its jingle: "The Ice-cream Truck of Oakland" to the tune of "The Yellow Rose of Texas". The family who owned the truck was Japanese. Vincent realized that he'd never bothered to introduce himself and welcome them to East 14th Street and invite them to Barbeque Saturday. Next to Parsegian's furniture store was an office building that housed mostly insurance and home mortgage offices. The truck always stopped in front of it. He decided when it did, he'd buy an ice cream bar.

No telephone call. He didn't want to leave his pop to close up, otherwise he'd have closed by now and driven to Sweets's apartment, two floors above Victor's and banged on the door.

His pop was happily showing a car to a man in an army sergeant's uniform who he'd overheard was headed to Vietnam for his third tour of duty and wanted to have a stable car for his wife while he was away. Checking out the car, the sergeant drove into the lot, Vincent could understand the soldier's concern for his wife's safety, a 1962 Plymouth Belvedere that looked as if it might have been in an accident and that the body shop had done a poor job matching the paint. After this year, Plymouth was no longer going to produce the model. They wouldn't be able to give the sergeant much of a trade-in for his new purchase.

Two previous tours in Vietnam, Vincent couldn't imagine how difficult going back would be. The war had escalated recently. About a month ago, President Nixon had ordered the invasion of Cambodia, the country to the west of Vietnam. It crossed his mind that the sergeant was trying to get things straight in the event he would not return. He imagined a last will and testament, a deed to a home and a dependable set of wheels, a list of all his possessions and the persons he wished them to go to. He beckoned to his father who excused himself, frowning as he approached.

Vincent took him by the arm and whispered in his ear, "Give the soldier a good discount, I'll take it out my profit at the end of the month."

His father raised his eyebrows.

"They just invaded Cambodia, Pop. The guy might die."

"You good boy," his pop said, patting him on the cheek. He turned back to his customer, announcing, "Mr. Sergeant, you very much in luck. My son just say to me this car is 25% reduced in price. Your most beautiful wife, she will love it."

Vincent hadn't expected his pop to be that generous, then thought, *oh what the hell*. He felt good. Done his part for the war effort. His twin would have been proud of him. Victor was forever the soft touch when it came to discounting cars if he thought the customer's need for a car was greater than his bank account could handle. Vincent wondered why his twin being proud of him meant so much to him. Was it the danger Victor was in? The thought that Victor could be thrown in prison or worse? Since 1968, there had not been any executions in the United States, but there was serious talk in the California legislature to start gassing again. He forced his thinking away from such morbid speculations. He wondered when Sweets would ever get in touch with him.

Toward closing time, the office phone rang. Vincent answered.

"You not going to like this, *mon frere*," Sweets said.

"I won't know until you tell me, *mon* brother," Vincent replied.

"*Nada. Rien*, nothing to do with Victor or Renee. Or any police matter of any kind. Now there were beaucoup Klan and Aryan propaganda and some anti-gay stuff from some outfit called The Proud Men, whoever the hell they are. His digs was spic and span. Bed made like he'd been a marine, bounce a quarter off the blanket like it was a trampoline, you dig?"

Vincent groaned. "I can't believe the guy is legit. That he isn't a crooked cop."

"I covered all the bases, Vincent. This morning, I called a *tres belle* mama I know work in a bank and checked his do-re-mi. Nothing unusual."

"How did you know what bank and account?" It was a dumb question to ask a burglar.

"I found his accounts in his desk. Got all his numbers. Vincent, the guy is a neat freak. Pencils all in a row, shit like that. Actually, I knew a guy like that. Turned out he was a serial killer been murdering all over New Orleans for years. Word was he cleaned his cell and made the bed before they hauled his ass out to Old Sparky and fried him."

Vincent thanked Sweets and hung up. Victor would be disappointed. Through the window he could see his father giving the car keys of a 1962 Ford Sunliner to the happy sergeant. Vincent told his father he'd close up.

After his pop left, Vincent sat disconsolately at his desk, staring out the window. The ice cream truck hadn't stopped at its normal place. He'd been looking forward to an Eskimo Bar.

Two hours later, he'd locked the office. He drove his car onto the street and parked then fixed the chain across the driveway. He should get home, he thought. Perhaps a beer would cheer him up.

Monday was not usually a big night for drinkers. This included Flynn's tavern, so Vincent was surprised to see the usual afternoon crowd sitting down at the far end of the bar, with Body and Stuart the night bartender behind the bar. Also behind the bar, standing with Body and Stuart, was Sweets Monroe.

Body turned toward him. "Vincent, this is a private. Go home to your wife and kiddies.

"Are you kidding, Body? What's going on?"

"You don't want to know what we're talking about," Body said.

"*Mon frere*," Sweets said, "do yourself a *favor* and about face."

"B-body is r-right," Jitters stuttered.

"True," Swanee said. "Make yourself scarce."

"Boy's telling you straight," Larry Hughes said.

Stuart added, "I second the motion."

"This is about Victor," Body said. "We have a plan, and you can't know about it. Now get your dago ass out of my establishment."

"Guys, he's my twin."

"Out," Body pointed to the door.

CHAPTER 30
THE DIOCESE

"If priests sin, all the people are led to sin."
St. John Chrysostom

"I'm going to fix you so you look a little Cajun," Miss Rhoda said.

"Why's that?" I asked.

"Because that's what you told me your friend with the sweet tooth got all buddy buddy with the good padré about, them both coming from Loosee-ana. Me having some Creole on my daddy's side, we'd better look the part when we talk to the people at the Catholic place."

"The Diocese, the Catholic headquarters."

"Yes, that place. I'll be your mama. We'll-"

"Whoa," I said, interrupting Miss Rhoda in mid-sentence. I must have missed the "we" part. What's with the 'we' and the 'mama'?"

"I know a bit about churches, Mr. Brovelli. Been singing in choirs all my life. Catholics no different than Baptists when it comes to handing out information. The head honchos' lips get tighter than a violin string when it comes to talking about their clergy. Young man by himself, don't stand a chance, but with his mama, he might be able to get the information he wants."

I thought about that for a moment. "You might be right, Miss Rhoda. I was planning on going in and asking about a Father Boniface who had helped me during a crucial period in my life as a young man in Louisiana. And I wanted to write him a letter of thanks now that I was no longer on drugs and living a clean life and going to mass. Like that. I'd pour it on thick about how much the Catholic faith was part of my being healed, yada, yada."

"Can't see any fault in that story," Miss Rhoda said. "But as your mama, I could add my own desire to thank the good priest. My yada,

yada would be sort of tearful, you know like a mama's joy over the return of the prodigal son."

I smiled at that. My being engaged to an African-American woman had made me the problem son in our family. "We'll have to practice," I said. "Get our lines down, so we sound real."

"You sit here while I get my makeup. We'll practice while I turn you a little more Cajun. I'll darken those eyebrows some. Good thing you didn't shave. Louisiana French very manly types."

Well, I'd been a stud from the neighborhood, and now I was going to be manly Cajun. I liked the idea of being a chameleon.

An hour later, Miss Rhoda and I were in my serviceable undercover Oldsmobile crossing the Oakland Bay Bridge to the Catholic diocese in San Francisco.

As we came out of the west side of the Treasure Island tunnel, I saw the approaching white glistening San Francisco skyline: Coit Tower in the distance sitting atop Telegraph Hill and nearer to us a recent high-rise, the triangular shaped TransAmerica building. San Franciscans disparaged the building as being too modern for "The City" as San Franciscans' arrogantly called their hometown.

As an Oakland resident, I get annoyed by our brethren from the west side of the bay for treating Oakland as someplace to be tolerated but not appreciated. One of our college professors pronounced that it was as if the east bay was the home of the proletariat and San Francisco was the home of the nobility. Jay Shirley, sitting in the next aisle over, had asked if a pro lariat had something to do with roping cattle. Nobility or not, I can't help getting goosebumps as I look at the City of Saint Francis sitting atop its many hills and beyond to the Golden Gate Bridge, and beyond that to wherever my imagination would take me when I was a boy.

Miss Rhoda voice startled me out of my reverie.

"I'm going to be your Girl Friday."

"What did you say?" I asked, hoping that I'd misheard her.

"Girl Friday," Miss Rhoda answered. "You know like Nora is to Nick Charles in *The Thin Man*."

This was a movie of an earlier generation, but I knew of it. On late night television, I'd started watching anything to do with private investigators. *The Thin Man*, was one of my favorite oldies. Not surprisingly, Vincent was also a late-night movie watcher, only he was not a fan of the P.I. flicks.

Give him an old time Western like *The Stage Coach* or *Shane* and he was a happy cowboy.

"Course, I'm no girl anymore," Miss Rhoda said and did her little giggle, covering her mouth with her hand.

I didn't reply.

"Did I say something wrong?" Miss Rhoda asked. "Oh, oh, my goodness. Dila was your Girl Friday, wasn't she? I'm terribly sorry."

Miss Rhoda must have sensed my sadness, but it was no fault of hers. "No, don't worry. You couldn't have known. You're right. I'd say Girl Friday and Dila would answer Detective Saturday."

"Well, heck, that sounds right to me, Mr. Brovelli. Now, don't you fret about your Girl Friday. These Black Panthers, they know how to take care of themselves."

"You can be my Girl Friday until Dila returns," I said.

Miss Rhoda reached over and patted my shoulder.

"More like Grandma Friday, Detective Saturday."

"Okay, Grandma Friday sounds good to me," I said, feeling relieved there would be a distinction between Miss Rhoda and Dila.

By the time we reached the Diocesan headquarters on Gough Street, we had our story lines worked out. I would explain what we were trying to find and Miss Rhoda would interject with commentary. Miss Rhoda had suggested that initially we keep up a chatter without letting the clerical person talk before our entire emotional story was complete. "Bureaucrats will always be trying to avoid doing extra work as much as they can," Miss Rhoda had explained.

• • •

A half hour later, I was following Miss Rhoda's suggestion, chattering away in front of middle-aged nun behind a counter and refusing her a chance to refuse my request to know how I could get in touch with Father Boniface. What I told the nun was that Father Boniface, bless him forever, had saved me when I was a kid heading in the direction of a life of crime and prison in Louisiana.

Miss Rhoda interjected a grateful mother's comments.

Looking back on it, I'd say Miss Rhoda and I were like well suited jazz musicians playing off each other.

The nun, who'd been unable to get a word in, looked to me to be stunned by our performance.

"My goodness, that is such a remarkable story."

She brushed at her eyes with the sleeve of her habit. *Hooked*, I thought.

"Let me see now," she said, pausing for a moment. "All right. I'll go to the records and see what I can find."

The nun left and Miss Rhoda leaned toward me and whispered. "You could be a salesman, Mr. Brovelli."

"Best car salesman in California," I said. "Can I interest you in a fine pre-used vehicle with low mileage?"

Miss Rhoda smiled.

We didn't need to wait long before the nun, who'd introduced herself as Sister Marie Rose, was back with a large binder. She placed it on the counter and opened it.

"Before we get started, can I have you sign in to our daily log? The Bishop is pretty strict who we provide information to. She reached under the counter and brought out a large leather-bound log book. She turned the pages to Tuesday June 9, 1970. Both of us printed and signed our fictitious names, addresses and phone numbers.

"You understand, I cannot provide you with personal information, but I can tell you that you are in luck, Mr. Monroe. Father Boniface, if this is the same priest you're looking for, was transferred from New Orleans to right here in San Francisco. He is rector of Saint Agnes's Church on the corner of Haight and Masonic. Isn't that good news?" she said, beaming.

"Thank the Lord," Miss Rhoda said, also beaming.

"The good Lord works in mysterious ways," Sister Mary Rose echoed.

"Indeed, he does," Miss Rhoda echoed.

I kicked Miss Rhoda's ankle, so she wouldn't continue the litany.

To insure she wouldn't, I said, "I've forgotten the name of the church in New Orleans. I'd like to write a letter to the editor of the New Orleans's newspaper about the good work the Catholic Church does."

"Not at all." Sister Mary Rose turned a page, then another. "Here it is," She said, "Saint Stephan's. I'll write the address. If you want to talk to the rector, you're also in luck, Monseigneur Duval has been at Saint Stephan's for a very long time. He would certainly have been there at the same time as your Father Boniface."

She turned to the next page.

I was about to ask another question when Miss Rhoda placed both hands on the counter and leaned forward moaning.

What came next was a series of exclamations by my Grandma Friday about feeling faint and thinking she might vomit, and Sister Mary Rose hurrying from behind the counter to assist just as Miss Rhoda slumped across the counter, then slid to the floor.

I would have been alarmed, but as Miss Rhoda fell, I saw she was clutching the binder in her hands. I bent down and fussed over her, me on one side, the nun on the other. Finally, Miss Rhoda struggled to her knees, then stood up. She promised the nun she wouldn't need to call emergency. When the nun turned her back to return to her place behind the counter, Miss Rhoda winked at me.

• • •

We were driving away from scene of Miss Rhoda's Shakespearian fainting performance before I said, "Okay, tell me what happened back there."

Miss Rhoda pulled some crumpled pages from her coat pocket and held them up. "I was only able to tear off the first couple of pages out of the binder before the nun got to me. I figured we might find some personal stuff."

"She'll raise the alarm once she finds the papers gone," I said.

"I was able to close the binder. I'm betting she'll just put it back where it came from. Why would she check inside? She didn't look suspicious when we left, still fussing over me."

"Okay, we'll take our chances," I said. "Good work, Grandma Friday."

Miss Rhoda nodded and smiled at my praise. It occurred to me that the two women that were central to my life at the moment, Dila Agbo and now Miss Rhoda Teagarden, were both actresses. "Did you ever take acting classes?" I asked.

"Not a one," Miss Rhoda said. "But singing, you're playing a role somewhat, aren't you? Fact is Black folk, especially if they're from the South, learn to act from early childhood. White people from my generation didn't like uppity Negroes, so you're a black brain surgeon and you talking to a white man in Alabama, you talk like steppin-fetch-it."

Miss Rhoda hung her head and began scratching at her hair and talking in barely understandable English.

"Like that," she said and winked.

Dila had explained this role-playing to me but not as graphically from the point of view of an older generation black. Watching Miss Dila's pantomime made me feel ill as if I was watching cancer.

"And don't you believe this act was limited to the South," she said. "It's a matter of degrees how much a black people felt they had to compromise themselves. I'm talking males now, Detective Saturday, because of male pride. Black men hated shuffling and acting stupid. It ground them down to dust. They'd rather be in prison and that's no lie. Leave their women and children because of pride. Not saying I don't have cause. No, sir, and lots of black women, they understand. It breaks their hearts."

As a white male, how could I respond to something so grotesquely tragic? A couple of years ago, I might have said, not my people, not the Brovelli family. Today, knowing what I know, such a response would have been obscene. Miss Rhoda stopped talking. We drove in silence.

To break the silence, I said, "Let's get something to eat."

"Acting does make a girl hungry,"

"How about soul food?"

"If you wouldn't mind," Miss Rhoda said. "I was raised in New York City. I'm not much into *poke* chops an' collard greens, no matter how great Nate the Great can cook. Never could figure out why black folks get all teary eyed over collard greens if it weren't for all the bacon used in cooking it. Collards just weeds as far as I'm concerned. And the pork chops are always overcooked with enough gravy a small boat could sail across it."

"I get the picture," I said. "How about the wharf?"

"How about Tommy's on Van Ness? I could use an end cut of prime rib."

Tommy's Joint on the corner of Van Ness and Geary was a popular deli-type restaurant that featured some of the best meat in the Bay Area. It sounded good to me.

After we'd taken our trays of meat and potatoes to our seats, we touched our mugs of beer and toasted our heist. Miss Rhoda removed the crumpled papers and smoothed them down on the tabletop.

The basic highlights did not provide us with anything to cheer about: Father Boniface had gone into the seminary right after high school. He'd been a decent student, but not exemplary. He'd served his first church in Los Angeles in one of the poor neighborhoods. After three years there, he volunteered to help a Catholic mission in Guatemala. He'd returned to New Orleans to serve at Saint Stephan's. Always Father Boniface directed his ministrations toward helping the poor and especially children of the poor.

We both agreed that the priest didn't sound like a murderer. But as we finished reading the last page, I said, "But his twin could be."

"Miss Rhoda returned to reading, then lifted her head. "I see what you mean," she said. "They were twins."

CHAPTER 31
CASTOR & POLLOX

"Identical twins do not have the same fingerprints."
How to Become a Private Investigator, chapter 10

"When Vincent and I were very young, our mom used to read to us out of picture books. One of her favorites was *Tweedledum and Tweedledee*. In some of the books, the two were cute little guys, but in some of the books they were fat and ugly, and a little scary.

"As we grew, our mom continued providing us with stories or information about twins. She found those individuals, both united and partitioned, in many mythologies. There was Artemis and Apollo and the lesser-known Heracles and his brother Iphicles. Our mom used to take Vincent and me on to the upper story balcony of our home on clear nights and show us the Twins constellation, Gemini. The constellation's principal stars are the twins, Castor and Pollux. Of course, she didn't tell us that they came from different fathers, which would have confused us at that age. They were the gods of sports, which pleased the Vincent and me very much since we were already playing Little League.

"From the Bible, she told us about Esau and Jacob. Esau came out first so he got his father's birthright, which entitled him to all the family land. Vincent, being the first ahead of me by a minute or two—an insignificant amount of time in my book—had said he thought that was fair. I remember punching him. My mom completed the story that later as a young man Esau came in from hunting one day very hungry. His twin, Jacob, was cooking a stew over an open fire. Probably *ciambotta*, she'd added as an aside, knowing how much we both loved her summer veggie stew. Well, she'd gone on, Jacob offered his twin stew, but only if he gave up his birthright to him. Esau agreed. When I'd remarked that

Vincent would have done the same stupid thing, it was my turn to be punched."

Miss Rhoda and I were halfway across the Bay Bridge. I was driving in the slow lane, so I could talk without some speed jerk crowding my rear fender.

I continued, "Even today, our mom never misses watching *The Parent Trap* on late night TV."

"I sort of remember the movie," Miss Rhoda said. "Got that actress with long red hair playing the mama."

"Maureen O'Hara, one of my pop's favorite actresses."

"So, you got a snoot full of twins stories, huh?"

"My mom tailed off after we'd hit junior high. By that time Vincent and I were well into all the tricks twins could pull on people. We made a point of dressing exactly alike, combing our hair the same way. And when people got us mixed up, we never let on. We drove some of our teachers to tears. We kept up these deceptions until I got hit in the face with a baseball and wound up with this scar." I pointed to my eye before remembering Miss Rhoda had covered it up for our trip to the dioceses.

"I miss the scar." Miss Rhoda said. "Looks like the leg of a rocking chair, but it ain't ugly. Makes you kind of mysterious."

"I thank you, ma'am," I said as we entered the Treasure Island tunnel. On the other side, the bridge view, obscured by the upper portion of the bridge, revealed the south bay and a long line of barges pulled by a tug moving slowly south. The giant cranes used for lifting ship containers were like gigantic tyrannosaurus rexes guarding the Oakland wharves.

"If I got you right, you're thinking that this man the people in the nightclubs said they saw with your ex-girlfriend Renee was Father Boniface's twin brother?"

"According to the records before he became a priest, Father Boniface's name was Louis. He had a twin named Charles. Boniface is the name Louis took when he was consecrated as a priest. So, Charles comes to San Francisco to visit his twin brother. He meets Renee. Father Boniface is handsome, so we know Charles is and perhaps a little more worldly. Unlike his twin, this Charles has a dark side. Renee was always attracted to danger. If I'm right, this could help us solve the crime."

"How would Renee have met this Charles?"

"I'm not sure," I said, "but my guess is Renee knew Merriam, which makes sense since Renee helped with the Oakland Youth Orchestra. Merriam was first violin. Renee must have looked around the Haight where she knew lots of hippie kids on the run hang out. That's what I thought when Sweets and I drove over. That's when we met Father Boniface. So, Charles is visiting his brother, right? Why have his brother stay in a hotel? It seems logical that Lewis, now Father Boniface, would offer his visiting twin a room in Saint Agnes's rectory. Right?"

Miss Rhoda was nodding her head. "Yes, I can see that happening. Probably did happen that way."

• • •

We arrived back at Miss Rhoda's apartment. Big Boy and his gang were there. Some were pitching pennies, an occupation that appeared to be one of the focal points of their lives. A few were circling the street on their bicycles, occasionally standing on their pedals and spinning their handle bars. The street was a dead end, so cars rarely turned onto the street.

"Why you boys not in school?" Miss Rhoda scolded.

They answered in unison, clearly delighted, "Teacher day, teacher day." They sounded like a choir of happiness. Big Boy looked at me expectantly. He was wearing a Black Panthers button on his T-shirt. A long key chain hung from his belt, ending in his jean's pocket. I dug into my pocket for two ones. He nodded. I nodded back. The tarp was no longer required. The Olds could remain uncovered.

"That boy, gonna be a millionaire one of these days," Miss Rhoda said as we walked up the stair to her apartment.

We settled into the living room. I leaned back on the couch. Miss Rhoda went to the kitchen. When she came back, she eased back into the La-Z-Boy and kicked her feet out.

"Put some cookies in the oven for the boys," she said, "Now, Detective Saturday, how are we going to prove this idea of yours?"

"That's the $64,000 question," I said. "God, I wish Dila was with me. We were together in the North Beach clubs. She might have an idea."

"You're welcome to use my phone," Miss Rhoda said.

I tried to imagine what Dila could be doing. I looked at my watch, but remembered it was in a drawer in my bedroom. I looked at the kitchen wall clock. It was 3:14 p.m., so 6:14 p.m. in New York City. "I won't talk long," I said.

I let the phone in Dila's apartment ring ten times before I hung up. Then I worried that I should have let it ring a few more times. She could have been just stepping out of the elevator and heading for her door. We'd be talking if I hadn't been so impatient. I dialed again. This time I let it ring a dozen times before I gave up.

I returned to the living room and shrugged. Miss Rhoda didn't say anything. I was relieved she didn't. I wasn't looking for reassurance, even though I could have used it because all of a sudden, I imagined a great evil presence in the world.

I almost spoke of it to Miss Rhoda. I would have liked to describe it to her. In my mind's eye, it looked like the continent of Australia only it kept changing its shape as if it was breathing. I closed my eyes and forced the evil to disappear. Miss Rhoda remained silent. From the kitchen, the refrigerator ticked and made a few clicking noises.

Miss Rhoda began humming, her voice carrying a tune. I knew little about gospel music, but I assumed that was what I was hearing, slow and mournful humming. When she stopped, she said, "Mr. Brovelli?"

"Yes,"

"How could a woman bear to have good and evil inside her? Lord, coming from the same egg and one murders and the other saves children. Don't rightly make any sense to me."

"Not to me either," I said. "But how would a mother know?"

"I'm not saying she would know at the time, but later just to imagine that time with the two inside her belly." Miss Rhoda paused, then continued, "I had a baby, a boy before my daughter. He died in childbirth. I was fifteen years old. Had no business being pregnant, but I was stupid. I think if I had had living evil inside of me, I would have felt it."

I didn't know how to respond to something that was beyond my capacity to understand as a male. "I'm sorry about your baby," I said.

Miss Rhoda shook her head sadly and changed the subject. "Could be you should go talk to that priest. He'd maybe knows where his twin is."

"So, what do I say, I'm looking for your twin Charles whom I believe raped and murdered my friend."

"You'd probably have to do better than that," Miss Rhoda said. "How about fingerprints?"

"If we could get them, it would help to establish Charles was in the area, that's for sure, but that's all. There is no law against traveling to spend time with your brother. There were no prints in Renee's apartment except mine and hers. Besides, how do we go about getting a set of Charles's prints?"

"Fingerprinting is required if you work for certain kinds of companies," Miss Rhoda said. "Or if you were in the military, or, you know. . . got in trouble with the law and incarcerated."

"Those fingerprints are part of personal documents," I said, "and are not just given out to anybody."

"It would still be good to have them, right?"

"Right, Miss Rhoda." Something told me having them would be better than good.

"What if your friend in the police force talked to the FBI? They could tell if he'd been fingerprinted and maybe get a copy?"

Jay would have to lie to the FBI. If the lie were uncovered, it could cost him his badge. I explained to Miss Rhoda that I wouldn't ask Jay to risk that. Besides, something else had entered into the dark part of my brain. It was something I'd heard recently or something I recently read. It was important, but I couldn't remember. I knew it would stay with me and turn into the annoying sound a car makes that no one can figure out where it's coming from. Dila called it my male intuition telling me to pay attention. *To what*, I wondered. *What the hell was it?*

The oven buzzer sounded and Miss Rhoda went to the kitchen. She came back and asked me if I wanted some cookies. I loved her oatmeal-raisin bran cookies, but I was full of *linguine con mari*. I shook my head.

"I'll open the front door. When they smell my cookies, they know I got some for them. They a smart bunch. They send their leader to ring my doorbell. Cute little brother. His name is Clarence. He and his mama living upstairs. Half those boys live in my apartment. Clarence, he thinks he big and tough. Just stands there waiting. I say to him, you just wait a second, I got something sweet for you. I hand him the bag. He says 'thank you, ma'am' and off he goes. Been this routine for as long as they grew out of their diapers and could walk on their own."

"I think I'm going for a drive," I said. "I want to think about what my next move is going to be."

"Our next move, you mean, Detective Saturday."

"My apologies, Grandma Friday, what *our* next move will be," I said, placing a heavy emphasis on *"our"* which made Miss Rhoda giggle. What a beauty she must have been when she was young, I thought. "I'll be back later. Maybe I'll have a better idea what to do."

I left the apartment. Walking down the stairs, I crossed paths with Big Boy walking up. He nodded. I nodded back. He had a cookies-expression on his face.

• • •

Normally, when I want to drive and think, I set out for Highway One, my thinking-highway I call it, but it didn't seem the same driving a nondescript undercover Olds Cutlass, and I couldn't chance getting my Cabriolet. I could have driven to Berkeley and the Grizzly Peak turnoff, another place I went to think. I sat in the front seat of the Olds.

The thought came to me that I really didn't need to think. What I wanted was information, something to stimulate thinking. I fired up the Olds, pulled away from the curb and made a U turn. I drove to the main Oakland City Library. I had to know more about twins. I would do some research.

The librarian asked for my library card. I told her I wouldn't be taking books out. She directed me to the right floor and section. The Dewey Decimal System led me to the correct bookcases. I picked out a couple of books and took them to a table. In college, I loved the library, not only for the books but also for the alone-time I found there away from my twin and the rest of the business majors. They spent their downtime sitting in The Barn, the local tavern down the road from the college, playing liar's dice and drinking beer. Nothing against either of those occupations, but it can get sort of boring.

The soft pale light of the reading lamp revealed a lot of information about twins. I finished examining a couple of articles about *Doctor Jekyll and Mr. Hyde.* I'd had no idea that Robert Louis Stevenson had thought of them as twins. Their terrifying dichotomy had been explained as having to do with a fearful struggle in the womb. This was not exactly what I was looking for, but it felt as if I was on the right track.

An hour later as I was reading through some Biblical essays about the *Genesis*, I came upon an article in *Anthropology Cooperative* that claimed there was textual evidence that Cain and Abel were twins. *Interesting*, I thought. I read on.

By the time I finished, the best that I could make of it was that the proof had to do with a Hebrew word, *Yasaph*, which is an adverb and means to continue. So, the writer contended it was written in *Genesis* that Eve gave birth to Cain, then (Yasaph) continued to give birth to Abel. As I read on, I imagined the look on Vincent's face as I explained to him that his birth model was Cain, the slayer who brought evil into the world. Not that I was very pleased with getting symbolically slain. I stifled a laugh and read on.

A moment later I stopped reading. What had happened? My annoying car noise was gone. I slapped the table and said aloud, "Cain slew Abel. Cain slew his twin."

From a nearby table came an irritated voice, "Keep it down, will ya, pal?"

I looked apologetically at the person I'd annoyed with my enthusiasm, but he was already back into his research. I closed the book and sat pondering what I'd just unearthed. *That was it! That had to be the answer.* I returned the books and hurried out of the library. I knew I had to find out if Father Boniface was the first born or born second, and I had to do it without Boniface knowing about it.

Half an hour later, back in Miss Rhoda's kitchen, I explained to her what I'd learned and come to believe.

Ignoring Miss Rhoda's doubtful expression, I said, "It's time to go to New Orleans."

CHAPTER 32
DAYS OF OUR LIVES

"If you don't think a day in your life, is not
a day in my life, you've missed the point of soap operas."
Anonymous

"God knows what the guys at Flynn's are up to," Vincent said to his wife. He hadn't meant to talk to Gloria about what was going on, but she had probably guessed that he was more deeply involved than he'd been letting on at home. Gloria came from a traditional Italian family and knew how family honor was baked firmly into Italian genes, especially in the more conservative southern parts of Italy where her family and his family had originated. Gloria confirmed his thinking.

"When it comes to your brother, you're like the guy in the chips commercial who can't eat only one. Especially now that Victor has been accused of that awful murder. I beg you, don't get involved with that gang from Flynn's."

"They don't want me around anyway, so you shouldn't worry."

"I worry, I worry. A wife worries," Gloria said. She was holding their recently fed happy baby. Their two-year-old daughter was in the living room glued to *Mister Rodger's Neighborhood*. They were sitting at the kitchen table. There was a glass of orange juice and Vincent's bowl of Grape-Nuts cereal in front of him. The morning Tribune was on the table open to the front page. "U.S. Invades Cambodia" was the headline. Outside the window, a humming bird batted its helicopter wings in front of the feeder Gloria had attached to the outside window frame a month ago. Vincent was feeling useless. Whatever his concerns were, from his own family to the business, they were always interrupted by thoughts of his twin.

Yesterday, a very large black man wearing an Oakland A's hoodie with the hood up had walked into the office and handed him a note from Victor, said, "For you," and left. Vincent was pretty sure that the man was the body guard for the Black Panthers' Minister of Education, Terrance Bowles. The note read: "Will be out of town for a couple of days. Not to worry. I'm onto something important." It wasn't signed. It was Victor's handwriting, so Vincent didn't know what Victor thought that not signing the note accomplished. He'd told Gloria last night about the note. She'd said, the P.I. thing was warping Victor's brain.

"Do you have any idea what I should be doing to help?" he asked Gloria, who was rocking the baby because the little fellow was getting fussy. Vincent didn't really expect much of an answer, he just needed to talk about it and sometimes the more he talked, the process itself produced an answer. He worked on his cereal while waiting for his wife to answer him. If Gloria wrinkled her brow, it meant she was thinking and not to interrupt her. It was one of her little habits he'd figured out early in their marriage after he'd impatiently started talking before she could answer his question. The baby quieted down. He finished his orange juice. Gloria's brow remained wrinkled. Finally, she looked at him.

"Your first assignment was finding information about Merriam. Let Victor handle the murder. You go find Merriam."

Gloria's answer surprised him. He'd not expected her to be that clear. Before he could ask her if she had any idea how he could do that, his wife continued.

"I've been watching *Days of Our Lives*."

"*Odio*," Vincent said.

"Don't be so condescending, husband, there's lots to learn from melodrama. You want me to go on or do you want to just figure things out by your macho self?"

Gloria's voice warned him that this was not a verbal battle he could win. "*Per piacere*."

"That's better. You might not believe it but I've kept up with what you and Victor have been doing. Well, to make a long story short, a couple of days ago, Mark fell in love with Laurie. I was stunned, you can't imagine."

A long story long, Vincent thought "And why was that?" he asked.

"You know, Mark Reddin is a Catholic priest, silly, and Laurie is married. I got at least ten telephone calls from my girlfriends that afternoon."

Vincent didn't need to ask his wife where she was going with this. He waited for her to continue. The baby began to fuss again. Somebody was singing a jingle on the TV, and he could hear Christina's little voice singing along.

"Well, talk about tense. We can't wait to see how it's going to turn out. We've created a pool, and we all have written our solutions and placed them in a sealed envelope with our five-dollar entry fees. Now, I know you're wondering how this relates to Merriam."

"I am on pins and needles."

"Sarcasm noted and filed. You'll hear back from me on the subject at a time of my choosing."

Vincent noted his wife's wicked smile.

"Back to the subject," she said. "It just came to me while I was talking on the phone. You two have been playing detective, you know, like concentrating on the blood in the Volkswagen, thinking all sort of bad things, when the solution is as easy as turning on the TV to *Days of Our Lives*. Merriam is deeply in love with her music teacher. He's a Christian Brother. You know, like Mark's a Catholic priest. You see the connection, don't you?"

"Go on," he said.

"Come on Vincent, it's plain as day. Brother Gaspare, like Mark, is torn with guilt. They may have already had an affair. Merriam ran away. I wouldn't be surprised if she isn't pregnant. If that's the case, she can't go home to her family. So, there she is in the Haight where a lot of kids run to. That's where Victor tracked her down, right? But she leaves suddenly. Why?"

"Why?" Vincent repeated the question.

"Because she can't live without him. You men are so obtuse about emotions. You find Brother Gaspare, and you'll find Merriam. I'll bet you that they are back together. Life is all about the complications of love. Soap operas present the world from a very narrow but truthful perspective. The absence of love creates all the problems of the world."

If he asked some of the questions he had in mind, Vincent knew he was in for a major plot analysis. What did he have to lose by following his wife's advice? At least he'd be doing *something*, instead of just worrying. He'd ask Pop to handle the lot, which he'd be perfectly happy to do. Theresa would groan, but she would oversee his father.

"You know, Gloria," he said. "I think I'll do exactly that. I'm going to Holy Names and talk to Brother Gaspare."

"Say hello to my alma mater for me," Gloria said.

"I'm sure the college will be happy to hear from you, since you haven't donated recently." Vincent leaned back as his wife's fist neared his shoulder.

"*Ti amo,*" she said.

"Me too," Vincent said.

• • •

The Dean of Faculty of Holy Names College had no idea where Brother Gaspare was. He'd not shown up for classes on Friday. On the weekend, according to Saint Mary's College, he'd not slept in his room, and this morning he missed both his Holy Names morning classes. Everybody was, of course, concerned. Vincent explained who he was and that he was working for Merriam's father. When he asked if there was anyone he could talk to, he was directed to the music department's secretary who, the Dean's voice implied, knew *everything* about *everything.* Vincent thanked the Dean and walked to the building housing the music department where he found the all-knowing secretary talking on the telephone. He waited until she hung up.

He explained who he was and his mission. She listened, all the while fiddling with a lock of her gray hair that kept falling over her left eye.

"I understand Brother Gaspare has been missing since Friday," Vincent said. "But I wonder if on Thursday he revealed anything to you about his plans."

The secretary, who'd introduced herself as Mrs. Dunnican, nodded thoughtfully. She smiled. "You're not by any chance one of the Brovellis from Alameda, are you?"

Vincent said he was, suddenly realizing why she had asked the question.

"My brother is Father Dunnican at Saint Joseph's."

"Small world," Vincent said.

"You're about the right age for the twin boys my brother said were hell on wheels."

Vincent was glad the woman was still smiling, which meant she was not of that group of unsmiling people who referred to him and Victor as The Holy Terrors.

"I wish I could help you, but I'm as much in the dark as the college is, and believe me, I keep my ear to the ground."

"Could I look in his office, Mrs. Dunnican? Perhaps if I took a peek at his calendar."

"It was the first thing I did this morning. Now, what do you feel is the connection is between Brother Gaspare and Merriam?"

Vincent was not certain, but behind her spectacles, he thought he detected a gleam in her eyes. Not only her ears to the ground, he thought, but her eyes and nose too.

He'd try coaxing her a little. "Well, you know, about teachers and students. Teachers have favorites, don't they?"

"We in education certainly wish they wouldn't. Unfortunately, it's the reality, and Brother Gaspare didn't make any secret that Merriam was his favorite. Many of the senior musicians in our orchestra, I must say, were pretty upset when he selected her, a freshman, as first violin."

"He didn't?" Vincent questioned, hoping he sounded horrified.

"Over Rachel Chabon, if you can imagine."

"I can certainly understand, my goodness, a freshman over a senior."

"You didn't hear it from me, young man, but there were a few rumors going around."

"Rumors." Vincent prompted.

"You know."

Vincent would have bet a month's sales that Mrs. Dunnican was addicted to soap operas. "You mean?" he responded, raising his voice slightly to form a question.

The secretary made a little coughing sound, "Well, it's only a rumor, you understand."

"If you mean what I think you mean, I *certainly* understand."

"As I said, you didn't hear it from me."

"Mum's the word," Vincent said, locking lips with his fingers. "About Brother Gaspare's office, is it possible?"

"Well, it's highly irregular, but in this case, a missing person and all."

"I'll need a key" Vincent said.

He took the key that she'd withdrawn from a large ring of keys and thanked her.

"His office is the third on the left down the hall to your right."

He left, promising her that he'd return the key shortly.

• • •

Brother Gaspare's office looked as if he'd left without putting anything away. It also looked as if it hadn't been cleaned. Theresa would have her vacuum humming the minute she saw this mess. He recalled that the other time he was here, the office had been much neater. If he had to guess, he'd say that Brother Gaspare left in a rush. Vincent searched. He found nothing unusual. If he didn't find anything here, he'd have to go to the college and climb into the crawl space from one of the student's room and crawl through to Brother Gaspare's quarters and search it. The space was full of spiders and he wasn't fond of the creatures. He continued looking. He found a couple of Grateful Dead albums, which could be related to Merriam, but he was already working under the assumption that there was a relationship greater than just a student and her teacher at work here.

There was nothing that stood out in Brother Gaspare's desk calendar except in the block for Tuesday, June 9th in which he'd written a time: 12:30 p.m. It could mean anything. He sat down at the desk and began doodling on a blank sheet of paper, thinking.

To his right, he noticed the wastebasket. He rolled his chair in front of it and looked in. Resting on top of other trash was an advertisement for *Music and Poetry in Golden Gate Park*. It was double underlined. Made sense, Vincent thought. There was a list of performers: two poets named Lawrence Ferlinghetti and Morton Marcus were headlining the poetry reading. The Grateful Dead topped the list of bands that included Southern Comfort, Santana and a band he'd never heard of before, The River Dogs. The date was today, June 9th, and the performance was scheduled to begin at noon and last until 4:00 p.m. Vincent checked his watch. It was 10:48 a.m.

He returned the key to the secretary, thanked her, promising to let her know everything, emphasizing the word *everything*. He walked quickly to where he'd parked his Dodge Charger.

In the town of Orinda, he stopped at a gas station and called Victor to see what he thought or any advice to give him how he should proceed once he was in the concert. No one answered. He really didn't need to call Victor, he decided. It was up to him. If Merriam and Brother Gaspare were at the concert, Vincent was not sure what he would do, but he'd cross that bridge when he came to it.

Crossing the Bay Bridge, the traffic was heavy, but he arrived at the entrance to Golden Gate Park and followed a 1950 Volkswagen Transporter bus, the same model as the one Merriam owned, disgustingly painted in candy stripes and decorated with peace signs. From his parking space, he followed the six young women who leaped from the hippy bus. They had flowers in their hair and were dressed in gauzy tie-dye dresses. They passed tennis courts until they reached the venue, a wide lawn and hillside.

There was a large welcoming sign that read FRONTIERS OF SCIENCE FELLOWSHIP. Next to it was a yellow and red International Harvester bus. Vincent guessed in was around a late 1930s model. The yellow and red paint job was overlaid with a variety of symbols and designs and pictures of animals and birds and sayings in swirling cursive. It had Oregon license plates that read: "Further", whatever that meant, like going farther but misspelled. Vincent thought the sides of the bus looked like photographs of the inside of an Egyptian Pharaoh's tomb he'd seen in *National Geographic*.

To the far left was a medical tent. He recognized the gaunt Native American from the Fillmore West concert who'd joked with him that his name was Tonto.

Some of the entertainers were on the stage testing the sound. The space was almost completely covered with people. Obviously, there was going to be a delay. Vincent walked slowly around the perimeter. Most of the audience was seated on blankets. Some were dancing to the music in their heads. The aroma of marijuana was already heavily in the air. He recalled his reaction to the last time he was at a Dead concert and inhaling too much of smoke. He had explained to Gloria when he returned home. She'd called it a contact high. He felt a little embarrassed not to have known that or perhaps forgotten from his college days. Unlike his twin, he'd never been much of a party guy. Vincent could see no police anywhere. Perhaps the San Francisco Police Department did not consider a bunch of Deadheads worthy of their time and effort. There were some pretty formidable-looking men standing in front and on either side of the stage. Every once and a while, they redirected a wandering Deadhead away from the stage.

Vincent found a place next to a tall stand of bamboo to observe. He looked at his watch. It was past noon. Some minutes passed. He felt a tap on his shoulder and turned to face a young man with five rings in his bottom lip. "Yes," he said.

"Are you a narc?"

"Am I a what?" Vincent asked.

"A cop. If you are, dude, the law says you got to tell me. Are you a cop?"

"No," Vincent says. "Do I look like a cop?"

"Yeah, sort of. You know if you lied to me, you could be arrested."

Vincent wasn't sure what this was all about. He highly doubted there was a law that stated an undercover cop had to reveal who he was if asked. He was thinking of something to tell this kid when the kid spun away and joined a group of teenagers dancing in a circle close by.

Five maybe ten minutes passed before a man wearing a dashiki moved out from behind the curtain at the rear of the stage and approached the microphone. He yelled, "Can you hear me?"

It acted as a signal for the audience on the ground to leap to their feet and the dancers to stop twirling. The audience began cheering and waving their hands in the air. There was so much noise that Vincent couldn't discern what exactly they were yelling. He and Gloria had been to enough music concerts that he shouldn't have been surprised, but it had been a while and he'd forgotten. It wasn't the marriage; it was the children. *The minute you have kids, that's it, you're middle aged and out of the loop. Well, so be it*, Vincent thought. *It is what it is.* He smiled hearing the voice of his twin repeating in Italian, *cosi, cosi.*

The members of the band trooped onto the stage to the cheers of the audience. Jerry Garcia led the way. Vincent knew what Garcia looked like. He had no idea about the rest of the band. The musician next to Garcia was holding an electric guitar. The musician nearest to him was holding a bass guitar. One member of the group peeled off and went to stand behind the keyboard. The drummer settled behind his drum set and began tapping. Another member of the band, standing close to the keyboard put a harmonica to his lips and blew a few notes. Garcia started playing the guitar, and suddenly, it was show time.

It seemed like forever before Vincent heard Garcia's voice. Hands and arms waving in front of him obstructed his view of the stage. The vocals continued the slower tempo, and the audience mirrored the flow of the music as if they had been hypnotized by golden bells and lady fingers dipping in moon light, the word down, down, down repeating and repeating. The song continued. Vincent was beginning to get a headache.

He recalled the Fillmore West concert and remembered he liked the song "Mama Tried" and some of the other songs that had a sort of country music feel to them. He didn't know much about music. In general, he liked lots of rock and roll, especially the kind you could dance to. He was a good dancer. It had impressed Gloria when they were courting. This song, "St.

Stephen", there was no way you could rock out with it. He guessed it was written with LSD in mind. He forced his thoughts away from the stage and music back to the audience. He was here to do a job for his twin.

He left his bamboo cover and slipped and slithered and pushed his way through the crowd a number of times, returning each time to the cluster of bamboo. "St. Stephen" ended and a new song began. He checked his watch for the fourth time. It was going on 3:30 and no Merriam and no Brother Gaspare. He thought about leaving.

Whoever Jerry Garcia was singing about was on his knees begging to let the light shine on him. Vincent liked the love-light, like head-lights showing the driver the way home. The thought of this pleased him. Perhaps his twin was not the only literary Brovelli in the family. This song was a hell of a lot better than the previous one, Vincent thought. *No frigging psychedelic complications.* Vincent made one more tour through the crowd and back. It looked like he'd wasted an afternoon.

Victor would be disappointed. He checked the time again. If he hurried, he might be able to beat the five o'clock traffic across the Bay Bridge. Then, he checked his watch again. It was probably too late for any real relief anyway, so he might as well stick it out. The crowd was so crazy, there was a good chance he'd missed Merriam and Gaspare in the hordes of Deadheads and poetry lovers. Vincent decided poets must talk in some kind of code ordinary people couldn't understand, sort of like whoever wrote that "St. Stephen" song.

He'd sort of understood the heavy-set poet with a beard when he recited a poem about boxers. Victor would probably have thought the poetry was cool stuff. His twin's love of literature bewildered him. His twin thought he didn't know about it, but Victor should know better than to hide anything from him.

Vincent was wondering if it was high time for him to confront Victor about this flaw in his character when he spotted Merriam. *Hallelujah,* he thought. No question it was her, that long deeply dyed ebony hair, that stately runway model figure? She'd turn heads wherever she was and the heads were certainly turning.

Two men were standing on either side of her with Brother Gaspare, no longer in his black robe but wearing a tie-dye T-shirt, trailing behind. Gaspare was not as tall as Merriam and was slender. The two anonymous guys were enormous. He could only see them in profile, but they were on his side of the lawn and close enough that it looked like Merriam was being escorted and not moving of her own free will.

Brother Gaspare's mouth was moving—a lot. The sound of a new song that began with a drum solo kept him from hearing what Brother Gaspare was yelling. He was definitely yelling. No one in the audience was paying attention. One of the men had his arm outstretched, pushing Brother Gaspare back whenever he tried to get close to Merriam.

Vincent ducked through the bamboo grove and jogged up the lawn using the bushes and other bamboo trees as cover. As he reached the end of the lawn and stepped out on to the path, he found himself standing no more than twenty yards away from Merriam and her escorts. Brother Gaspare was gesticulating wildly. It was then that Vincent saw that Merriam was handcuffed and that one of the men was holding something in his hand covered by his jacket. *A weapon of some kind*, Vincent thought, *probably a pistol.*

Vincent thought, *no way.*

Then he thought again. There were people all over the place, walking, sitting. This guy wasn't about to pull the trigger. He remembered back to a few times in the past when he was confronted by danger and had to make a quick decision. *Si deve in ballo, si deve ballore.* And each time he had been in for the penny.

He stepped quickly toward Merriam and her captors. When he reached the guy holding the backpack, he tapped him on the shoulder and said, "Hey dude," The man swung around in surprise, and Vincent kicked his balls through the uprights for a field-goal. He didn't wait for the man to drop, lunging at the second guy and head-butting him. He fell on top of the man's bleeding nose and yelled, "Run, Merriam, run, run!" The guy below him was struggling to get free. The man he'd kicked was on his knees vomiting.

Vincent heard voices yelling, "Fight, fight!"

He watched Brother Gaspare grab Merriam by the arm and they began running. While running, Brother Gaspare turned his head around and yelled, "Thank you," then together, holding hands, they continued running.

Vincent rolled off the guy beneath him and stood up. The guy attempted to rise and Vincent kicked him in the head. *That felt good*, Vincent thought as he sprinted away. The last thing he saw when he looked back was Tonto, the Native American medic, waving at him. Vincent was experiencing an adrenaline high. It was the 100-yard dash. The wind couldn't have caught him. He wished his twin had been there to see him. There had been times growing up when the two of them had battled together. He'd always been the better boxer, but Victor was the better street fighter. Victor would have enjoyed seeing that last kick to the head.

Vincent wished Gloria had been there to see him rescue Merriam. He wished all the guys at the tavern had been there. "Don't mess with Vincent Brovelli," he yelled, laughing at the sky.

Vincent arrived at his car panting and feeling a little delirious. He drove out of Golden Gate Park. He figured by now Brother Gaspare and Merriam would be in the wind. It was probably a good bet they wouldn't go to Merriam's parents. Chances were Nick Parsegian and his wife wouldn't see their daughter for a long time, if ever. And whose fault would that be? In his mind, Vincent closed *The Case of Merriam Parsegian and Her Lover.* The first case of Vincent Brovelli's career as a P.I. Vincent smiled. He could hardly wait to tell Victor that this wouldn't have happened if Gloria hadn't steered him in the right direction.

Soap operas, Mama Mia. Perhaps a whole new way to solve mysteries. *Silly,* he thought. Then he thought, *why the heck not?*

CHAPTER 33
THE BIG EASY

"Spresso l'amore exessivo puo transformarsi in odio.
Often excessive love can turn to hate."
Italian proverb

When I said we had to go to New Orleans, I was not using the Papal We. I had also not been thinking. I was a wanted man, a fugitive from the law. If Miss Rhoda was captured with me after crossing a state boundary, it would be a federal offense, and she would be arrested as an accessory to murder. I pointed this dire consequence out to Miss Rhoda, but her only answer was a stubborn shake of her head and a "no self-respecting Grandma Friday would let down her Detective Saturday." Stubborn is a trait I recognized, having been afflicted with it since childhood, as witnessed by my parents and any nun that taught me in elementary school. I gave up trying to change Grandma Friday's mind and turned my attention to my twin. Vincent needed to know what I was up to.

I suppose I could have trusted the age-old twins' communication system called, for lack of a better term, dual carbs-vibes, which was an automotive version of two children talking into tin cans on either end of a tightly stretched string.

Vincent, it's me, copy?

Copy, Victor, hear you loud and clear, over and out.

In elementary school, we really didn't need that string and the two empty 24-ounce Italian tomato paste cans with their labels torn off. We *felt* each other in ways that drove our older sibs crazy. *How did Vincent know?* Carlo would ask in frustration. And I'd answer with a smug smile and a shrug. In the seventh grade, Vincent broke his arm horsing around with his friends climbing the cliffs near the Golden Gate Bridge. Back in Alameda, I didn't need to know why my mother had looked worried talking on the telephone. The twins down the street from where we lived, Louisa and Lorretta, swore they could hear each other think. They claimed all twins were aliens from the planet Zedonia.

Of course, that was only a silly thought. I had to be certain that Vincent knew where I was going and the risk. My solution had been to ask Miss Rhoda to call Big James for me and asked him to take a message to Vincent. Big James was not my biggest fan, but Miss Rhoda had assured me "he doesn't refuse his auntie". On that same call, James had informed Miss Rhoda that he was planning to fly to New York City to be part of something that had remained unexplained, and Miss Rhoda hadn't probed.

This *something* was on my mind as we drove across the border through Texas. I cannot describe how desolate northern Texas is. Its landscape made me thirsty and my thirst did not abate until we crossed over the border into Louisiana, and I saw some green things called plants. The Oldsmobile Cutlass had purred nicely so far. My Grandma Friday was sitting in the passenger seat with her eyes closed. I didn't think she was asleep. We'd made the first leg of our drive with a sleep-over in a motel in Shamrock, Texas, across the border from New Mexico. We'd driven hard the next day across the Texas panhandle. We'd be in the Big Easy before sundown with some time to spare.

As the Louisiana miles passed, the vegetation became more dense. Trees had moss on them. You could see the heat rising from the side of the road.

Because of Miss Rhoda's magic makeup, the scar below my left eye was close to invisible. I'd gone unshaven and with my swarthy southern Italian skin, I could easily be creole or Cajun, which was the effect Miss Rhoda was trying for. With one of her son's sports coats and a porkpie hat, she'd achieved her objective. I had a copy of her son's old drivers license that might work if the person didn't pay attention. In my disguise, I looked enough like him to pull it off. Mother and son drove on, and I followed Miss Rhoda's advice to think of the *casino* I was in and stop obsessing over Dila.

• • •

We checked into the *Maison Rouge*, a two-star hotel, within walking distance of the French Quarter. It was a little past three o'clock in the afternoon on Thursday, June 11th, I noted on my pocket calendar. We'd made good time. We freshened up, then began our search for Father

Boniface's mother.

We knew from the page Miss Rhoda had pilfered at the diocesan headquarters that the priest's father was dead, but his mother, Mrs. Eugenie Dubois, was still listed as living. Before we'd left Oakland, I had considered calling Sweets to see if he knew of anyone in New Orleans who could find out where this woman might be living but nixed the idea because Sweets would have insisted on being part of the investigation, and he would have somehow managed to join us. That would have been out of the question. I'd called Terrance Bowles who had a connection in the telephone company. His connection had found no record of a Father Boniface of Saint Agnes's Catholic Church making calls to anywhere in Louisiana or to any of its contiguous states.

That had left us on our own.

An hour later, we were sitting in a cafe, having just returned from visiting Saint Stephan's Catholic Church where Father Boniface last served, and we'd found out nothing we didn't already know about the priest. They had been very complimentary and were willing to talk about how good a priest Father Boniface had been. We could have been there hours listening to praise. They had no idea how we could locate his mother. The secretary thought that the woman had moved out of New Orleans but that we should check other Catholic churches to be sure. She'd handed us a long list.

A yellow and green streetcar rumbled past us, following its tracks around the corner. There was a park across the street filled with some sort of bush resplendent with purple flowers. In the middle stood a statue of some notable citizen from Louisiana's past. As far as I could tell from where we were seated, it was not Sweets's supposed relative, the pirate Jean Lafitte nor General Andrew Jackson, the hero of the Battle of New Orleans. We were having New Orleans version of high tea, a beignet and café au lait. I had the list of all the Catholic churches in my pocket. In all, the Archdiocese of New Orleans had 112 churches and 12 missions in the city. I wondered aloud if we'd get some information about our elusive mother at one of these churches.

Miss Rhoda answered. "God knows. It's too late to do anything now. We'll start early in the morning."

We finished our snack and went back to the hotel. Both of us were too tired to think of dinner. We'd said good night to each other, promising to meet in the lobby by seven for breakfast and get an early start.

• • •

For a two-star hotel, its restaurant called *Tout Sweet* had a full menu of various Louisiana breakfast fare: crabmeat cheesecake, breakfast po-Boy, *pain perdu*, which translates to *lost bread* and was nothing more mysterious than French toast. Miss Rhoda had biscuits and gravy. My choice was the po-Boy. The coffee was strong. We both felt refreshed after sleeping nearly twelve hours. We decided to leave the Olds in the hotel parking lot since neither of us knew the city. Miss Rhoda followed me to the taxi stand down the street, and we began our travels.

By late afternoon, exhausted, our taxi dropped us off in front of our hotel with no additional information about Father Boniface's mother. On the other hand, our heads were full of more praise for her son, the priest. Many of the priests and nuns often used the word "saint" when referring to Father Boniface. This version of Father Boniface was Lewis Dubois. If my theory was correct, I didn't think they would have had the same response regarding Charles.

Two hours later, after a short nap and dinner at a nearby restaurant called Nicole's that, according to the hotel, served authentic Creole food, Miss Rhoda and I wound up on Bourbon Street in a tavern listening to blues. Toward the end of the evening, the drummer approached Miss Rhoda, whispered in her ear, and much to my surprise, she stood, winked at me, and followed him onto the stage. The drummer introduced her as Rhoda Teagarden, granddaughter of Jack Teagarden. After that, I was treated to Miss Rhoda's voice singing jazz vocals none of which I recognized but enjoyed thoroughly.

"How did you manage that?" I asked.

"I recognized the drummer from my days in New York City. Guess he recognized me."

"You have a great voice, Miss Rhoda," I said.

"I should have kept singing. I wanted a family. I wish my husband had had the same idea."

I could have asked but didn't. Her marriage was her own business. We said our good nights. I went to sleep still listening to Miss Rhoda singing.

• • •

On Saturday morning, we were having breakfast in the hotel dining room.

"You are my son looking to find a place for mom now that she's getting on in years," Miss Rhoda said.

Before leaving Miss Rhoda had spruced up the makeup concealing my scar and darkened my eyebrows some. I had checked myself in the mirror. In some ways, Miss Rhoda and I actually looked related. Dila would have thought that hilarious. What was it about skin color that seemed to be so important to white people? My people? Or maybe Italians from South Italy were considered by whites as colored. Not true. But I knew the Portuguese often were mistaken for people of color.

In the eighth grade, Sister Xenobia, our English teacher gave us a novel, *To Kill a Mockingbird* to read and to write a book report about it. The father in the novel, an attorney defended a black man who'd been accused of raping a white woman, had instructed his young daughter not to jump to conclusions about other races until you spent some time in their shoes. Miss. Rhoda's had disguised me well enough that I'd experienced what that dad meant. I didn't need to be completely black to understand the deep hole of prejudice so many white people had dug for themselves and could not get out of and in many cases did not want to, which was the worst part of it. I thought of an entire life spent mostly with Caucasian people. I was going on thirty.

I felt a hand of my shoulder. I'd had my eyes closed. "Penny for your thoughts," Miss Rhoda said.

"I don't have enough pennies," I said. I removed the list of homes for the elderly from my pocket. Miss Rhoda unfolded a city street map. There were seven homes within the city limits. If we couldn't find what we wanted in them, we'd continue with those outside the city. If that failed, we'd try and homes for old folks in nearby towns. We had not given ourselves any time limit but were hoping to discover Farther Boniface's mother within a few days, giving ourselves three days on the outside. Miss Rhoda had to be back in Oakland by Monday.

"Saint Jeanne's Home for the Elderly, first," I said.

"Is Saint Jeanne the patron saint of old folks?" Miss Rhoda questioned.

"You got it," I said. "Nothing there we'll move on to Clear Horizons."

"Strange name for an old folks' home," Miss Rhoda said. "What kind of horizons you think they're talking about?"

"Not the earthly kind, I suppose," I replied.

"After that, if we don't find her?"

"Gentle Living," I said. "They claim their home has won numerous Bridge tournaments. Old people love playing card games."

"Not me," Miss Rhoda said.

"Wait until you get old," I said, which brought a smile to Miss Rhoda lips.

"You ready?" I asked. Miss Rhoda put down her coffee and stood up. We walked to the corner of Royal Street and found a taxi.

On the drive, the taxi driver treated us to the history of New Orleans' stately mansions and some of the ghost stories that accompanied them. As we drove through the French Quarter, our driver pointed out the home of Madame Dauphine La Laurie, which was home to the socialite and serial killer's ghost. Further on, he slowed down in front of a Bourbon Street bar called Lafitte's Blacksmith Shop which, he explained, was the oldest operating tavern in America. It was haunted by an unknown woman dressed entirely in black. I mentioned that I knew a guy who said he was related to the pirate Lafitte to which the driver's response was him and half the male population of New Orleans. I would not mention that to Sweets.

We arrived at Saint Jeanne's Home for the Elderly and told our driver to wait for us. I explained that if we found the person, we were looking for we'd tell him and he could leave. I gave him a ten spot so he wouldn't think we were trying to scam him. Ten minutes later, we were back in the taxi heading back the way we had come in the direction of New Horizons. This home also didn't pan out. Neither did Gentle Living, where we ran into a clearly racist administrator who looked horrified when we asked him if a Cajun or Creole woman named Eugenie Dubois was living in his home for gentle people.

"Guess gentle is a synonym for white," Miss Rhoda quipped as we left.

We got back in the taxi. The driver who was of mixed race and looked like Billy Eckstine said, "I didn't think you folks would find your kin in that place."

"You could have warned us," I said.

"My daughter's birthday coming up. You're helping me pay for her present. The kid is picky."

Our sly driver, perhaps feeling a little guilty, suggested another home for the aged.

"It's economical. Takes in all sorts of religions as long as it's not Vodun."

Miss Rhoda turned to me and raised her eyebrows.

"Is he being comedian?" I whispered.

She whispered back, "I don't think so."

"Take us to that comical place," I said.

"Out of town aways," he said. "If you find her, I stay and wait for a discounted price; otherwise, you folks will be here a long time waiting for another taxi."

We made the deal. Five minutes after walking through the doors of Bayou Bay Senior Living Residence, I walked out of the building and told the driver that we'd found her and to wait. I gave him a twenty this time.

• • •

Mrs. Dubois greeted us warmly. Her hair was completely white and cut short. Her complexion was swarthy—much like Father Boniface. She was plump and dressed in a print housecoat. She walked with a limp but did not exhibit any pain. Her apartment was about the size of a large studio, but it had a separate small bedroom. Her furniture was old but not antique. For Mrs. Dubois, I changed our story back to my being a writer. I introduced Miss Rhoda as my camera man. Miss Rhoda immediately reached into her purse and withdrew her Brownie Automatic. I stifled a laugh. Mrs. Dubois directed us to a small settee facing the TV set. I was not sure she believed us, but I got the feeling that she didn't have a lot of visitors and was happy having a chat with us.

She pulled over a chair and sat down. "*Moi*, I am always *tres joli* to talk about my little boy. Still call him a boy even though he become a grown man and a priest no less. *Probablement*, I should be more respectful, no?"

Mrs. Dubois spoke with the same accent as our taxi driver. Sweets too, but the burglar mostly used his accent when he was playing a role. He could deliver a speech in the King's English if he wished. Shakespeare had that the world was a stage.

"He is the pastor of Saint Agnes's Church," I said. "I write for the Catholic Archdiocese in San Francisco. We are going to do a feature article on him."

"Oh, ma goodness. You are such a blessing. My little Louie, so famous."

Miss Rhoda touched my knee, in recognition that half our mission was complete. The next question might solve the remaining half of our mission. "You had an older son, is that correct?"

"Charlie, he one scampering child, he was. Before my husband died, we lived happy in Arnoudville. The boys shared a room. Louie, he played nice in the corner with his blocks; Charlie, he be throwing the blocks in the air, jumpin' around. Little monkey, he was."

"I assume he didn't go into the seminary," Miss Rhoda said.

"Oh, goodness me, no. Charlie? He go in the army. He real proud in his uniform just before he leave for Vietnam. See, over on the wall? I have all the pictures. Charlie and Louie from time they be little ones." Madame Dubois stood up and went to the wall and returned with a number of framed photographs.

"This be Charlie in his uniform," she said, holding it out for us to see.

"And this be Louie, in his first cassock. Handsome, *non*?"

"Yes, he is certainly handsome," Miss Rhoda said, smiling broadly. She began clicking her Brownie at the photographs. I said, "They are twins, I see. I wasn't aware of that."

"Oh, they be twins all right. Charlie, he come out fighting, Louie just slipperin' out calm as can be. Don' get me wrong, Charlie, he a good boy, just rambunctious."

The old woman frowned. "Oh, they were a pair all right. You couldn't tell them apart no how. Me too. They play games together. *Mon Dieu*, how they play strange. Made up their own language. Couldn't tell 'em apart, not their faces, not their voices and couldn't tell what they talking about. My dear husband chase them around with his belt, he get so mad."

Mrs. Dubois' voice trailed off and she stared ahead as if she was seeing her twins fleeing their father.

One last question, I thought, just to be sure. "Mrs. Bouchard, how many minutes was Charles older than Louis?"

"What a question. We mamas don't be countin' time doing what we be doing, *vous savez*," she said, turning to Miss Rhoda and repeating, "You have babies, you know, madame?" Miss Rhoda nodded vigorously in agreement.

The doctors told me less than a minute before Louie he came into the world like a little lamb.

The word sacrificial came to mind.

We had what we came for, but I had a couple of more questions. Madame Dubois, do you keep in contact with Charles? I'd like to interview him.

"Charlie, ah he come home from Vietnam all sorrowful-like. And angry too. Like to scare me sometime. Charlie stay wit' me for a while. Sometime, he go meet friends from the army call themselves *Les Tigres*, come back home more sad. Make me *tristess*, sad, too. One day he say he go to the store for cigarettes, and he never came back. Poof, gone."

The story of a soldier returning sorrowful and angry reminded me of Mario, my older brother. The war did brutal things to soldiers. Mario was dead. He hadn't died in the war, but after what happened to him last year, I would have preferred he had.

I asked a few more questions about her life. There were letters from her priest son with all sorts of promises to come home for a visit, but "*Lord Almighty, he be a busy priest, saving those runaways.*" Mrs. Dubois liked it here. There were lots of bingo and some zydeco dances, she explained, tilting her head and batting her eye lashes flirtatiously. She did not seem unhappy.

She hugged us as we said our goodbyes, asking us to send the article when it was finished.

Our taxi driver was waiting for us. On the drive to our hotel, he said he'd have lots of money left over after he bought his daughter her birthday present.

Back in the hotel, we went to the bar for a celebratory drink. Two glasses of the house Bordeaux. We clinked glasses.

"Vincent and I used to invert words so people wouldn't know what we were saying to each other. Like Epod for Dope. But Charles and Louis went to greater trouble inventing an entirely new language."

"I've never heard of such a thing," Miss Rhoda said.

"My mother knew about it. She called it an anonymous language. Let me think for a sec. Oh, yeah, she called it Crytophasia."

"Sound like a disease."

It was strange to me how close the Dubois twins, Charles and Lewis had been, then suddenly in their teens, they had drifted apart until by the time Charles joined the army, they barely spoke to each other. I couldn't imagine a life not talking to my twin.

"If you're right, Mr. Brovelli," Miss Rhoda said, "it's going to break that nice woman's heart."

"I'm right," I said. "But being right is not proof. We need to think of some way to actually prove Charles murdered this brother and is impersonating him."

Miss Rhoda said that she was too tired to think about it. She wanted to get some room service and go to bed early. I had another drink at the bar then found a restaurant down the street called Fats' Grille. After dinner, I stopped in a jazz club. It was too early for the show, but an old black man was playing tunes on a trombone. I ordered a coffee with a shot of bourbon and listened. The bartender came over and poured me a complimentary shot of bourbon. I asked him about the music.

"Comes in about this time most days and plays old Jack Teagarden tunes. He's good. Word gets around and people come to listen. Half an hour, this place will be filled up."

CHAPTER 34
ALL FOR ONE AND ONE FOR ALL

"Those friends thou hast and their adoption tried,
grapple them to thy palm with hoops of steel."
Polonius to his son Laertes

The headline on the third page of the Oakland Tribune read: "Missing Oakland Police Detective. Foul Play Suspected." Vincent finished reading and rubbed his eyes. Then he rubbed his temples, hoping he could avoid the headache he knew was on its way. The guys at the tavern couldn't have been so stupid.

"Who couldn't be that stupid?" Gloria said as she placed his toast and bowl of Grape-Nuts cereal in front of him.

He must have been thinking aloud, that or his wife had turned into a mind reader. "The guys at Flynn's."

"What did they do that was stupid?"

Vincent considered whether he should tell Gloria. He decided his wife already knew all about the case, and she could perhaps come up with some advice the way she'd done helping him locate Merriam. "A couple of days ago, the guys were concocting some kind of scheme to help Victor. The missing cop in this article is Detective Mark Halperin, you know, the cop who arrested Victor and found all the evidence against him. He's hated Victor ever since Victor connected him to the cops who caused that riot last year at the Bobby Hutton vigil."

Gloria said she remembered.

"If the fools at Flynn's had something to do with his guy's disappearance, hell, they could go to jail until they are too feeble to walk."

"They're not that dumb, are they?"

Vincent wished he could be certain. He stood up. He left his cereal uneaten and went to the bedroom to get dressed for work. He'd be standing in front of the tavern when Body arrived to open the door. If they had been that stupid, he'd have to warn Victor, but his twin was, according to his message, out of town. Today was Wednesday. Victor had left on Tuesday. He wished Victor would have told him how long he'd be gone. He was probably following a lead. There would be a highway in the picture and his twin's elbow sticking out the driver's side window. He'd be in his Porsche Cabriolet going over the speed limit, Credence Clearwater Revival, Victor's favorite rock band, playing on the car radio.

• • •

Three hours and one sale, a 1967 Ford Galaxy, later, Vincent was standing where he'd promised himself he'd be, in front of Flynn's, watching its owner Body Flynn drive into the driveway to the back of the tavern where he parked his car. Vincent made a note that Body needed new wheels. The '66 Pontiac GTO coupe he was driving was looking a little seedy. As Body stepped out from the side of the tavern, he stopped and looked at Vincent.

"Don't give me that fake surprised look, Body. You know why I'm here."

"I have no idea what you're talking about, Vincent."

Body put the key in the door and opened it. "Come in. I'll make coffee and you can explain to me what in the *fook* you're so excited about."

Vincent followed Body in and sat at the bar. "What did you fools do?" Vincent asked.

From the end of the bar, Body repeated himself, "I still don't know what you're talking about."

"This morning's Tribune," Vincent said.

"What about it. I haven't had time to read it yet."

"Detective Officer Mark Halpern gone missing. Two days now and no sign of him."

"Breaks my heart, but why should. . . Oh, I get it. You tink me and the boys had something to do with it. Is that right?"

Vincent was starting to feel a little foolish. It sounded as if Body really didn't know what he was talking about. "You're not responsible?"

"Vincent, give us some credit. We're not all smart Eye-talians like you, but we're not crazy. You're talking about offing a cop or kidnapping him or some daft ting like that. I didn't know you held us in such low esteem."

Now Vincent was feeling really foolish, recalling at breakfast how certain he was. "Well, what do you make of it? Cops just don't stop showing up for work. Especially that bozo, being in charge of Victor's case, missing a chance to get even."

"Well, I'll level with you, Vincent. We did have a meeting to put our heads together to formulate a plan of some kind. When you interrupted us, we had decided we would try to plant kiddy porn in his apartment. Sweets said getting into the arsehole's apartment was a snap. We didn't want you involved. But we finally dropped the idea and then we just sat around an' drank a lot of beer. Sweets said he knew a guy for the right amount of cash would break the sonavabitch's legs. But by then we were all so drunk. No, Vincent, as much as I like that the asshole is disappeared, it was none of our doing. Sorry to disappoint you."

Vincent sighed. "You sure. Maybe Sweets?"

"Nah, I don't see it. Sweets might be capable. . . Nah. But you should ask him. I can tell you for Swanee, Jitters, Larry and Stuart, we didn't have anything to do with Halpern gone missing. Okay with me if he was fish food at the bottom of the bay. That cop was as mean as a junkyard dog."

Vincent was not sure about Sweets, but it was a relief to know the guys were not involved. "Glad to hear you guys didn't do anything dumb," Vincent said. "How is that coffee coming?"

"Coming right up, Vincent. Oh, by the way, boy-o do you know what the difference is between an Italian grandmother and an elephant?"

Vincent shook his head.

"Fifty pounds and a black dress."

Sigh.

• • •

After a couple of cups of coffee and some conversation about the A's and the Giants, Vincent was back on the lot showing a 1968 Mercury Monterey to a tubercular looking man who said that the owner of the Chevron station on the corner had promised him that the Brovelli Brothers had the best used car deals in Oakland. Vincent knew this was going to be wasted time. Guys who came onto the lot with deals on their mind, never found the prices low enough for them. He continued his sales pitch anyway. It allowed him to go through the motions while thinking of how he would explain to Nick Parsegian that his beloved Merriam had run off with her music teacher, a Catholic Brother. *Better that than a priest*, he thought. At least her father would have to take some solace in the fact that his daughter was alive and seemingly happy. She too had looked back at him while the two were running, and she was smiling.

Parsegian would have to break the news to his wife. Over the time it had taken Vincent to find Merriam, he'd learned that Merriam had little respect for her parents. They'd spoiled her, but they'd also kept a tight rein on her and demanded her total obedience. Merriam was not likely to worry about her parents now that she was free of them.

The Mercury remained unsold, and Vincent went to the office where his father was once again making cold calls that were, by any standard of sales irrelevance, excessive. On the other hand, Vincent had never seen such irrelevance turn into relevance as his father's voice found its way across telephone lines to a person unaware that he was about to be convinced to leap into his car and drive down to Brovelli Brothers. Sales were up some, so he shouldn't complain. Even so, Vincent felt that his pop's motive had more to do with having a conversation and the sales were as much of a surprise to him as they were to the customers. Vincent decided he'd discuss his father's behavior with his next-door neighbor, the shrink. Maybe his pop was lonely.

He turned from the puzzle of Big Sal Brovelli to the puzzle of Victor Brovelli. On his desk was a note Theresa had handed him when he came in to work that had been slipped through the mail slot.

Your brother is with my aunt Miss Rhoda
In New Orleans If anything bad happens
to her I will bust up you and your brother.

James

No date. It sounded like Big James had delivered his first message, then thought about it and decided he need to add a postscript. Vincent was certain gigantic James could make good on his promise. He crumpled the note and chucked it into the wastebasket.

"Where the heck are you, Victor?" he asked aloud.

"You're mumbling, Vincent," Theresa said as she walked in the door. "There's a customer on the lot if you and your father haven't noticed."

Big Sal Brovelli's voice came out of the shadows. "Is my customer. I call him, he say ten minutes he be over for 30% off." The sun could not get through the door when Big Sal stood in it.

From her desk by the door, Theresa said, "We don't have any 30% off cars on the lot."

"I know," Big Sal said. "Don't worry, he take 15% off."

The sunshine returned as Big Sal turned from the doorstep in the direction of his customer.

"I swear to God, Vincent, you have *got* to get Victor out of this mess, so your dad can go home to his tomatoes."

"Sales are up since he started," Vincent said.

"So is my blood pressure."

Vincent asked Theresa if she'd had any messages from Mr. Rossellini. She shook her head.

● ● ●

Vincent was the last off the lot. Before he left the office, he'd called his wife and told her he was going to run a few errands and not to wait on dinner for him. He explained that it was Victor business, and she'd sounded less upset. He'd have to boil his own pasta. She'd leave the meat sauce on the stove on low. Vincent smiled. If he'd traveled to Italy, he'd not have found an Italian wife better than Gloria Mancuso.

He had decided to take a couple of hours to find Sweets. Sweets had told him that he had rented an apartment in Victor's building, but Sweets was born a liar. He wouldn't be surprised if he found the burglar reclining on Victor's couch, eating everything in Victor's refrigerator and drinking Victor's beer.

Which was exactly where Vincent found Sweets when he unlocked Victor's front door and walked into the living room—Sweets Monroe, asleep on the couch and on the coffee table, a plate with something brown on it and two empty bottles of Anchor Steam. Sweets's mouth was wide open. Vincent was tempted to drop one of Sweets' candy wrappers in it. Sweets would probably choke and die, then he and his twin would both be tried for another murder. He shook Sweets by the shoulder.

"Wake up, you scumbag," he yelled. Sweets opened one eye. A frown creased his forehead. His other eye opened.

"Daddy-o."

"You never rented an apartment in this building, did you?"

"*Au contraire, mon ami, au contraire,*" Sweets said, sitting up. "The apartment is directly over Victor's, but the furniture has not arrived. All I have is a mattress."

"And when do you plan to steal your furniture?" Vincent asked. Before Sweets could respond, Vincent began laughing. *That was a good one, his twin would appreciate. Proof he had a sense of humor and was not always the serious first-born that Victor often accused him of being.*

"You think that be funny, you?" Sweets said. "I'm hurt. My heart hurts bad that you believe Sweets Monroe would stoop to stealing sofas and sheet like that. Me, I'm a high-class burglar."

Looking at the fake expression of disbelief on Sweets's face, Vincent found it hard to stop laughing.

"Go on, mistreat me. You Italians think you are special because you born at the teats of a fucking wolf, so you tink you hotter than sheet We Creoles, we know different."

Bringing his laughter in check, Vincent said, "I thought you told us you're Cajun?"

"Cajun and Creoles, we all mixed up now. All peoples will be soon enough, you see. Big Easy folks be the model for the future world."

If the burglar was right, Vincent didn't like the idea at all. Italians should remain Italians. Then, he thought of Victor who might marry what their mother referred to as that *donna nera*. So maybe Sweets had a crystal ball.

Sweets stopped talking and offered him a hard candy. Vincent declined.

"What you want of Sweets, *mona mi*? You got a question mark in your eyes."

Vincent decided to bluff. It was something his twin once told him was a good technique if you were interviewing a suspect. "I need to know what you did with that cop. Victor is already in such deep water, there is no way he can be saddled with some dimwit plan you decided on to help."

"You talking to the wrong guy, Vincent. You can ask the dudes at Flynn's, we're all clean. If the cop is AWOL, he's missing on his own."

Vincent studied Sweets's eyes. Habitual liars believe their lies. He stared.

"Cross my heart," Sweets said. "I didn't touch a hair on his greasy wig."

"He wears a wig?"

"It's a good one, but it don't fool old Sweets. I'm a hairdo specialist."

Vincent looked at Sweet's cockatiel haircut and burst out laughing.

"You tink that's funny, you?"

"Hilarious," Vincent replied. "Okay, so do you have any ideas what happened to the cop?"

"Not a one."

Vincent left and drove home. At least he'd determined that Victor's friends had not done anything stupid to Officer Mark Halpern. He was looking forward to Gloria's meatballs. At home, he took his pasta to the living room to watch the news while he ate.

He was halfway through his dinner when an announcement came on. The Oakland Police Department had found the body of Detective Sergeant Mark Halpern. He had been shot. The police had no suspects at the present time, but Halpern was known to have made enemies of the Black Panthers. The reporter continued. Recently, Officer Halpern had arrested a suspect in the murder of Renee Sorenson, a graduate student at Mills College. The suspect, Victor Brovelli, an Oakland automobile dealer, had forfeited his bail and was at large.

Vincent had no doubt what the implications of that last sentence were. Not only was his twin being hunted for the murder of Rene Sorenson, but now he was a person of interest in the shooting death of Oakland police officer Mark Halpern. Their mom and pop would hear about it in the morning, as would his two older siblings, Carlo and Constanza, and *her* sons who adored Victor. He'd have to get on the phone and break the news now. Victor was innocent of both slayings. They would insist they didn't need to be reassured, but Vincent knew they would. Ever since Victor had become interested in becoming a private investigator and getting involved with a female member of the Black Panthers, his parents had begun lighting extra candles; his sister had told his wife that she hardly recognized Victor anymore, which was disingenuous, considering she, as well as Carlo, rarely came to Alameda except on holidays and never to the lot.

Vincent turned off the lights. He knew he wouldn't be able to sleep tonight. He wouldn't bother Gloria with his tossing and turning. He took a blanket out of the hall closet and returned to the chair in front of the TV. He hoped there would be a good old western. He'd watch until the screen turned to snow.

CHAPTER 35

DETECTIVE SATURDAY & GRANDMA FRIDAY

"Piu ti avvicini alla verita, piu e lontana.
The closer you get to the truth, the farther away it is."
Italian proverb

We parked the Olds in front of Miss Rhoda's apartment. It was late morning on a sunny Bay Area Day. Big Boy Clarence and his gang were nowhere in sight. We trudged wearily up the stairs. Monday's Oakland Tribune was laying at the foot of the apartment door. It fell open as I picked it up. I spotted a headline at the bottom of the page: *Hunt for Slayer of Oakland Police Officer, Mark Halpern Continues.* "What the hell," I said.

"What?" Miss Rhoda replied as she opened the door.

I didn't answer. I dropped my carryall and hurried into the kitchen. Seated at the table, I read, Miss Rhoda, reading over my shoulder. It didn't mention me. I was relieved. Miss Rhoda left the kitchen and brought back the previous day's newspapers. I began with the Wednesday's edition, hoping Halpern's body had been discovered while we were on the road, but no such luck. His corpse had been found near the Alameda estuary on Tuesday in time for Wednesday's front page, so I could have been the shooter. I had explained my relationship with Halpern.

"*Minchia,*" I cursed.

Miss Rhoda said, "Oh, my."

This turn of events was so unexpected, I wasn't sure what to do. I considered prayer. I'm Catholic and a believer. I grew up praying; Vincent said he grew out of it. I re-read the article. I was definitely the prime suspect. I was already wanted for the murder of Renee. It took me a while and a couple of cups of Miss Rhoda's coffee before I could think straight.

"It can't be a coincidence that Halpern was the cop shot to death and left by the estuary not far from East 14th Street," I said. Miss Rhoda agreed with me.

Miss Rhoda said. "You still got the rest of the day, Detective Saturday. I don't know where that murderer Victor Brovelli is hiding, but my nephew has got some work cut out for him if he's going to help this Brovelli person prove his innocence."

I touched my cheek where my scar was no longer visible. Miss Rhoda gave me a pick-me-up smile. It didn't entirely work, but I felt a little better. The beginning of Dickens's novel came to mind: "*It was the best of times; it was the worst of times.*" Best because I was certain beyond a shadow of a doubt that Charles Dubois, aka Father Boniface, had murdered Renee. It was the worst of times because I had no solid proof that Charlies had murdered his twin brother, Louis, and assumed his identity.

Now, to make Dicken's worst *even worse*, I was being hunted for the murder of a police officer. *Che fottuto casino,* I thought. Then I immediately edited my thoughts; *fucking mess* was an understatement! The worst of times was winning. My thoughts turned to Vincent and my parents. I could count on Vincent to use his twins-antennae to monitor my present state of health. But my parents would be worried sick. I'd have to take a chance and call. Rhoda cautioned against it.

"You must stay undercover working on the case. I'll go to your business, pretending I'm looking to buy a car."

It was a good solution. I felt better. I turned my attention back to the case. I told Miss Rhoda that I would take a quick nap then go to Saint Agnes's to see if I could talk to the girl, Ginger. She had to know something.

Miss Rhoda said she was no longer tired and would drive to East 14th. She'd take a nap when she returned. I offered to drive her, but she said she'd take her own car. Up to now, I had no idea Miss Rhoda owned an automobile. "Nothing fancy," she said. "An MGB roadster convertible."

"Wow," I said.

"We have a garage in back," Rhoda patted my shoulder and wished me luck, leaving me alone to mull over my condition.

I stretched out on her son's bed and closed my eyes. That Charles Dubois would kill his twin sickened me. What would he gain by being a priest in a hippie neighborhood in San Francisco? Whatever the reason was, Miss Rhoda and I had decided it would have to have been the reason he murdered Renee. Unless a killer is a psycho, he or she has a motive for killing. Whatever it was, Renee must have found out, and he could not let her live.

I thought back to what I knew: *The priest helped runaway teenagers, so he claimed, but that was verified by the owner of the sporting goods store. Sweets and I saw all the beds. The priest told us the place filled up every night. No reason to doubt him.*

According to him, when Merriam was a runaway, she stayed in the basement of Saint Agnes's. He told us she played her violin. He wouldn't have known that unless it was really Merriam. According to the priest, Merriam told him she was relieved to find a sanctuary. That too sounded like the truth. So why didn't Merriam stay more than a night? Could it have been that Renee discovered that he was impersonating his brother? That didn't compute because how did she know he was a twin? Means, motive and opportunity; I needed the motive, maybe more than one motive.

These thoughts kept circling in my mind like a dog chasing its tail. I closed my eyes tightly and pictured Renee, tall, long-legged Renee Sorenson. *Renee, how did you meet this phony priest? And what did you find out about him?* I opened my eyes and there she was standing by the door. She was wearing a straight black cocktail dress and high heels that accentuated her height. She was tapping her right foot and pointing a finger at her shoe, something she used to do when I was late picking her up. Inevitably when I arrived, she'd stick her tongue out at me then smile. It never failed to charm me. After Dila came into my life, I no longer thought of Renee in terms of romance, but here she was all dolled up like she looked so often when we first dated, heading out to a club for dancing or a concert and later, *ah, Madonna,* it was something.

What took you so long? I wondered. I had been waiting for Renee's ghost to show up to haunt me. *Multi fantasmi,* my Great Aunt Madelena had said to me on one of our family's visits to Italy after reading my tea leaves. I would see many ghosts.

I was overcome with a fury toward the fake priest. "*Filglio di puttna,*" I said aloud, "What kind of vile *cretino* are you?" I was no longer sleepy. I grabbed the letterman's jacket and took a Giants' baseball cap from the hall coat rack and put it on backwards. I had now gone five days without shaving and a beard was beginning to grow along my jaw line. Miss Rhoda's makeup still concealed my scar. My eyebrows were darker and she'd added a few wrinkles at the corner of my eyes. I was either her nephew or a recent arrival from Latin America. I looked in the hall mirror. A hipster version of Vincent stared back at me. Good enough that I would not be instantly identified. Renee followed me out of the apartment to the Olds.

Clarence was by himself pitching pennies against the wall. When I approached, Big Boy said, "I be guarding your wheels." He stuck out his palm.

"Where are your buds," I asked.

"School."

"And you?"

"I'm sick." He reached out his hand.

I withdrew three one-dollar bills and held them out to Clarence far enough away that he could not reach them. "That's the new going rate for watching a dude's car," I said. Big Boy nodded.

"Good," I said.

"You look funny," he said then sprinted away, faster than a sick boy should.

"Cute kid, huh, Renee," I said. I didn't expect an answer. In three years since I'd been seeing ghosts, not one had said a word to me. It was like being in a silent movie without the subtitles.

• • •

I arrived at the Haight District, closing in on 9:00 a.m. I found a telephone booth and called Saint Agnes's rectory and asked to speak to Father Boniface. I was happy to hear he was not in. I asked if he might be at the church. No was the reply again. Father Boniface had driven away last night to visit a friend and was not due to return until this evening.

Okay, I said to myself as I hung up. I could catch Ginger alone. But how would I approach her? Tough guy? Scare her? Probably not. A lot of these street kids grew up on fear. They knew all the kinds of pressure, from physical abuse to mental harassment. Being Mr. Nice Guy would never work either. She'd be too suspicious.

I thought of bribery. Maybe if I bluffed like I knew she was involved in some real criminal behavior, even if she wasn't, maybe I could scare her. Then if I offered her money to leave town if she told me everything she knew. I'd hint about Father Boniface. I imagined the balance of my checking account. How much could I offer her? She wouldn't accept a check. But I'd seen a bank a few blocks away as I drove in. She'd drive with me. I'd give her cash and take her to the bus station.

I was playing the scenario over in my mind when I heard a loud banging. I'd forgotten I was still in the telephone booth. A guy with blond hair down to his shoulders held in place by a rainbow head band had his knuckle ready for another onslaught. I opened the door and sidestepped out; he side-stepped in and banged the door shut. I walked up and down the street playing and replaying what I'd say to Ginger, if she was there. I hadn't thought of that. I was wasting time. I changed direction and walked toward the church.

Most of the beds were empty, but curtains were still drawn around several of the sleeping areas. I was in luck. Ginger was sitting alone on the couch on the stage. I walked slowly across the basketball court. When I arrived at the bottom of the stage, I waved. She was reading, but I knew she'd seen me. Kids like her were always vigilant. How did I know? Sweets had explained street life to me. We'd been driving back from the Haight and he'd explained, "*Moi, I was on the street a lot as a kid in New Orleans. We developed peripheralized vision see behind our ears on both sides.*"

"How goes it, Ginger," I said. She stared at me and said nothing.

Then, I remembered I was now Miss Rhoda's nephew. I was about to explain.

"What are you dressed up as?" she said. "Without that scar you look like a guy I know."

I said, "And you told him your name was Lydia."

"It is. But down here, I go by Ginger." She tossed her ginger-red hair to make her point. "You two look-a-likes some sort of undercover cops?"

"No, my twin brother. . ."

"David?"

"That's not his real name," I said. "It doesn't matter, he's a P.I. I work for him." It was a reasonable lie.

"Two P.I.s trying to find one missing teenage girl. Seems a little much. What do you want from me?"

"You promote this safe haven. I saw you handing out cards at the concert."

"So what? Saint Agnes is righteous place."

"But you know it's not, don't you?" I frowned at her. "You know what's really going on."

"What the fuck are you talking about?" Ginger said. "I don't know shit."

"Well, if she don't know shit, I do."

The voice came from behind me. I turned around and saw a head, hair shaved on the left side and Rasta braids on the right-side dangling lose past her ear. She looked biracial but of an extra-terrestrial variety from a galaxy far, far away. Despite the weird hairdo and numerous facial piercings, she could have been a model for a Renaissance angel, with bow lips and huge round eyes.

"You go back to sleep, you junkie," Ginger said. "Or I'll be over there and kick your ass."

"Yeah, yeah, hard ass, but you tell that fucking priest to stop trying to get up my skirt."

"You're dreaming. What would anybody want with you?"

"Fuck you, Ginger," the other girl yelled. "This place isn't as safe as you said it was. I'd like to know where the hell Jennifer and Georgia-Rose went last night with that bald guy, huh? Huh? You tell me. All their clothes and gear are still under their beds."

"If you haven't noticed, freak, people around the Haight disappear all the time."

"Yeah, but they don't leave their stash behind."

Back and forth, the two went. I felt like I was watching a tennis match. No doubt Ginger or Lydia was an alias. Or maybe Ginger was also an alias. I assumed Jennifer and Georgia-Rose were not the girls' real names. Who was the bald guy? My strategy to intimidate Ginger had devolved into something else. I listened as they continued arguing.

"Who knows and who cares," Ginger yelled. "Get some sleep so you can shoot up tonight."

"Screw you, Ginger," the extra-terrestrial said and retreated behind her curtain.

I was getting a queasy feeling, not like my usual frustrating undetectable car-noise-feeling, but something more sinister. Girls being escorted away in the dead of night, leaving their possessions behind—that smelled like kidnapping to me.

Ginger raised the book she was reading so it covered her face and leaned back in the sofa. It was time to push the girl. Kidnapping, but to what purpose? I recalled my mistaken belief while trying to solve my brother Mario's murder that Vietnamese women were being smuggled into the U.S. to be turned into prostitutes. I had been completely wrong, but what about now? Were hippie teenage girls being kidnapped and turned into whores? I was certain that Father Boniface was guilty of killing his twin brother and the murder of Renee Sorenson, which meant he was capable of any other heinous crime. Had I discovered my missing motive? I watched Ginger. I was thinking of the kind of question I would ask her. I didn't want her to bolt, but I needed some answers. I swung up onto the stage and sat of the coffee table in front of her. She didn't take her face out of the book, but she managed a "fuck off, will you?"

"I will," I said, "if I can get some answers from you."

Silence.

"You know kidnapping is a federal crime, don't you?"

Silence.

"FBI will get involved. Long prison terms." Silence I took a gamble. "Your friend, the bald guy, if he goes down, so do you."

She moved fast. I almost didn't catch her. I had her firmly by the wrist and swung her back onto the couch just in time to receive a roundhouse fist from her other hand that caught me on the side of the jaw. I fell backward, stunned. I looked up through bleary eyes and Ginger was gone. From beyond the curtain stage left I heard a door slam.

"*Minchia*," I groaned.

"You shouldn't swear in a church."

I followed the voice to extra-terrestrial's head sticking out from behind her bed curtain.

"You got to be Italian to know that," I said.

"Yeah, on my mom's side. She swore all the time."

I hopped off the stage. As I walked toward her, the girl stepped out from behind her curtain. She raised her right hand with a set of brass knuckles on it.

"See these," she said. "I know how to use them. There are bad vibes in this place. As soon as I get a little straighter, I'm packing up and blowing this joint. I should have known better than come here. Religious people give me the hives."

I was close enough to see those wide eyes, and the pupils were black pin holes. This girl was still seriously whacked out. "So how did you choose this place then?" I asked.

"Ginger gave me one of her pamphlets at a concert, and I liked her. Everything was fine, good chow and good sleep until I woke up and heard all this noise, crying and swearing. I was so out of it, it must have been pretty damn loud to wake me. I poked my head out and this bald-headed guy and another dude were hauling off Jennifer and Georgia-Rose. I thought cops at first then maybe private cops like some of those rich parents hire to find their kids. That's what I decided. Since they weren't after my ass, I wasn't worried."

"What about Father Boniface trying to seduce you?" I asked.

"That was totally weird too. I was back in bed. I had the chills. I heard more noise. I looked out real quiet like and saw the priest up on the stage. I thought I better tell him what happened. He was real nice, comforting like, you know, like taking my hand and patting it and stuff and telling me not to worry. That's when he tried groping me. Shit, I gave him a slap and got away, back to my cot."

"How come you didn't run away then?" I asked.

"Da'know, still coming down pretty hard, and streets at night 'round here are not so good for girls alone. I figured I'd straightened his ass out. The priest sort of acted like he was embarrassed, y'know, like he'd never done something like that before. I figured if I needed to I'd leave in the morning, but I woke up a little while ago thinking I knew those girls, and they came from real poor families. That got me worrying because I'd pretty much decided those men weren't police or private cops."

I almost asked her how she knew, then I remembered Sweets saying he could smell cops a mile away. The only scent I could identify on my friend Detective Sergeant Jay Ness was the vanilla citrus of his Old Spice aftershave. I thought of the priest and wondered if evil had an aroma.

"Then what?" I asked.

"Then, you came and I heard you and Ginger talking."

"So, you believe your friends were kidnapped?"

"Look, mister, I'm hurting and need some sleep. Just a couple of hours."

"Aren't you afraid of staying here?"

"If I was in better shape, yeah, I'd be outta here."

Extraterrestrial held up her brass knuckles.

"And I got a straight razor under my pillow," she said.

"Look, why don't you pack of your gear and let me take you to a motel. I'll pay for however many days you want."

"What's the catch?"

"You got to tell a cop friend of mine about what you saw last night."

"No way. I don't talk to cops. Never."

"I promise you he's one of the good guys. Honestly. Would one Italian lie to another Italian?"

I could see from the expression on her face that she was giving this some thought. I waited. I crossed my fingers; I crossed my heart. I said, "Hope to die." Finally, she smiled.

"I'll get my stuff," she said.

"*Bene*," I said. That earned me another smile. She stepped behind her curtain. When she came out, she was dressed in jeans and a Deadhead shirt that read "Mama Tried". I wondered what percentage of The Grateful Dead's fans there were living as runaways on the streets. On our walk to my car, Extraterrestrial, who'd told me her name was Neptune, kept her distance enough space between us that if I tried anything, she'd have time to bolt—or slug me with her brass knuckles.

Neptune got in the car and sat with her back against the door, keeping her backpack on her lap. There were stickers from just about every state in the union on it. You could have made it across the country going east to west from one sticker's location to the other. "Been around," I said pointing to the stickers.

"Been over the moon," she said. "Where are we going?"

"Oakland, that's my territory. You'll be safe there." I was already thinking imposing on Miss Rhoda instead of a motel. She could have her son's bedroom. By the time I got to Fell Street that led to the Oakland Bay Bridge on-ramp, Neptune was asleep, bent over, her head resting on all the states of the union.

It took me some convincing to get Neptune out of the car and up the stairs to Miss Rhoda's apartment. It took only a couple of minutes for Miss Rhoda to convince Neptune she'd be safer with her than at a motel. There are people in this world that are magnets. You don't have to meet them more than once to know you have been drawn into their field of caring. Of course it helped when Miss Rhoda mentioned she'd have a Black Panther keeping an eye on the place. She had walked Neptune to her son's bedroom and tucked her in. She returned to tell me the girl was fast asleep.

• • •

Miss Rhoda poured her second coffee. We were musing over what my next step would be.

"What do we do next?" Miss Rhoda asked.

"I had to talk to Jay."

"And he is?"

"Oh, right," I said. "I don't think I've ever mentioned him to you. He's Jay Ness, my friend who is a detective sergeant in the Oakland Police Department." I saw the look on Miss Rhoda's face. "I understand the Oakland cops are not on your Christmas card list, but Jay is a good cop."

"Rare bird," Miss Rhoda quipped. "We folks in West Oakland haven't spotted many of those flying around here."

"Trust me," I said.

"Okay, so what does he do for that poor child in the bedroom and all the others this Boniface guy is kidnapping? He can't go in and arrest him. First of all, this is the word of a big-time junkie. I saw the marks on the child's arms when I put her to bed. She's going to wake up looking all over for her stash. Lord, she'll be craving. No one will believe anything she has to say. That priest will be all holy, telling your friend this and that about how he helps these desperate kiddies. Your good cop be crying and reaching into his pocket for a donation."

"You're not being very helpful," I said.

"I'm being realistic. I know you're right about this. And, there's only one reason for kidnapping young women and that's to sell them."

"I figured that out on my own," I said.

"Good for you, Mr. Brovelli. This is not anything new for people in poor neighborhoods. A good-looking teenage girl is worth money to the cartels. Next to drugs and weapons, it is the third most lucrative illegal business. You got to understand poor folks are more likely to be victimized, often by their own kind. The Black Panthers have been really good for us down here in West Oakland, scare the crap out of the police and scare the crap out of our villains too. Except for some petty crap, crime has dropped significantly since they arrived. We might be better off getting the Panthers to help us. For one thing, they don't have to play by the same rules that your cop friend does."

The last point Miss Rhoda said made sense. I didn't have any proof other than the word of a teenage junkie and my own suspicions. Until proven, Father Boniface would remain the rector of Saint Agnes's Church.

He'd still be *Lewis* Dubois. The Archdiocese would back him up. What did his mother say? Even she couldn't tell her twins apart.

Still, I thought I needed to talk to Jay, just to run things by him, get some advice. But how to do that? Could I gamble on Jay not arresting me? As good a friend as he was, he was also sworn to do his duty. In the wild west of my mind, my Wanted Dead or Alive poster was nailed to every storefront and gatepost, and a hangman's noose was waiting for me beneath the branch of a tree.

"Let's go talk to Minister Bowles first," I said. "Maybe he has some ideas. Then I'm going to talk to Jay."

"You got to go on your own, Detective Saturday. Don't forget we have Neptune now and I clean forgot I have my book club coming in a couple of hours. Got baby sitting and baking to do. You want me to spruce you up?"

"I'm okay," I said. "I'm going to clean up and shave. The people around the Panther's office are used to seeing the Italian me."

$$\bullet \; \bullet \; \bullet$$

Terrance was not in his office and wouldn't be for the next three or four days. I was informed by some very nervous Black Panthers that their boss had flown back to New York City. It looked like New York City was going to be the setting for some kind of confrontation between the Panthers and the various branches of police.

I left the office frightened for Dila. If only I could have been in New York. There was no way, except for four days of nonstop driving, and as badly as I wanted to be with my fiancé, Miss Rhoda was right, I owed it to my family to clear my name.

$$\bullet \; \bullet \; \bullet$$

When I got back to Miss Rhoda's apartment, I explained to my Grandma Friday about Terrance flying to New York City. "The Panther that Bowles left in charge of the office said helping me was not on the To Do list his boss left behind for him. He wished me good luck."

Miss Rhoda was at the sink washing dishes. I asked her about Neptune.

"I got the girl to eat something. Then she upchucked it. I put her back to bed with a little something from my medicine cabinet. She'll sleep through the night. You'll have to sleep on the couch."

The couch would be fine. "A woman at the Panthers' office named Dora told me to say hey to you."

"A good woman. You know that country song, "Mama Tried"? Well, that be Dora, only she got two boys in prison without parole."

"Country music is not my thing."

"Just *Days of Our Lives* set to music," Miss Rhoda said.

"That's funny," I said.

"Problem with Country Western is that there are not enough really good singers to put any soul into their tunes. They need some black singers. There's a boy named Charlie Pride starting to sing some good country tunes, but that's about it."

"The only Charlie I'm interested in is Charlie aka Father Boniface."

Miss Rhoda began toweling the dishes.

"Coffee's hot," she said. I could smell dough baking in the oven. Most likely Miss Rhoda's oatmeal raisin-bran cookies.

I walked to the counter and filled a mug and took a sip. "What if we bring their mother here from New Orleans? She's bound to be able to tell if he is her sweet Lewis or her angry Charles."

"We talked about this before," Miss Rhoda reminded me. "The way I remember Mrs. Dubois talking about them, it was almost prideful the way she said they were like the same human being, down to their voices and body language. And, remember, she's pretty old and could easily get confused."

"If that's the case, I guess I got to rely on Jay. He's smart. He'll listen to Neptune."

Miss Rhoda turned from the sink. "What can your cop friend do with a junkie's story?"

"I know Jay. He may not do anything right away, but he's a curious guy. He meets once a month with a bunch of cops from all over the bay area that graduated from the police academy at the same time. He's always talking about them. They call themselves *Knights of the Round Table.* Jay could get the cops from San Francisco interested, checking things out. Putting the spotlight on the church. Get the beat cops to pay better attention."

"Okay, it wouldn't hurt, Mr. Brovelli. I sure can't think of anything better to do for the time being."

"If I go see Jay myself, he might have to arrest me. I wouldn't want to put him on the spot like that. I can't risk calling Vincent or other friends.

Warrants for wiretapping in criminal investigations had been passed into law a couple of years ago, and I couldn't chance the cops had tapped our office and all the Brovelli residences. I'm going to find a phone booth. If I can reach Jay, I'll be gone awhile. I don't want to interrupt your book club. Would you mind if I just read in your bedroom while you folks have your meeting?"

"You're welcome to sit in and comment."

"I haven't read the book. I've always wanted to. If you have an extra copy, I'll catch up on my reading."

"There's a hardback in the living room bookcase. The book club will be disappointed. They were looking forward to meeting a bone-a-fide wanted dead-or-alive fugitive. "

"Funny," I said.

• • •

The Shell station two blocks away had a telephone booth. I slipped in a dime. As I heard Theresa' voice, I said, "This is Mr. Rossellini."

"Ah, come stai, signor Rossellini?"

• • •

I returned to the apartment. I waved to Rhoda in the kitchen and went to the living room bookcase for the copy of *Catch 22* and took it to Rhoda's bedroom. I sat in her easy chair and opened to page one and read: *It was love at first sight.*

"Oh, hell," I said. I put the book down and closed my eyes and saw Dila two years ago in the Black Panthers' office looking down at me, stretched out on a couch with her halo afro and her mismatched green eyes. I was barely conscious. I'd been kicked in the head by a cop named Halperin. "You're an angel," I had said at the time. And she'd yelled something about the white guy being awake and talking stupid.

It took me awhile to leave that time and return to the Second World War and the airbase on the Island of Pianosa in the Mediterranean. I fell asleep sitting up, and sometime during the night remember stumbling to the living room, and the couch and a pillow, two blankets and a glass of warm milk on the coffee table.

CHAPTER 36
JAY NESS

*"I'm a copper. . . as honest as you can get in a world
in which it is going out of style."*
Raymond Chandler, *The Big Sleep*

I woke up the next morning on Miss Rhoda's couch with Renee's ghost standing by the fireplace. She was wearing a Grateful Dead "Steal Your Face" Lightning Skull tie-dye shirt over Levis with holes in the knees. Startled at first, I sat up but fell back and closed my eyes just in case I was dreaming. When I opened them, she was still there.

"Welcome back, Renee," I said. "I hope you're here to help me because I can sure use it. You'll pardon me if I go take a shower." Then I remembered Neptune was in the bedroom. I peeked into the bedroom. The girl was curled into a fetal position and fast asleep.

I took a quick shower then found some new duds in the closet and came out. Neptune hadn't moved. She was breathing heavily, so I wasn't worried. I returned to the living room. Renee had changed into a Grateful Dead Roadies '70 Fillmore West tie-dye shirt.

"Are you trying to tell me something?" I asked. It was a foolish question because so far, my ghosts never talked to me. Why would Renee's ghost be any different? "I'm assuming you think I need to focus on the roadies. Correct? Correct," I answered for her. "I got to talk to Jay Ness first, okay. You remember Jay, don't you? Big belly, wide shoulders. You called him loveably ugly."

Miss Rhoda's voice came from my left, "Detective Friday."

I looked over to where she was standing at the entrance of the living room. She was wearing a silk dressing gown with half the Amazon jungle on it. The gown was the kind Renee had worn once when we'd treated

234

ourselves to a night at the Clairmont Hotel. I took a quick look at Renee's ghost. Was her ghost reading my thoughts? Her dress had been pink. She had called it a peignoir and was wearing it so she could look like Grace Kelly in *Rear Window*.

"Yes," I said.

"You either talking to yourself or you snuck a woman into my apartment while I was asleep."

"Talking to myself," I said. "Don't worry, Grandma Friday. I'm not going over the edge."

"Good, then I'm going to check on Neptune. Coffee will be ready soon."

I could smell the chicory. Miss Rhoda's coffee rivaled Mame's coffee at Ole's, my breakfast restaurant of choice. I went to the kitchen and sat down. Renee's ghost was watching me from the door. I was reading the *Oakland Tribune* when Miss Rhoda entered leading Neptune by the hand.

"You sit down here, girl. That man over there is Mr. Brovelli in case you don't remember. He doesn't bite. I'll get you some coffee."

Neptune whispered, "I remember."

"Lots of sugar, I'll bet," Miss Rhoda said.

Neptune nodded. Then she bent forward until her forehead rested on the kitchen table.

"Oh, Lord, I've been there, honey," Miss Rhoda crooned, placing the coffee in front of Neptune and adding three tablespoons of sugar. She drew a chair up and coaxed the girl to take a sip, all the while talking softly to her. I stayed behind the newspaper. I didn't want to intrude on such tenderness.

Two cups of coffee and half of a hot-cross bun later, Neptune looked a little better, although from time to time she clutched herself and shivered.

I figured she was well enough to listen to me. "Neptune, do you remember what we were talking about at Saint Agnes?"

"I think," she said. "Remind me."

"You saw two guys leading your friends away during the night."

"Yeah, they didn't want to go, that's for sure. The men were real mean looking. I was scared."

"I need you to remember all of that night as much as you can in detail."

"I can tell it to a cop, right?"

"Good, you do remember that."

"Good girl," Miss Rhoda said and hugged Neptune.

Neptune began to cry. There were tears in Miss Rhoda's eyes. There were tears in the eyes of Renee's ghost. How could that be? Perhaps I *was* going over the edge.

• • •

Jay had told Mr. Rossellini aka Theresa Bacigalupi, that he would meet with us at 6:00 p.m. at Grizzly Peak Road turnout. Through my rear-view mirror, I could see Neptune and Miss Rhoda in the back seat of the Olds, Miss Rhoda with her arm around the girl. The girl's head was resting on Miss Rhoda's shoulder. Jay had conveyed he message that his was a one-time deal. If he saw me again, he'd have to arrest me.

I'm not sure why he chose Grizzly Peak. It was a place of memories for me, the scene of last year's family tragedy. It was also the place where Renee and I used to go to make love. Why making love in a car turned Renee on had always been a mystery to me. I was thinking that Renee's ghost would approve of this choice of meeting places. Her ghost was sitting in the passenger seat. When I pulled in to the parking area, the ghost smiled.

Jay's car was already there. I parked next to him. He got out and slid in to the place occupied by Renee's ghost.

"This better be good, Victor," Jay said. "As bad a cop as Halpern was, he was still a cop. Every cop in the Bay Area has your photograph. No one is saying it out loud, but it's shoot to kill."

"*Merda*," I said.

"Yeah, shit is right," he said. "You're up to your Italian neck in it." He turned around in the seat and said hello to Miss Rhoda. "Is this the young lady who has something to tell me?"

"Her name is Neptune," I said. "Jay, she's made a deal with us. She'll tell you everything she knows about Saint Agnes's Church and in return I will pay for her rehab. Miss Rhoda knows a place with a great track record for helping with addiction."

"I'm going to use a tape recorder. If what you tell me pans out, young lady, we'll have to figure out how I got this recording."

It didn't take long for Neptune to describe that night in the basement of Saint Agnes's Church, adding a better description of one of the suspected kidnappers. She recalled he looked Hispanic and had an ear ring in his left ear. After Jay turned off the tape recorder, I told him that the bald guy with the earring sounded like one of the roadies who confronted me backstage of the Grateful Dead concert. We needed to talk to him—and we definitely had to find Ginger.

"Hold on, Victor," Jay said. "I'm not going to start hassling people just yet. Let's take a walk. You tell me your theories, I'm going to think about things, and then you are going to disappear and this meeting never happened."

We got out of the car and walked to the edge of the lookout and sat down on the log, which served as a bench and a barrier.

"Okay, so tell me about what you think is going on, Victor."

By the time I was finished explaining, Jay was holding his head in his hands. It was not a good sign. "Look," I said. "I know this sounds strange, but I'm positive I'm right."

"Victor, Victor, positive of what? That Father Boniface is a stone cold killer and heads up some kind of kidnapping ring because he is a twin and Cain came out of his mother first and Cain frigging slew Abel, which is a story in the Bible? The Bible, Victor, three-fourths of the population of the world doesn't believe in the Bible!" Jay's voice had increased about a couple of decibels. "Jesus, Mary and Joseph, do you have any idea how stupid that sounds?"

"No, no, no, listen, Jay. Boniface definitely was the guy seen by the bartender with Renee, right? Then, there's Ginger recruiting runaways at Grateful Dead concerts, right? Then, this kid Neptune seeing a couple of thugs hauling two of her friends off in the middle of the night, and now this recent description of one of the thugs that fits the guy Grillo, one of the band's roadies."

Jay groaned.

"Plus, you know me, Jay, over the last two years, haven't my annoying car noises been right? Tell me I'm wrong."

I watched Jay chewing his bottom lip, a sign he was thinking. I waited a while longer before asking, "Will you say something?"

What he said surprised me.

"Vincent told me at Saturday barbeque that he solved the Merriam mystery."

"He found Merriam?"

"Yeah, alive and well," Jay said. "He'd figured out that the music teacher and her were getting it on, and they were going to run away together."

"Has he told Parsegian?" I asked.

"Not as far as I know. But here's the thing, he found them at a Grateful Dead outdoor concert in Golden Gate Park, and he had to rescue her from being kidnapped by two guys Vincent described in detail. One of them that Vincent hit in the nose sounds like the bald guy your junkie described."

"My brother punched some guy in the nose?"

"Head-butted him was what he told me."

"Jay, you said there was another guy? What about him?"

"According to Vincent that guy is looking for a new pair of *cajónes*."

"*Mama mia*," I said. This was sounding like one more in a long list of Vincent Brovelli surprising tales of heroism that have thrilled the denizens of East 14th Street for years. Surprising because most people who've known the Brovelli twins have always dubbed me the wild one.

"Your mama and my mama," Jay replied.

"Was Vincent hurt?" I asked.

"Not at all. He and the girl and her boyfriend escaped without a scratch. Too bad for Parsegian, his daughter and her lover escaped for good. The last Vincent saw of them he said they were running away holding hands. Vincent told me he doubts they're going to go to Nick and his wife for their blessing."

What a stud, I thought, thinking of my twin.

"Vincent told me that Merriam was handcuffed, which matches the story your little junkie just told me."

"So, you believe me?" I said hopefully.

"About kidnapping, yes, to a degree. Something is happening for sure. But it could be just that Ginger is involved. It doesn't have to be the priest too. As for the priest and Renee, if a Christian Brother can lose his vows over Merriam, why not a Catholic priest over Renee? You understand what I'm telling you, Victor. This is *not* cut and dried by any means. Kidnapping young women is one thing. That's been going on for a long time. Big business in San Diego and LA and in Texas close to the Mexican border.

"But the priest being a murderer seems a little farfetched. You have absolutely no proof that Father Boniface is not who he says he is. If I start talking about Cain and Abel, and my captain will have me walking a beat. And how do you tie him to Officer Halpern's murder? Why would he kill a cop?"

"How about because all the evidence points to me?"

"You mean, the priest knew about the bad blood between you and Halpern. How?

"All right, maybe that's a stretch, but I believe Boniface murdered Renee, and according to my theory, Boniface murdered his twin brother, Louis. . ."

"And assumed his name and became a priest. You already told me. And I'm telling you again, it sounds like fiction."

"What are you going to do?"

"You and Vincent have convinced me about the possibility of kidnapping. The more I think about it, the more it makes sense that kidnappers would find a new crop of candidates hanging out in the Haight and at Grateful Dead concerts. I'm not going to go through chain of command. First, I'm going to talk to the San Francisco Knights. I'll start making calls tonight. By tomorrow we might have a few off duty undercover cops on the job, but you can't count on it. Like me, my guess is they're not going to be interested in trying to involve their captain without proof. Plus, these days most police departments are stretched to the max trying to stay ready for all the protests and antiwar shit. But you can rest assured the Knights of the Roundtable will sniff this out if it's true."

I should have been thankful to Jay, but I was not satisfied. The murder of Renee was foremost on my mind. "Boniface murdered Renee," I said.

"Prove it, and I'll arrest him," Jay said.

I knew Jay was right. I also knew I was right. I wish ghosts could talk. Renee would settle the question. Instead, my ghosts tended just to hover around me, occasionally providing me with some obscure encouragement or displeasure, like *hurry up and solve this damn thing, I've got a meeting at the pearly gates.*

I watched Jay drive away. Back in the car I asked Miss Rhoda for directions to the addiction clinic. It was not far away in Hayward, a town just south of Oakland. I took the Nimitz freeway. On the drive down, I listened to Miss Rhoda whispering to Neptune that she was doing the right thing and that she would visit her. Renee's ghost remained in the passenger seat.

After we dropped Neptune off in the care of a woman that looked like Aunt Bee in *The Andy Griffith Show*. Miss Rhoda took the passenger seat. It was a quiet drive back to her apartment.

In my head, I kept hearing Jay's voice saying, *"prove it, prove it."*

CHAPTER 37

HARD EVIDENCE

*"Before crime is committed, conscience must be corrupted
and every bad man who succeeds in reaching a high point
of wickedness begins with this."*
Henri-Frederic Amiel

I slept fitfully before I woke up and sat on the side of the bed thinking. My best bet to find the kind of evidence Jay needed was with the roadie that Neptune identified as the bald Mexican wearing an earring. I make a quick bathroom run and went to the kitchen where I found a note from Miss Rhoda telling me that she was off to her church for choir practice. I looked at the wall clock. 8:46 a.m.

The coffee was cold so I reheated it. I pulled a couple of oatmeal raisin-bran cookies out of Miss Rhoda's gigantic ceramic cookie jar shaped like a red delicious apple. The Oakland Tribune was open as usual to the *Dear Abby* page. A woman was in love with two men equally and need Abby's advice.

I skipped the advice and turned to the news section. Nothing about Halpern's murder on the front page. On page six, I found a small column that said the investigation was ongoing.

Renee's ghost joined me at the table. She was wearing a mini skirt and crossed her legs. "Are you going to be with me the rest of the way?" I asked her. "It's not a rhetorical question," I added. At least Renee's ghost was a smiling ghost, unlike the gloomy or impatient ghosts of my past. "Why don't you make it easy on me and tell me who murdered you?"

What happened next was something I would always remember. I heard Renee's voice, or I heard my voice that sounded like Renee. Whatever it was, my imagination or a spiritual encounter, it went like this:

"*I knew Merriam from the youth orchestra. When she disappeared, I went looking for her in all the obvious places, the most obvious in the Haight. That's where I met Father Boniface. Well, you know me, Victor, I've always craved a little excitement, so when he came on to me with those dark, dangerous eyes, what was a girl to do? It was all fun and games until I found out what he was up to. He started getting suspicious. And the next thing, well, you know what happened. I wish I could tell you why he wants to pin my murder on you. I swear I never mentioned you, ever.*"

I cut my reverie short. *Wait a minute*, I thought. That last part could not have been my imagination. Renee *must* have told him about me—*must have* because if she didn't then the attempt to frame me for her murder didn't make any sense—and framing me for Officer Halpern's murder made even less sense. I remembered that Jay had also brought this up. I looked at Renee's ghost. "I suppose you're not going to explain, are you?"

It was at this point that I began to wonder if ghosts really existed. In Napoli and throughout southern Italy, people take the spirits of the departed very seriously. Okay, so I was Italian and my family was from Naples.

I stood up and paced the kitchen. I drank another cup of coffee. By now I was pretty wired.

The doorbell ringing startled me. I went to the door and looked through the peak hole. On the other side was someone who looked a lot like a cockatiel. I opened the door.

"Daddy-o."

"Sweets, what the hell? How did you find me?"

"My brothers at the Panthers' office told me."

"Your brothers?"

"You haven't noticed all these years, I'm bi-racial."

Total bullshit, but I was happy to see Sweets. I waved him into the apartment and ushered him into the kitchen. "You want some coffee?"

"To be sure, *mon ami*. Half and half with lots of sugar."

I made his to his specs and brought it back to the table with two cookies "What brings you here, Sweets?"

"I had a feeling. Victor Brovelli needs the services of Sweets Monroe, flashing in my brain. I think to myself, Victor doesn't have enough of a criminal mind to find out the real killer. This killer be very smart. Could be you got a killer wit' two brains, you see what I'm saying?"

I didn't. But, I had to admit that Sweets had a point that I could use some help. While we drank coffee and ate cookies, I explained my research. He didn't blink except to say Cain was sure enough a bad dude. I filled him in about New Orleans and what Miss Rhoda and I had uncovered.

"You probably blew any chance of talking to the roadie or that girl Ginger. I'm betting they're halfway to Mexico City by now."

"Maybe," I said, "But we need to find out for sure."

"We'll take a run to Fillmore West later," Sweets said. "Shindig be going on for the release of the Grateful Dead's new album, *Working Man's Dead*. Sort of a private party sing-along kind of teeng. Doesn't start until 9:00 p.m. Gives us lots of time. You got more of them cookies?"

I pushed my plate toward him. "You think Ginger and her pal are in the wind?"

"Criminals live on their animal brains, you know that leetle stem at the base of their skulls that says 'here come the lion, time to boogie.'"

"Would they have told Boniface before bolting, do you think?"

"Fifty-fifty. Depends how scared they were. You know that your bro put a hurt on a couple of bad guys trying to haul Merriam off. You know that, right?"

"Jay told me yesterday."

"And Vincent told me last night," Sweets said. "Tough guy, Vincent, no?"

"Tough guy, yes," I said.

Sweets looked toward the kitchen door and made the sign of the cross.

"You see Renee?" I asked.

"*Non*, but I feel her good spirit. Renee be a stand-up lady. Some folks, you know, make fun of Sweets Monroe, you dig. Not her. She always say hey and give me smiles. A real lady and that's the truth. I help you find this killer with two brains."

Sweets stood up. He put a couple of cookies in his jacket pocket.

"I'll be back around eight, *mon ami*," Sweets said and stood up. "Renee, one fine lady," he repeated as he headed for the door.

Perhaps Sweets was my *ami*, my friend. I'd have to give that some thought.

• • •

Rhoda returned. I told her of Sweets' visit. She said he sounded interesting. I told Miss Rhoda I had hours before Sweets' return. I decided to use the time doing more research at the library. Perhaps I might find something new to support my theory.

"It wouldn't hurt," Miss Rhoda said, but she wouldn't let me leave until she did her magical makeup transformation, covering my scar and darkening my eyebrows. This time she placed a mole on my right cheek. "A beauty mark," she called it. I dressed in my West Oakland attire, buttoned my shirt at the top. As I left, I took the McClymonds letterman's jacket off the hook in the hall. My A's baseball cap was on backwards.

Outside, Big Boy Clarence said, "McClymonds gonna kick ass in football this season."

I handed him three dollars. He nodded. So did I.

The morning commute had already cleared up and I'd be at the library in twenty minutes.

• • •

Most of the books and articles about twins dealt with the normal phenomenon: Sisters who gave birth to twins on the same day; the British school with 20 sets of twins; twins that had been separated at birth about 30 years, reunited. It was enjoyable reading but nothing that I felt had anything to do with my set of twins, Charlie and Louie. I turned to the mythology of twins and planned on reading the rest of the afternoon.

Two hours later, I'd found only one myth that held my interest. It was from West Africa and called the *Ibeji*. According to the myth, twins were one soul shared by two bodies. If one twin died, the parents carved a doll to represent the dead twin. If they didn't, the remaining twin would soon die. As long as the doll existed, that twin could live a normal life span. This tradition, I read, had made its way from Africa to the Caribbean, then to Louisiana. It was still part of the Voodoo religion. I was not sure why this felt important to me, but I wrote the details in my notebook.

• • •

I was back to Miss Rhoda's in time for meatloaf, green beans and mashed potatoes. When Sweets arrived, he and Miss Rhoda hit it off immediately. They sat at the kitchen table and swapped New Orleans stories while Sweets ate all of the leftovers. Miss Rhoda was raised in New York City, but her father's side was from Louisiana. Sweets, well, where else would you find the descendant of the pirate Jean Lafitte except in the Big

Easy? I enjoyed Miss Rhoda's' family tales. Sweets's tales I'd heard so often my eyes began to glaze over.

• • •

By eight o'clock, Sweets and I arrived at Fillmore West. The event was free. The interior of the upstairs hall was crowded. A light show was going on and Grateful Dead songs were coming out of loud speakers.

The Dead were not here, but somebody had to put this show together. The roadies probably. We made slow progress inching in the direction of the stage. We arrived and were immediately halted by a large security guard. I began to talk, but Sweets interrupted.

"*Mon frere,*" he started and continued until the guard help up both his hands in surrender.

"I'll see what I can do," he said and disappeared behind the curtain.

As is the case with Sweets when he's on a verbal roll, it is hard to understand his eloquence. He becomes part preacher, part good friend, part psychologist, the latter having to do with saying just the right thing at the right time. I asked Sweets about this one time, and he told me it was a matter of knowing when to push a person off a cliff or keep him from falling. I've never figured that out.

The guard came back. Behind him was a man who introduced himself as a manager.

"Why are you looking for Brillo?" he asked.

My lie that an old friend from Mexico had asked me to bring him some money he owed him was met with skepticism.

"I'm sorry, mate. Brillo is AWOL. I'm not really happy. We just hired him and now he's gone, and we're about to go to Hawaii for a series of concerts. Not easy to find a solid replacement."

I didn't think he was lying, so we thanked him and Sweets and I inched our way back to the entrance and out into a world without strobe-lights.

"We boogie to the church," Sweets said. "If we be lucky, they left without telling the priest. He thinks he's safe."

I was beginning to wonder who the private investigator was, me or Sweets. Sweets answered my question with his next statement.

"If he's around, I cut the muthafucka up. Renee be your woman, but she be Sweets's friend."

"Whoa, whoa, Sweets. Nobody said anything about cutting anybody. We need evidence so Jay can arrest the creep. We got to do this legally."

"Some big-time lawyer gets him a reduced sentence; he be out in ten years," Sweets said. "Remember you told me there's no way to prove he's not the real priest. They don't gas priests, *mon frere*, you dig?"

"Are you serious? If we can prove he raped and murdered Renee, a magician couldn't keep him out of the gas chamber."

"You one living fairytale, Victor. You got money, you got power. I cut him up, drop him in the ocean at land's end. Sharks take care of justice. When you live in the fourth world as long as I have, the rules are different."

"What the hell's the fourth world?"

"It's the shadow world, *mon ami*. Everybody has a shadow. Folks too fearful to climb into their shadows, see the other side."

I could feel a headache coming on. I raised my hand to stop the journey into shadow land. "Enough, Sweets," I said. "You do it my way, legal, or you can go home. I appreciate you coming to assist me, but we're not killers."

Sweets cocked his head and squinted. Was his brain saying "*maybe you aren't*"? I couldn't get into that cockatiel head.

Finally, he said. "Okay. We do it legal. Now what's the legal plan?"

That was the question. So far, I'd been moving on instinct. "Well, before we get to that, we have to be sure Father Boniface has not flown the coup like Brillo and Ginger. If he has then I'm screwed. I'm going to call the rectory. The housekeeper will know."

There was a telephone booth down the street. I was in and out in a couple of minutes. I gave Sweets a thumbs up. "Not only is he not there, he's away from the church doing confessions at an old folks' home in Daly City. It sounds as if he's doing his priestly duties, which means to me he doesn't know Ginger and the Mexican roadie are gone."

"Agreed," said Sweets.

"That one time you and I were there," I said, "remember Ginger had a friend sitting with her. Do you remember her name?"

"It was something that started with a K, like some veg-ee-table."

"Like kale," I said.

"Yeah, like that." Sweets said. "Rabbit food."

"Boniface called them assistants. Maybe she and Ginger worked together."

"You think you can get her to confess?"

"Sarcasm noted, you *chooch*," I said. "You got a better idea?"

"I don't see no beeg plan, Victor. I don't. Boniface don't stick around unless he damn confident he covered his ass. If that veg-ee-table chick is still there and she's in on the kidnapping, she don't be there either unless she knows her butt is safe. You dig? We talk to her about the padré and she gets hip to it, she tips him off. Then they both fly like the birdies."

I hate it when I'm wrong. I hate it more when Sweets is right. "So, we find out that Brillo and Ginger have skipped town and that's all we've accomplished."

"Not all," Sweet said. "That veg-ee-table might know some teengs that can help."

"I thought you said if we talked to her, it would tip off Boniface."

"*Moi*, not you, Victor. She see me only once. I go like I be New Orleans friend of the priest. She remembers that we talk Cajun. I smooth-talk her. You stay in the car and wait for Sweets."

We drove to Saint Agnes. I parked a couple of blocks away from the church. Sweets got out and ambled down the street, his cockatiel hairdo swinging side to side. He stopped and gave something to a kid on the sidewalk with his hand out. Probably money, but it could have been some hard candies or perhaps both.

Sweets's boom box sat on the passenger seat. I pushed the on button. Zydeco. Thank God it wasn't the Grateful Dead. I listened for a while then turned it off. An hour later, Sweets opened the passenger side door and slipped in.

"Got the scoop, *mon ami*. But you not going to like it."

"Tell me you didn't let on and she's running to tell Boniface as we speak."

"What you think Sweets is a dumbass? She dig what I was after from the get-go."

"Damn, you just said she's not going to be suspicious and tell Father Boniface."

"She a cool one all right. Unless I'm stupid, she truly is his assistant. She tells me like this, 'Mr. Monroe,' she say, 'Ginger is gone for good,' like she know what for good means like forever. Then she say real proud like, 'Father Boniface will be here helping teenagers for a long, long time. He's not worried at all.'"

"That sounds like she is talking only about the safe-house."

"Why she say that fake padré not worried? Why those words?" Sweets added.

"What do you think she meant?"

"*Moi*, I tink she meant Ginger and Brillo going to wash up on some beach someday soon."

"Really?"

"I'd put money on it," Sweets said. "That girl no burnout, come to the safe-house and get saved then go to work for the priest. There's nothing hippie-dippie about her. Smart veg-ee-table, looking and her eyes be laughing at me."

"How do you think she figured out they were in trouble?"

"I'm guessing that Ginger and Brillo come here to their boss. They talk. They never talk again. See what I'm saying?"

Sometimes I get so exasperated with Sweets's Cajun-Creole-Seminole-interplanetary accent that I don't see at all what he's saying. This did sound possible. I was disgusted with myself. I should have formulated a real fool proof plan before talking to Ginger. But then, I wouldn't have found Neptune. I started the car and pulled away from the curb.

"Where we go now?" Sweets asked.

"Back to Miss Rhoda's apartment, and I'm not leaving until I have a solid plan to bring down Father Boniface."

CHAPTER 38

TO GHOST OR NOT TO GHOST

"Nel corso della vita, una persona incontrera almeno un fantasma.
In the course of a lifetime, a person will encounterat least one ghost."
Sicilian proverb

At midnight, I left Sweets and Miss Rhoda still sitting at the kitchen table and went to my bedroom. We had put our three heads together and come up with three empty heads. I fell asleep to the muted sound of Miss Rhoda singing some blues number and Sweets singing harmony.

• • •

The next morning, I showered, dressed and went to the kitchen. The wall clock read not yet six in the morning. I put the coffee on then retrieved the Oakland Tribune from the hall and returned to the kitchen. I read while drinking my coffee. The front-page stories were about the endless Vietnam War and the economy. I was about to turn the page when I felt a breeze on the back of my neck as if someone opened the front door. I turned around and looked down the hall. The door was closed. When I turned back, Renee's ghost was sitting in front of me. She was not wearing Grateful Dead clothes. "I always liked that dress," I said.

I turned back to the newspaper. Surprisingly, I found it was now open to the sports page. I had been reading the news.

Okay, Renee what do you want me to read? There was a story in the sports' page about a Little League baseball team. The entire team was made up of students from one elementary school. There was a photograph of the team with their beaming coaches standing on either side of the boys. The point of the article was how unusual it was for all the kids coming from one school. It reminded me of my elementary school, and that reminded me of my fifth-grade teacher, Sister Josephine or as she was better known as Sister Jo, Rocking Jo or Kick-Ass Jo, our baseball coach. She could hit home runs and pitch fastballs and curves. And. . . and. . .

There was something else in my mind about Sister Jo. I stared at the photograph. *Come on, come on, what is it?* I stood up and began pacing. I knew this was important. Renee's ghost had left the page open for me to read for a reason. I walked out into the hall and came back. I sat down, I stood up. I sat down again.

"Renee, help me out here," I said aloud.

"I missed what you said, Mr. Brovelli."

I turned around as Miss Rhoda entered the kitchen. "I was talking to myself. The coffee is hot."

"I smelled it all the way back in my room."

A sleepy-looking Sweets Monroe stumbled from the living room where Miss Rhoda must have tucked him in on her couch the previous evening.

"Café au lait for me, Victor."

"The cream is in the refrigerator," Miss Rhoda said. "We got no waiters here."

When we were all seated and drinking coffee, I explained about the photograph and that it had triggered something important in my memory which related to our murder case. I was sure of it, but I just could not remember.

"It's like on the tip of my tongue," I said. Both of them looked at the photograph.

"I can't hardly remember my elementary school," Miss Rhoda said. "They were all numbers in New York City. P.S. 65 maybe, or was it P.S. 56?"

"I went to a Catholic elementary school," Sweets said. "One through eight. Those nuns beat crap outta me."

"I had a 6th grade teacher name of Martha Wiggins," Miss Rhoda said. "She was my guardian angel. I swear I loved that woman. She ran the choir. She encouraged me to sing."

"I do remember one Sister who was nice to me," Sweets said. "I was always getting in trouble even back then, but she said she could see inside me and knew I was good at heart."

"That's it," I shouted, leaping from my chair. "I got it. When Vincent and I were in elementary school, none of the teachers could tell us apart. Except Sister Jo. She said there was something that gave Vincent away. I can't remember what it was, but I can find out. As far as I know, Sister Jo is still teaching."

"What's the point, Victor?" Sweets asked.

"Don't you get it?"

"I get it, Detective Saturday," Miss Rhoda said. "It's a bit of a long shot, but what if there was an elementary school teacher in New Orleans like your Sister Jo who knew how to tell Charlie from Louie? "We might have to drive back to New Orleans," Miss Rhoda said. "It's going to take some leg work to talk to all the elementary teachers that those two boys had."

I saw the highways stretching out in front of me. "Well, we know their ages, right? We have that off the stuff you snatched at the diocese. They're both 41. Elementary school starts at first grade, six years old about. Right? It's 1970. Go back 35 years."

"Class of 1935," Miss Rhoda said.

"Dude, that's a lot of classes," Sweets said, "and you don't even know what elementary school they went to."

"Their mama would know," Miss Rhoda said. "I'll call. It's almost noon in Louisiana." Miss Rhoda found her purse and brought out a brochure for Bayou Bay Senior Living Residence. She went to the wall phone and dialed. She asked to speak to Mrs. Eugenie Dubois then listened.

She hung up and returned to the table. "Mrs. Dubois has suffered a stroke. She may not live."

I made the sign of the cross. "I liked her," I said.

"We know the high school," Miss Rhoda said.

I continued her thought. "All Catholic high schools have feeder elementary schools. We start with those."

"Eight years of classes," Miss Rhoda said.

"Can't be helped," I said. "At least the way it looks, Father Boniface thinks he's safe and is sticking around. We might have time, if we get right to work."

"It's best if all three of us go," Miss Rhoda said. "There's a good chance that many of the teachers are retired and living elsewhere. Three of us will cover more ground."

"Some of the teachers could be dead," Sweets said.

"You can talk to those," I said.

"*Tres amusent*," Sweets said.

"We go to the Bayou Bay home anyway," I said. "Mrs. Dubois would have memorabilia stored. My mom has boxes in the attic. Teacher's write letters to parents about how good their child is, like that. I bet we could talk them into letting us look through her stuff."

"Leave hotel reservations to me," Sweets said. "I got deals."

"Victor, wait here," Miss Rhoda said. "I'll need to get cover the scar better and touch up your eyebrows some, and don't shave today."

CHAPTER 39
THE NUNS

*"Tutti gli student bruseranno luminosi finche ci
sara un insegnanta ad accendere il fuoco.
All students will burn brightly as long as there is a teacher
to light the fire."*
Italian proverb

Mr. Rossellini had made another successful call to the Brovelli Brothers' Used Cars. No reply was required. Theresa was informed that Mr. Rossellini would be out of town for a few days.

Miss Rhoda and I packed then drove Sweets to his place to do the same, dropping him off a block away from his apartment building, which happened to be my apartment building, much to my regret. Having a burglar living in the same building as a future P.I. seemed sort of counter intuitive.

By early afternoon we were on the road. We drove straight through as I was still wanted for Renee's murder, taking turns sleeping in the back seat and driving with rest stops only for food and bathroom breaks. Rhoda brought pillows, blankets and a little boom box along a collection of jazz vocalist. Sweets brought a few Zydeco tapes. We drove south on Interstate 5 as far as Barstow where we turned east onto Route 66 towards Flagstaff, Arizona.

We listened to Rhoda sing "(Get Your Kicks on) Route 66". By Gallop, New Mexico, Jay McShann entertained us with "Hooties Blues" and "I'll Catch the Sun". From Gallop on, the New Mexico landscape was burnt orange and dotted with mesas and juniper trees. Sweets spoke of his Navajo cousin, which interested Miss Rhoda but I ignored him. There was no ethnic group that Sweets did not belong to. We reached the town of

Grants with Clifton Chenier doing the "Zydeco Cha Cha".

I spent more time than I should have thinking about Dila. The good memories mostly, but sometimes good memoires can be painful. Sweets entertained us with a history of burglary. The first account of a well-known burglar Crispus Leonidis, the Elder had been recorded by the Greek historian, Herodotus.

We raced across the Texas panhandle, stopping only once in Amarillo that Sweets christened Armadillo. We hit the border of Louisiana listening to "A Good Man is Hard to Find" by Helen Hume. By the time we arrived in New Orleans, I felt as if I was an expert on jazz vocalists. And if I heard another Beau Solei Zydeco tune, I would commit suicide.

The last two hours of the drive, Miss Rhoda and Sweets slept. I woke them up. Sweets mumbled something about jambalaya. He gave me directions to the DeSoto Hotel, which he announced with pride was the most expensive and fanciest hotel in the city of his youth. I was not going to argue about the expense at this point of exhaustion. We pulled up to the entrance and were greeted by a bellman who was dressed like the tiny man pictured on the back of Phillip Morris cigarette packs. We checked in and were shown to our rooms. I might have been asleep before I hit the bed.

In the morning, Miss Rhoda and I were sitting in the lobby waiting for Sweets.

"Leave it to Sweets," I said to Miss Rhoda, waving her hand over our regal surroundings.

"I love those marble railings," she said. "The clerk told me they came from a hotel in Paris. Imagine." The lobby was full of antique furniture, elegant oriental rugs, Renaissance art and marble sculptures.

"That Sweets Monroe must have some connections," she said.

"Sweets is a wealth of surprises," I said. I wasn't kidding. Our neighborhood burglar never had more than a few bucks on him at one time, but he had a financial portfolio; he ate mostly at pancake houses and burger joints but was often treated to free meals at the finest restaurants in the Bay Area; he'd drink cheap jug wine but could tell the difference between a 2015 Chateaux Margaux and a 1982 Chateau Rothschild Paulliac. How do I know this? I was at Ozzie Averbuck's A & B Liquors in the wine section watching Sweets on a bet do a blindfold taste test.

The police hated Sweets, but he was on a first name basis with many of our most influential Bay Area politicians. Years ago, he had saved our pop and his business from a Mexican gang called the Amigos, and the Black Panthers referred to him as Brother Sweets. He sucked on hard candy constantly, leaving the wrappings wherever they fell, which drove Theresa nuts, never paid his bar tab and was an unreliable boyfriend.

"But here's the kicker," I said to Miss Rhoda, "after every burglary, single moms found bags of groceries, toys and clothes on their doorsteps, that included envelopes filled with cash."

"That's some history, Detective Saturday," she said.

History for our East 14th Street neighborhood was news to Miss Rhoda, and she was impressed. "I could go on and on," I said.

"Another time," Miss Rhoda said. "I'm having difficulty digesting what you told me."

A bellboy walked by crying out in a loud voice for a Mr. Louis Prima to go to the entertainment desk for a message. Sunlight was streaming in through the tall windows, brightening the leaves of giant potted ferns. A couple of minutes later the elevator doors opened and someone who looked a lot like Sweets Monroe stepped out and walked toward us.

"*Mais ami,*" this elegantly dressed, beautifully coiffed gentleman said.

"Where is Sweets Monroe, descendant of Jean Lafitte?" I asked.

"He is going to talk to *Les Soeurs*. If I go as myself, the nuns will hit me with rulers. Nuns frighten me," he answered.

A grown man afraid of nuns. Miss Rhoda and I began laughing at the same time. When I finally caught my breath, I stood up. "Let's get going," I said. Miss Rhoda was still laughing.

"I miss your usual lovely hairdo," I said.

"I disregard your sarcasm," Sweets said.

We left the Olds at the hotel and found a cab. We stopped first at Bayou Bay Senior Living. Sweets stayed in the cab while Miss Rhoda and I went inside. We were met by good news. Mrs. Dubois had recovered. She was weak but able to talk, though only to one person at a time. Miss Rhoda told me to wait. She returned a few minutes later to tell me that Mrs. DuBois could not remember the boys' elementary school.

"I'll stay on and talk to her," Miss Rhoda said. "You guys go ahead. "You never know what the old girl may remember. I'm just going to hold her hand for a while." She'd meet us back at the hotel.

Sweets and I went on to the elementary school that served the twins' high school. We had an appointment with Sister Maria Innocentia for 9:00 a.m., and we were a little early. I walked to the church for a quick look. Sweets said he'd pass since the roof might fall on him if he stepped inside.

I entered, genuflected and sat for a while. *A small prayer wouldn't hurt*, I thought and whispered a quick *Hail Mary*. I was praying and hoping that I would find the murderers and finally be cleared of what I was accused of by the Oakland police department.

A half hour later, Sweets and I were sitting in front of the principal. Even seated I could tell she was tall. Her shoulders were wide. Her wimple framed a strong-jawed woman.

"I need for you to explain what kind of an article you are writing, Mr. Teagarden. Our telephone conversation did not clarify enough for me"

I took my time, trying to add additional impressive details.

"And this is on behalf of the San Francisco Diocese, correct?"

"Yes, Sister," I said. "I finished the article, but on rereading it, I decided I needed to dig deeper in Father Boniface's life. It's my belief that one's best traits are nurtured in elementary school as far back as first grade."

Sweets added, "Elementary school was when I learned about morals and ethics."

I almost choked. The principal's stern face softened, and she smiled.

"I just had to be certain," she said. "I have asked our librarian to pull out all of the class photographs for each grade level Father Boniface was in. I was not the principal back then, but you can talk to Sister Augustine who was. She now teaches 3rd grade mathematics." The principal stood up and so did we. She asked her secretary to escort us to the library.

Two hours later, Sweets and I had no candidates. None of the teachers' year-end notes contained anything that would help us tell the twins apart. Most of the time, the nuns relied on Louis to own up to who he was, never Charles. And Charlie was always the boy mentioned as being naughty. In my mind this confirmed that Charles was the bad seed, but as Sweets reminded me such an observation would not hold up in court. This was not to mention all of my research as it was so eloquently pointed out in no uncertain terms by Detective Jay Ness, who'd turned apoplectic when I explained to him about Cain and Abel.

The principal's secretary telephoned for a taxi, and we rode back to the hotel in silence. I hoped that Miss Rhoda had come up with something or we'd wasted our time coming to New Orleans. Then, where the hell would

I find evidence to support my theory?

Miss Rhoda was sitting in the lobby in an armchair that looked as if it once held the French Sun King. Two similar antique chairs were arranged around a small marble table. A tall drink with a tiny umbrella in it stood on the table. When she saw us, she smiled broadly. My heart soared.

"Have a mint julip," she said, lifting the glass.

We ordered two from a passing waiter and sat down beside her. "Well," I said.

"Not until the drinks come back. We have to toast."

My heart soared.

The waiter returned with our drinks, Miss Rhoda said, "I got what we wanted to know."

"Tell us," I said.

"Mrs. Dubois had a trunk of memorabilia. She was in no condition to show me but told me the trunk was in the back of her closet. Looking through it was a long haul. All very organized. It took me a while just to get through baby pictures and the terrible twos and the easier threes until I got to elementary school. I took the bundle to Mrs. Dubois. Once she got started, it was hard to keep her from showing me every single photograph and commenting. As well as photos, there were letters from teachers. Most of the letters were about Lewis, praising him for this or that. I was about to give up when we came to a drawing of a nun. No great drawing, but it was done by Charles in the fourth grade. At the top of the drawing, he'd written in big block letters: *My Favorite Teacher Sister Mary*. And on the bottom, he'd drawn a heart."

"Just Sister Mary? How old do you think this sister is now?"

"I asked Mrs. Dubois. She didn't remember a Sister Mary at all. So much of her memory is gone. I hope it comes back. She's got a lot of spirit, but you know. . ."

Sweets interrupted, "If this nun is dead. . ." His voice trailed off.

"We must find out," I said. I looked at my watch. It was late afternoon. Classes were certainly over, but knowing the nuns, the administration would still be at work. "Let's go up to my room. I'm going to call the elementary school, and you two cross your fingers."

Fifteen minutes later I hung up the phone. Luck was with us. At the time the Dubois twins were in school, Sister Mary Rose was a first-year teacher. She was still teaching art. If we could get here before five, she'd be pleased to talk to us. I was the first person out of the door. I gave the taxi driver the address and told him I'd tip big if he got us there the quickest way. It was a scary ride, but we pulled up in front of the school a little after four-thirty.

A young nun escorted us to the art room. I introduced myself, Sweets and Miss Rhoda to a short, slender nun with a café au lait complexion. Large black-rimmed spectacles peered out of the perimeter of her white wimple.

"I'm pleased to meet you," the nun said. "Our principal explained this is for an article about Lewis Dubois.

"We actually have all we need about Lewis. As your principal probably told you, these days Lewis is Father Boniface."

Sister Mary Rose nodded.

I continued. "We decided that as a twin, some mention of his brother, Charles, would add to the background. Our readers would be interested in what their relationship was. You know how curious people are about twins." I had said this so many times recently that I was beginning to believe I was actually writing an article.

Sweets said, "Two Cajun twins, one becomes a soldier, the other a priest, you see how very intriguing, n'est pas?"

"Je comprend. Are you from Louisiana?"

"Born and raised," Sweets replied. "I almost went into the seminary myself."

"I am Creole, but we lived close to a Cajun community, so I learned French."

I saw Miss Rhoda roll her eyes. Like me, she was probably thinking this nun was willing to help us. Sweets was wasting our time doing his Cajun, we-all-one-big-Big Easy-family thing.

I interrupted. "What was Charles like? Lewis was a good student and never a discipline problem. Was this true of Charlie?"

"Charles. I never called him Charlie. He didn't like the diminutive. But for all the other teachers, it was always Louie et Charlie. Charles was not a good student in his academic classes, but he worked hard for me in art. He didn't draw well, unlike his twin, but he was talented with clay and carving. Some of his wood carvings were quite excellent. I have to tell you I felt a little sorry for Charles. All the other teachers clearly preferred Louis."

The question had to be asked. "Tell me, Sister Mary, were you able to tell the two apart?"

"Oh, no. Those boys were the most identical twins I'd ever had seen in my life, let alone in my teaching career, which I was just starting at the time. Unlike some twins, who make an effort to create ways for people to tell them apart, you know like combing their hair differently, dressing differently, the Dubois boys delighted in being identical."

"Was there no way you could tell?" Miss Rhoda asked. "Their mother told me if anyone could, you could."

I lifted my head up slightly and let the prayer "*please, God*" rise in the direction of heaven.

"I had a few teacher/parent conferences with Mrs. Dubois. A lovely lady. No, I couldn't tell them apart, but there was a way finally. I discovered it by accident."

"And how was that?" Miss Rhoda asked.

"When Charles became angry, he stuttered. I noticed it a couple of times on the playground when he got into a confrontation with another student."

I let Sweets and Miss Rhoda continue the conversation until we could politely take our leave. I had what I needed, a way to prove to Jay that Father Boniface was Charles Dubois and not Lewis Dubois. The question that had to be answered now was how to make Father Boniface angry and how to do it in front of witnesses.

In the taxi heading back to the hotel, Miss Rhoda said. "It's good, but not good enough. We must see Mrs. Dubois again. There is no way she wouldn't have noticed this in Charles. You can't tell me Charles and Lewis never got angry as children."

Sweets agreed. Grandma Friday had a point. Jay would be more impressed if we had the mother to back up the teacher's word. I directed the taxi driver to Mrs. Dubois' retirement home. When we arrived, Miss Rhoda explained it would be better if she talked to Mrs. Dubois alone. Sweets and I waited in the taxi with the meter running. By the time Miss Rhoda returned, the taxi driver and Sweets had become best friends and Sweets had invited him and his family to visit him in California.

Miss Rhoda slid into the back seat with me and said, "Sister Mary was telling the truth."

"Why didn't Mrs. Dubois tell us in the first place?"

"She didn't want to embarrass her son," Miss Rhoda said.

"She hasn't heard from her son for years," Sweets said.

"That doesn't matter. She's a mother."

"The mother of a killer," Sweets said.

CHAPTER 40
THE WAR CABINET

"We are so accustomed to disguise ourselves to others
that in the end, we become disguised to ourselves."
Francois de la Rochefoucauld

On Sunday afternoon, the telephone at the Brovelli Brothers' car lot rang. Theresa answered. It was Mr. Rossellini back from his business trip leaving a message for Mr. Vincent Brovelli. After the call, Mr. Rossellini drove to Saint Patrick's Church in Oakland to attend late mass.

There, I lit a dozen candles for the success of our mission and for our future success. Miss Rhoda began baking, even exhausted as she was from our nonstop drive. Sweets was asleep on Miss Rhoda's living room couch. When I returned from Mass, I called Jay and explained what we'd discovered. We made plans to meet at Rhoda's the next day.

Rhoda finished her baking and went to her room. I tried to read but could not keep my eyes open. I fell asleep in the recliner and woke up sore around midnight. The next time I woke up, it was Monday morning and the sun was shining.

• • •

By afternoon, the war cabinet was assembled around Miss Rhoda's kitchen table. Besides us, it included Homicide Detective Jay Ness and one of his San Francisco police officer friends named Drew Darby, and much to my surprise, my twin who'd arrived from Oakland with Jay. And, standing by the door to the kitchen was Renee's ghost. She was looking very pleased.

Miss Rhoda had made what she called her version of high tea: scones with large slices of thick honey-baked ham along with a variety of cheeses. She'd baked a shepherds pie and an apple pie. Miss Rhoda offered coffee and soft drinks; no booze until we were finished reviewing our plan. She had set out her best china and cloth napkins. We had all laughed when Jay said planning war doesn't usually start with scones.

It had not taken me as long as I thought it would to convince Jay that we now had enough evidence to support my theory that Charles DuBois had murdered his twin brother Louis and assumed his identity for the purpose of kidnapping hippie teenage girls and selling them to a Mexican Cartel. I would leave the cartel part to law enforcement. It made me happy to know Vincent and I would be working together to bring this case to a close.

Still, I missed my Girl Friday, Dila Agbo. If our plan worked, and I was exonerated, the first thing I was going to do was take a flight to New York City. Whatever Dila was facing, I would face it with her.

"Let's go over it one more time," Jay said.

"All right. Before we go to the church this afternoon, you're going to put a wire on me, so everything Boniface says will be recorded."

"Check," Jay said.

"You have fellow officers who will be there to make sure Kayla doesn't escape through the backdoor before you arrest her. Is Kayla her name?"

"I've got that covered," Darby, Jay's officer friend said.

"I've called to see if Father Boniface will be in tomorrow hearing confessions," Miss Rhoda said. "I told the secretary I was a poor old sinner."

"That's perfect," I said. "It will be my job to lure him down into the basement."

"You know how you're going to do that—all squared away?"

"Absolutely," I said. "The confession I have for him will not be one he wants to hear."

"Remember, our goal is to anger him," Miss Rhoda said. "If we have him on tape stuttering, we'll have enough to pressure Kayla into being a witness against him."

"That's what we've decided," I said. "I promise you I'll prime him." Vincent asked. "What about Sister Mary? Didn't you say she's going to be here?"

Sweets smiled broadly. "We don't need the real sister, we have our own Sister Mary, don't we Sister Rhoda?"

Rhoda nodded. "No worries, Vincent. I have a friend who owns a nun's habit. She wore it for last Halloween. I'm going to wear it and present myself to him as his art teacher Sister Mary Rose who cares for him and wants him to give himself up."

"By then," Sweets continued, "he'll be so spooked that he'll be stuttering all over himself."

"Theoretically." Jay said. "We're only going to have one chance to make this work."

"I'm a pretty good actress," Rhoda said. "With a little makeup and the wimple, he'll believe I'm his elementary school teacher."

Vincent said, "But is Sister Mary black?"

"She is Creole," Miss Rhoda said. "She must have some African in her. Our skin color is not much different. And it has been a lot of years since the priest has seen her. I'll be wearing those black-rimmed glasses she wore even as a young nun. I'll put a little rouge on my cheeks. What does Boniface possibly remember? A kindly young face, now grown old, glasses and a nun's habit."

"Inside those wimples," Sweets said, "they all look kind of the same."

"What's a wimple?" the San Francisco cop, Officer Darby, asked.

"A bonnet like a hoodie with little white wrinkly things all around it," Sweets said.

Jay said, "Sweets, this might be a first for you."

"What is that?"

"You said something intelligent."

"I take deep offense," Sweets replied. But he smiled and nodded to all the people around the table, his renewed and invigorated cockatiel hairdo back in place and shaking as if there were more than a ghostly wind in the room.

"My friend lives in this apartment on the sixth floor," Miss Rhoda said. "I've called her. She's excited to have her habit involved in a murder case. If you'll excuse me, I'll go fetch it."

"We should all get a little rest," I said. "We'll leave around three when confessions begin.

"*Mon Dieu*, this going to be the *coup de gracias*, the nail in his coffin, the arsenic in his lace, his. . ."

"Shut the fuck up, Sweets," Jay said. "I've made a commitment to my fellow officers that this is going to be a righteous bust."

• • •

Officer Darby told us that he'd be back at the following day at 2:00 p.m. with a couple of his fellow officers. Jay and Darby did some kind of double backhand *Knights of the Round Table* solidarity handshake before he departed. I was thrilled that my twin was with me. Like Vincent said from the beginning, he had my back.

Before Jay left, he said, "If this doesn't work, Victor, I'm arresting you."

"This bust is going to get you promoted to lieutenant," I said.

CHAPTER 41
WILL THE REAL FATHER BONIFACE PLEASE. . .

"Nowadays, no one believes in evil. It is considered,
at most, a mere negation of good. Evil, people say,
is done by those who know no better – who are under
developed – who are to be pitied rather than blamed."
Agatha Christie

D Day, Tuesday June 23, 1970, 4:15 p.m. The Oakland Knights of the Round Table in plain clothes were in place in the alley behind the church guarding the two basement exit doors. Sweets had done an advanced search and found that Father Boniface was in fact in the church hearing confessions. Our plan would start with Jay arresting Kayla on some invented charge, hauling her to the alley exit and turning her over to one of his police friends for safe keeping. Then Jay, Vincent and Miss Rhoda, in full nun's habit, would hustle to the basement. Jay and Vincent would stand guard on opposite sides of the stage close to the exits but out of sight. I had explained to Miss Rhoda the way the beds were set up in the basement. She would pull the curtain around a bed and hide there until she would make her entrance to confront Boniface.

I was nervous, not quite as sure of myself as I had been earlier. I had never run track in school, but I thought that this was the way a runner felt just before the starter's pistol went off. I reminded myself that it was my life at stake. Jay was wrong about arresting me if this failed. The gas chamber was not for Victor Brovelli. Pop had friends in Naples who would hide me.

Sweets said, "Time to go, Victor."

I gave Jay the signal.

Jay took off. Twenty minutes later he was back. He gave me a thumbs up.

I gave him a thumbs up in return.

Jay, Sweets and Vincent escorted Miss Rhoda aka Sister Mary Rose into the church. We had agreed on fifteen minutes for the three of them to get settled in the basement, before I went to confession.

I didn't know if the old priest was hearing confessions as I stepped into the confessional, and said: "Forgive me, Father, for I have sinned." But when I heard the voice, I knew it was Boniface.

"And I plan to sin some more," I said.

"My child," the priest said. There was such kindness in his voice, I wondered if somehow I'd entered the wrong confessional.

But I stuck to the script. "And I wouldn't confess to a sinner like you even if I didn't want to sin again."

"Who is this?" the priest asked, his voice no longer kind.

"The man who's going to stop your evil game, Father Charles Dubois."

"If you are on drugs, my child," the priest said. "Let me help you. We have a methadone clinic."

I laughed. "You are such a fraud. You want to know who I am. I'll be waiting for you in the basement."

I jumped up and hurried out of the confessional. As I reached the door of the nave, I felt the priests' eyes on my back. I bounded two at a time down the stairs to the basement and joined Sweets. My forehead was covered with sweat and my shirt was sticking to my back. I've been in some hairy situations in the past, some with bullets flying all around, but this was different. This was Victor Brovelli hoping to find justice for a murderer and being a free man again or living in hiding in Italy for the rest of his life. I checked the inside of my shirt for the tape recorder. It was on. The stage was empty, but Jay and Vincent would be waiting behind the curtains. One of the beds had a curtain pulled around it. I left Sweets standing in the shadows to the side of the entrance. I moved to the center of the basement and waited. I knew the target I was making of myself. I waited.

And I waited.

Opposite the beds was a row of windows close to the ceiling through which the afternoon dust motes of sunlight streamed to the floor.

And I waited.

Then, just as I was about to give up hope, the priest entered. He looked calm, both his hands were tucked inside his soutanes in a priestly pose. I had never seen him in his priest's robes wearing his Roman collar. No man looked more like a priest than him. I didn't wait for him to speak.

"That's a pretty good disguise you have there, Charles Dubois." He didn't reply but walked toward me. He stopped a few feet away and smiled.

"I remember you," he said. "You came to find the runaway, Merriam. You had a Cajun friend."

"*C'est moi*," Sweets said.

The priest swung around, looked then turned back to me.

"You need to explain what you're talking about, my son," the priest said. "Why are you calling me by my brother's name?"

"Why did you murder your twin brother, Lewis, and assume his identity?"

"Have you lost your mind? You're on drugs. If you don't leave, I'll be forced to call the police."

"The police are already here," Jay hollered from the back of the auditorium, stepping out from behind the stage curtain and hopping down from the stage. He was followed by Vincent, who moved to the exit and stood there holding his trusty aluminum softball bat.

Jay has a presence. If he were not a cop, he could have a career in Hollywood playing the role of a cop. Jay's voice was loud and clear. "We have your assistant, and she's singing like a little birdie," he said as he approached.

"I don't understand. I'm going upstairs to call the diocese. I will talk to Bishop Turner." The priest turned around, but Sweets stepped in front of the door, blocking the exit for the stairs. He said, "You can't use these stairs, Charlieeee."

"Stop calling me that," the priest yelled. "Why are you calling me that?" I could see he was getting excited.

"Charlieeeeee," Sweets yelled again.

"Charlieee," Jay yelled.

"Sister Mary," I called in a loud voice so he was sure to hear me. Miss Rhoda stepped out from behind the bed curtain and approached him.

"Charlie, you have been a naughty boy," she said.

Father Boniface or Charles Dubois stared. He frowned. Then his eyes widened. "S-s-sis-ster M-m-mary," he stuttered.

"You're Charles Dubois," I said, "You kidnap young women and sell them to a Mexican cartel. You raped and murdered Renee Sorenson, my good friend."

I saw a fearful look on his face, his jaws clenching and unclenching. Suddenly, one hand appeared out of his soutane holding a pistol. He didn't hold it for long because it was knocked out of his hand by a karate side kick administered by a flying, screaming Sweets Monroe. Jay was there before Charles Dubois, no longer Father Boniface, could run. Officer Jay Ness of the Oakland Police Department's homicide division was there pinning him to the floor, reading him his rights. That moment felt like a year. We stood around Jay and his prisoner, staring down on them as if we'd just discovered this odd tableau and were trying to decide what it meant. I broke the silence.

"Sweets, where did you learn karate?"

"Army Rangers. I was young and stupid."

Vincent said, "For real?"

Jay had his prisoner in handcuffs. Two Oakland Knights of the Roundtable were hauling Boniface away.

"Is Kayla really singing like a bird?" I asked Jay.

"No, but she will now, Victor. It looks like I won't have to arrest you."

CHAPTER 42
FREE AT LAST—OR NOT

*"We must be free not because we claim freedom but
because we practice it."*
William Faulkner

The first thing I did when Jay called from the police station that he had all he needed and that I was free to go, was drive from Rhoda's to Alameda to visit my mother. She wept, but shortly thereafter had me sitting at the kitchen table eating lasagna and sighing over my good appetite. *What is it about Italian mothers and food?* We left the house together, she to Saint Joseph's where she was going to pray and light candles.

I drove to East 14th Street and the lot where I embraced my pop and received one of his enormous bear hugs that happily took the wind out of me. Theresa kissed and laughingly called me Mr. Rossellini. Vincent, who'd driven ahead of me, was standing at the door of the office grinning. I exchanged the Oldsmobile for my Mustang, but to tell you the truth, I was getting used to the Olds. It was nothing to look at, but its engine was every bit as worthy as my Mach Two.

Promising to call my older brother Carlo and my sister Constanza, I drove to my apartment, made my two obligatory calls, and a few minutes later, I was in my bedroom fast asleep.

• • •

When I woke up the next day, it was close to noon and I was clammy with sweat and groggy from dreamless sleep. I took a long, very hot shower. I made coffee. I turned on the TV to see if there was any news of the arrest of Charles Dubois for murder and kidnapping. The only news was that the San Francisco Police Department had broken a Mexican cartel kidnapping ring, but no mention of the fake priest. I thought that was odd, but then I remembered that the San Francisco Catholic Archdiocese would probably have intervened to keep its name out of the press. It didn't really matter to me. Renee's killer was in jail and would probably go to the gas chamber. I could go back to being a car salesman and continue studying for my P.I.'s license.

I dressed in my salesman attire of blue blazer, gray slacks, white shirt with my blue and red striped college tie. All morning, I was a salesman. I made cold calls, I showed two automobiles and sold one of them, a 1968 Corvette, for a neat profit. I took Theresa's usual job going to the bank to make deposits and listened to the clerks whispering my name and felt grateful to our banker who'd told me he was never in doubt. *Of what*, I wondered as he didn't finish the sentence. I returned to the lot and headed to Flynn's for lunch.

I felt like a conquering hero, as I entered the tavern and heard the applause. I even welcomed Body's stupid Italian joke that I knew was on its way as the large Irish presence of Body Flynn lumbered from the other end of the bar toward me.

"Victor, me boy-o, now that you're no long the post office billboard poster child, can you tell me what you call a Roman with a cold?'

The tavern was full except for the one stool I found next to Larry Hughes. The guys sitting at the bar stopped drinking and eating to listen. I recognized most of their interested faces and thought I was home.

"You're dying to tell, Body, so lay it on me."

"A Roman Snezzer," Body said proudly.

Hughes laughed. The rest of the guys looked like, *huh*?

"Julius Caesar, you uneducated donkeys," Body said.

Cat calls and boos sounded all around. Sounded like music to my ears. It was Thursday. I ordered a bowl of I-Dare-You-Chili and a mug of Anchor Steam.

"On the house," Body said, as he placed my beer and chili in front of me.

"We missed you, Boy-o. Not a single man in this tavern ever thought you were guilty. We knew you'd prove the garda wrong."

The tavern echoed with "Damn Straight!" and "Here, here!"

"Jay had a hard time dealing with this," Body said, "You know, being a cop and your friend. He and Jitters almost came to blows over Jitters telling him he wasn't doing enough to help you."

I looked down the bar where our genius mechanic was seated playing liars' dice with one of the two salesmen from Sears nicknamed Shoes and Trousers for the departments they worked in. I caught Jitters's eye and raised my mug. He saluted me back.

"Jay came through in the clutch," I said.

Larry Hughes' large head looked up from his bowl. "Word gets around the neighborhood pretty quickly. It's hard to believe a priest could have committed that awful murder. We all liked Renee."

"Did you hear that on the news?" I asked.

"No. I'm not sure where I heard it. Body, maybe. Vincent might have been by earlier."

Hughes stopped talking and continued eating. My chili tasted like the best chili on earth. It felt good to hear the sound of dice slamming on the bar top and smell the aroma of whiskey and beer. The jukebox was playing Loretta Lynn singing about some guy coming home drunk with loving on his mind. Pool balls were clacking against each other. The players were Ben and Ozzie Averbuck who owned A & B liquors.

"Where's the pool shark?" I asked Hughes.

"Haven't seen him around for some days. Maybe he got embarrassed after Jitters beat him at Nine Ball and took his money. Guess he wasn't as great as he made out."

"Can't say I liked him. Too much phony cowboy talk."

The Loretta Lynn song ended and Waylon Jennings began singing "Mama Tried". If I never heard another Grateful Dead song again it would be too soon. I left my chili unfinished. I thanked the guys for their support and left. I was still exhausted. Vincent had told me to take a day off, and that was exactly what I was going to do.

I'm not sure I can remember Friday.

• • •

On Saturday, instead of going to the lot for the Brovelli Brothers' Barbeque, I went for a long run along the east shore of the bay to the end of Alameda Island and back through the city's streets with a stop at Versailles Ave and a visit with my mother and more Italian pasta. She asked about Dila, and when I was slow responding, she'd taken my hand and patted it without saying anything except with her eyes.

Back at my apartment, I took another long shower and nap. In the afternoon, I tried calling Dila. There was no answer. I called the Black Panthers' Headquarters and asked them if they'd heard from her. They hadn't. Had Terrance Bowles or Big James left a message about Dila? No, they hadn't, and they reminded me that Bowles would not appreciate his messages being shared with anyone who was not a Black Panther.

It was time for my Porsche Cabriolet and a drive along the Pacific coast to get Victor Brovelli back in sync with the world he'd been hiding from. I drove with the windows open and the wind blowing through the car. I drove as far as Carmel, had a quiet and peaceful lunch at a little café called Germaine's and returned along the same costal highway. The rhythms of driving the curves of the highway had been soothing.

At home, I resisted trying to call Dila again. I went to sleep believing that what would happen to Dila and me was already decided. I would just have to be patient to find out what the result would be.

On Sunday, I went to mass with my parents. This time I said my confession to a real priest.

Another ordained priest gave me communion. Then, I decided these few days away from the lot sufficed. I was there in time to watch Vincent sell a 1962 Caddy El Dorado 2 door hardtop. Vincent had relieved our pop of his duties, much to Theresa and our mother's relief.

Around noon, I was busy with paperwork when Jay Ness drove onto the lot. He entered the office and sat down at Vincent's desk opposite me. I could tell he had something on his mind. I had a bad feeling.

"How're you doing, Victor?"

I recognized a soft ball greeting and threw one back. "Ducky," I replied, wondering how that old time expression came to mind.

"Ducky?"

"Yeah, really. Tell me. You're here with bad news, aren't you? "

"It's not a huge deal, but the DA is having a lot of problem pinning Renee's murder on Dubois."

"What, for Christ's sake, he has the bartender's statement placing them together, right? Kayla admitted that Charles and Merriam were seeing each other."

"True. Dubois isn't denying having a relationship with Renee. There were no fingerprints of his in the apartment other than hers and yours."

"*Minchia*," I swore. "You're not telling me. . ."

Jay cut me off. "No, no, but Renee's underthings in your apartment is still an issue. The DA is a political animal. Losing a case will not help him run for governor in the future. And you should know, Victor, Dubois insists he didn't rape and murder Renee. He's adamant about it. He claims he loved her, that they never had sex. He liked her sense of humor, he told us. He also said he she reminded him of a nurse in Vietnam. The guy had a Purple Heart. I got to tell you, Victor, I pushed him hard. He was persuasive. The DA says all we have is circumstantial evidence and we should be satisfied with a conviction for human trafficking."

"You gotta be kidding," I said. "You going to believe a guy who killed his own twin brother?"

"That's another thing. The DA has had a conversation with the DA in New Orleans. Without Lewis' corpse, there is no case. They're treating it as an unsolved missing person. As far as our case against him is concerned, I don't know where the money is coming from, but the phony priest got a top lawyer, a crooked one, but real clever. We did manage to arrest Brillo and Ginger trying to cross the border in Waco. No matter how clever his attorney is, theirs and Kayla's testimony will put Dubois in prison for a long time."

"Dubois is going to get away with murder," I said.

"Maybe, but you might want to consider this, and I'm just saying, Charlie Dubois may not be the murderer."

"Why would I do that, Jay?"

"Well, you're a PI, right?"

"I don't need your sarcasm, spit it out."

"Okay. You're pretty much off the hook for Renee's murder, but you don't really have much of an alibi for Halpern's murder."

"But a couple of the cops who originally searched the apartment swore there were no women's underwear in the closet."

"Yeah, good cops," Jay said. "They wouldn't lie. I just said you don't have a solid alibi."

"What's the problem?" I asked.

"Victor, you're not paying attention. If Charles Dubois didn't murder Renee and it wasn't you, and it wasn't Halpern and Lazlo, who the hell put her underthings in your apartment and who murdered Halpern?"

I closed my eyes and said, "*Mamma mia!*" Some clever P.I. I was.

CHAPTER 43
ON A FIRST NAME BASIS

"I knew when I met you, an adventure was going to happen."
Winnie the Pooh

After Jay left, my annoying, undetectable car noise paid me a visit, louder than I'd ever heard it before. Hearing such a noise in reality, any mechanic worth his salt would have been able to follow the sound to its source, no matter how undetectable it was supposed to be. In my case, the noise was located in the pit of my stomach.

It didn't shock me when Renee's ghost appeared, perched on Theresa's desk, those long, slender legs, encased in tight Levis, crossed. A Willie Mays long sleeved T-shirt was tucked into the jeans. The bemused look on her face seemed to be saying, *Victor, I thought you were smarter than this.*

I turned away from her to the window and the Monday morning traffic moving along East 14th Street. Out of the window, I could see Vincent walking in and out of the cars, checking spots, checking doors. What was he thinking? After Merriam had been found, and I was no longer the suspect in Renee's murder and the phony priest had been arrested for human trafficking, was he thinking things would somehow get back to normal? I suspected this was what Vincent devoutly wished. Renee's ghost would have disabused him of that notion. I imagined him also thinking of me coming to him and saying, *"Vincent, I will never play detective again. You and I will go on with our lives selling the best pre-used vehicles in the Bay Area."*

My twin also might have been wishing that we started a new car franchise and moved the business away from the city to the suburbs where daughters didn't run away to become Deadheads; where good friends were not raped and murdered and older brothers didn't die; where people didn't shoot at each other and motorcycle gangs didn't exist; and where the sound of anti-war protests and the roar of airplanes taking off carrying troops to Vietnam and returning bringing dead bodies to grieving loved ones also did not exist. In the pure heart of my twin, a simple life was what he wanted most, and he deserved it. His ambitions were modest, a good business to support his family, the love of his wife and kids. My twin's soul resided in the heartland of America while his body lived in the State of California—the heart of a changing country.

The world presented to the public by bands like the Grateful Dead was too complicated, too full of regret and sorrow and confusion. I put aside my reverie. I would join him. For now, the two of us would walk around our lot together. I would not tell him of the dark mood I was beginning to feel. Today's clouds had moved in from the Pacific, and the weather had turned cold. I took Vincent's blue blazer from the coat rack and carried it out to him. We were dressed similarly with our college ties, button down Oxford dress shirts tucked into finely creased gray slacks. *GQ, all the way*. Me in my loafers, he in his brown Florsheim's wingtips. We didn't speak much and only car talk when we did. We circled the lot a couple of times and at the end, I told him to go home and play with his kids. I watched him drive away and felt a little jealous of him.

I returned to the office and closed the door against the change of weather. I was not about to bother Vincent with the terrible feeling that I was once again in some kind of serious danger. What and why and by whom was a mystery to me.

Two years ago, Dila helped me bring a murderer to justice, and last year she had helped me identify and solve a major international crime. In the process she almost lost her life. I was glad enough that she was not here, considering the kind of danger I was sensing, but I wanted to talk to her. This time it had nothing to do with our relationship.

From her desk, Theresa asked me if I was alright. "Of course," I answered.

She returned to what she was doing.

I had been pacing. Now, I was standing in front of my father's large poster photograph of his neighborhood in Naples with the house he grew up in circled in black. It had a yellow door. My pop's younger brother, my uncle Marco, and his family were living in it. Our family had visited Italy a number of times while I was growing up. We stayed in that house. Vincent and I bunked in our cousins' bedroom. They insisted we take the beds and they slept in sleeping bags on the floor. On the street, houses faced each other so close it seemed like people could lean out their window and shake hands. Laundry hung on lines that stretched from the facing windows. Your eye could follow the hanging sheets and trousers up the hill to the end of the street to a white church that seemed to me as if it was looking down on the neighborhood and blessing it.

I had seen this photograph every day of my working life. Often, I had taken a nap on the couch positioned beneath it. Today, there was something about this photograph that caught my attention. It was important. I tried to think what it could be. It was as if the poster was telling me something. Did the reason for my annoying car noise have something to do with our family home in Naples? Not likely. I crossed it out of my mind. If my Girl Friday was not around my Grandma Friday was. I called Miss Rhoda. She said come over when I got off work.

• • •

Rather than drive the Nimitz freeway that I could see was bumper-to-bumper, I took the city streets. I parked in front of Miss Rhoda's apartment. Big Boy Clarence and his pals were playing in the street. Big Boy held out his hand and I placed three one-dollar bills in it. He nodded. I nodded back and entered the apartment.

Miss Rhoda answered the door bell.

"I was just thinking of you, Victor," she said.

Not Mr. Brovelli, I thought, but Victor. It sounded right. "I was thinking about you too, Rhoda," I said.

"Now that we are finally properly introduced," she said. "Come on in. I am about to take some oatmeal raisin cookies out of the oven."

I could smell the sweet aroma that I had come to associated with Miss Rhoda's apartment. I followed her to the kitchen and sat down at the table. Rhoda went to the oven and peeked in.

"Another five minutes or so," she said. She sat down opposite me. "Coffee will be ready soon too. Now, tell me what's wrong."

I wondered if I was that easy to read. A twin I could understand. Dila could read my thoughts and now Rhoda. I looked over to the kitchen door at Renee's spirit-self and wanted to say, *"well, Rhoda, since you asked, you see that apparition over there, that's what's wrong."* She might have understood, but the spirit-self was my responsibility.

By the time I was finished explaining my conversation with Jay and the way I was feeling, the cookies had come out of the oven and were piled on a plate on the table and the coffee was in a mug in front of me.

"Do you remember years ago, Victor, when you and your brother repossessed a car in front of this apartment?"

"Yes," I said.

"I'm telling you this now. I had a strange feeling you were going to make my life a lot more interesting."

"I'm not sure about interesting. More dangerous, for sure."

"Well, that's okay too. At my age I can stand a little excitement. Danger qualifies. Let's review the present danger you can't pinpoint the source of. Start with your po-lice friend."

"Jay has a lot of experience judging whether criminals are lying," I said. "I trust him when he told me he believed Charles Dubois was not lying when he said he didn't murder Renee."

"Which means somebody else did," Rhoda said. "And that somebody intended for you to be blamed for the crime."

"Yes, and that same person put Renee's underclothes in my apartment just to make sure I would be arrested."

"Somebody hates you a lot, Victor."

"For the life of me I can't figure who it could hate me that much to frame me for murder. The way I see it, it is completely unrelated to either Merriam or Renee. A couple of days back, I remember this thought crossed my mind, but I didn't pay attention to it because I was certain I was on the right track with the phony priest."

"If it has nothing to do with Merriam and Boniface, Detective Saturday, where do you start looking for it?"

"Damned if I know. And my annoying car noise is back big time, which means there is something I'm missing, a clue of some kind."

"Cookies stimulate the thought processes," Rhoda said. "Have another. I have to put in another batch. I promised Clarence and his gang some."

"Yeah, Clarence is making a business out of watching my car."

"Clarence is no dummy. He lives with his grandma a couple of floors up. All the kids he plays with, they all be part of his chess club."

"And I thought they were little wannabe gang bangers."

"They good kids, just play acting, like most grownups do, right? At the rec center, Clarence takes on the adults at speed chess, beats their pants off and takes their money. Gives every cent to his granny."

I could just hear Big James laughing, "*Jokes on you, White Bread.*"

Rhoda returned from the oven and sat down. She took another cookie. "I do like my own baking." How Rhoda kept her slim figure, the way she ate, was another mystery, but not of the deceptive kind.

"You have any ideas, Grandma Friday?"

"If this is unrelated to what's going on now, it must have something to do with your past."

"I can go back a couple of years and describe them to you. Perhaps you'll hear something that connects to the present. I'll try to be brief."

"No, Victor, don't be brief. There's an old saying the devil is in the details. Just talk. Let your mind wander. I went to a shrink when I was going through some hard times before I moved out west. He had me on the couch with my eyes closed talking and talking. I swear there were things I came up with that I had totally forgotten. He got me to the bottom of my problem and I felt a lot better climbing out. You don't have to lie down on the couch, but why don't we go in the living room and get comfortable. Put your feet out on the Lazy-Boy. I'll sit in the armchair and take notes like I'm a shrink. Then we can go through the notes together after you run out of steam."

I agreed. I took one last cookie before moving to the living room. I sat in the recliner and leaned back.

"Now, close your eyes, Victor, and start where ever you want."

I did what Rhoda ordered and began. I started with the first time I met Renee Sorenson at a wedding reception in the summer of 1966. I was just out of college, and she was a junior at Mills. So many memories.

I let my mind roam. 1967 became 1968. Vincent and I found Sweets ex-girlfriend in the trunk of a '61 Chevy Impala. Although I didn't know it at the time that was the start of my first detective case.

I met Dila. So much to remember about that. Looking up at that halo of hair into those mixed matched green eyes. Our first date. Our first kiss in a playground not far from Rhoda's apartment and just up the block from the Black Panthers' office. Dila with an M1 carbine in her hands. How I admired and sometimes feared her determination for a just society. She'd chosen the Panthers over all the other African American movements from the extreme conservative Black Muslims to the peaceful resistance of Dr. Martin Luther King Jr.

I spoke of Dila in my arms. Of Dila showing me the scarification over her womb, with pride, not anger or remorse. I went on too long about Dila, and Rhoda stopped me and told me to move on to other parts of my life.

I spoke of my immigrant parents and Vincent and their importance in my life and my recent interest in becoming a private investigator. I spoke of my religion, of my doubts and beliefs.

Another sheet of cookies came out of the oven. Rhoda returned.

I picked up where I'd left off heading toward Christmas of 1969 and my older brother Mario's death and then came January of 1970 and I was back to Dila on the wharf in Monterey laying on the sidewalk bleeding. I could feel the tension in my gut.

"I was stupid to let her come with me."

"She survived, not your fault, Victor. What I've heard of your young woman, she has a mind of her own. You can't expect women like her to take a back seat to any man. Certainly not to take orders from him. Women done changing if you haven't noticed. You're almost caught up to the present. Talk to me about the last five months."

I'd already discussed my frustration about Dila going to graduate school all the way across the country and her silence. Aside from that, I couldn't think of anything, except that Renee had returned from Europe and we'd renewed our friendship.

"Friendship?" Rhoda questioned.

"Just friends this time around," I said. "Dila and Renee knew each other through their interest in music and were close. Dila knew about my past with Renee. I've tried calling Dila but no one answers. She'd want to know that the cops have arrested the priest for human trafficking. I was hoping to tell her that he was also Renee's killer, but it's turned out that he isn't."

"You said Dila's father hates you. Do you think he hates you enough to hire a killer and set you up?"

The thought shocked me. *Mr. Agbo? No doubt he hated me.* And once he had threatened me with his African sword.

"No," I said. "He might want to cut my head off. He's too arrogant to be hire a killer. He wouldn't stoop so low."

That drew a laugh from Rhoda.

"He wouldn't, but there's someone who's trying. You must think of a person who hates you so much that he *would* stoop so low. Think hard. It has to be within the last two years. Before that you were just selling cars and hitting on women."

"There was this woman from January by the name of Carol Housty."

Rhoda looked through her notes.

"Is that the one who tied you up and left you overnight in the PeaceLinks' office?"

I nodded.

"Maybe she decided she couldn't take a chance on you not talking to the police and returned to the Bay Area to take care of business. Is that a possibility?"

"I doubt it," I said. "I have the feeling she had her hide-away already planned in some distant country."

Rhoda looked through her notes again. "You were responsible for the killing of that Satan gang leader, Sunny what's-his-name. How about one of the gang members looking for revenge? If not a gang member, how about one of his family members? Bad guys have brothers and sisters and parents."

I thought about Sunny and how generally unlikable he was. Again, the idea of any of the gang going to all the trouble of framing me didn't make sense. They were not that smart or devious. I didn't know where Sunny was originally from. He could have been a local, but he could have been from anywhere in the United States. One of the guys at Flynn's tavern out of curiosity had gone to Sunny's funeral. He said it was all the gang, no older people. A couple of younger women who could have been sisters or old girlfriends.

"No, I don't think they're the ones," I said.

"How about that secretary accountant of yours that got blown away?

"Sylvia? Nah, her family and my family are related."

"Then I've run out of ideas," Rhoda said. "But you have got to keep thinking. Keep in mind, Victor, whoever is doing this is smart and ruthless."

My Rolex told me it was going on 8:00 p.m. There was a knock on the door. Rhoda got up.

"That'll be Clarence. He'll want his cookies. I clean forgot. She moved to the door and let Clarence in. He looked at me and nodded. I nodded back. "I heard you're a champ chess player," I said.

"You have some money? I'll play you," he said.

I said, "My mom didn't raise a foolish child."

Clarence grinned. Rhoda returned holding a brown bag. She gave it to Clarence. He thanked her and left, closing the door behind him.

It was time for me to leave too. I stood up and stretched. I didn't think we'd accomplished much. No doubt I was looking for a smart and evil person. Rhoda was right about that. I had not even brought up the murder of Officer Halpern. It was possible that it was Halpern who'd put Renee's underwear in my apartment. Possible, but unlikely.

Outside the apartment, Clarence and his gang were eating cookies and watching my Mustang.

"On the J.O.B," Clarence said.

I tipped Clarence two bucks, which he gave back with the statement that we'd agreed on a price. Okay, I was impressed.

I was halfway to my apartment when I realized that something Rhoda had said was important. The rest of the way, it nagged at me. It continued nagging at me when I arrived home. The driveway to the parking area was blocked by a large, unmarked van. Two guys were hauling furniture out of the back and placing them on the sidewalk. It was already dark. The quality of the furniture looked high-end. I heard a familiar voice calling out for them to be careful with the "sheeeeet."

"What the hell are you doing, Sweets?" I asked as he stepped out of the lobby.

"Vincent not told you, *mon ami*, we be neighbors."

I'd have to speak to my twin. Sweets a neighbor! I loved my apartment. I'd miss it, but living in close proximity to Sweets, as much as I often depended on him, was out of the question. "What floor?" I asked.

"Sixth, the penthouse."

"We don't have a penthouse, you *babbo*."

"We do barbeque on the garden roof, you and me. Invite all the gorgeous dollies, *non*?"

"We don't have a garden roof."

"I already talk to the manager. We make one. Roof plenty solid and easy access. I'm real good with plants."

News to me, but I wasn't going to go into this any further. I had more important things to consider, like my life. I brushed by him and sprinted the stairs to my floor and noticed the door to my apartment was unlocked. Sweets no doubt, looking through my refrigerator for my mother's lasagna.

From my fridge, I took out an Anchor Steam and went to the couch. *What was it Rhoda had said?* Two beers later, I gave up. I turned on the ten o'clock news, watched Vietnam body bags, felt sick to my stomach and turned it off.

I was sound asleep, then I was startled awake by the phone ringing. I don't know how I knew but the moment I picked up the receiver, I said, "Dila?"

"Victor, it's me. Sorry it's so late."

"Late, who cares? How are you? Where are you? I've been calling you."

"So much going on, Victor, it would take years to explain. I've not been in my apartment for the last week, I've been sleeping at a friend's place. We've been in the process of planning a major protest. It's been Chinese takeout or pizza and very little sleep. Terrance is with us and so is Big James, but they're heading back to Oakland tomorrow. Lot of West Coast stuff to do on their end. I've signed on to the protest core."

"What does that mean?" I asked,

"Sixteen of us have put our names on the dotted line. We might get arrested, but don't worry. It'll be a peaceful protest. We might have to spend a night in jail but we'll be out the next day, our attorneys promised."

I felt slightly relieved, but not excited with having Dila being the target of the police. It just depended on the officers themselves. It seemed to me as these protests continued, it was a crap shoot what kind of cops showed up, the ones who abided by the law or those who made up their own laws.

"I'm going to regret saying this but could you ask Big James to hang around?"

"Big, small, in between is not going to matter, Brovelli. We're not going to confront the police. But. . ."

Dila left the "but" hanging in the air of my imagination. I didn't like what I saw. "That's not helping to calm me much," I said.

"Please, Victor, don't worry. We'll get this done and I'll be back and we'll find Renee's killer."

"That's what I've been trying to call you about," I said. Dila listened as I explained everything that had happened up to Charles's arrest.

"Halleluiah, you're free," Dila exclaimed.

"I'm not completely off the hook yet," I said and explained the rest of the story.

"What are your plans?"

I didn't have anything firmly in my mind. I told her about hearing my intuition-car noise, so I knew I was missing something. There was that *something* again. I was beginning to hate the word. Dila gave me some brainstorming ideas which in the past had helped a lot. I promised her I would try them. We talked for a while longer. I brought up marriage that she told me we'd discuss later after we got through this insane period in our lives. Her tone of voice sounded like a dismissal. I didn't like it but said nothing.

"I've got to hang up now, Victor," Dila said. "Oh, before I go, remember I told you about I'd remember where I'd seen that pool shark guy at Flynn's."

"I remember," I said.

"Well, I remembered. I saw him on television once when I was visiting a cousin in LA. He was doing a commercial for that big Volkswagen dealership in San Diego. He was wearing a cowboy hat and had an ugly bulldog that sat on his lap."

Dila said goodbye and hung up. I stared at the phone for a while. Then, the poster of my father's family home in Naples entered my mind in full technicolor, and I said aloud in the direction of the phone, "*La famiglia.*"

CHAPTER 44

THE WORLD ACCORDING TO BIG SAL BROVELLI

*"Asperta il tempo e il luago per vendicarti, perche non
e mai ben fatto in fretta.
Wait time and place to take your revenge, for it is never
well done in a hurry."*
Italian proverb

I had not been able to go back to sleep, so when my bedside alarm clock read 5:30 a.m., I rose and took a shower. I dressed for work. I was in my Mustang by six, but I wasn't going to our lot; I was driving to my parents' home. I knew I wouldn't be waking them up since they were always up and going by five. What I wanted to discuss with my mom and pop was family business.

They were sitting at the kitchen table. Big Sal with his daily espresso with a small glass of *grappa* next to his cup and my mom drinking her milky coffee and dunking her brioche. Both were reading the newspaper.

"Vittorio," my mom greeted me as I entered. "What is upsetting you? You have anxiety all over your face." Like I was a kid again, so easy to read.

"I have to talk to both of you. It's urgent. It's about family and about honor or perverted honor."

"How can honor be perverted?" my mom asked.

"Listen to what I have to say and then decide."

My pop put down his newspaper and hooked his loose suspenders up over his shoulder, which was a habit of his when having to deal with something of importance. The way my mom put it, it was as if he'd be able to understand better if his pants were secure.

I explained my theory that I had worked out most of my sleepless night.

"*Madonna*," my mom said when I finished.

My pop said. "*Dominic Vitali* is not blood, only family by marriage. This is *infama*, this is disgrace."

My mom said, "My parents warned my sister not to marry him."

"What I must know is if you believe Mr. Vitali is capable of such evil." I was talking about the father of Sylvia Vitali, our one-time mercenary office manager and accountant. Her death at the hands of Sunny Badger, the head honcho of the Satans' motorcycle gang, was always blamed on Vincent and me by Mr. Vitali, her father.

"I have always felt he was a violent man," my mom said. "I know he strikes my sister. She will not divorce him. It is a sadness."

"If this is true, *Vittorio*," my pop said, "how do you intend to prove it?"

"Mr. Vitali would never admit it," I replied, "but if there was some way, I could get his henchman to turn against him." The second I said it, I knew that would never happen. Why would the pool shark admit to being hired by Mr. Vitali? Why would he admit to raping and killing Renee, planting false evidence against me and maybe even murdering a police officer? "Not a chance," I told my parents.

My pop rose from the table and puffed out his chest. "*Vittorio*, it is 1970. In Italy, even now, even as life in the South is changing, it does not change. You have visited often. My brothers in Naples and I write much and talk on the telephone. There are government commissions starting investigating the *Mafioso*, but it is a struggle. The code of *Omerta* is deep inside all Italian people from the South and in Sicily. Your mama's family is originally from Sicily. *Omerta* is worse there. People do not cooperate with the police or officials of government. Is long time way of doing things that if you are wronged you take care of the wrong by yourself."

My mother waved her hands at Pop. "Salvatore, do not go on like you are expert. We live in America. Don't suggest to your son to take this wrong done to him into his own hands. He has a friend in the police department, remember, a very nice man. He has a big appetite, remember."

"I don't suggest to *Vittorio* nothing. I explain what is in the mind of your sister's *marito pazzo*."

"I agree her husband is crazy. But be brief, *per piacere*."

"His daughter was crazy like he is. Two years now, he broods about this. Is that what you think, *Vittorio*? Each day he thinks of you, it makes things worse. There is an old Italian proverb: *La vendetta e un piatto che va consumato freddo.*"

"You eat vengeance cold," I said.

"*Non,*" my mother translated. "Vengeance is a dish best eaten cold. Stupid males make that up. No woman would."

"Even today, my brother says, people don't like to talk about vengeance. People who have a score to settle do it on their own or they find a patron who will do it for them. They are then forever in that person's debt."

"It is not our world anymore, *Salvatore.*"

"I know, but it may be the world *Vitali* is still living in, even with his fancy dealership in San Diego and fancy house on the beach."

"I'm glad that you don't have to live in that world any more, Pop," I said. "I'm sorry if I made you two worry. Look, I'll figure this out."

"You go to your police friend,"

"I will, Mom." She looked relieved. I said my goodbyes. Pop lowered his suspenders and sat down. My mom walked me to the door and told me again to go to the police.

I drove away, thinking of *Omerta*. What if I did go to Jay with this information? Unproven, it was just a theory. He wouldn't be able to do anything about it. Proving the priest had assumed his brother's name and started a kidnapping ring, in retrospect, seemed a piece of cake compared to proving our secretary's father, out to avenge the death of his daughter, had concocted a scheme to send me to the gas chamber and he'd found a man to do his dirty work.

Then, I realized that car salesman doubling as a pool shark was still around. His job would not be complete until I was in prison sitting in a cell in death row. "*Che casino,*" I said. At the tavern, the pool shark that Jitters had proven a fraud introduced himself, but I couldn't remember his name. I didn't really care. Murderer was good enough.

The clock on my dash read 7:52. I turned on to Broadway Street and headed to the bridge and Oakland. It was Barbeque Saturday. Theresa and Vincent would already be there preparing for the noon crowd. I wouldn't say anything to Vincent. I didn't want to worry him. I would have to find a way to bring these criminals to justice. It would take whatever P.I. skills I had acquired in two years to do it. I hoped it would be enough.

CHAPTER 45
CAJUN STOMP

"Don't mess with my toot toot"
Buckwheat Zydeco

Normally I suffer Body's awful Italian jokes without responding, but today I was feeling vengeful. A bunch of the guys from the tavern were standing together listening to Body talking about how Flynn's dart team was going to cream the dart team from Scotsman's Bar & Grill. I interrupted him by asking him what an Irish seven course meal was, and when he shook his big head, I hit him between his smiling Irish eyes with "a six pack and a potato." I must admit looking at Body's startled face and hearing the rest of the guy's jeering was enjoyable. Which reminded me, I hate to say it, of my pop's Italian proverb about revenge being eaten cold.

Some of the bar jockeys were chuckling and giving Body a hard time when Jay walked onto the lot. I told him to get his barbeque and come into the office. I wanted to ask him something. He looked at me suspiciously, then went to the serving table. He came back with his usual Mount Everest serving of barbeque, sausage and chicken and Theresa's Italian pasta salad. He followed me into the office. I motioned to Vincent's desk. I sat down at my desk facing him.

"If this is about your Black Panther lady. . ."

"No, it isn't, but what about her?"

"I hope your lady is doing fine and not getting herself in trouble. In the last 24 hours, FBI has sent out information to all law enforcement that the Black Panthers are about to stir things up."

Merda, I thought. I said, "Dila is smart. She'll be okay. But listen, here's what I need to talk to you about. Dila called from New York. She told me something that she remembered and it may mean that I know who really murdered Renee."

Jay hung his head, and for a moment I felt sorry for him. If I put myself in his shoes, I'd be damn tired of hearing about Victor Brovelli theories too, but I had promised my mom I'd talk to the police and more importantly I needed to bounce the whole thing off Jay and see what he thought. As much as he griped about me being a P.I. and interfering in police business, I knew he listened to my opinions and for the most part took them seriously.

Jay ate while I talked. I explained how Dila's revelation had focused my attention on family. I explained about standing in front of the poster of my pop's home in Naples and how that too triggered the idea of family. I emphasized the word, by repeating it in Italian: *La Famiglia*. I might have gone on a little too long because Jay told me he was growing old, but I could tell he was interested. Jay had been very much a part of what I now referred to as the Case of the '61 Chevy Impala. He knew Sylvia Vitali and had briefly tried to date her. He was aware of all the details of that case and its violent conclusion.

I finished and waited for a response. I was gratified when he said he'd have to give this some thought.

"But, of course, Victor," he said. "It's all about proof, not theory or hypothesis or that dumb-ass car-rattle-intuition stuff you've read in your detective novels. How are you going to prove this?"

"Does that mean you believe me?"

"Let's say I don't disbelieve you. I didn't like that phony cowboy-talking pool shark, and I recall now that he asked too many questions about you and Vincent."

I was on hyper alert. "He asked about Vincent?"

"Yeah, both of you. You know how you often entertain the guys with stories about Vincent and some of the fixes he gets himself into? Well some of the guys told him those stories. He was real interested. Come to think of it, a little too interested. I guess that's why I'm thinking your theory might have legs."

"You'll help us then?" I asked. My twin was now part of my thinking.

"I'm pretty damn busy. You know what's happening around the country, but I'll try. My captain is happy with me for my role in breaking that kidnapping gang. I can probably get away with some independent digging. With all the action going on, many of us are operating without partners, which means I can do some snooping on my own."

"We have to find the pool shark. We ought to be able to find out his real name from the TV station he worked for in LA. If we find him, we can convince him that Mr. Vitale is going to throw him under the bus, maybe he'll want to cut a deal," I said.

"You're back reading those detective novels again, aren't you?"

"All right, all right; you're the homicide dick, how do we go about proving he's the killer?"

"If he did what you think he did, Victor, he's a hard nut. He's not going to crack. The best bet is to catch him in a crime."

"Like what?" I asked. "Another murder?" Jay shrugged. "Mine?" Jay nodded. "Vincent?"

"Could be," Jay said. "If he's following the instructions of Sylvia's father then both of you are in his crosshairs."

"I have to talk to Vincent," I said.

"Not a bad idea," Jay said.

I stood up and hurried out the door where the lot was thinning out.

"Jay and I have been talking," I said as I came around the serving table next to him.

"If it's about crime, Victor, I don't want to talk about it. Unless Jay wants to buy a car."

"Hear me out, will you," I said. "Don't be a *chooch*."

"I have to start cleaning up, Victor, make it quick."

He started putting stuff away while I explained.

"Is my family in any danger?" he said when I finished.

"I don't think so, but I don't know and I have no idea. The guy is in the wind, but Jay definitely thinks I'm still a target, and he thinks you are too. He believes it's possible that he'll go after you, since setting me up didn't work. And, maybe your family. I didn't mean to frighten you, but I thought it best you go home. You will be safer there than on the lot. Besides, I didn't know if your family is in danger. The pool shark was clearly a stone cold killer."

"I'm going to send Gloria and the kids to her parents." Vincent said.

"You do that. I'll finish cleaning. Go home. Take care of your family. I'll handle the lot." Vincent was gone before I could say another word, and I was left with sudden heavy bundle of guilt. To put myself at risk was one thing, but to risk the life of my twin and his family and maybe even my parents and friends because I wanted to be a private detective? Victor, the unsatisfied wanting more excitement in his life. Was that what this was all about?

I slammed my hand on the tabletop, sending a container of condiments flying into the air. I caught a bottle of catsup on its way down. The rest hit the asphalt. Two mustard bottles broke, turning the ground into a yellow Rorschach Test. I stared at the growing goop. Maybe I needed one of those tests. I sure as hell needed to give this private detective business some thinking beyond the sign I fantasized atop our building: Brovelli Brothers' Used Cars and Detective Agency.

• • •

"I don't like it," Vincent said.

He had returned to the lot after seeing his wife and kids off at Gloria's parents.

My twin and I were walking around the lot. I had explained the possible plan Jay had agreed to if he could square it with his captain. It called for us to be sitting ducks. Jay figured the pool shark guy couldn't wait too much longer to finish the job. That this time around he wouldn't spend the time and energy on some kind of devious plan but would come after us shooting. Two bullets, one for each of our Italian brains, and he'd head to San Diego for his payday.

"Why does Jay think he'll try for us at work?" Vincent asked.

"Jay wasn't sure, but he said it made sense that he hit us at the same time."

Vincent exhaled. "I'm taking Gloria and the kids on a vacation to Hawaii after this is over. If I'm not dead."

"I'll man the lot," I said. "You'll never see me be a P.I. again. I promise."

"I'll believe that when I see it." He answered.

"You asked me to make up my mind. Well, I made it up."

"*Bene.* That's good to hear, Victor. Okay, when do we start?"

"As soon as Jay gives us the go-ahead," I said.

"We can't put Theresa in harm's way," Vincent said. "We'll give her a week's vacation."

"She'll want to know why," I said.

"We tell her the truth. She's family. That's what this is all about, isn't it?" he said.

"We act normal," I said. "Keep to a daily routine. There's no reason for him to believe he has been identified, so he probably believes he's safe, just another guy. I wouldn't be surprised if he simply walks onto the lot and starts shooting."

"I'm going to talk to Theresa."

Ten minutes later, after hugging me and calling us "*due stupidi gumbahs*," Theresa drove off the lot. A few minutes later, Vincent went to the office. He said he was keeping the door open.

The lot was eerily quiet, which was only my imagination as the traffic on East 14th was always a jamboree of noise. Across the street I saw the nose of a yellow Volkswagen Transporter bus appear at the edge of the driveway facing East 14th, stop, then pull out, turn west and disappear in traffic. It was not Nick Parsegian behind the wheel because only fifteen minutes earlier I had seen him leave his store and jaywalk across the street to Flynn's. If it wasn't Parsegian, who was it? Merriam must have had a second set of keys, I thought. The answer made me happy for her and her man. *Good luck, Merriam.* Parsegian would certainly be surprised when he found the hippy bus gone.

Jay's call came close to six. Vincent had already left, explaining that Gloria was frightened and wanted him. Jay informed me that his captain had approved the plan but would not approve plain clothes cops to guard Vincent's home, my apartment or the lot during working hours. Vincent would not be happy to hear this.

I was locking the door to the office when a powder-blue Mercedes Benz pulled into our driveway and stopped. The distant relative of Jean Lafitte stepped out and waved. Sweets strode towards me with a huge smile on his face.

"How do you like my new wheels, Victor?"

"I don't want stolen property on the lot," I said.

"Oh, you funny man, you. Bought this baby this afternoon from a *bon ami*. Two years old with low mileage. The car, not my friend. That's a joke, Victor, you dig?"

"Pretty weak, Sweets. You bought it legally. What bank did you rob to pay for it?"

"Ha, ha, again with the Italian humor. I admit to a sudden windfall, the details of which are too complicated for you."

"The same windfall that helped you pay for that antique furniture for your new apartment?"

"How did you guess?"

"Sweets, Sweets, you should write a book called the *Greatest Uncaught Burglar in the World*."

"I will think on it. There may be a better burglar in Africa or China, but you are right. None better than Sweets Monroe in the You-nited States of America. I could sell a lot of books, *non*?"

"I'm about to close up," I said.

Sweets said, "I was thinking of taking you and Miss Rhoda out to a fancy dinner tonight. What do you think? On me, of course."

The thought of Sweets Monroe paying for anything, let alone dinner in a fancy restaurant, was so amusing, I couldn't resist. Anyway, I had nothing to do, except be a sitting duck for a killer. He probably wouldn't want to shoot me in a five-star restaurant with lots of witnesses. "I'll call Rhoda," I said. "If she agrees, I agree."

I unlocked the door to the office. Rhoda answered my telephone call and told me she'd be delighted. I told her we'd be on our way and to put on her best finery.

Through the office window I saw Sweets pointing to a silver Chrysler 300 driving onto the lot and pulling up behind Sweets Mercedes. The first thing I saw of the man stepping out of the door were two cowboy boots and I didn't need to see the rest of the person. I rushed to the door yelling to Sweets. I leaped down the two steps. Sweets turned to me, a look of confusion on his face.

The man approaching us was Mr. Pool Shark-Killer-Cowboy, home of the fucking range, but he was not holding a pistol in his hand as I expected, and he was smiling broadly.

He reached us and spoke softly and almost kindly. I thought of John Milton's description of the snake talking to Eve.

"Now, I know what you're thinking. Y'all think I've come to do you harm, right?"

I was now standing shoulder to shoulder with Sweets. I couldn't think of anything else to say except, "Yeah."

Not a very cool response. It occurred to me that at any moment a weapon would magically appear in one of those empty hands.

"I'm an excellent private detective," he said. "I've kept up with you and your investigation. You have potential."

"You're not a detective, you're a car salesman," I said. "You work for Dominic Vitali's Volkswagen dealership."

"Oh, I did a little work in that area for a while. Can't say I liked it much. My boss finally told me I had to make up my mind, be a P.I. or be a car salesman."

"What do you want?"

"I won't keep you. For some reason my employer has taken me off the case. No skin off my nose since I'll still be paid. I'll be leaving the area. I just wanted to say goodbye. I'm sure you'll eventually find your girlfriend's murderer, and the police will surely find out who murdered one of their own."

"Why don't you just confess," I said, "and save us the time and trouble."

"I wouldn't want to interfere. I must admit you are a little smarter than I thought. Perhaps we'll meet again someday. I'd shake your hand, but I know you wouldn't. Give my regards to your brother and your fat cop friend. I surely did enjoy the chow at the Irishman's tavern. Best damn Irish stew I've ever had."

Cowboy-killer turned back toward his car. I charged, and he pivoted. This time he did have a pistol in his hand.

"Y'all don't move another inch," he said.

I didn't. Sweets leaped to my side. From some pocket of his wardrobe, he'd pulled a switchblade.

"You too, Mr. Monroe, not an inch closer."

Sweets had his blade extended, but he didn't advance.

Cowboy-Gunslinger backed into his Chrysler and fired up the engine. He leaned though the open window.

"You might be interested, Renee put up a fight. She was a tiger. Tigers turn me on."

The car backed up fast, fishtailed into East 14th and sped away.

I was barely breathing.

Sweets put his hand on my shoulder.

"That dude, he be the one who raped and murdered Renee?"

I nodded.

"Muthfuka," Sweets whispered. "Muthfuka."

The switchblade snapped shut in his hand. "Dinner will have to wait, Victor," he said.

I watched Sweets do his own version of a fishtail into East 14th. I was numb. It was all over. No sitting ducks' plan. *A murderer for hire free to kill again. Dominic Vitale free to keep selling his Volkswagens.*

I turned back to the office and sat down on the office step and looked up at the sky. In the distance I could hear the planes from the naval airbase taking off for Vietnam. The clouds over the Bay Area were turning orange. It would soon be a purple sundown.

CHAPTER 46
JUSTICE

"La guistiza non mangia sempre alla tavola con la legge.
Justice does not always eat at the same table with the law."
Italian proverb

For the last two days, I'd been unable to shed my fatigue that was both mental and physical. The Case of the Volkswagen Hippie Bus, which is what the guys at Flynn's tavern named it, had come to an unsatisfying ending. Nonetheless, a conclusion of sorts. Charles Dubois, aka Father Boniface, fake rector of Saint Agnes's Catholic Church and human trafficker of young women, was in the hands of the FBI. He'd go to prison. His brother, Louis, the real priest, would remain a missing person.

As far as Renee's murderer, his body was found in Stockton in an empty lot, his throat cut. The Stockton Police attributed the murder to the rise of gangs in their city, which the Police Chief lamented had once been a peaceful university town. I had my suspicions. I was tempted to share them with Vincent but decided it was best he didn't have to deal with the ethical considerations, so I kept it to myself. As far as I was concerned, justice was served.

Whoever employed the cowboy killer would remain a mystery to everybody but Big Sal Brovelli, his wife and their twin sons. As I looked out the window of our office at the familiar urban landscape of East 14th Street, my pop's words came back to me from the last time we spoke a day ago. What he said was more of a statement than an explanation. Big Sal was standing in the kitchen in our family home on Versailles Ave in Alameda. His suspenders were up. On the table were three small glasses and a bottle of chianti. This was our pop at his serious best. He began in a voice that my mom and I knew heralded something *estremamente serio*.

"The husband of your mother's sister," he began, "Dominic Vitale, has decided to sell his Volkswagen dealership in San Diego and return to Napoli."

He had raised his hand and stopped me from speaking.

"Non mi interrumpere! Ascolta! Listen to what I explained to him over the telephone yesterday. I say to the husband of your mother's sister. I tell him, such a decision would be wise. I am a good salesman. He did not argue with me. I tell you now, *Vittorio,* what I did not tell him. Your Uncle Marco and your cousins will be meeting his plane. It will be of some surprise to him."

My mom followed Pop's statement by filling our glasses and offering a toast to her beloved sister Gabriella who had surprisingly informed her husband that she would not be traveling with him to Italy. She was planning to move up to Northern California and live with her sister. I knew better than to ask either of our parents to elaborate. I remembered the time after I'd graduated from college when my pop called me a *good American boy.* It was clear to me that despite the many years our pop, Big Sal Brovelli, had lived in the United States, there was too much Italian in him to completely accept America's way of dealing with life's injustices. No matter how long he had lived in America, Salvatore Brovelli was still a good *Italian* boy.

I was already living with one secret, now I would be living with two, the demise of a certain cowboy pool player and now our pop's announcement. As this was family business, it was impossible to keep Pop's resolution a secret from Vincent. All he had to do was see my face later that day, and he became alarmed.

Pazzo, pazzo, he kept repeating as he listened to me explain our pop's words. I didn't necessarily think it was crazy. But *pazzo* or not, it would be something my conscience would have to deal with for a long time.

When the law and justice conflicted, I had chosen justice. For this reason, I had decided I would *not* become a licensed private investigator. How could I, if I believed more in justice than I did in the law? I kept my reasoning from Vincent, but he was delighted to welcome me back to the business. I think he knew that I would not fully give up detecting. He was right, of course, but when I did, from that time on it would be on my terms.

In front of me was a United Airlines' ticket Flight 86 nonstop to La Guardia Airport in New York City. The plane had departed without me. A day ago, Dila Agbo, my fiancé along with fifteen other members of the Black Panthers had been arrested and indicted for the assault on police officers and police stations. Newspapers in New York City were calling it a copycat of a similar assault by the Black Panthers in April of 1969.

In that year, twenty-one Black Panthers were charged with conspiracy to kill several police officers and to destroy a number of buildings including police stations and the Bronx Botanical Gardens. I remembered Terrance Bowles, the Panthers Minister of Education saying to me at the time, "Victor, why the hell would we want to destroy flowers?" And Dila had nodded vigorously in agreement.

The idea of it had definitely seemed stupid to me. Bowles explained that there had been a great deal of sympathy for the twenty-one among many individuals and groups. Abie Hoffman had raised money for their defense and so did Leonard Bernstein, the conductor of the New York Symphony. Dila had told me that Tom Wolfe had written an article called "Radical Chic." She'd added that the term now was in popular use to describe rich white folks who enjoyed hanging out with radical blacks.

But in April of 1969, twenty-one had meant only a blackjack game to me. The only Hoffman I knew was the manager of the local bowling alley. I *did* know Bernstein was a conductor, but when it came to radicals, I was a novice. Dila and I had only been dating seriously for less than a year, and I was nervous about the political left. I was hoping there would be similar groups and rich individuals willing to fund the defense for Dila and her group of Black Panthers that were being called *The Foley Square Sixteen*. The twenty-one of 1969 had finally been exonerated because it was proven they'd been set up by the police. What I wasn't sure about was if Dila's sixteen were similarly innocent or if the assault they were accused of was real. It made my stomach lurch thinking about it.

Last night, I had gone to dinner at the Top of the Mark with Sweets and Rhoda. Sweets had combed his cockatiel hair down and worn an elegant black pin-striped suit. Rhoda had matched elegance with elegance in a black silk cocktail dress that made her look twenty years younger than her sixty-plus years. After dinner, we'd gone to the Basin Street West to listen to the Dewey Brown Quintet. Rhoda had been recognized by the bass player and asked to sing. She sang "Smoke Gets in Your Eyes". As festive as our evening was, I couldn't keep Dila out of my mind, so there was more than smoke in my eyes.

What had caused me to cancel my plans to fly to New York? Dila had. "*Victor*," she'd said to me. "*Victor*," repeating my name in a way that I knew what she was about to tell me would hurt. *"I'm with my people now, where I'm supposed to be. Don't come."*

"Why," I had asked her, "in God's name, why?"

And she had answered that there was more than three thousand miles between us.

I knew she was right.

The End

About the Author

TOM MESCHERY is the author of five books of poetry: *Over the Rim, Nothing We Lose can be Replaced*: *Some Men*, and *Sweat: New and Selected Poems about Sports* and *Clear Path*. Meschery was born in Harbin, Manchuria in 1938 and immigrated to the United States after the Second World War. Meschery played NBA basketball for the Golden State Warriors and the Seattle Supersonics from 1961 to 1971. After his playing days, he earned his MFA from the University of Iowa. He  taught literature and creative writing for 25 years in Reno, Nevada, and he was inducted into the Nevada Writers Hall of Fame. In retirement, he continues to write poetry and fiction. His debut novel, *A Brovelli Brothers' Mystery: The Case of the '61 Chevy Impala* was published in October of 2022 to an enthusiastic review from *Publishers' Weekly*. The second in the Brovelli Brothers' series: *The Case of the '66 Ford Mustang* was published in October of 2023. The third Brovelli Brothers Mystery, is *The Case of the 1950 Volkswagen Hippie Bus*. Meschery lives in Sacramento, CA with his wife, artist and art historian, Melanie Marchant.